"BANTUS"

The untold HiStory of Africa and her People from Creation

abaNtu

Vhathu

Wanhu

Bathu

AbaNtu

Anhu

Anthu

baTwα

Vanhu

Batho

Watu

Dr Takalani Dube
Mukololo wa Luvhalani

Printed in the United States of America

ISBN:	Softcover	978-1-63871-450-7
	Hardback	978-1-63871-452-1
	eBook	978-1-63871-451-4

Republished by: PageTurner Press and Media LLC
Publication Date: 08/17/2021

To order copies of this book, contact:

PageTurner Press and Media
Phone: 1-888-447-9651
info@pageturner.us
www.pageturner.us

Nota Bene!

This Book is Vernacularised...

(Various amaNguni Languages used)

If you do Not understand the Language,

Don't worry,

the Explanation is Bracketed.

Otherwise google Translate the word

and

you should be sorted...

Happy Reading (Learn some Vernacular)

Contents

Disclaimer 1

Dedication 5

Gratitude 6

Truth 7

Prologue 15

Part 1: Afrika 43

- The name 44
- The Continent 47
- The People 50
- The Culture: kiNtu/isiNtu 71
- The Philosophy: ubuNtu 108
- The Contribution 124
- The Afrikan Renaissance 139

Part 2: The unTold (Hi)Story 145

- Origins 146
- Ancient History 154

Part 3: The Glory and the former Days 181

- Bronze, Iron Age & Classical History 182

Part 4: Imperialism 220

- Muwene we Mutapa falls 221
- Formation of Colonies and Republics 243
- The Union of South Africa 270

Part 5: Political Change 283

The Genesis of Apartheid 284
Republic of South Africa and Anti-Apartheid Movement 303
Constitutional Democracy 324
Part 6: Scrambled Eggs 332
Part 7: New Beginnings 350
Bibliography 378
Ndi u fa ha Lungano! (What Seemed like Myth is actually Truth) 386

"There's really No such thing as the 'Voiceless'...
There are only the Deliberately Silenced or the Preferably Unheard."
Arundhati Roy

unsilenced

Disclaimer

Yes, Imperialism *in its purest form* has ended, Colonialism *in its purest form* has ended, Slavery *in its purest form* has ended and Apartheid *in its purest form* has ended... but have their notions and legacy been erased in the Soul of Africa? What about in her Psyche? Her Economy, Her Social Fabric, Her Worship of God, Her Technological Advances, Her Legal environment and... NO! Their Painful Wound lingers on in both Continental and Diaspora Afrikans.

The Pain of a wound is known by the wounded. Those who are not wounded find it convenient to tell the wounded to get over it and forget it. "It is in the Past"; "That has ended"; "It is no longer like that"; "You have to stop blaming Colonisation, Slavery and Apartheid for everything that's wrong in Africa" They quickly Admonish... Leaving us stung even more and unable to defend ourselves or explain why that wound is still there. **You will notice mine in my ramblings...**

The Wounded know they have to open their Wounds; Debride them; Wash them out and Apply dressings that need to be cleaned often until healing begins and until that healing is completed, and sometimes, even that scar may still be painful on inclimate weather. This writing is that surgical treatment of our wound. The Place to talk about why we are still bemoaning things that happened thousands of years ago... The Place to talk about the things our written History covers up, denies, erases or ignores. It is writing Necessary to stop the septicemia that we are already dying from in the form of Murder; Gender-Based Violence; Substance Abuse; Economic inequalities; Greed; Poverty; Inequality before the law; Fear; Anger; Corruption; Inferiority; Self-Loathing; Poor Technological Progress; Looting of State Resources; Theft; Racial Tensions; Xenophobia...

If you are interested in curbing this Septicaemia and Healing, allow me to take out the Surgeon's knife and open the wound. It will be painful for both the descendent of the Colonial Imperialist and the descendant of the Continental and Diaspora oppressed, as Truth is laid bare without apology. In the End, it will Help us to Find each other. My sister Tshiwela loves reminding me of this luVenda adage: *"U amba Livhi, ndi uri Livhuya liwane vhudzulo"* (One utters unwelcome words in order to make room for the words of Life). I encourage the brave to "take it in the chin" in order to Learn their History and be Empowered Holistically, so that we are Re-Humanised and #**NolongerSilent**, but can rise up together in a Healing Revolution for the Reconstruction of Afrika for Global Impact.

"Your Choice to Hold this Book in your Hand Here, Now and in this manner, is a unique experience that has Never been since creation, and that will Never repeat itself in this exact same manner in the future, for Today, happens only once, Savour it!"
Dr MC Neluvhalani, 1981

Picture of Mvumi Dr M.C Neluvhalani and Mrs. S.P Neluvhalani taken at a family gathering by Anza. Author's Property

Foreword by Dr Vhonani Sarah-Jane Neluvhalani-Caquece

The Truth enunciated in this book, the first of its kind, written from an Afrikan's perspective. A crucial read for all Afrikans that want to have a deeper understanding of who they are. This book takes one on an epic journey of Afrika of yore... it includes a detailed analysis of Ubuntu and the humanity and hospitality extended to the coloniser upon his arrival to the none the wiser indigenous people of Afrika. It brings to light the antics of the coloniser and their bid to strip off the dignity of the Afrikan when they "sliced up Afrika like a cake" and declared it "Terra Nullius" no-man's land. It exposes the strategy of the divide and conquer rule and the incessant dismissal of anything Afrikan such as Afrikan culture and customs as evil, yet Afrikans have always been spiritual beings who acknowledged "Nwali" the almighty. The "Truth" as recorded by the coloniser dispels and distorts history as written from a perspective that records their truth as truth. This book exposes and brings to light Afrika with its people who have always been advanced in many aspects. The calculated manner upon which the coloniser stole and dismantled Afrika of yore into haphazard boundaries, is the reason why authors such as Mukololo wa Luvhalani, Dr Takalani Dube are needed. This fearless, bold Afrikan female warrior has heeded the call in her heart to put things in perspective and dispel the coloniser's "Truth" as the untruth that it is.

Foreword by Bishop Emmanuel Vusumuzi Dube

I Applaud my wife for this Labor of Love. Needless to say, I endured a Long, Cold 2020 whilst she languished in the Labor Pangs of this Work of Love... All I could do was watch, Pray and quip occasionally: "Write Love!" and She wrote.

I Invite the reader to allow themselves to be Transported by her words, to the Volcanic Africa of yore, to Hear the Life-giving Drums of the Ancients, See the Spirit enchanted rock paintings and Travel their Millennial Trade routes to emerge today in the 4th Industrial Revolution...

Thank you Sweety, for setting the record Straight. Thank you for jumping into the Murky Waters of the Misinformation holocaust of Africa, to search for survivors and to resuscitate the dying. This Writing, is the Clarion Call for Africa to Arise and take her God-given Position as the First of Humanity.

Foreword by Charles Ngobeni

I have known Dr Taki Dube for 32 years, as a friend, sister and an academic. I have always admired her passion for humanity, which manifested in her humanitarian response to the HIV/AIDS pandemic in 2000, when she established the 'Centre of Hope" to address the problem and when she sacrificed her Medical Career to support her husband in building eThekwini Community Church.

"*Bantus*" is another manifestation of her continued dedication to the welfare of humanity, especially the "Black" African.

If you do not know where you come from, you will be doomed to having no sense of direction or of where you are going. If you do not know where you are going you will have no sense of accomplishment, because anywhere you arrive at, may as well be your destination. The sad part of this, is that it is true for most of the African children that have grown up to be adults and who themselves have given birth to their own children, for whom they have nothing tangible to show as their heritage.

Misrepresentation and Misinformation has left the African child taken advantage of. This has been the case not only in the southern parts of Africa, but across the entire continent and the Diaspora, to the extent that the African children have had to grapple with what seems to be an inheritance of untold levels of poverty. Since up to now, the African child has not had his true value and identity re-exposed to him, he has remained in the shadows of other nations. The African Child has thus been relegated to a life of crime and thievery just to survive. This Lifestyle, further destroyed the values and culture that he was brought up to believe and be defined by, leaving him incongruent within himself.

Dr Taki does a wonderful job of debunking the myths propagated by misinformation about the roots and value of the African, which has left him in doubt about his identity and existence. If well defined, the African has more value to give than could ever be imagined possible in order to make this world a better place to live in. May this work of art find its rightful place in the history of mankind, and may it facilitate a rehabilitative role in the life of one of the most gracious and powerful species of the human race, the "Black" African.

Dedication

I Dedicate this book to you the Reader first and foremost! Thank you for your Support

I also dedicate the book to: all Continental and Diaspora Sub-Saharan Black people, also classified as: **Bantus, Blacks, Niggers, Pygmies, Hottentots, Bushmen, Negroes, Coloureds, Caffers and Kaffirs** who are in Truth **abaNtu; Banu; Wanu; Antu; baTwa; Vhathu; Batho; Vanhu; Antu; Wanhu; Anthu; Setshaba; Sewochi; Buhuenyong; xxx.** May you lay the names of the Imperialist to Rest and take back your Identity, **Afrikan abaNtu/baTwa (Afrikan People)!**

You did not fall from the Sky, neither did you come to live where you do by annihilating and colonizing another...Your Ancestors were born here and have persisted here through all generations since creation. Some of you are Still Continental whilst others of you are in the Diaspora and the Islands...

You are the first Nations of (South)Africa: The autochthones, Aboriginals and Natives of this Continent and the First Nations of the World.

As you Read the Book, May the eyes of your understanding be opened, so that you, with unveiled faces can freely Reconnect yourself to yourself, your Maker, your Next of Kin and your Land and be Re-humanised as you are restored to ubuNtu.

I also dedicate it to our Asian, Arabic and Indian brethren as well as all Those who have come to be known as white people all over the world who are burdened by the injustices they can see meted against their brethren and who wish to hear an authentic history of the so-called Black people from black people themselves.

This book is also Dedicated to the **Governments of Africa and their Institutions**, as well as the **African Union** as they work to fulfill the Prophecies of Old, captured in Ashiýa (Isaiah) 19: 19-20 & Ashiýa 66 and as espoused in the aspirations of Agenda 2063, “The Africa we want”.

Gratitude

1. YHWH... Thank you for Commanding me to write!

2. eThekwini Community Church, Thank you, for Maturing me into a Mother and Re-Humanising me. Thank you for enabling me Financially to be able to write this Book. This is the Fruit of your Labor of Love.

3. Dube e limthende, Mbuyazwe, Nzwakele, okhushwayo ... wena ogeza ngobisi abanye begeza ngamanzi! (Praises) My Love, My Friend, My Sweetheart and Darling Companion, whose willingness together with your brothers, Gugu Baba's Sun-Sons Neluvhalani, Mhlantla, Caquece and Netshimbupfe, to listen to him talk for 3 hours non-stop is Legendary. Your Patience, Love, understanding and willingness to allow me to take the time to Research and write this work... Aaa, Ndi a livhuwa!

4. Tehillah, Mafungwase wami, Dlubuladledle nje nge ngonyama...
   I started writing this book on your 21st birthday (20.02.2020) and I completed it the day you did your Experimental Virtual Festival... surely there is some significance in that! Thank you, for agitating me toward this work with your demand for the explanation of how you came to be in Africa, if African History denies your presence in Africa. Thank you for your Wokeness and ubuNtu Emotional Intelligence

5. Ruth, Thumbu wami, Nyamazane entle, Shiri ya Denga...
   Thank you, for having Afrika in your heart. Thank you for your passion for storytelling. Thank you for using your Colorism privilege, to sow the seeds of reconciliation and cohesion of the Human Family.

6. The full List of all the People who made this work Possible is an entire Chapter... If not a Book. I have taken time to Thank you at the end of this Book. I ask that in the spirit of ubuNtu, the reader helps me Honor these heroes by reading their names out loud as a Prayer. If you do not find your name, it is not because your contribution is less... Forgive me and acknowledge yourself in the bigger pictures that I have painted in the Book. Your desire to locate yourself in History is what pulled this Book out of My Dad since 1971, pushing him to write and defend a Successful Doctoral Dissertation on some of the subjects that inform this work in 2017 at the age of 78, and finally in this format, out of me in 2020/21.

   I Thank you

Truth

"One sees that the moment is not far, when the learned world will admit that the black race is the first race of Homo Sapiens to exist; the others are derived from it by a process that science will specify. It is no longer necessary to populate Black Africa and Egypt at the beginning of time by mysterious whites or non-negro races." Nnamdi Azikiwe

When his Excellency, the first President of Nigeria, Nnamdi Azikiwe spoke the words quoted above, it was at the height of Scientific erasure of "Black/Negro/Bantu/Sub-Saharan" African people from all the Archaeological sites that proved Africa's Pre-historical and Ancient civilisations. It was well before anyone thought the Out of Africa Hypothesis could one day be the Predominantly accepted Theory of the origins of the human Species.

Today, Scientific Consensus favors this Theory over the Multi Regional Theory.

What we currently accept as Truth, is an Accumulation and Distillation of various knowns and unknowns that have been "proved" over time to be "True", based on their Credibility; Validity; Reliability; Justifiability; Verifiability and Replicability, through three (3) main methods: Spiritual; Scientific (Deductive or Empirical) and Philosophical methods, until an acceptable standard is reached which is then accepted as Truth.

Some of what is accepted as Truth is Hypotheses, which may go unchallenged and be presented as truth until new findings challenge them and a new Truth emerges.

Let us do a quick experiment that I "developed" in 2016 to Expose Truth

You might enjoy doing this experiment before you continue reading further. If you choose to do it after you have read further, do not worry, you will still enjoy doing it.

Take an Onion and Peel it. Layer by layer to its core...

Notice the Appearance, Texture, Smell, Taste, Effect on you.

Write out your Observations. Ask someone else to do the same experiment and compare your observations. Based on your Experiment, what is an Onion? What Truth have you learnt about an Onion?

Some of the things you may observe are that:

1. Your onions are different.
2. If the second person used the onion peeled by the first observer, they are affected by the bias of the first observer in how they peel the onion. Yet, they may still discover some things about the onion that the first observer missed.
3. The Conclusions drawn about the onion experiment may or may not be the same, even if the same onion is peeled by the two observers.
4. One observer may rush through the peeling process, taking the natural "peel" lines of the onion and missing out on the finer lines, whilst another may discover even more lines.
5. The Peel followed may deny or expose the peeler to smells and excretions that may not be found by another peeler.
6. The peeling experience may provoke revelation and the revelations may or may not be similar and these may affect the conclusions reached by the observers.
7. In all that handling of the Onion, The Peeler may start smelling like an onion and thus believe they know the whole realm of the Onion's story, yet, perhaps if the onion could speak, the onion might tell a better story…
8. The God who created (gave) the seed, The Seed itself, The Farmer who planted the onion, the soil in which it was planted, The Air and water that provided some of the nutrients, the harvester who harvested the onion, the retailer who bought, Transported, Packaged, Stored and finally sold the onion as well as the buyer who brought the onion to your home and packed it and the Onion itself, may also have another story to tell, if you do not have their input in distilling your Truth, you may miss out on important facts about the onion.

In this manner, Human Truth behaves. As we peel each layer of Truth, we discover new Truth. This New Truth may corroborate or deny previous Truths.

There are several types of Truth:

Historical, Philosophical, Scientific and Spiritual. This Book delves into all these aspects of Truth, Albeit Superficially in some areas, whilst it does so, deeply in others.

Historical Truth

- No human being alive today knows ALL the Truth about Afrika's History or the origins of Man in general. We do have enough information from Oral Historical Records, Indigenous Knowledge Systems, Archaeology, Genetics, Written History, Anthropology and other areas of Study to deduce some Historical narrative. Our deductions however, are just that, deductions. The Truth is known by those who lived it and their descendants to whom they passed the knowledge.
- The picture of Truth can't be complete when we dismiss, out of hand, chunks of Knowledge repositories in favor of "scientific truth" only, when Scientists themselves do not Present their Findings as Truth but rather as Findings... They are the first to acknowledge that a True Scientist, "Never says Never." What is true today can be obsolete tomorrow.

Scientific Truth

- Science as Collins, FS (2006:58) puts it, "is Progressive and Self-Correcting." It is unfortunate therefore, that History Books, tend to present their Theories, Findings and Hypotheses as Truth. They are NOT. They are Just Findings, to which a multitude of meanings, can be imputed. Some are just Hypotheses that can later be disproved.

Spiritual Truth

- Truth is Revealed by Truth in small incremental doses, to Assist the Recipient of Truth on their journey according to their capacity to fathom truth.
- Spiritual Truth is based on the written or Oral Scriptures of the devotees.
- Yeshua ha Mashiach (Jesus Christ) is the only person to have Claimed that He is the Truth and the revealer of Truth (through His Holy Spirit). John 14:6; John 16:13

Philosophical Truth

The Word, Philosophy, Means: The Love of Wisdom. It is the Study of the fundamental Nature of Knowledge, Reality, and Existence. Every Culture has a Philosophical View point/Theory which acts as a guiding Principle for behavior.

The Global Philosophical outlook espoused currently is that which is rooted in Academia and which focuses predominantly on Western Philosophy. This Philosophical outlook credits Socrates as the Father of (Western) Philosophy. Afrikan and Asian

Philosophies are however, starting to be taken seriously, with Asian Philosophy having been recognized longer than Afrikan Philosophy.

Ancient Greek Philosophers regarded Afrika as a Place of Wisdom and Philosophy. Pythagoras of Samos is Credited by Socrates as the first to bring to the Greeks all Philosophy, having learnt it in Egypt. The dismissal of Afrikan Philosophy therefore, creates a Barrier or Blind Spot, to an observing Non-Afrikan, as to the Clear perception of Truth regarding Afrika. For Non-Afrikans to gain a better view of Truth in Afrika, they need to be immersed in Afrikan Philosophy, otherwise, the Conclusions they arrive at are Biased to their own Philosophical outlook.

African History in Particular is written by Imperialists on behalf of their Subjects that they Colonised, as Van Jaarsveld (1975:62) asserted: "The history of the "Bantu" had to be recorded for them by civilized whites from Western Europe, from the time of their first contact.

- In this Version of the Reconstruction of History (Dominions History), The voice of the Colonised is ignored, silenced, misheard and misinterpreted whilst the observer's voice is Amplified, Accepted and Promoted as Truth.
- Nabudere (2012:120-121) explains it this way: "Writing History for others is an expression of power by the Self over the other and it is the basis upon which Anthropology as a discipline is founded. It is an Arrogant Ascription of European Superiority over the Afrikan who is instructed to understand themselves through the eye of the coloniser. This is the reason why Racial Classification had to be created, for the European to exercise power over the native. Race became the mirror through which they could be identified regardless of how they identified themselves." Basically: "Why are you Black?" "Who says I am Black?" "You, are Black"
- The Colonial Voice is the Authoritative and Acceptable voice that has Chronicled Afrika's History. This is more so in South Africa where influential Historians such as Van Jaarsveld (1975:19), insisted that: "The History of South Africa must disregard all Indigenous Knowledge, oral History and archaeological findings and be recorded only through the Colonial lens."
- Afrikan abaNtu's means of Self-Identification and Self-Determination were brutally butchered for them to emerge with "Christian" Names and Surnames in order for them to Access "Created" Privileges of: Legitimacy; Employment; Recognition as Legitimate Royalty; Education; Health; Economic Access and acceptance as "civilized Africans".
- In Historical Records therefore, Afrikan abaNtu/baTwa Identity is:

Obscured and recorded as: unknown civilisation, Homo Sapiens; Prehistoric man; Advanced Civilisation; Iron, Stone or bronze age man

Changed and recorded as: Bantus, Hottentots, Bushmen, Pygmy, Nilo-Saharan, Congo A, Congo B, Afro-Asiatic, Austronesian, Sub-Saharan, Coloured, Berber...

Covered up and or Erased: Human Remains and Material Culture have been Stolen, Defaced, Destroyed or Appropriated to Private farms, Game and Nature Reserves, World Heritage sites as well as Museums, where they are archived under Eurocentric names: Coloured Saartjie Baartman; Black Oprah Winfrey, Rosetta Stone; Lynton Panel; Mapungubwean Rhinoceros; The Sphynx... The Balance of the Material Cultures lie buried under Cities.

Denied: as in the following popular narratives: "An advanced Black Civilisation that is NOT "Bantu"; "No Bantu genetic Material was found" or "Does not match Bantu genetic Material" Nguni, and ancient civilization that is not Zulu; The people who once lived at both K2 and Mapungubwe remain a mystery as they lived before the time of written record and there are no known oral traditions recorded further than a thousand years back.

Ridiculed: The dominions view dismissed all of Afrika's Culture, Traditions and Way of Life as Barbaric and unworthy of Study or understanding. Whilst this Perspective is slowly changing, it is doing so, at a time when the Repository of indigenous Knowledge is finally becoming depleted.

This elaborate Narrative is woven into all disciplines: Paleontological Science; History, Anthropology, Medical and Social Science, so that there is one cohesive Narrative that obscures the Genealogical History of Afrikans from Creation to date. Therefore, an Afrikan reading any of these Scientific Findings and Historical narratives is unable to identify themselves in them.

Afrika's Evidence buried in the Sahara; Protected in World Heritage Sites and Buried under cities and Private Farms still cries out to be: Remembered; Re- Discovered; Re-Investigated; Correlated to oral historical records and indigenous knowledge systems to be Reconstructed Appropriately by Afrikans from an Afrocentric view.

The time to dismiss Afrikan knowledge and wisdom out of hand is long past. "**It is no longer necessary to populate Black Africa and Egypt at the beginning of time by mysterious whites or non-negro races.**"

It remains the responsibility of Afrikans to assert themselves and their knowledge. It should be: "Nothing about us, without us" where Historical and other "Truths" are written about us. Our Names as we call ourselves, not as assigned to us should be used in all writings about us.

The Truth Presented in this book, is long stated, but previously ignored Oral History which is now woven together with ancient written history as found in scripture as well as in scientific writings, to produce a coherent and seamless Narrative from Creation/Emergence of Human Beings to Present History. We will Narrate in a Cohesive Chronological manner the History of the Afrikan abaNtu/baTwa Nation Family since Creation from Primary and Secondary Sources: Archaeological Evidence of Dated Human Remains, Foot Prints on Rocks, Remains and Artifacts found in Stone-Walled Citadels all over Afrika with particular focus on Southern Africa in Gauteng; Limpopo; Mpumalanga; KZN and the entire North, West and Eastern Cape areas; Ethnographic Oral History; Biblical History; Literature Survey of written African and South African History; As well as Recent Documented History.

We Systematically and Objectively Locate, Evaluate and synthesize this evidence, establishing facts and drawing conclusions about past events of Antiquity. This Reconstruction implies a holistic perspective that encompasses the whole realm of the Past of Afrikan abaNtu/baTwa in a way that greatly accentuates their Social, Cultural, Economic, and Intellectual Development.

This Seeking of and exposing of Afrikan Truth, is what "Human Progress" is about.

To thwart the Truth of another, is to Deny Oneself Wisdom and Understanding.

Uncovering Afrika's past and acknowledging the descendants of its civilisations is a Necessary step toward Re-Humanising Afrikans (who have been de-Humanised by Colonisation, Slavery and Apartheid). Re-Humanisation involves the Anchoring of the Souls of Afrikans in Hope, The Restoration of their Dignity as well as the Restitution of their Erased History. So that, the Afrikan can re-connect to their God, Fellow humans, themselves and their environment. This gives them the same sense of permanence experienced by all other people, in order for Afrika to believe in her future and to live Responsibly today. *Karibu! Kena! Wamukelekile. Aa!*

Writing style

1. abaNtu in the True sense bearing a Meaning of: The Human Race (Human beings/ People) and;
2. abaNtu in the bastardised Bantu sense, being descendants of 4 sons and having been separated from each other through Colonially motivated Political boundaries and further having been colonized by people of differing Languages and Intentions; and
3. The Author having been born and confined to Political South Africa by "Citizenship", There is a South African Bias in this Historical Narrative; and
4. The Afrikan Continent being one of the Largest and Oldest, its History could not be contained in one small book like this one, the Reader must be invited to understand that they are reading a synopsis rather than a detailed narrative of everything Historical about Africa; and
5. luVenda being the Parental tongue of the Author whilst English is the Author's colonial second Language; and
6. Afrikan Languages having been reduced to a written language using different orthographies that make them seem different;
7. The Author writes this book in Vernacularised English.
   Sometimes pure luVenda is used with Translation with the hope that Afrikan abaNtu will be able to recognize the same words/terminology or spirit thereof, in their Languages. Sometimes isiZulu as the Majority South African abaNtu Language which is similar to isiNdebele, isiXhosa na xiTsonga, and it being the Author's Language by marriage, is also used with Translation for the same reasons explained above....
8. Words are Spiritual Creative forces and sometimes the spirit and essence of the words is lost with Translation. This is the struggle Translators of all Books of Scripture find themselves battling with. It is also the reason there is a movement toward encouraging use of the original languages in which scripture was written for the Impartation of the Spirit of the Letter to the readers. Anyone who has had the privilege to Listen to Translations or be a Translator will understand the Bias that creeps in with any Translation no matter how rigorous.
9. The Author being of the Christian Faith and being a Scientist, Both Scientific and Biblical Knowledge and Wisdom have been used extensively to inform her work, Other Faith Traditions are alluded to but not dealt with extensively due to the Author's ignorance. "Afrikan Traditional Religion" as it has come to be termed is treated in more depth in separate chapters as it informs ubuNtun and kiNtu. As much as Possible, Original Aramaic words for Biblical Names of Afrikan abaNtu

are used, to enable umuNtu to recognize themselves. where applicable, Anglicized names are bracketed.

10. The Author requests every umuNtu to replace LuVenda and isiZulu words and names with those similar to theirs in their language so that every reader may be better able to discern themselves in the pages of this book.
11. The Author departs from English writing convention and Capitalizes Words for Emphasis. The concepts of: abaNtu, ubuNtu, kiNtu and the "Bantus" are the subject of this book and are dealt with rigorously throughout the Book.
    To borrow from the words of Lane, Belden C, "This is a highly textured, multidimensional narrative which draws heavily (with a naked honesty at times) from the Author's experience. I simply don't know any other way of writing this book. This unusually personal involvement of the author in his research raises important questions of Bias. Thus, an extensive Bibliography is on hand to prove that this is not just a work of Emotions, but of fact." Sölle, D (1990:35) sees nothing unusual in this type of narrative, arguing that she considers separation of the personal from the professional of one's own experience, from reflections that then vaunt themselves as scientific or philosophical thought, to be a fatal male invention.
12. Lane, Belden C states in The Solace of Fierce Landscapes that "The Aim of this writing is to bring the reader to Attention and to nudge them away from a place where his/her concern is simply to move as quickly (and freely) as possible from one place to another, to where they can restore rituals of entry that allow them to participate fully in the places they inhabit."
13. It is my Hope that as you read this book, you will restore rituals of entry, by Dwelling on each Chapter, drawing on it what you need for your Journey and leaving in it, the weariness deposited on you by the Erasure and Denial of your History, so that you, can Boldly and Confidently Tell the Story of your Ancestors to your Progeny, Restoring them to their Place in Human History.
14. We will begin with a Prologue, that carries much Vernacular... Persist and you will get the hang of it, as everything is interpreted... Though fictionalized, it is steeped in verifiable facts.

Prologue

Yesterday for Tomorrow...

Your name reminds you of names like, Pelegi (Peleg) who was named as a prophecy of the Continental Drift and especially Tshawe (Jabez) whose mother named him in Pain and the Painful time his people would experience. Your people always use the opportunity of the birth of a Child to tell a History or a foretell the future.

You were born in the year of the Locust, duvha lintha ha thoho (When the sun was above the head/midday) It was a 1000 moons since your Mom's relatives relocated from Mapungubwe because of the constant Flooding and the expansion of the Nation which dispersed to Vhulozwi (today's Zambia and Kongo), Lifurudzi (Lefurutse, Botswana), Dzimbabwe (Zimbabwe), Mitshilinzhi ya Venda (Venda) into most of the current Venda Dynasties. Some People, however did remain until Asili displaced them.

Your Mom loves singing you the song they sang when they finally dispersed, for it was a difficult decision and a tearing of relations as Son followed father! She says it reminds her that Nwali always provides and never abandons Thakhayawe (His People), That is why your people named themselves Thakhayanwali (The Lord is our Husbandman)

Mapungubwe ro vha ro dzula, ehe, ha! Rovha rodzula oho...
Ri tshi la Nama, Ro vha ro dzula, ehe, ha, Ro vha ro dzula!
Mapungubwe ro vha ro dzula, ehe, ha! Rovha rodzula oho...
Ri tshi la Mashonzha, Ro vha ro dzula, ehe, ha, Ro vha ro dzula!
Mapungubwe ro vha ro dzula, ehe, ha! Rovha rodzula oho...
Zwiliwa zwo dala, Ro vha ro dzula, ehe, ha! Ro vha ro dzula!

xxx

Mapungubwe ro vha ro dzula, ehe, ha! Rovha rodzula oho...
Ri na Musuku, Ro vha ro dzula, ehe, ha! Ro vha ro dzula!
Mapungubwe ro vha ro dzula, ehe, ha! Rovha rodzula oho...Vho salaho
vhashakuliswa nga vhatsinda, Ro vha ro dzula ehe, ha! Ro vha rodzula..!

It is a Song of Remembrance. An Historical Narrative, a Song of Worship and Thanksgiving. It Narrates how your life experience at Mapungubwe was like, what you Ate, who you Associated with, what you did, what you owned and how and when you moved from there.

You are content to live in the Stone walled Fortified Citadel (City) of Thulamela, on the Mountain, in safety with other members of the Community where you experience a fully settled lifestyle.

Your Family is a Family of Metallurgists. Your daughter has a unique gift in Smelting. She makes the most beautiful ornaments of all Thulamela. Your wife loves boasting to her friends about them. She sells all Vhukunda that her daughter makes. That one has a very strong business sense too! (Google, Vhukunda to make an online order of the ornaments her descendants still make).

Your Mom Cultivates the Land Magovhani na Mitangani (Undulating Plains and wetlands). You love the Food she produces; it is very Medicinal. Your Children are very strong and healthy because of it. It is famed for its anti-Malarial effect.

The cattle herders Graze the Livestock and together with the Hunters, they hunt in the plains below. These are punctuated with perennial water streams and rivers, that supply all your water needs.

Your family is well fed, Adjusted and Content, observing a rigorous Spiritual life. Makhadzi insists on honoring the Creator, "For it is He who provides the Earth, the Fire, the Water and the Air that is so necessary for our existence." "She always says she is the Keeper of the Memories and Words of the Past. On Remembrance Nights, she recounts the story of creation and the dispersal of the peoples into the 4 corners of the earth. She always insists: "This is your Heritage, it is what makes you Human and you must preserve it from Generation to Generation… Nwali visits those who remember His ways with His People."

When she can't convince you on something, she just says: "Zwi a ila!" (It is an Omen)! Ha, that used to get you all the time when you were young. Your Children don't seem to be too phased by it though. They always retort: "Zwi 'ila zwiri mini?" (What says the Omen?) Ngoho nga Khaladzi anga Maemu, (You swear by your sister Maemu), You don't know what is happening in this Generation, but they also seem to be more obedient in spite of not being afraid of Zwiila (omens)

You love Family gatherings in the evenings when everybody returns from their Day's work.

You are prepared for the upcoming City Wide Celebrations. Surely your Children will know most Ng'ano, Mirero, Maambele, Thai, Khube, Ndode, Mifuvha, Mapfatshane na zwinwe, because their Mom is always speaking in the various riddles and she always wins all the Games for Calculations. Mudzimu (God) knows, even you don't get her sometimes, let alone when she starts: Thai... Ha! Nobody ever gets those.

Your son and daughter will be participating in the Madomba and Zwikona/Nanga this year. Tshikona is your people's Symphony orchestra. Sometimes up to a 100 members play the Nanga, usually Men. Each person has their own Tune that they stick to. When everybody plays their tune, a heavenly melody descends which directs body movements that everybody adheres to, forming an undulating orchestrated movement as people move as one... You always find it so thrilling. You are passionate about Tshikona. It is a Healing Dance. Some say it helps regulate the body's systems. It is accompanied by Drummers who are usually women and who are the Choreographers... You can spend a day just talking about Tshikona. It is a pity that these things are not being formally preserved for posterity... one day, others will appropriate them as their own. Enough... you caution yourself as you notice the depressive nature of your line of thought.

You blame your wife (of course!) that only one of your sons wants to follow you in your Tsimbe footsteps! You would be a few cattle rich from the winnings. You can Practically wrestle anything down.... You should try a Lion perhaps? You chuckle to yourself. You have heard stories of Maasai people who walk with Lions as with Men. Shucks, maybe you are just wiser... hahaha... this is the land of the untamed. It is the main reason your Citadel is on the Mountain.

You are able to share with your neighbors what you have and you love one another and respect one another and trade what you have in excess with other communities, Locally, Regionally and Internationally.

Apart from the few Skirmishes, especially with the various Nomadic bakhoe, and baSan when they are new in the area and have not been introduced, you generally live in Peace and Harmony with your neighboring Nguni and Barolong Communities. Disputes arise also with these when some men do not have enough cattle for iLobola and they resort to ukuThwala, (eloping and or kidnapping) and sometimes for Grazing Lands and or stock theft. The battles are hardly protracted. Nguni people believe more in dialogue than military warfare. God knows, there are more things to battle in this world than to battle each other.

You are grateful that you have all the Implements and Technology you need for a settled Lifestyle. Children are home schooled according to a Family's Call (ubizo) and Specialty in various sectors of Industry: Mining; Philosophy, Religion and Culture;

Technology; Fashion Couture including Bead, Copper, Gold, Ivory and Wooden Jewelry (Most families collect these to Create Heirlooms passed from generation to generation as they usually tell significant stories and are symbols of Covenants), Hair Dressing; Manufacturing of Mats; Utensils; Implements; Farming and Animal Husbandry; Hunting and Trekking; Medicine; Justice and Righteousness; Astrology and Meteorology; Building and Architecture; and Business; Entertainment; Sports; Environmental Care and Environmental Preservation.

You Dress well for your environment with various types of apparel for various occasions, adorned with jewelry and with Hair Styles that designate your position in the Community; tells the history of your people; Your Social Standing; Your Profession and your Values. You are a written open Letter that anyone who meets you can read.

You are Happy and Content in who you are and your Purpose in the Earth.

You are preparing for Davha la Mutale, which has been called for mutual enrichment and (Davha is when the entire Community rallies around a Project to assist the Project owner), But right now, you are at the Lookout. You have been sent by the King to assist them, "When the time comes".

She seems to be sensing the same thing that you have been sensing for a while now... something is unravelling in the Land... Shepherds have reported a run in with her. This, is very unusual behavior, usually you would never know she is there. The only way you can tell is by her Spoors. Leopards are fiercely territorial but, she seems to be marking a larger Territory these days... refusing entry to passersby. She, is completely Belligerent! This is more than what you expect from her when she is just trying to protect her young.

Animals are more astute than people you know... They sense all manner of Natural disasters, days before they happen. vhaVenda say you must follow the Animals if you are running away from a Natural disaster.

kaHasani (at a place named after King Hasani), an elephant rampaged through a Town without provocation. Elephants are gentle creatures and they never attack without provocation.

The Crops are failing more and more and ubuNtu is eroding as people and families seem to just disappear overnight...It is an evil omen!

It is the 1800s according to the Reading of years by Asili (Asili is short for Asi wa ili, directly translated: One who is in not of this land/this continent). Your people know it as the Century of the great Crushing.

Your family has lived in Lukungurubwe (The Land of Molten Rocks), Afruika (Africa/Afrika), since Creation. They have grown from 4 families to 26 Dynasties, 120 Empires presiding over 10 000 Nations/Kingdoms. Your Fathers have lived in this part of the Continent for tens of thousands of years... Granddad just says: "Zwigidi zwa zwigidi zwa zwigidi zwa minwaha" (Thousands upon Thousands of years). He is fond of invoking the sayings of his Ancestors that they used whenever they spoke of their enduring presence in the Land... "Ndi Mubikwa na ive, ive lavhibva nda sala (I have been here in the times of Molten Larva that melted the Rocks and still, I endure), Ndi Ntangi wa kugala (The First of the People), Nganiwapo (From hence I originate), Tshidzatshapo (My Ancestral graves are here)" He always chants these words, before sharing any great Teaching and Concludes by saying: "This is our Land, We named the Mountains and the Rivers and the Forests."

The past 300 years however, have been very turbulent and the Storm is gaining Momentum... Afruika (Africa) is going through the Birth Pangs of something which thus far is unclear to Tshifhe (Priest) and Layman.

Asili from Portugal have built many Forts on the Coastline of Afruika (Africa). This has undermined Millennial Trans-Saharan Trade Routes with the South that depended on the Intra-Continental Water ways. As a result, Misanda ya Tshipembe kha la Muwene we Mutapa a i tsha luvha Musanda Muhulu Dzimbabwe (Most Southern Royal houses in the Domain of the Regional Polity, no longer pay homage to the great Monarchy in Dzimbabwe). Dzimbabwe had risen with the rise of Trade on the Eastern Sea Board, contributing to the fall of Mapungubwe. Now, it too, is falling!

Because you are not a Trader, you have not yet laid eyes on Asili. However, in this past few weeks, two have been sighted inland and in your area. In view of the evil omen, everyone is on edge and wants to know: Why are they here? "If my name and my Dad's names are anything to go by, we are certainly headed for a Perfect Storm" is the opinion you always give to anyone who enquires about these rumblings, and you believe, that, these two, may well be the Start of the end.

The Leopard's unusual behavior, has triggered the King's Summon, to you, to be on the lookout for them. You have been at it for the past few hours now. His Instruction is simple: "Find them. Follow them. Do not interfere with them. Assist them when the time comes." His rationale to you was: "Although we know not whether their mission be for good or for evil, they are in our Land and are therefore our guests and our Responsibility..."

You have found her, at the watering hole. "What a beauty!" You almost exclaim out loud. It is as though she is walking on Air. Her Strides are measured and deliberate... Self-assured like one who owns the Land. That, is how you feel right now as well.

Your eye is distracted from the Leopard as the two men appear suddenly in your line of view...

They are exactly as !Xarra had described them. You Remember how prior to him reporting that he caught sight of Asili in your area, you had both joked about the fact that you had yet to see them. "Remember, I am not as well travelled as you are, !Xarra." you complained as he laughed at your lack of exposure. !Xarra, whose name means Unity, belongs to amaGoam family of the Nomadic San baTwa. baTwa is their name for abaNtu. abaNtu means People in Afruika (which Asili mispronounce as Africa). Various Nations pronounce abaNtu in accordance with their language, but because all the languages here descend from one, you can see the similarity of the word in each language: **abaNtu, Vhathu, Wanhu, Bathu, Batho, Anthu, baTwa, Watu, Anu, Banu, Vanhu, Wanu, Antu...** Some Nations refer to people as Nation and thus call themselves: **Sewochi, Sechaba, Buehyong...** and other variations thereof.

You have heard that Asili refer to abaNtu as **Bantu,** and they use this, to separate Farming Communities from Herder and Hunter Communities. They seem to think you are different unrelated people because you speak different languages and follow different callings in life... They do not realise that this, is the beauty of it... The Difference, is what makes you live at Peace with one another... Everyone does what they are created for.

baSan, being Nomadic travel extensively, with most of them traversing the entire continent at least once in their lifetime. At 20, !Xarra had travelled as much as a 40-year-old amongst your people, so, "he had an advantage" you feel.

Due to the fact that they travel so much, they are in the habit of Writing pictorially on Rocks, especially Landmark ones, in order to share their experiences in that area with the next family that will pass through the area. It is also an act of worship. Their Pictorial Narrations are thus present all over Afruika (Africa).

You had attended the Night of Worship when his family added to the Rock at Matjulu and you were amazed by the similarity of your rituals and recording styles... Fascinating stuff!

"It must be fun to be so well travelled," you had remarked to him. "Yes... it is..." he had answered forlornly. "What is it my brother? You had enquired. "Sometimes," he said, in a measured tone: "I envy your settled lifestyle, you get to see the Trees grow old my brother…" He released. You both fall silent as you acknowledge each other and the moment.

"What do you mean they are without color?" you had asked, !Xarra after a while. He had laughed and said, "Tell me when you meet them."

That fellow is a great Tholi (Watchman). In fact, his whole family are Trekkers and Watchmen. Your Dynasty have relied on them to be watchers of the woods as Millennia of their lineage have always lived closely with you when in the area and they always pass on valuable information, whenever they come to trade their valuable superfood of medicinal roots, barks and leaves… of course, you do trade much more than that.

Your face suddenly lights up as you remember the bark you purchased from him. Your wife will be very happy tonight. The Last time you brought the bark home, Makhulu's (Grandparent's) appetite and energy levels increased tremendously. It has become a valuable commodity and amaGoam won't say which tree they get it from, suffice it to say, the Great spirit of uThixo (God) reveals it to them, deep in the Forest where your people dare not tread.

"Makes great business sense anyway." you think to yourself. But, it is getting more and more expensive, This Stash cost you an Arrow and a goat, amaGoam have no use for tshelede (Money) They call the copper ingots from the Coast used for trading, "trinkets" and laugh in anybody's face who dares offer them as a medium of exchange.

"Focus!" you chide yourself. The leopard has now draped herself on a Branch and is fully Camouflaged. Asili are dangerously close to her lair and she is with young, so, she will be highly provocable. You have to warn them, this is why you are here… to "Assist them when the time comes" according to the words of his Majesty, the King. They are in your territory and according to isiNtu/kiNtu they are your Visitors and Responsibility.

Judging from the position at which amaGoam first sighted them, you surmise that they probably arrived on your shores from Lwanzhe Mbwandaa (The Deep Ocean known to Asili as the Atlantic Ocean). Portuguese Asili who Trade at Lwanzhe Vhimbi (The Ocean of the Whales, known to Asili as Indian Ocean) do not travel so deeply into the continent because of they have built Trading Forts on the Coast. Traders like your uncle who is a Mining and technology mogul, go to the Coast to trade at these Forts. Your Uncle trades at the one in Malindi (what the Portuguese re-named Delagoa Bay), Sofala is too far and the Arabic people are great at negotiating a price, "you don't gain the requisite value for your goods there, as you would at Malindi." he always says.

Constant visits to the continent from Asili date millennia back.

The North being closer to other continents has attracted international invasions and settling by Asili for a millennium and a half now. Most people in the North are now of mixed heritage, you've heard. The East Coast which is also accessible by sea however has not suffered as badly because of its tempestuous waters. Besides which the baKushi Khandake (Kushite Queens) famous for their war faring managed to repel most settling invasions.

Asili from Arabia and recently Portugal only increased on the East Coast due to Trade. The Portuguese people, with their Forts, have settled some people at the coasts as permanent workers. Some of these settlers, have married local women, thus the higher level of mixed heritage abaNtu (people) on the East Coast. One of the King's Muzwala (Cousin) in Luonde, Maravi (Malawi) consorted with Asili from Portugal and being of a Matriarchal lineage, she raised the six children from the various consorts, accordingly. When the Children became of age, she let the fathers take them to their Native Land. You wonder if she will ever see her children again? Will they remember whence they came from, their language and Traditions? "Rothe ri vhathu (We are all people)" you encourage yourself. "Surely, vhana vhawe u do vha fara nga vhuthu/ ubuNtu (he will care for his children humanely)" you decide. Arabic Traders have also been marrying abaNtu for Millennia now. On the North Eastern Coast, most people think of themselves as Arabic because their fathers are Arabic. Majority have also adopted their fathers' Religion of Islam.

By the look of things, the Ancient Northern Settling style of invasions are now happening here in the South. Some say it is because of the Gold, whilst others say it is the Slave Trade. Slavery is old in Afruika. There are different types: People selling themselves off due to poverty or debt, People being carried off as war conquests or to fulfill Treaty agreements and Recently (the past 300 years), with the Portuguese Forts along the entire African Coast line, Slavery has become a Commercial Sport. Taking over from the Millennial Arabic Slavers in Zanzibar the Portuguese have increased Slavery in this region and on the West.

You remember very vividly the story of the near enslavement of your Nation that Granddad told you about. Had it not been for the bravery of vhoMakhadzi, the great warrior, the whole Nation would have been carried off to Slavery. Khadzi (The King's sister and Chief Counselor) ya Thulamela, Bwerina (The Rock is with us), alerted the armed guard that something was amiss when the young maidens under her care who were undergoing u imbelwa (Right of passage at Menarche) did not return after their ritual bathing. The armed guard, after confirming the Abduction of the maidens and learning from amaGoam, that a greater invasion was planned, evacuated the city to Mashubini a Tshimbupfe (The Past Royal Place of Tshimbupfe), while they remained in the city to defend it. The Great Queen and King Makahane the second (now named Losha and Ingwe by Anthropologists) refused to flee, choosing to guard the city to the death. Unfortunately, they were slain there. After their burial, by those who returned to do so, it was decided that Musanda (the Royal Citadel) uteya u ilwa (must be subjected to a Holy abandonment) until the days of its Cleansing are fulfilled when descendants will return to it.

The King has informed the Nation, that reports have reached him, from amaNguni aka Zwide; amaNtshungwa and amaKhoenamaTwa, about the Settling of their land by Asili at their respective coasts. Wars have ensued in these areas between Asili and the various Nations. Nations are losing Territory and civil war is breaking out as a result, as they are pushed against each other and align themselves with Asili to gain advantage against each other... greed and betrayal have become very common place. abaNtu are becoming effaced from ubuNtu.

amaXhosa, those great of warriors, had been overcome after their 100-year continuous resistance of the takeover of their land. Many had been carried to the new Colony at llHui!gaeb (The Cape), as Slaves. Here they Joined baTwa (baKhoe and baSan) who had already been enslaved, desecrating their way of life as Hunters and Herders. The other slaves were from Malindi, Sofala, Zanzibar and vhubva duvha (Far East). What precipitated the Conquest of amaXhosa was their mass ritual slaughter of their cattle to cleanse the land that had become defiled because of ubuti (Dark Magic). They undertook this National Cleansing in obedience to a word that came from God, which was told to Nonqawuse in a vision, by the spirits of her Ancestors.

The Poverty that ensued, the scorched land tactics of Asili wherein homes and farms would be laid to waste with fire and the Harsh winter and subsequent drought, saw many amaXhosa volunteering themselves as indentured labourers, as Instant Catastrophic Displacement and Famine ensued.

To think amaXhosa waged a war for 100 years to defend their land and still lost it, is a trauma in all of Muwene we Mutapa. In all of your History, this is unknown. Dynasties usually quickly reached a Treaty when there was a dispute or if one Dynasty wanted to Assert itself over another... "These Asili who invade and will not relent in another's land are strange people indeed." You think to yourself.

The Fall of Dzimbabwe when King Nyatsimba Mutota established the new capital at Zvongombe left a Vacuum which together with the Invasion by Asili on the West Coast and their arrival on the Shores of Indodana ka Senzangakhona iNkosi uShaka Zulu, has caused a great crushing among the Nations. !Xarra told you that some fleeing from iNkosi uShaka are now called Amamfengu and have found Rest kwaXhosa. Being foreigners there, they aligned themselves with Asili against amaXhosa... Some people from other nations would be stunned to see each other alive and ask: "Le wena o sothogile mabapeng a leso?" (Have you also survived the great Slaughter?) Thus becoming known as Basotho(gi). Your people had also assisted amabutho ka Mzilikazi as they fled to Dzimbabwe, establishing themselves as amaNdebele in Dzimbabwe.

Your Neighbor, Kgoshi (King) Sekhukhune successfully repelled Asili until they brought a multinational and international army to subdue his Nation and imprison him. On release from prison, his brother Mampuru Assassinated him to settle succession scores with the help of Asili. In a confusing turn of events, Mampuru was then Executed by Asili for Assassinating his brother. The Law of Asili is now the Law of the Land apparently... and it is confusing.

You are convinced that these events are a fulfillment of your grandfather's Prophecy when he did the unthinkable and took over the duty of Makhadzi of naming Children from her and named your father Lavhengwa (Turbulence and Hatred in the Land) and you Thivhilaeli (unperturbed). He said: "Turbulent Times of Hatred are coming. When they do, we Must remain unperturbed because He who sees All things, will see, strengthen our Loins and turn around our fortunes at the appointed time..."

It is important therefore that these Asili be Monitored. Yet ubuNtu dictates that you consider them first as brethren until they prove themselves otherwise. To this end, you have come to Watch and Assist, when the time comes...

They seem to be on a journey, "Whereto?" you wonder. Anyway "Kholomo ya ndila a i fhedzi hatsi (A Passing Cow does not deplete the Graze lands)"

They are a party of 2, riding some animal similar to those ridden by baTuareng Amazigh. Your people ride, Zebra and Cows... The sun is already going down and you can see that they do not know the Highways (Mizwila) in these parts of the world. Because of the prowling leopard, you consider that this is the time the King alluded to when he said, "Assist them when the time comes"

They seem armed but you are not concerned as you are not at war, besides which, you are confident that you can handle yourself very well against two armed men.

Everyone carries a weapon here, for hunting and defending themselves against animals and occasional marauders.

The Visitors are startled when they see you, Your Stealth did not allow them to prepare nor give them a chance to draw their arms.

You Crouch to minimize yourself and appear less threatening as they try to reach for their weapons. These are not like any weapons you have seen before. They are possibly similar to those that Portuguese Asili are rumored to carry. You wonder how they work because the men are not holding them the way one holds a weapon around these parts. !Xarra told you about these weapons which were used effectively against his dynasties in the llHui!gaeb at the Coast of Lwanzhe Mbwandaa (Cape Colony area at the Atlantic Ocean). Apparently they are quite lethal. They shoot their arrowhead from a distance and make a terrible noise too. Most Nations that have been subdued thus far, were defeated because of these and apparently they also have ox drawn ones that devastate entire landscapes. You are curious to see them.

At this distance, you figure you can disarm these two before they have a chance to shoot though.

You Call the Name of your Great Grand Father who is Resting with His Fathers in the Life beyond and Ask him to intercede before Nwali (The Great God) on your behalf so that he can Protect you as you obey Him in this Act of Hospitality Wherein He nudged the strings of your Heart even at the King's command.

The Men seem to capitulate as you continue crouching and silently pray whilst maintaining eye contact because you regard them as a threat.

You speak to them but they stare back in Confusion. You introduce yourself:

Ndi Muthu (I am a Person); Muredzamavu (My Complexion resembles the soil of my Land); Ndi Mungona (I belong to the vhaNgona, Bakone, amaNguni Dynasty) wa Lukungurubwe (of the round earth that was created by Volcanic eruptions); fhano Afruika (of the African Continent); fhasi ha vhuranga phanda ha Mune wanga Makahane wavhurathi (under the leadership of His Lordship our King Makahane the sixth who leads his people on behalf of God). Mune wanga ndi Lavhengwa (My Father is Lavhengwa the Turbulent), son of Mupetanngwe (he who folds a Leopard), son of Muratha ngwena (he who steps on crocodile's backs as one does a bridge), son of Bwerinofa (he who is as old as the rocks but who like all succumbs to death), son of Ranwedzi (he who belongs to the creator of the Moon), son of Shiri ya Denga (he who is the eagle of the sky!), Son of Ntu, the son of God! My Name is Thivhilaeli, the unperturbed, a citizen of the second Thulamela.

They respond in an unintelligible tongue.

You smile and Acknowledge them nga u Losha, Ndaa! (Bowing in Greeting)

You use hand signs to ask them to follow you. The sun has now gone down. They Contemplate their decision a little and are interrupted by an eerie growl which makes the decision for them... They follow you.

You Lead Them Home where your wife has Already Prepared Meals.

You can't wait to show off the Cuisine. She has also prepared Water for bathing and a Place for them to Sleep. You Invite them to that evening's Dance and Lessons in Philosophy and History by the fireside.

You are confident that at daybreak, they will carry on with their journey. For now, it is a Privilege for you to House Angels in your Home.

You are reminded of your favorite Fireside Story about showing ubuNtu to others. There was this man who entertained Angels unknowingly. The Angels saved his village from catastrophe. Perhaps these "Angels" will also save your Nation from the Catastrophe that seems to be surrounding every Nation these days.

The following day, they make no effort to leave at the Crack of Dawn as it is Customary with people on a journey, so that they cover much ground whilst it is yet light. You do not ask, Zwi a ila! (It is Taboo). They will tell you when they are ready to leave and you will accompany them until they are on Mizwila/imzila (the Highways.)

After Brunch, you invite them to follow you around. They are happy to do that and they show keen interest in your daily life. Reports from Tholi indicate that the Visitors are truly alone. The threat of invasion is excluded and you host them freely.

By the end of the month, you have started learning each other's languages and you introduce them to King Makahane the 6th, who officially welcomes them in the Nation, in a lavish Ceremony of Dance and Worship.

You answer all their questions honestly. They seem interested and they write everything you say with interesting pens on thin papers... You have never seen this before. The King's scribes only Note Major Events of the year annually on Mvuvhelo (Clay Drums) when these are still wet, before they are baked to immortalize the words. Some Families especially of the Priestly order also do the same.

You notice also that the writing style is different from yours. You show them the writing on your Father's Mvuvhelo. It is a record of your Genealogy. You explain, that your people also write their History on their body Parts, using various decorative Markings and hairstyles; on Clothes, using decorative beads and Pictorially on Rocks, especially in Sacred places where they keep a Record for Thimudi (The unknowable, unknown God). "But, the most important place for Recording History, is in the Heart and ears of one's Children." You conclude.

History Recorded in the Heart can't be lost in war and natural disasters, it cannot be defaced, as you have heard the great sculptures commissioned by Khosi pfareli Khafre (Pharaoh Khafre) of Kemet, Musuru (Misr, Egypt) have been. You have not travelled that far but you have heard of its Majesty and you shudder to think what kind of people could attack such great Monuments to Nyadenga (God, Creator of the Heavens who dwells in the Heavens)?

You explain that the Historical Repository time spent with the Children also forms part of the opportunity for family to spend time together and worship together as the father or Mother or Elder of the village shares exploits of abaNtu (people), in the sight of 'Nwali (God the Almighty).

You know a lot of History of Afrikan abaNtu (People) in general, as well as the History of your family. Your Grandfather being a Tsimbe (wrestling) Champion like yourself, inspired you with stories of Nimurut (Nimrod), the Mighty Hunter before God. Your Grandfather always maintained, you can't be a great hunter unless you know how to hold your own ground. This is the reason he taught you Tsimbe.

The Newcomer Visitors (You no longer call them Asili, because they are now your guests) seem less interested in investigating your writings. You understand, they have their own way of writing and you know that deciphering your writing takes a full cultural immersion because one symbol can speak volumes, and you are grateful that you do not have to teach them all that. In any case, it is written in the Priestly sacred language.

The visitors remain with you for several months, so, you approach the king to see if they can't be given wives and land to build their own homes and start their own Nations, as they do not seem to be in a hurry to leave. The Community would Sisela them of course. The Custom of ukuSisela, is when the Community comes together to help a newcomer start their own isibaya (Livestock Kraal) and Homestead. They would donate various domesticated animals: Chicken, Cattle, goat and even puppies. Then they would hold a Dzunde, where they come together to help the newcomer plough a field. Whilst waiting for their first harvest, the Community will also give the newcomer sufficient Vhukhopfu (dried mealie meal) and Mikusule (various dried vegetables and Insects), Mikoki (various dried Meats) and Muno (salt) to last them, until they can start producing their own food.

The custom of giving wives, disarms a potential enemy. You chuckle to yourself as you remember a story that young men are always told as a caution against marrying a foreigner without it being an arranged marriage. It is a story of a young man who was very hot blooded and a law unto himself. He is another Tsimbe Champion that one and your own personal Hero. It would be safe to say, your father always worried that you would turn out to be like him.

Perhaps you would have, if you did not meet the Most gorgeous iNdoni ya manzi (Dark Beauty, like a Blue Starling) on earth, at your first Domba (Vogue Dance). Domba lasted about a month. Young Men and Women of a Marriageable age who were deemed compatible and whose likely marriages had sometimes already been arranged, were brought together, to meet and to undergo Premarital and Responsible Adulthood Training.

Domba is where you were taught how to be a self-controlled man. "There is a difference between Men and dogs," your father was fond of saying. "Dogs will smell a bitch (female dog) in heat from miles away and will jump over any hedge, no matter how high, to mate it whether it wills or not." Your father would conclude. "Not so, for men, my son" He would admonish. Men, you were told, "are spirit (Ntu) which lives in a body and which have a mind/soul and a Conscience that can differentiate right from wrong". At Domba, Men were taught how to tame their dragons, to emphasise this teaching. "Here, your manhood is not allowed to respond in kind during Dance, if he does, my keen eyes will see and I will humiliate you immediately right here in front of this Domba of 60 young men and women! Are we Clear!?" the head Warden had howled.

She had this most radiant of smiles...it reached her eyes. She also had this deep laughter that came from her belly and reached directly into your heart and nudged it ever so gently. It made you quiver at the knees and sent butterflies up to your chest from your belly. You loved discussing Philosophy, Politics and Natural Science with her. She was an Astrologer and you were always fascinated by her understanding of the signs of the times.

The Domba wards had been observing you, so, come time for dance, they placed you right behind her.

Cruelty!

Much like Asili's ballet, Domba is a Contact Sport. Barely 10 minutes into the Dance you were pulled to the side amidst giggles from the girls. By the third Dance, your situation had become Legendary. Your Mentor decided to tell you the Punishment meted a man deemed untamed. It is told that King Makahane the 3rd, who was also Tshifhe (Priest) whose Holy Pool was Tshitongadzivha on the Luvuvhu river as one goes to ha Lambani, did not tolerate men whose dragons were not tamed. He would take these men atop the mountain that has a precipice on one side. This Precipice was home to Madondindo birds, a type of Guinea fowl that nestled there. Vhafuwi (King Makhane the 3rd) loved Madondindo Bird meat and eggs. Any man found to have violated the Self-Control code would be sent to fetch Vhafuwi a Madondindo bird or eggs.

To reach the area of their abode, a Mountaineering Team was usually necessary and that team would be availed to the errant man with the instructions however to make him descend the precipitous mountain-side where Madondido nestled, with hands tied and holding the Mountaineer's rope with his teeth. Once on the precipitous ledge, he would be warned, that he was going to receive a beating for the violation of the Self-Control Code. Today, is his chance to learn self-control or perish. They would then proceed to give him a beating. If he learns self-control, he will not scream and will be saved, but if he does not learn, he will scream from the pain of the beating, lose his rope and crash down the mountain-side. This practice, he told you, was still in force and you may be subjected to the same fate. After hearing that, you became the master of self-control and you passed Domba with flying colors and a Match. Two years after Domba, rigorous courting and Relationship building visits between the families including ukuCela (Requesting the hand of a maiden in marriage), iLobolo (Paying the Dowry), uMembeso no uKwaba... (Various gift exchange Celebrations), you married the love of your life at age Twenty. She was seventeen. A Twenty-year-old, in your time would be like a Thirty-eight-year-old these days because your home based practical education, permeated every facet of life and you had family support for life as you lived communally and not in nuclear families.

Anyway, back to your Tsimbe champion hero... This guy wore his Locks Long... He did not shave because 'Nwali had locked his Physical Strength in his hair. As a young man you also kept very long Locks because you hoped that you also had the same Special powers... Maybe you do.

The Practice of vhaNgona (your people), to marry their daughters to Nations that were deemed Potential threats, had also worked to the advantage of vhaLemba,

Vhatshimbili na Misi, vhe Mituli, ri do I wana phanda (The Nomadic Men, who go out to Trade and prospect the land without their maidens, believing that wherever they go, they shall find wives). Most vhaLemba are from Senna in (today's Yemen in the Middle East). They are descendants of Shem (Semites) and some of the ten Tribes of Israel, that dispersed to the Afrikan Continent, during the Persian and Babylonian Captivity and being joined by others after the fall of the Jewish Temple at Jerusalem. They are termed "Black Jews", when, in fact, they are some of the real Hebrew Israelites. Other Israelites were dispersed to West Afrika and especially Ghana as some Igbo (descendants of Eber) who were carried off to slavery. Many are fully Assimilated in the local (K)Hamitic vhaNgona/ baKone/amaNguni and do not know their own identity for now.

VhaLemba (Those who refuse to do evil) have assimilated your language and some of your customs. "That is why it is called the mother tongue," you chuckle inwardly. They practice a rudimentary pre-Judaism, Israelite culture and religion. They are responsible for the transmission of much of the oral history you know about Kanaan and Kemet and all your Tsimbe heroes. Anyway, the intermarriage practice seems pretty effective. You have lived in Peace with your Neighboring Nations for Generations now, because of it. Maintenance of Peace through Marriage is the reason for Polygamy amongst Afrikan Kings.

You are hoping that this Proposal to the King will be acceptable and you will have neutralized these visitors if they have ill-intent in their prolonged stay.

Thovhele (The King) is positively disposed toward your suggestion and he Proceeds to Allocate them a Piece of Land each, sufficient to sustain 4 to 5 generations. It takes about that long before descendants have to go and start a new Dynasty. Land is held in Custody by the King on behalf of the people for precisely this reason, so that no one, kin or foe, is treated unfairly and denied the opportunity to be able to sustain themselves by reason of landlessness.

The Visitors accept the wives they are given as well as the Land and other gifts, graciously. They settle down to life in Afruika, bear mixed heritage children that speak LuVenda fluently. You soon learn that these men are "Missionaries" and that they have come your "ways" specifically for the purposes of converting you to their Religion and to further the ends of their sending Nations. They oppose your Spirituality vehemently even though they do not understand it, with a Blanket judgement that it is demonic.

They build a School and a Church. As People convert to their religion, they are forced to cut ties with their "heathen" families and move to the land the King Allocated to the

Missionaries, which is now called a Mission Station. The Mission Station quickly aligns itself with other Mission Stations, which had been established in the Lands of other nearby Monarchs as well as to Asili's Magistrate who had become the new Judiciary in the Land (You have reverted to calling them Asili, because of their Acts, which show that they see themselves as separate from your People. Nobody, saw this coming... Conquest by taking advantage of Kindness.

You figure that their Religion is similar to yours: One God, who is Creator of all; Other Spirits in the Universe who have various functions in the maintenance of balance in the Cosmos; The Call for people to live out the will and purpose of God and to Worship Him; The need for Atonement to restore man to right-standing with God, when this is lost as well as The Acknowledgement of genealogical heritage that roots one in the Call of God and in the land. Where you find their religion fascinating, is that it provides for eternal propitiation for the restoration of relationship between man and God...This is exciting for you.

This new revelation makes sense to you, but you are troubled by the Visitors' unwillingness to really understand your Spirituality, Culture and way of life so that they can see the gap that their piece of religion closes in yours. Their insistence that you be stripped of everything you are, in order to receive their Gospel, does not seem God-like? God always visits people within their culture and helps them see what it is He does not want them to continue with, in their culture and what new revelation He wants them to walk in... their Scripture as recorded in Acts 17 seems to attest to your opinion. This has been the experience of your people thus far whenever God has visited them.

You believe God had indeed visited that young umXhosa maiden Nonqawuse within her culture, when she prophesied and mobilised her people to abandon ubuti in order to cleanse the land with the slaughter of their livestock. Although Asili took advantage of the weakened state of amaXhosa to force them into their labor camps, thus defeating them, you believe that the prophecy will be fulfilled one day... Who knows how Mvelinqanqi (The Alpha and omega who comes before all things and is at the end of all things) will do it? With Him a day is like a thousand years...

This Approach of Missionaries, to sharing their gospel wherein people are stripped of their identity reminds you of the Islamic Religion that was transmitted by the Arabic Traders about a millennium ago and that is now very prominent along the East Coast. They also stripped abaNtu (People) of their names, culture and traditions and gave them new Arabic names, separating them from their "unbelieving/kaffir" families, as they took up Arabic culture. Even now, most see themselves as Arabic rather than

Afrikan. You wonder if it is not possible for one to Accept God's mercy within one's culture? You wonder if God is Arabic or European? (You have learnt that these Asili are from Europe).

You do not understand why European people and Arabic people want you to abandon your culture in order to serve God in this new way if they maintained their cultures. For example, Europeans do not use Hebrew names, they do not dress like Hebrews nor do they follow Jewish traditions which their savior followed, but they maintain that they are His followers... yet for you to follow the savior, they want you to embrace their European culture, which is not the culture of the savior... "Something very wrong with that horse!" you muse.

You decide to Accept the Teachings of their Book but Practice it within your Culture... unbeknownst to you, you are joining a growing number of Afrikans who have done this, like Nehemiah Tile of abaTembu who started the Tembu Church kwaXhosa.

"I tell you this story Matshikhiri, so that you can write it in your heart and repeat it to your Children and your Children's children after you. They need to know who we are and how we have persisted in this continent since creation. There will come a time when Asili will write your History for you. They will do so in such a way that dispossesses you of your Land and Heritage, leaving their History as the legitimate Afrikan History. Your voices will be Deliberately Silenced, Preferably Unheard and you will be erased from the Land as you become European as the North has become Arabic. Your children, will lose their identity and great will their turmoil be, unless you retain this knowledge I tell you here today." Your GrandDad Thivhilaeli had concluded.

So, you have told Granddad Thivhilaeli's Story as if it were yours... because it is, yours... his blood courses through your veins, your DNA has been impacted by the events of his life and you will keep telling it until they will hear and believe and begin to speak. You will No longer be Silent!

Your name is Matshikhiri a Nndwa (Behold a Legion ready for War).

You were born in 1920. Granddad Thivhilaeli told you this story of the arrival of Asili, when you were 12. You had asked him what your posterity was now asking you... "How did Asili come to live and be prosperous in the land of your Ancestors whilst you became landless and have been re-named invading Bantus?" His words have become an eerie prophecy, as indeed your History is now written by Asili to serve Asili objectives. Most disturbing of all, for you, is when you see the names of your Ancestral homes, Rivers and Mountains changed to names in the language of Asili. Sometimes they just bastardise the name… eZimbokodweni becomes, Umbongintwini, Phando vhuria becomes Punda Milia…

It was perplexing for you and being a man of war, you were restless about it.

"Your best weapon now", GrandDad Thivhilaeli had admonished, "is your mouth and your Pen, 'nwananga! (My son!), Do not pick up Arms. Bloodshed begets Bloodshed and what is done is done… we can only change the future. Remember, All People are one and they come from you. We are now looking for Peace… a return to our Settled Lifestyle."

Your Granddaughters have asked you the same question you asked your GrandDad Thivhilaeli with wider ramifications.

They want to know:

- What are the names of their fathers/Mothers to the 89th Ancestor?
- "Can you locate your family in the Quran, the Bible or in Scientific journals?"
- Why are we: "Black"; "Bantus"; "Bushmen"; "Pygmy"; "Caffers"; "Niggers"; "Hottentots"; "Coloureds"?
- What is this ubuNtu and kiNtu, you keep yapping about?
- How did this Continent become known as Africa and who named it that?
- Why is North Afrika Arabic and the Arabic Identity increasing daily in Africa?
- Why are Afrikan Traditions similar to Jewish Customs?
- Why is it that, Non-Afrikans who have lived in Africa for several generations, do not speak Vernacular but you speak European and Arabic languages?
- They want to Know where and how they can Learn Afrikan Proverbs, Idioms and Ngano (Folklore) which tell their History, Teach Wisdom and Train in Righteousness
- Where is Israel and who are its original inhabitants?
- Where is Eden?
- Were you created or did you evolve or fall from the sky? They want to know.
- What/Who is Homo Sapiens? Homo Naledi? Lucy? Eve?
- What is the difference between: inyanga, isanusi, umthandzi, isangoma and umthakathi and are they evil? How are they different from Western trained doctors, witches, warlords and wiccans?
- Who is Jesus? Why is he white when he was born in Kanaan and his parents had Kanaanitic and Shemitic heritage?
- What is the Out of Africa Exodus and who does it affect?
- Why do all Afrikan countries have so-called "Traditional Leaders"? but European Kings are called Monarchs?

- Could Afrikans Read, Write and Count before Colonisation?
- What is Civilisation and were Afrikans civilised before 1652?
- Why is Afrika in such turmoil and lagging in Industrialisation today?
- What does it matter if I aspire to live in Europe or America?
- Why do you persist with this "African way of doing things" when we have moved on and we are all basically the same? Shouldn't we all just be South Africans, Speak English and follow Western Culture which is already the Standard for our Politics, Media, Religion and Socialisation?
- Can I Practice Afrikan Culture and still be authentic to my Religion as a Moslem, Christian, Baha'i...?

Their questions reminded how the final phase of the loss of Land came to be.

It came after King Makahane the 7th Rested with his Ancestors (Died).

"Mavu, uyadunguzela (The Soil/King, is unwell)." The King's aide who came to inform Dad's uncle could barely look in his direction. Dad's Uncle Ramulayo knew. As the great Priest and King's Counsellor, he takes his Medicines and the special golden spear...

When he arrives in the Courtyard, the aides escort him to the Royal chambers. Upon entry of the King's Chambers, he crawls toward Mavu (the King) whilst singing the Royal Praises. He continues until he gets to him. There is no response. He examines him. After examining him and getting consensus from the elders present, it is confirmed that the great one has departed. He punctures the king's main Vein to let out the Blood and inject the embalming Mixture. Afterward he crawls out backward in silence to confirm that Musanda wo Dzama (His Royal Highness Has Rested), Makhadzi begins a Song, the Drums beat in a deep rumbling tone like the heartbeat: "Dungununtungu, Du! Dungununtungu, Du!" Dad's uncle Ramulayo proceeds to the Danga (Cattle Kraal) and points at the beast with the golden spear. Before he is out of the gate, the bull is down, to the sound of ululation. It is a different type of ululation. Not the usual vibrant and joyful type. This has a Mournful ring to it...

Dad's Uncle Ramulayo returns to the Royal chamber with the hide of the bull to wrap the King's body in a sitting position and Sew him in after both the body of Musanda and the hide are thoroughly prepared for Mummification. His body is left in state... it will lie here and several layers of hide will be added upon the previous as the former dries up and tightens, over several weeks whilst the Nation Mourns. The Nation will not be told until after the Royal Council has confirmed the Successor. Coronation will take place immediately after the Nation has been formally informed. Some Nations bury their king immediately but keep this secret from the Nation until the Successor is Appointed and secured. The burial rites differ from Nation to Nation and they are always kept secret. In this case, the King would be buried seated and facing his Palace to become a Trusted Ancestor for the Palace as it is believed that he will guide future generations as iThonga elihle. He would be buried with several articles and may be accompanied in death by his Royal Food Taster or Chief Counselor.

It was not to be so, for King Makahane the 7th.

Barely 2 months laying in state, there is a raucous in the Streets, Mbulungeni's name is being chanted in the Streets as the new King. People are rushing to the Church. He is being coroneted as the new King by the Magistrate from Makhado. Mbulungeni (Nurture Me), is the son to the late Musanda's (King's) cousin, He is not the legitimate Successor. His Lineage is not a lineage of Kings. Although the King had not Converted to the religion that you now know to be Christianity, he had encouraged those in his nation who felt so led, to convert, and Mbulungeni had converted and worked well with the Missionaries at the behest of the King. The King's son and rightful heir on the other hand had questioned the advancements of the Missionaries and their Government, in the land and he was generally unco- operative with Asili Missionaries and Government.

At the sound of Coronation announcements, the King's son fled to his Mother's people in Gaza, what is today Mozambique, for fear of Assassination.

The New King and the Missionaries advance the new way of life. Asili from Makhado move people from their lands and push them to Arid areas, appropriating their homesteads; grazing lands and Holy Forests as Farms for themselves. They Destroy Archaeological evidence or build atop it, as they see nothing sacred in the land. People watch in bewildered amazement. Without a Legitimate king and the Military in disarray, they are defenseless. Much of the land is now inaccessible and they are no longer able to graze their herd of cattle and are forced to sell them as they are Taxed for everything. They are forced to pay these taxes using Asili money, so once their herd of cattle is depleted, they join Asili labor force to earn this money to pay the Taxes. The Great Sir Steven Hamilton fences off Thulamela, to separate the wild animals from the people and ecosystems are irreparably damaged.

The Closure of Thulamela behind fences is a request by the new Asili reignal king of Afrika Tshipembe (The Southern African Domain), King Paul Kruger, and is thus aptly named, Kruger National Park. This effectively Closes people off from their Mines, Farms and Trade Routes. baSan Nations disappear into the Forests and continue their nomadic lives as some of them do to this day. Most become indentured labourers and slaves in Asili Farms. They become Classified as Coloured. baKhoe Nations who are Semi pastoralists suffer the same fate becoming assimilated into amaNguni Nations, being designated coloured and becoming indentured Farm labourers. This is how baKhoe and baSan become erased and expunged from South African History and their numbers are now claimed to be less than a few thousand, when in fact their offspring is expressed in Today's few baSan and baKhoe and the multitudes of "Coloured", "Black" and some "White" People.

Today as you sit in your Garden, you are Mesmerised at the Kaleidoscope of color. They are from all over the world... Yet they are all yours. Tshisikule with his pitch dark skin is a sight for tired old eyes and he loves clambering on GrandGumommy...a word he created for Grand Great Mother. "How Innovative", you think to yourself. These names for Grandparents were first innovated by his grandparents who called you GuguMma and GuguBaba for Grandmother and Grandfather respectively, because the Luvenda Makhulu, does not infer gender and being western encultured, this was confusing for the children, so you let them call you GuguMma and GuguBaba (Gugu being the other name for Grand Mother), "What's the harm?" you had thought. It was enchanting anyway. Little do you realise that in your enchantment, you are also feeding into the loss of culture or is this evolution of culture?

His Cousin sister (as they call each other, In kiNtu she is just his sister, full stop) Paulette, with her adorable million questions was headed your way! You love it. It Keeps your mind sharp. Her burnished bronze skin, green eyes and Red hair are startling but Mesmerising.

For a 92-year-old, Grandgumommy's Knees Are Strong. She owes it to !Xarra's bark and all those years of Kneeling to Cook, Polish the floors with cow dung and mud cement as well as Painting the house with Clay. You suddenly realize that it has been a long time since you last saw the different colors of Clayey Soil: Red, Yellow, Black, White, Green... it came in all sorts of colors, just like this Kaleidoscope of Great Great Grand Children in your Garden.

GrandguMommy was an expert at decorating a house, a great Cook who loved Entertaining. You were the envy of the Town! Everybody used to just rock up around Lunch time because they knew she was quite Hospitable. She served up a Storm. Various Vegetables: Thanga, Muroho wo kodeliwaho, Delele, Murudi, Vowa... Types of Porridge: Vhuswa ha Mutuku na vhutshena na ha makhaha... "there must always be a choice" she would insist. Then there would be the different Meats, Mukoki wa nguluvhe ya daka, Khuhu ya mukokoroshi na gwengwelele la hone, nama ya mbudzi, ya nngu, kholomo...Even if she is serving Meat, sometimes she would still serve the edible insects, just for good measure: Thongolifha, Nzie, Madzhulu. These would be Served in several Courses...

The drinks always flowed too, mukumbi wa Mufula (Amarula Spirits), Mabundu (Sorghum beer), Mahafhe (Gin) and Amasi (Sour Milk). For Dessert she had a variety of specials: Thophi (a Pumpkin Relish); Various types of Fruit; Tshidzimba (a Mixture of various beans); Sweet Potato; Afrikan Potato and various Cheeses. For more on some of the recipes her descendants still make, you can buy the book: South African Indigenous Foods by Bomme baseMzansi from amazon.

The men loved her, always commenting: "Vha na mafunda, vhathu vha Dzata" (The Dzata people are Hospitable). Sometimes you would feel jealous at all the attention she got, but that would soon fizzle as you felt this deep sense of pride in her ability to hold a Community together. Everybody would stay on until sunset, when the entertainment from zwikona na zwigombela Dances Would Start. The elaborate dances and exquisite music was very spiritual. One always felt renewed after a day of Celebrations.

Your Granddaughter Vhugala (Glory) one of the authors of GuguMma and GuguBaba fame told you the other day that after discouraging your people from all these types of Music and Dance because it was deemed evil, Asili were now Researching and Confirming the Therapeutic effects of Song and Dance on Cancer and Mental Health... It explains why abaNtu are so sick these days, their DNA is no longer receiving the daily healing Musical Waves...

Your eyes wander off as a neighbor Hollers a Greeting from the Street. He has been a neighbor for close to 50 years... ever since the forced removals made you to take up residence here. He spends close to twenty minutes standing there on the Street, speaking to you over your low hedge to enquire about your life and your family that has come to visit you for their annual Christmas retreat.

You are reminded of your wonderment every time you visit Vhugala in the suburbs, at how high their boundary walls are... yet there are no lions there. "Who or what are they trying to keep out?" you had asked her. Even when lions used to roam about, you never built walls around your homesteads, the bushy hedges and feda la muthu (Natural human odor) were sufficient as territory markers. Only Misanda (the King's Citadels) were walled with massive Stone Walls that Stretched for Kilometers around the ruling city. Some are still Standing to this day in what have become Private farms and Game Reserves. Few such as the Dzimbabwe ruins are well known whilst others like the Phalaborwa and Dzata ruins are starting to catch the eyes of the scientists.

What is remarkable, is that you have never seen her neighbours. Their walls are higher and they have an electric fence over them. They have cameras mounted on the walls as well. She tells you that she only sees the neighbours when they come in or leave their house. She was hoping to have a Street Meet and greet, but she does not even know how to introduce herself to the neighbours, 18 years later. Being a doctor and her husband a School principal, they were some of the first "Black" people to move into this neighbourhood.

"How do you get help if you are in danger or something" you had asked her. "Oh, heee..." she had chuckled, "I have to call my security company and the police. If I am in danger, I Press this Panic button here."

You worry about her because she is always exhausted. Her body aches and she constantly complains of headaches, dizziness and fogginess of the brain. She is only 50! Pity you have not maintained the culture of using !Xarra's bark and all that intellectual property has been lost. Fortunately, some knowledge has been painstakingly collected and your children can learn about it from the book: People's Plants, a Guide to useful plants of Southern Africa, available at Loot.co.za. In your youth, you all used to chew on it. It was good for everything, Appetite suppressant, Immune Booster, Cure for Colds and minor ailments and good for age related aches and imbalances. Surely it would have done her good. She tells you the doctors could not find anything wrong with her except that she is menopausal and has high blood pressure. Some of her friends have even suggested that it may be that she needs to ukuthwasa (undergo Afrikan Spiritual Training).

You know that your mother who was a Medical doctor herself (She would be called a witch doctor by Asili), would have known exactly how to manage her. Menopause was not a big deal in your era. Your wife sailed through it. Besides, you think that she just needs to Rest and take life easy. She is always busy... both she and her husband who is now a Pastor and a Member of the Provincial legislature. They have no work-life balance. Those poor children were practically raised by their caregiver, Television and Technology. You remember very vividly how you always found the girls home alone with only the caregiver and their technological gadgets for company when they were young. It did not help that the neighbors' children were "white", older and at high School or Tertiary.

Fortunately, they met another "Black" girl at the Preschool and then began the camping... they camped at each other's houses for weekends. That helped and also didn't... as they became fully self-parented.

Her children, Munaka (The beautiful one) and Matenzhe (The Mighty one) were some of the few "Black" girls in their private school. You shudder even now when you recall the Micro-aggressions they reported to have experienced: "You are different from the other blacks" (you are The Better Blacks); "You are so pretty, well-mannered and speak so well, you can't be black!"; "I have called all of you here to let you know that xyz (the white girl)...is depressed, If her hygiene seems otherwise, let me know, We all have to support her... but of the "Black" girl in the same predicament... xyz is very lazy and unhygienic, Make sure she reports to you to prove she has bathed"; "Why don't you do drugs like the others?"; "I like and prefer your hair Long and silky like that"; "You will not fit into that, It is size 36"; "I love Blacks, my Maid is Black"; "You people must not speak vernacular on the school grounds"... It was incessant. Ultimately, they were left feeling inadequate, unworthy, Anxious and Depressed. Their Mother was left confused. "Their Confidence will be amazing, they will be taught by white teachers and associate with white Students you know" She had told you when she registered them at the school. Now, she was getting the opposite impact and it was deeply upsetting for her.

They still have to work so hard to remind themselves that they are worthy and they belong. It does not help that they feel alienated to their own Kin who call them coconuts or white. You are very proud that they are now... "what do they say...? Yes...! Woke."

They are starting to ask you relevant life questions. This is why everybody is gathered here... You are grateful to be able to share this knowledge before you go and join your Ancestors.

Mboneni (Be Mindful of my being in yourself), Vhugala's (Glory) Mom, will have to Translate. Munaka and Matenzhe do not speak Vernacular and this message is best narrated in vernacular. You never understood it, Vernacular was their First additional language at school. It was taught by a white teacher who did not speak vernacular. They achieved distinctions in it but are not conversant in it...You wonder if even Mboneni will understand some of the Traditional concepts? Three generations of Western Enculturation have left her bereft of Afrikan Cognition.

One has to be immersed in kiNtu culture to really understand it and the ubuNtu spirit within which it operates. God will help you though. It is time. You can no longer be Silent. You have Unsilenced yourself and you will be heard!

You are grateful that you have lived long enough to have the repository of the History of abaNtu and baTwa in Afruika since Creation because of all that oral history passed to you from generation to generation. Mboneni has confirmed for you that most of your oral history is corroborated by Scientific studies. It is this History you wish to Narrate with the corroborating Bibliography.

"Grandguby, Grandguby!" Paulette disrupts your thoughts. "Look, there's Daddy!" she chimes spiritedly as she also clambers atop GrandguMommy.

Logan steps forward and Kneels beside you, Ndaa! (Venda Male greeting) Your heart melts. You never know what to do with him... Ndi Muthu (He is a person) and not only is he a person, he is now part of your family!? How can this be? Logan is Asili from Scotland... How ironic.

At 98, your eyesight is still good, you do wear glasses for reading, but otherwise, you can still see a Lion even if it was camouflaged behind a shrub. Your hearing is nearly perfect and your mind is Lucid. As for your memory, all that recitation of the Genealogy must have helped. You take a good look at Logan's wide smile as though you want to immortalize it, and you acknowledge him: Ndau ya Nduna! "Take a Seat my son" you direct him.

"Pholetha, ni khou lemela zwino, iyani ni yo tamba na vha'nwe (Paulette, my knees are tired now, go on and play with others)" GrandguMommy Chimes in...

Looking at Logan, your thoughts go back to that fateful day... The last time your Grandfather Thivhilaeli saw !Xarra and the day of their arrival...Thulamela is now Kruger National Park. Your Ancestral home is now a World heritage site of a "Prehistoric advanced people who are obviously NOT Bantu and could possibly be the Khoi and the San" reads the Plaque placed at the Information desk for tourists who wish to visit Thulamela.

Your Descendants 300 years from now will surely not be able to make any connection of self with that place. They will believe the Lie that Bantus arrived in South Africa in the 1800s when Trek-boere Clashed with them upon the latter's arrival eCacadu (Zuurveld). This is the story many Afrikaners grew up on and which has been told in School History Books and which make Racial Reconciliation and Re-Appropriation of Land in South Africa such a Minefield. It is also what traps "Black" people in a cycle of poverty, anger and violence as they remain: Landless, Poor, Unable to access the Economic value chain landless and their History and Identity is erased.

Looking at Logan and the love between him and your great granddaughter Munaka, you remind yourself: "We have to find each other, and it starts with the Truth..."

It is time!

The Drum Beats!

Makhadzi sings: "Dziphathutshedzo dzenedzi, ni nga dzi vhala naaaa!?" (God's Blessings are innumerable): Hymn 146 from the Lutheran LuVenda Hymn Book.

"Salungano, Salungano! (Let me tell you that which sounds like a fable, but is actually, Truth)" you begin...

"Salungano! (Tell it, as if it is a Fable)" They Respond.

"Ndi Muvenda Mubikwa na ive, ive lavhibva Muvenda a sala (As Muvenda, I have been here in the times of Molten Larva that melted the Rocks and still I endure), Ndi Ntangi wa kugala (The First of the People), Nganiwapo (From hence I originate), Tshidzatshapo (My Ancestral graves are here)"

You begin. You are **#NolongerSilent**

You hope that all those who hear this History, will tell it to their Children and their Children's Children as you have been faithful to your GrandDad Thivhilaeli and his friend !Xarra, in telling the History that they received from their Ancestors and which they lived and they Transmitted to you orally. It is also the History that you lived through and are now capturing in the written word by the hand of Vhugala. A History that is now being proven True as more people research honestly about Afruika! A History that one Day will Grace the School Curriculum and help guide a New (South) Afrika and bring Healing to her.

Salungano...

Salungano

In what ways have you felt that the current Historical Narrative of your Country has Negated, Erased or Unheard you and your people?

Who and What are you Grateful to/for in your life? Do you know the History of your Family?

Could you Start Writing your Family/Community/National History?

What else could you write to help advance knowledge about your People? Journal it for yourself.

Why is it important to know and understand your History? How will you use the Information you learn from this Book? Will you Commit to learning a/your Vernacular Language?

Construct your Family Genealogy: Do this, as a Work in Progress. Start by buying a Nice Journal and Entitle it: Our Genealogy. Take Time and visit several Relatives and try to Reconstruct this as far back as possible. If you only know your Parents or Grandparents, do not despair! it is time to Start...

Part 1: Afrika

"Kingdoms in Afrika are the oldest Political Institutions which emerged before time began."
Davidson B (1994:41)

The name

3 Schools of Thought:

Indigenous African origin:

Afruika, from: Afurakanu and Afuraitkaitnut (Male and Female)

Indigenous name since Creation as found recorded on the Medutu of Kamit (Hieroglyphs of Egypt) (http://www.odwirafo.com)

This is supported by:

- Massey in 1881 stated that Africa derives from Egyptian Af-rui-ka which means to turn to the womb's opening. The Birthplace;
- In luVenda, u pfuruka means Agitated by birth pangs and nyika means land (Apfurunyika) Land of the Birthing or Birth pangs;
- Jewish historian, Flavius Josephus Asserts that Afrika was named after Abraham's grandson Afar (Epher) whose descendants dwelt in Libya as per Genesis 25:4;
- Robert R. Stieglitz at Rutgers in 1984 proposed that Aphi-ir-ca derived from Ophir (The Land of Ophir) Genesis 2:10-11; Genesis 10:7 & 1Kings 10:22, Land of Gold.

Travelers' descriptions of the Continent as they visited it. (tripsavvy.com)

- Romans named the (Northern part of the) Continent after the indigenous Afri Berber people who lived in Kart-hadasht (Carthage) and Libya. The Afar people;
- In Sanskrit Hindi: Apara means the land beyond (Beyond India);
- In the Roman Empire languages: Latin and Greek, Aprica means Sunny and Aphrike means without Cold and horror;

Other Names used to name the Continent, Concurrently and over time

Egypt/Aegyptos

Was the name for the entire Continent? Not just the currently demarcated area named Egypt whose size has been changed several times over the years, on successive Political Maps.

Egypt is the English Bastardisation of Hwt-Ka-Pta. Hwt (House/Temple/Mansion) Ka (of) Ptah (the Spirit of Ptah/Tata/God). It is also known as the Garden of God. Genesis 13:10 and (www.worldhistory.org/egypt). Afrikans understood themselves to be God's stewards on earth. God had said: Multiply, Increase and fill the Earth. Everything Afrikan abaNtu do, they do for and on behalf of God. Their kings were called Khosi Pfareli (Pharaoh), because of this very understanding... The King who rules in God's stead. This is why it was not enough to honor God with the Pyramids, the whole Land was named after Him. Indlu ka Tata (Hwt-ka-Ptah). The Garden of God. God in turn used Egypt as the Land of Refuge Genesis 12:10; 39:5; Matthew 2:13-23 and the Land of Judgement Exodus 1:8; Deuteronomy 6:12

Kmt (Kemet) after Kham (Ham) also Khamit. This name has been in use since the dispersion of people when Afrikans populated the whole Afrikan Continent. Genesis 10; Psalm 78:5; 105: 23-27; 106:22

Misr after Misraim the second son of Kham. The Citizens of Cairo have known Cairo by its original name, Misr (Misraim) from Antiquity and to date they still call it Misr. Misr is the Capital City of Egypt. It is the Home of Tutankhamun and the Great Sphinx of Giza. When the citizens of Cairo are in the city, they refer to the Rest of Egypt as Cairo. When they are outside Cairo, they refer to Cairo as Misr.

Havilah

Havilah is the son of Kushi (Cush). Havilah is the Land of the sons of Kushi, it is the entire continent of Afrika. This name has been in use since the birth of Havilah. Genesis 10:7 & 11:29

Alkebulan: Since 1400 years ago, with the Arabic Colonisation of North Africa

In Arabic, Alkebulan means Land of the indigenous Black people; Garden of Eden (Qabl = Before / Al = the / Lan = here: The ones who were here before or first) Land of the ones who were here before or first. (Courtesy of Names.org)

Aethiopia

According to Annales d'Ethiopie, 27,2012 (305-306) and Biblically, Aethiopia is the land of the sons of Cham (Ham/Kham). Medieval Mappaemundi, before the 13th century, mostly represent the five zones of the sphere or only the inhabited part. This is represented as a large latitude region, occupying the Southern half of Afrika, West to East and sometimes including Arabia (the Kingdom of Saba or Sabeans) and India, "between Egypt and a torrid equatorial zone, or the circular Ocean."

Azania

This name has been in use since AD 1000 Applied mainly to the South Eastern parts of Afrika (Mozambique and KwaZulu) apparently by the Greeks who transcripted the Arabic name: Ajam, one who is mute, whose native tongue is not Arabic (wordpress.com). The Muteness also refers to the focus on Listening instead of talking. Azania(h) means God Listens (Names.org).

Africa

English Imperialism and Convention Popularised the use of **Africa with a C** instead **of a K,** for the name of the Continent whilst the French retained the French version of **Africa: Afrique**

Afrikans, have known the Continent as Afruika and variants of the same as well in their own Language in a Manner that honors its Geography; History and God's purpose for them, in the Continent.

Understanding the History of the Name, allows Afrikans to Re-Appropriate the Name of the Continent: Afrika!

In this book, the name Afrika, will sometimes be spelled with a C to follow convention or as per quoted Text... and often if not always with a K, to reclaim Identity.

The Continent

Geography and Culture

1. There are 54 countries and 4 "non-self-governing territory/ Dependencies" During the writing of this book, Western Sahara went into war on 01/11/20 to assert its sovereignty.
2. All of Afrika was colonized by foreign powers during the "scramble for Africa", except for Ethiopia and Liberia.
3. Before colonial rule, Afrika comprised upward of 10000 different states and autonomous groups with distinct languages and customs.
4. The Pharaonic civilization of ancient Egypt is one of the world's oldest and longest-lasting civilizations, it succeeded the Sudanic, Kushitic civilisation which are the oldest.
5. The Afrikan continent is the first and world's oldest populated area. Humanity proceeds out of Afrika and all people are descendants of Afrikan abaNtu/ baTwa (People).
6. The Sahara is the largest desert in the world and is bigger than continental USA.
7. Six of the top ten countries with the largest annual net loss of forested areas are in Afrika.
8. Over 1270 large dams have been built along the continent's many rivers.
9. Lake Victoria (Naalubale)is the largest lake in Afrika and the fourth-largest freshwater lake in the world at 68000 square kilometres.
10. Afrika has the most extensive biomass burning in the world, yet only emits about 4% of the world's total carbon dioxide emissions.
11. Afrika has approximately 30% of the earth's remaining mineral resources.
12. The continent has the largest reserves of precious metals with over 40% of the gold reserves, over 60% of the cobalt, and 90% of the platinum reserves
13. Afrika has eight of the 11 major biomes and the largest-remaining populations of lion, elephant, rhinoceros, cheetah, hyena, leopard and hundreds of other species.
14. Megafauna like giraffe, zebra, gorilla, hippopotamus, chimpanzee and wildebeest are unique to the continent and only found in Afrika.
15. Afrika has over 85% of the world's elephants and over 99% of the remaining lions are on the Afrikan continent.
16. Afrika is the world's second largest continent covering about over 30 million square kilometres. China, India, Portugal, Spain, Great Britain, Germany, France, USA, Netherlands, Italy, Switzerland, Japan and Eastern Europe together fit into

Africa in terms of Landmass. (Asia is the largest Continent at 44.8 million square kilometres). The Below Map, Courtesy of World Economic Forum, 17 December 2015, shows True Size of Africa by superimposing maps of known countries on the Afrikan Map.

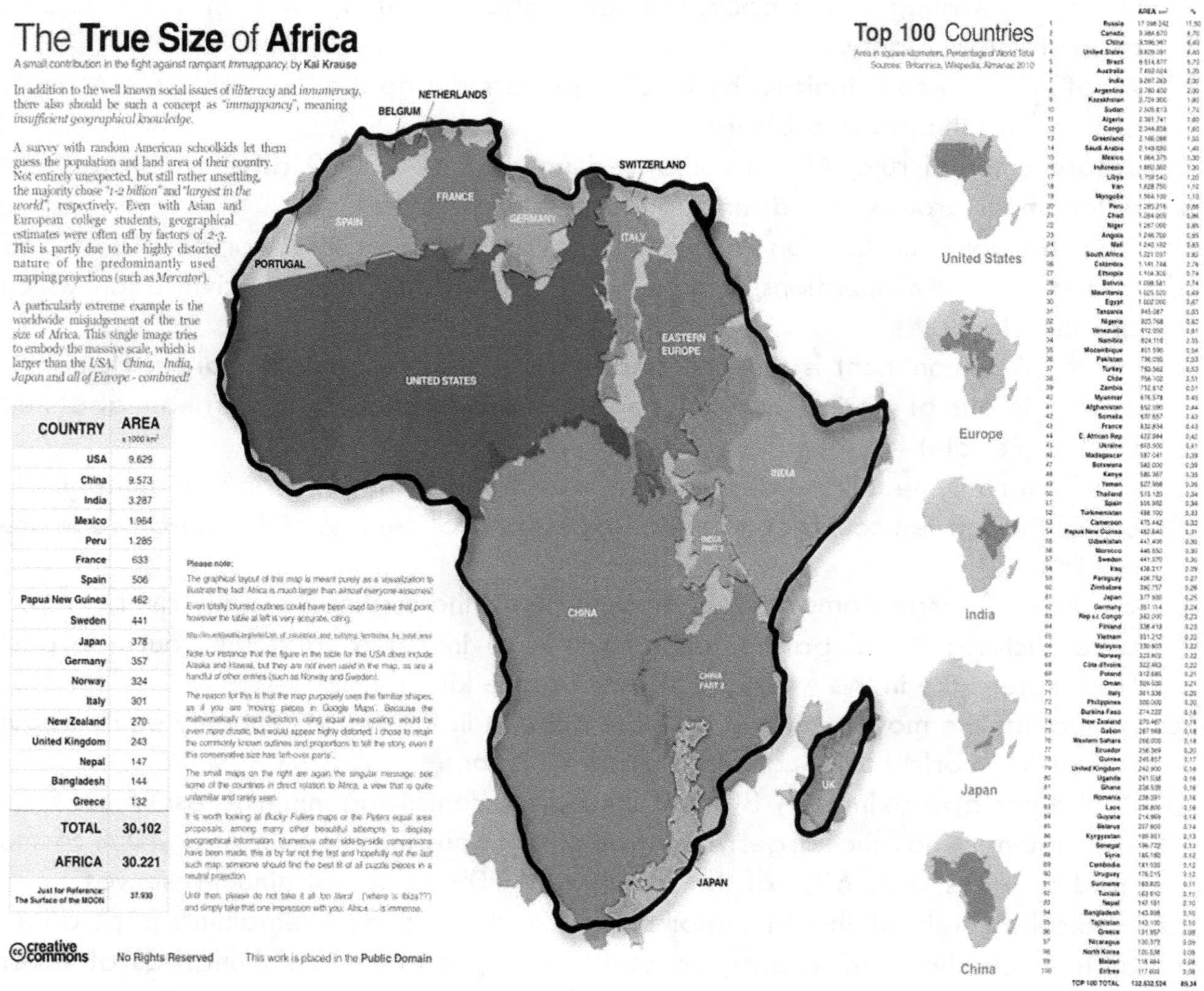

Courtesy: World Economic Forum, 17 December 2015: True Size of Africa

17. Afrika is home to the world's largest living land animal, the Afrikan elephant, which can weigh up to 7 tons.
18. Afrika has over 25% of the world's bird species.
19. Eight of Conservation International's 34 biodiversity hotspots are in Africa.

20. The Serengeti (Tanzania) hosts the world's largest wildlife Annual migration on Earth with over 750 000 zebra marching ahead of 1.2 million wildebeest as they cross this amazing landscape.
21. Lake Malawi has more fish species than any other freshwater system on earth.
22. The Nile River is the longest river in the world with a total length of 6650 kilometres.
23. There are over 3000 protected areas in Africa, including 198 Marine Protected Areas, 50 Biosphere Reserves, 129 UNESCO World Heritage Sites, and 80 RAMSAR "Wetlands of International Importance". Most of these are also home to most of Africa's past civilisations that have yet to be examined.

Religion

- 49% of Afrikans are Christian: Mainly Sub-Sahara Africa; 42% are Muslim: Mainly North Africa;
- 8% are: Afrikan Traditional, 1% Hindu, Baha'i, Atheist and other religions (Both descendants of Migrant people who brought the Religion and converts).

Population

- In 2020, Afrika was the second most populous continent in the world, with about 1.341 billion or 16% of the world's population.
- In 2020, the world population was estimated at 7.8 billion.
- IN 2020, the most populous continent was Asia at: 4.672 billion people. (this accounts for 59% of the world's population)
- The least Populous Continents are: Europe with 447.8 million; South America with 422. 5 million People; USA with 331million and Canada with 39.7 million.
- Afrika as a Young Population, with Over 40% of Africans under the age of 35. It is estimated that the continent's population will more than double to 2.3 billion people by 2050 (in 30 years 'time).

The People

The People of Afrika are Afrikans. Afrikan Herders, Hunters, and Farmers.

Although it should be obvious as to whom the Afrikan Identity refers to, in reality, the Afrikan Identity is a Contentious Painful subject. The reason for this, is the Conquest and Settlement of Afrika by other Nations from 343 BC to 1994 AD, a Period of about 2300 years. Afrikan Oppression officially ended in 1994 (27 years ago). Its Emotional, Spiritual, Social and Economic toll is only now, beginning to emerge, as Afrikans seek to Re-Humanise from the 2300 years of Conquest, Settlement and Slavery; 500+ years of Trans-Atlantic Slavery; 360+ years of Colonisation and Apartheid.

The descendants of the Conquerors, Traders and Settlers of Afrika, who are either mixed heritage with Afrikans or not, have persisted in the Continent and have Naturalised as Continental Afrikans. Some of these descendants have been made to believe that they are superior and better than the Aboriginal, Autochthone, Indigenous and Native Afrikans who have been Classified as Sub-Saharan, Black and xxx, following Racist Classifications and Derogations of Afrikans over time.

To be Afrikan, is to be the Progenitors of all Humanity; The First People in every Continent; The Architects of the Many Pyramids and Great Walls Strewn throughout the Continent; The First Language Speakers; The First Mathematicians; The first Writers; The first Astrologers; The First Physicians and Surgeons; The First Miners; The first Artists; The First Industrialists; The first Civilisations; The First Government, Culture and Religion... This, is irreconcilable with the image given to Afrika, of Poverty, Backwardness and 3rd world Darkness.

In order for those who imagined Afrika as the Dark Continent, to make sense of its Great Civilisations, Afrikans were displaced from their Afrikan Identity by being Named, Classified and or Derogated as: Black, Kaffir, Negro, Bantu, Pygmy, Hottentot, Coloured and Sub-Saharan...Anything, but Afrikan. The Afrikan Identity was then used in relation to the Conquerors, except as far as it relates to: Pestilence, War and Famine.

Afrikans are the descendants of (K)Hami's 4 Sons: Kush; Misraim; Phut and Kanaan. The 4 Nations became 26, then 120 and 10 000, each with a language of their own, which was related to the initial Proto-Kintu Language. Today 3000 of the 10 000 Languages survive.

In Literature, one finds these People named: Kushutic/Kushites; Nubians; Hamitic (rendered (K)Hamitic by the author); Ancient Egyptians (Misraimi); Ludites/Lubim (Libyans/Phutites) Bantu and Sub-Saharan. The Kanaanitic people who are also (K) Hamitic, tend to be Classified in literature as S(h)emetic. This understanding is recent and is caused by the "Removal" of the Arabian Peninsula where the Kanaanites and some Kushites settled, from Afrika and the renaming thereof as the Middle East. The Middle East was occupied by both (K)Hamitic and S(h)emetic people and it was part of Afrika, North East Afrika until the 1800s when North Afrika and North-East Afrika became Caucasoid and divided into North Africa and the Middle East (MENA: Middle East and North Africa). Literature further distinguishes Pastoral/Semi-Pastoralist Khoe and Hunter San Nations from their Farmer (So called Bantu) Brethren. This is incorrect. Farmer, Hunter, Trader and Herder sons of (K)Ham are the sons of (H)Kam. One People. They are Not Different People. They are one People who grew into various Nations with different and Complimentary Callings of Hunting, Herding, Farming and Trading. All These Terminologies Are Artificial, created from the Dominions Paradigm to Classify, Box, Analyse and Package Afrikans in Labels that the Imperialist can understand and use for their Agenda of World Dominion. We are Not who they say we are. We are who we say we are: Afrikans. People of the Afrikan Continent. are referring to Black People. All these, are Afrikan People.

Afrikans are of varying Phenotypic Characteristics, Histories and Occupations/ Callings, but they are one people.

- From tall Maasa'i, to short baTwa;
- From the broad-lipped, broad-nosed to the thin-lipped and pointy-nosed;
- From very yellow hues to Red/copper, to very dark green and blue hues of skin tone that have been Classified as Black and Brown or Dark Skin;
- From very coarse and dry, water resistant, to loose curled, and wooly Hair Texture;
- From Dark Brown to Red/copper to black and even Blonde (yellow) Hair Color;
- From the rare, but very present, Blue and Green, to the predominant, Dark Brown and black eye color;
- From Hunter to Herder to Farmer, they are one Family.
- From unmixed (K)Hamitic Heritage (if such a thing still exists) to Mixed Afro-S(h)emetic; Afro-Asian; Afro-European; Afro-Indian; Afro-American; Afro-xxx to Austronesian and xxx.

They have always lived Symbiotically with one another in the Continent, as well as with S(h)emetic people of the Arabian Peninsula. S(h)emitic people have a wide

Phenotypic Spectrum that can easily fit into the Sub-Saharan look and the Asiatic look and everything in between. They Migrated in and out of the Continent from time immemorial for Hunting, Shepherding and Trading Needs and intermarried with Afrikans, becoming one with them. They can be found in every part of Afrika. Some of them are part of the 10 Lost Tribes of Israel and the Hebrews, the so- called Black Jews, who are in Truth: Hebrew Israelites, who may or may not be Jewish (as in Judean and or follower of the Jewish Religion) abaNgoni (The Righteous ones) or vhaLemba (Those who keep themselves pure/Righteous by not partaking of/in unclean things)

How did Afrikans become: Arabic, Berber, Sub-Saharan, Negroid, Black, Pygmy, Hottentot, Bushman, Kaffir, Coloured and White?

The Arab Identity

In 4000 BC, Ta-Seti in Sudan, was Afrika's Continental Polity. Here Afrikans built their first Pyramids. A Total of about 255 Pyramids are still in existence in Sudan. From this Centre, they helped to Establish the other recognized three main Ancient Civilisations of: Sumeria (Middle East/Arabian Peninsula), Indus Valley (India) and Iberia (Southern France, Portugal and Spain Iberian Peninsula) Hermel, H. Black Sumer: The African Origins of Civilisation (2012). Hwt-ka-Pta (Egyptian), was then established as an Afrikan Continental Religious and Trade Centre, due to its Strategic Position as a Gateway to these new Civilisations. Goods from West and North Afrika were transported through the Trans-Saharan Trade Route, whilst Southern Afrikan goods came through the Water Ways of the Great Lakes and the Nile River to be Transported through the Via Maris to establish these new Centres of Civilisation.

In the Sumerian Middle East, together with the Aboriginal Autochthone and Native S(h)emetic people of the Arabian Peninsula, Afrikans built the cities of Erech, Calneh, Babylon and Akkad. They were joined by the Indo-European descendants of Japheth: Persians, Greeks, Romans, Scythians, Macedonians, Indians and Asians. (These are lighter skinned people with long straight hair, what became classified as Caucasoid and Mongoloid and later some became classified as white) Thus the Mixed look of Arabic people who have a spectrum of phenotypic features from very swarthy to very lightly pigmented and from very coarse hair to very light hair)

Sumer later became known as, Mesopotamia (Meso = between and Potamos = Rivers: Tigris and Euphrates Rivers, The so-called fertile Crescent, in today's: Iraq, Kuwait, Turkey and Syria). During the time of Tiglath Pileser, a united Identity of the people of the now Cosmopolitan Arabian Peninsula, began to emerge with a diffuse Afro-Semito-Euro-Asiatic Culture and Language. The Lingo-Cultural Identity became known as Arabic (Lingo-Culture of the Arabian Peninsula). The Cosmopolitan (K)Hamito– S(h) emito – Indo-European People, became known as Arabian/Arabic People (Arabs). The Native Arabs however are the S(h)emetic Arabs who are Abraham's Children by Hajra, the Ishmaelites, 12 Nations. These are predominantly part of the ancient bedouins. Islam later Solidified this Identity as most Arabic people became Muslim, so that the Arabic Lingo-Culture, became the Lingo-Culture of Islam (Much like the Lingo-Culture of Europe became the Lingo-Culture of Christianity).

Between 632 AD and 1100 AD Islam had Spread through Missionary Campaigns; Military Campaigns, Trade and Pilgrimage from the Arabian Peninsula to as far West as Spain, East to North India and South to North Afrika. Muslim forces built Imperial Structures in these various territories, so that the territories became Muslim and Arabic, Lingo-Culturally. This Process has been termed: Arabisation, but the other Process has not been termed Europeanisation...

The Nations of Afrika that have become Assimilated into the Arabic League of Nations Are Predominantly in or near the Sahara and they are:

- North Afrika: Morocco, Algeria, Tunisia, Libya and Egypt. The lands West of Egypt (Morocco, Algeria, Tunisia and Libya) became known as the Maghreb. Maghreb is Arabic for: West of.
- The Sahel (Although Sahel literally means Coastlands, some of the lands grouped in the Sahel are further from the Coastland). These are the nations of – Senegal, Southern Mauritania, Central Mali, Northern Burkina Faso, Niger, Northern Nigeria, Northern Cameroon, Central African Republic, Central Chad, Sudan.
- The Horn of Afrika – Djibouti, Eritrea, Ethiopia and Somalia. Some of the people who dwell in these Countries, now Identify as Arab.

A Total of about 420 million People in these Countries are now identified as Arabic, rather than as Afrikan, which is their Genetic and Continental Identity. They are denied their Mixed Heritage as well as their identity with their fellow Afrikans and their Continental Identity. They are Neither European, Afrikan, Asian nor Indian They are neither Black nor White... forever denied an Identity because of the Politics that wish to Appropriate North Afrika. These people are Continental Afrikans and Afrikans by Heritage with other mixed descent which they do well to know and assert themselves in. They may or may not be Arabic Lingo-Culturally, but they are Afrikans. They may or may not be Muslim by religion, but they are Afrikan

The Berber Identity

The Afrikan Continental (Misrami, Kushitic and Phutitic) and Afrikan Kanaanitic (Phoenician) Civilisation of the Iberian Peninsula (Modern day: Spain, Portugal, Gibraltar, Andorra and Southern France), which is responsible for the Beaker Civilisation that revolutionized European Civilisation, Attracted the Visigoths from their Germanic lands to join in. The Intermarriage between the Visigoths and the Afrikans in the Iberian Peninsula, gave rise to a mixed Heritage people of the Iberian Peninsula: French, Spanish and Portuguese. In North Afrika: Morocco, Algeria, Tunisia, Libya, Mauretania and Western Sahara, these people were later derogated as Berber, a Term used by the Romans to describe everyone who did not speak Latin as Barbaric (Barbary). The entire North Afrika became known as Barbary. One finds therefore, a wide Spectrum of "Berbers" in Afrika of (K)Hamitic; S(h)emetic as well as (K)Hamito-S(h)emetic-Iberian Heritage. Berbers are now starting to re-claim their Original Afrikan Amazigh (Imazighen), Tuareng, Lubim, Sukiim and many other Identities and their languages such as Tamazight are becoming recognized as official languages. Berber which like Afrikaans and Swahili is a mixed language that took various words from the languages of the various people has also become official in some North Afrikan Countries, such as Algeria and Tunisia. Like the Arab Identity, the Berber Identity denies people their true Heritage as Afrikans of mixed descent. They also have the added burden of having to identify as Arab, whether they believe they are Arab or not. Black or White? Caucasoid? These people are Continental Afrikans and Afrikans by Heritage with other mixed descent. They may or may not be Arabic Lingo- Culturally, but they are Afrikans. They may or may not be Muslim by religion, but they are Afrikan.

The Sub-Saharan Identity

Arab writers in the 12th Century AD, referred to the region, South of the Sahara, as bilad al-sudan (Land of the Sudan). Sudan in this instance, referred to all the Savannah Grassland areas South of the Sahara Desert. The 18th Century British Cartographers, then Translated this area as Negroland. Subsequently, this area became known as Sub-Saharan Afrika, as it became politically "separated" from Northern Afrika, which was perceived to be Arabic and Saharan. I don't even know what to say about this Classification…!? What is the intention except to say: You do not belong in North Afrika? It is impossible for you to have lived and contributed to the Civilisations found in North Afrika. North Afrika is part of the Arab world and or Europe and the civilisations thereof belong to these Nations?

The Negroid Identity

Negroid was part of the Early European World Racist Classification, of the 1800s, when people were Classified into three Categories: Mongoloid: Caucasoid or Negroid. This was a Hierarchical Classification with Caucasoid Nations at the top rung of Civilisation, followed by Mongoloid and Negroid as the least Civilised/ Advanced Nations. Europe, Western Asia, Central Asia, South Asia and North Afrika were Classified as Caucasoid, Appropriating the Ancient world civilisations (North Afrika, Iberia, Indus Valley and Sumer) into Europe. Afrikan People, South of the Sahara Desert, as well as some South Indians and South East Asians, were Classified as Negroid. This Classification is responsible for the North- South sense of Inequality, wherein North Afrika and East Afrika are seen as superior to Sub-Saharan Afrika.

It has also become a Policy decider that influences the decisions of such organisations as The World Bank and International Monetary Fund, as the UN divided Afrika into 5 Regions, where North Afrika is part of MENA.

The Black Identity

In 1580 AD, the word: "Race", was first used. Derived from the French, "*Rasse*" and Italian "*Razza*", It was used to describe people of Common descent. When Settling European Merchants and explorers began to pour into America from 1519 AD onward, they were not united as they came from different and often warring regions of Europe: Spain; Germany; England; Netherlands; France.

This made each group on its own, a vulnerable Minority, compared to the growing Afrikan Slave population, the European Indentured Labourers and the ever- present threat of the Native Americans.

To Protect themselves from these people, whose land they were appropriating or whom they were oppressing as slaves and indentured laborers, they fortified themselves as a Superior Race, the White Race, to which belonged all who had no drop of Negro or Indian Blood and were of a certain Social or Economic Standing. As the White Race, their numbers were suddenly large and they became a united and formidable Front, attracting even more "White" Settlers...

Whiteness was then used to legitimize and separate those entitled to privileges, from those whose exploitation and vulnerability to violence could be justified. Anyone who did not fit the White Category, became Black. The Blacks, however, were divided into various hierarchical Classes that weakened any sense of solidarity, that could have come from their shared sense of Marginalisation. Instead, they competed amongst each other for white favor and privilege. These divisions became structural and institutional as people were denied the right to self-identify and were forced into racial Classes that enabled their marginalization. Afrikans then became, Black and Negro.

At this time, the Western Church was of the opinion that Africans and Indians, were Pagan, and Soulless. This understanding justified the Enslavement, Killing and general Abuse of "Black" people by White People. This position, which was changed in 1741, had done the necessary damage of entrenching Racist views and Institutionalising Racism, without a sense of guilt, amongst white people, such that, the Superiority mentality and attitude has not been expunged from the Psyche of some White people to date.

Over time, Black has become a Political Social Construct that has been institutionalised and describes people with what is understood to be a Sub- Saharan look. This Look includes a spectrum of these broad features: Dark Skin tone; Curly water resistant hair; Broad noses; Thick lips... using this description includes a wide spectrum of people in the Black Identity. These are people of Afrika and its Diaspora, some people of the Middle East (Predominantly, Yemen Iraq and Palestine/Kanaan), as well as People of Oceania, the Afrikan Islands and the Afrikan Diaspora.

My friend Nhlanhla Mncwango puts it this way: Black "umoya wobumnyama nje abafisa ukusithelela ngawo!" (Google Translate should help... Zullu to English) "Kasimnyama, asikaze, sibemnyama." siNsundu (We are Brown). "If a person's skin color is deep, kuthiwa uyi Ndoni yemanzi because their color is like that of a Blue Starling... It is a Shiny Blue green and it is the richest of colors and most loved. It is understood that all colors originate from this color, as you know doc... It is considered a symbol of Strength, power, health and fertility. I suppose because it has the best capacity to absorb Vitamin D which is so fundamental in all the pathways of Hormonal production, and the Afrikans have always known this."

The Kaffir Identity

According to Van Jaarsveld 1975 (p.58), "The Arabs who first came into contact with them, called them Kaffirs, a word meaning, Heathens, who were not followers of the Islamic faith". Referring to someone as Kaffir, of course, is an Othering, that Disregards the fact that we are all heathens to each other's belief systems.

The Dutch Applied the Term Kaffir with a wider meaning to include uncivilized, savage and barbaric, reminiscent of the Berber terminology of North Afrika. The English Anglicised it to Caffer. This term was first applied in South Africa, to amaXhosa, baKhoe and baSan, as the first indigenous people that the Dutch encountered in Southern Afrika.

Bushman, Hottentot, Pygmy and Coloured Identity

In Southern Africa, the Cape Colony Government Named Khoe people: Hot Ten Tots (Hottentots), based on the practice of the Dutch of Remunerating Semi- Pastoralist people with 10 hot (Alcoholic) Tots, as wages for their labor.

This Practice ultimately left whole communities Alcohol dependent. This Alcoholic legacy is still a scourge amongst their descendants and that of the Nomadic Hunters who were also remunerated in the same manner. The Nomadic Hunters because they lived in the Forests Were Named Bushmen, whilst their Brethren in Central and East and West Afrika were named Pygmies.

Khoisan Identity: This Identity evolved over time to distinguish Nomadic and Semi-Pastoral Afrikans from Farmer Afrikans. When it became Politically incorrect to name people Bushmen, Pygmy and Hottentot, as it became clear that these people did

Identify themselves differently as various Khoe and various San Nations, Their Nations were lumped together as Khoisan.

Coloured Identity

This Identity is uniquely South African, wherein: Mixed heritage descendants of Black people (Farmer, Herder and Hunter Afrikans) with: White people, Indian people and Chinese people were Classified by the Apartheid Government as Coloured. Some mixed heritage people who carry White and Afrikan Heritages, were Classified White, because they were "White Passing". Amongst the white people who divorced themselves from their Continents of origin and Claimed the Afrikan Identity for themselves, this Afrikan heritage is Claimed to be a Khoisan Heritage. This is because Khoisan people are understood to be the first Nations of South Africa according to the Bantu Migratory Theory. This Identity is therefore prized, as it confers upon these White people, a legitimate Afrikan Identity, whilst maintaining their white privilege. See implications later in the last pages of the section: Cape Colony and the first Resistance Wars.

It has been done to the "Coloured" people of South Africa what has been done to the Afrikan Berber and Arab... To impute upon a people, an Identity that completely Erases them and renders them illegitimate and None Existent. They can't call anyone Brother... The White say: "You are neither my Daughter nor my Brother" The Black say: "You think you are better than us... We will dehumanise you in the manner we feel de-humanised, we will call you Boesman and Basters as they did, you are not our brothers, you are not Black, you are not Afrikan, you do not belong". These people are sons and daughters of Afrika... Our Sons and daughters. Let us stop disowning our own Flesh and Blood. They are Afrikan and They have a rich International Heritage which they should not be made to feel ashamed to own. Neither should they be denied their Identity. They are Continental Afrikans and Diaspora Afrikans. Genteic Afrikans. They belong.

Bantu Identity

This is a Philologically Spawned Identity, wherein Sub-Saharan Nations who identified themselves as **abaNtu, Antu, Wanhu, Anhu, Vanhu, Batho, Vhathu, Bathu, Manhu, Watu...** in reference to them being People, were Classed together as an Ethnic group. These were then separated from their brethren who used other words, such as Sewochi, Buehyong xxx to identify themselves and from Khoe and San Nations as Nomadic Nations and who identify themselves as baTwa.

The Root Word, Ntu and its variations in Afrikan languages is what inspired Bleek in 1862 to coin the term: "Bantu" as He decided that, because these people use the same root word **–Ntu/Nu**, their languages are Bantu Languages and they are the Bantu Ethnic group.

Greenberg and Guthrie later helped him perfect it to a Science. McCall Theal is the one who, Hypothesised the Migration of these "Bantus", from South-Eastern Nigeria or the Great Lakes Area, where it was believed the Language and Culture originated, to spread to the rest of Sub-Sahara Afrika, where they are theorized to have displaced and or Assimilated Khoe and San Nations, Meeting the Dutch Trek boere in Terra Nullius (No man's land) in what is today South Africa.

The Bantu Migratory Hypothesis:

Although the Bantu Migration is a Hypothesis, it is widely captured in many scientific sources as a Theory. Theories and Hypothesese are not exactly the same however...

A hypothesis proposes a tentative explanation or prediction of something.

A scientist, upon observing a specific event, makes an educated guess as to how or why that event occurs or has occurred.

Their hypothesis may be proven true or false by testing and experimentation.

A theory, on the other hand, is a substantiated explanation for an occurrence. Theories rely on tested and verified data, and scientists accept theories to be true even though they too are not unimpeachable.

Hypothesis and Theory will be used interchangeably in this book as it is the case in Literature where Bantu Migration is Concerned. Bantu Migration Theory/Hypothesis presupposes that because the Dutch first encountered baSan in Today's Western Cape of Southern Afrika, that they are the first Nation of Southern Afrika and the entire Afrikan Continent. All Rock Paintings of Southern Afrika and Material Culture attributable to a Hunter-Gatherer Lifestyle are then Credited to baSan as proof of their enduring presence in Southern Afrika and the entire Continent. baKhoe who were encountered second are then presumed to have arrived in Southern Africa about 4500 years ago followed by the Farmer "Bantu" who are presumed to have arrived in Southern Africa later. According to this Theory, "Bantus", who unlike their Khoe and San brethren, were Farmers, and who led a Settled Lifestyle, Dwelt somewhere in the Niger – Congo area or Great Lakes area. For some unknown reason, about 2000 years ago, they began "the world's largest ever Migration" that took place over a period of 1000 years in 2, 3 and 4 waves to arrive in their current countries of abode between 1000 years ago and 350 years ago. The Theory presupposes that Bantus, did not live in Northern Afrika or Southern Afrika prior to this Migration.

In South Africa, this Theory is stretched further in a Terra Nullius Notion, whereby "Bantus" only arrived in Today's Eastern Cape in the 1700s, where they met the Trekking Dutch Vryeburger boere, who later named themselves Afrikaners. The Boere (Afrikaans for Farmers) had arrived in Southern Afrika in 1652 as Dutch people indentured labourers to the Dutch East India Company (DEIC), to set up a Layover Station that ended up becoming a Colony. The Colony was named, the Cape of Good Hope. These Dutch Vryeburger Trek Boere, were venturing further into the interior of "Kafferraria" to free themselves from the unrealistic demands of the DEIC, when they met the "Bantu" Farmers at Cacadu (Zuurveld), between the Nukakamma (Sundays) River and the Oub (Great Fish) River. It is then alleged that "Bantus" began to steal the cows of the Trek Boere and fight with Trek Boere, having earlier displaced Khoisan (sic) from their paths.

With his book, *The Past and Future of the Kaffir Races* (1866), W. C. Holden turned this conjecture into Fact. He is one of the early writers of South African history to publish a book that used the Theory of empty land as an explanation for land ownership in South Africa. This Notion had been used in Australia to Dispossess the Australian Aboriginals of their land. Based on the Terra Nullius (Empty Land) Notion, it is argued that both Boer and Bantu were foreign to South Africa and had arrived into South Africa by conquest of baKhoe and baSan Nations and therefore there are no 'original' inhabitants with an 'original' right to the land in South Africa (since baKhoe and baSan were imagined to have been exterminated) There are only two migrating groups who have equal claim to the Land.

It is for this reason that one South African Advertiser, found it appropriate to Air an Advertisement which was later banned as Inflammatory, showing South Africans of various Ancestry, disappearing from South Africa in a puff of smoke, as each questioned the legitimacy of the other's presence in South Africa. First the Indian people disappear, then the white people disappear. They are then followed by the "Black/Bantu" people and only the "Black/Khoisan" man is left in South Africa and he exclaims: "I'm not going anywhere... You, x#%7! found us here." This Advert belies the prevalent Sentiments held by some South Afrikans that like the European and the Indian people, "Black/Bantu" South Afrikans have no Claim to South Afrika, because according to the Migratory Theory, "Bantus" Migrated into South Africa just like everyone else, at the same time as the White South Africans. In this Imagination of the South African History, Black people are foreign to South Africa and San People are the first Nations of South Africa.

The Below Snippet (Reproduced with permission) from SA History on line, confirms this Notion as recorded in our History Books by the Whites from Western Europe on behalf of the Bantus, as per van Jaarsveld's Testimony (1975:62) wherein he asserted: "The history of the Bantu had to be recorded for them, by civilized whites, from Western Europe, from the time of their first contact." (namely: 1652 instead of recording it from creation).

This is an example of how our History currently stands recorded in all official South African Documentation, our History Books and All Books on African History internationally.

The Narrative is repeated for all countries in Africa. If you search Name of Country and Precolonial history, this is the type of Narrative you will come across.

https://www.sahistory.org.za/article/people-and-culture-south-africa

South Africa has early human fossils at Sterkfontein and other sites. The first modern inhabitants of the country were the hunter-gatherer San ('bushman') and the Khoi ('Hottentot') peoples, who herded livestock. Bantu-speaking clans that were the ancestors of the Nguni (today's Zulu, Xhosa, Swazi, and Ndebele peoples) and Tswana-Sotho language groups (today's Sotho/Basuto, Tswana, and Pedi) migrated down from east Africa as early as the eleventh century (archaeological evidence recently confirmed this through pottery specimens). These groups encountered European settlers in the late eighteenth and early nineteenth centuries, when the colonists were beginning their migrations up from the Cape. The Cape's European merchants, soldiers, and farmers wiped out, drove off, or enslaved the indigenous Khoi herders and imported slave labor from Madagascar, Indonesia, and India. When the British abolished slavery in 1834, the pattern of White legal dominance was entrenched. In the interior, after nearly annihilating the San and Khoi, Bantu-speaking peoples and European colonists opposed one another in a series of ethnic and racial wars that continued until the democratic transformation of 1994.

Conflict among Bantu-speaking chiefdoms was as common and severe as that between Bantus and Whites. In resisting colonial expansion, Black African rulers founded sizable and powerful kingdoms and nations by incorporating neighboring chieftaincies. The result was the emergence of the Zulu, Xhosa, Pedi, Venda, Swazi, Sotho, Tswana, and Tsonga nations, along with the White Afrikaners. Modern South Africa emerged from these conflicts."

Another example of that Narrative

www.turtlesa.com/migration.html:The Migration of Africans into South Africa.

Traditionally the Western Cape has not been inhabited by black people in large numbers. This is however changing at a rapid pace as a migration is currently underway. Black people from the Eastern Cape and other parts of South Africa are moving into Cape Town at a rate of about 50000 people per month and with no housing available for them are building shacks on any piece of open ground they can find. This influx is causing the local authorities major headaches as they strive to house the influx of people. The Cape Flats has taken the brunt of the migration and as more people arrive more and more squatter camps are springing up in other areas of Cape Town as well. Cape Town authorities will soon have to take some major decisions as to how they are going to control the influx of people as the infrastructure in Cape Town is already taking strain. Cape Town is starting to experience gridlock on its roads, power cuts as electricity supplies are shared out and water shortages due to the lack of rain. Why not visit Cape Town and witness the current migration for yourselves?

Notice how definitive this Narrative sounds, as though the writer was Present as these events unfolded and that there is definite evidence for what they say. Our History books intentionally use language that makes us believe everything written in them is Truth, when in some cases, it is Conjecture and Postulations/Hypotheses/Theories. This Languaging, introduces Bias in the Interpretation of Genetic Studies, because they are done on the backdrop of an accepted Migratory Theory. Genetic findings are therefore interpreted based on the Accepted Migratory Theory to confirm it.

"Black"/ "Bantu" (K)Hamitic amaNguni and Sotho South Afrikans have always Asserted themselves as Autochthone, Aboriginal and Native to South Africa. They have always Rejected and will continue to reject the Migratory Theory as a Myth and a Fallacy with no basis in Truth. They Confirm that they have been in South Africa from time immemorial with their KhoiSan brethren and that they have persisted together with them in this Country in a Symbiotic Relationship since Creation/Emergence and that they together are the First People of South Africa and every African Country. Their Indigenous Knowledge is backed up by much ongoing Scientific discovery that will be unpacked in the upcoming Chapters.

Deconstructing the Theory of the Migration of the Black Bantus into South Africa (and every other Post-Colonial African Country):

In his dissertation for Doctor of Philosophy, The Examination of the Migration of Black Africans into South Africa: A deColonial Perspective (2017), Neluvhalani argues extensively against the Migratory Theory and below is a synthesis of his Arguments supplemented by other external sources as credited.

First, let us consider what other Non-Bantuist Anthropologists have to say about this Theory, which according to de Luna Kathy M (2016) quoting Dubow (1995) was influenced by racial thinking in the 18th Century. According to her, Nurse (1997) Linguist & Eggert (1981) Archaeologist, offer alternative perspectives on the development of Scholarship on the Spread of "Bantu" Languages, Their Speakers and their Material Cultures.

In his Journal Article: Bantu Origins and History: Critique and Interpretation, Published in the Trans African Journal of History, Vol. 2, No. 1 (January 1972), pp.1-9, Ehret, C. argues that "A further analysis of the Materials presented by Guthrie indicates that, in fact the (Migration of Bantu people into Southern Africa) Hypothesis cannot be made to follow from the proffered evidence and that the place of heavier concentration of the so-called "Common Bantu" vocabulary has no necessary coincidence with place of origin."

https://www.journals.uchicago.edu/doi/abs/10.1086/201717, In the Article: The Bantu Problem Considered, Author(s): Samwiri Lwanga-Lunyiigo's Analysis also disproves the Migratory Theory as he avers, "The Physical Anthropological evidence favours the view of an Ancient and widespread Proto-Negro group from which the Bantu and other Negroes emerged" He concludes by saying: "We should abandon the Greenberg/Guthrie hypothesis and look for other ways to explain the Bantu presence."

Based on a Multidisciplinary Approach, Neluvhalani Argues that The Theory of the Migration of Black/Negro "Bantu" Africans into Southern Africa is NOT: Credible; Valid; Reliable; Justifiable; Verifiable nor Replicable and should be discarded. He argues that "Bantus" are autochthonous to Southern Africa and have persisted here since creation.

I have summarized his 200 plus page Dissertation on the matter as follows, Regarding: Credibility, Reliability, Justifiability, Validity, Verifiability and Replicability

A: Credibility, Neluvhalani argues that the Theory does not offer reasonable grounds for being believed or being convincing for the following reasons:

1. There is no sound Archaeological evidence for the Migration of Black Africans "Bantus" into South Africa. Evidence of Material Culture (think: Pottery Specimens) found does not prove Migration.

2. Nobody knows when or why the 3 wave Migration of "Bantu" people into Southern Africa happened. There is No evidence of: An Intrusion into an area by new cultural groups; There is no evidence that the intruding culture shows an actual relationship to some other region and, ideally that there are traces of the culture along the route or routes of migration; and that a reasonable chronological relationship exists between the cultural donor and recipient, as criterion for Migration suggested by Rouse (1958).
3. There is No indigenous knowledge Tradition or history that agrees with the Theory. Rouse (1958) argued that the possibility that some other hypothesis might better fit the facts of why people are where they are must be eliminated first before Migration is proffered as a reason. The Migratory Theory does not do this.

B: Reliability, Neluvhalani argues that the Theory is not Consistently good in quality or performance and therefore able to be trusted because of:

1. Constant Revision of the Narrative to fit in with new scientific evidence (first, 2 migrations were suggested, then 3 and 4... Bantu A & B and later C, Revision of Names, Dates and Maps (1652 to 1931) as well as the discarding of evidence by anthropologists as outliers whenever they do not fit in with accepted theories (Samwiri) renders the Theory Unreliable.
2. The Separation of abaNtu (People) on the basis of Tribes and Ethnicity, in South Afrika, created arbitrary differences between Khoe and San baTwa Nations and abaNgoni-vhaLemba and amaNguni-baSotho, creating new and arbitrary "Bantus" and "KhoiSan" separate and unrelated people. Wells (1969) as cited by Samwiri in above link, notes that both the Tuinplaats and Border Cave (Cape Province, South Africa) skeletons can be Classified with the Asseler Specimen, as well as some central and East Afrikan Material, in an undifferentiated proto-Negro, proto-Bushman group. Drenan (in Brothwell 1963) noted that the Cape Flats (Cape Province, South Africa) Late Stone-age Hominid skeletal material recorded as showing European and Negro characteristics, probably represented a Pre-Bushman, Pre-Negro type.

A re-examination of the Oakhurst, Matjes River Rock shelter, Bambadyanalo (Fhambananalo) and Leopard's kopje material has recently convinced Wai- Ogusu that the Black/Negroes "Bantus" were already in existence, in South Africa in the late Pleistocene/Early Holocene times (129 000 years ago to 11 700 years ago (Biblically: 5000 BC)). This evidence is seen in East Afrika as well (Ishango hominid fossils).

The Chronology would be:

Hominid that is Pre-Negro, Pre-Bushman differentiates to Proto-Negro and Proto-Bushman (Siblings) who then differentiate to various Negro and various Bushman.

Basically, one Afrikan family co-existing in Afrika and more so, South Africa and the Cape Province in particular from as far back as 129 000 years ago.

C: <u>Justifiability</u>, Neluvhalani argues that the Theory does not offer reasonable grounds for it to be considered right, reasonable and defensible because:

1. Egyptians practiced the same type of Agriculture as the "Bantus"; Painted themselves looking like Black Africans; their Mummies have Melanin levels of Black Africans; their Sphinx has features of a black person; their culture and language has Bantu similarities. If Migration is necessary, why is it that the Bantu farmers are not considered to have migrated from Egypt into Southern Africa? or from Southern Afrika to Egypt? There is certainly nothing that makes that scenario implausible.
2. The Sahara Desert has never been an unassailable frontier, especially in comparison with the forests of the Lacreustine area. Using it and the Arabisation that has brought in relatively new linguistic differences to separate people into Nilo-Saharan, Afro-Asiatic and Bantu is unjustifiable.

D: <u>Validity</u>, Neluvhalani argues that the Theory does not offer reasonable grounds for being a sound basis in logic or fact;

1. There is no Ethnographic Black/Negro "Bantu" Afrikan Oral History that supports the Theory. The current Black/Negro "Bantu" Afrikan who share such Oral History cite their source as "What we were taught at school." Others cite familial History as in Grandparents who moved to South Africa from Malawi, Mozambique and Congo after the dispersion at Mapungubwe or after the Scramble for Africa created boundaries and differentiated Afrikan abaNtu or the Black Hebrew Israelites who Migrated Southward from Senna and Kanaan. This is not sufficient to create blanket assumptions of a Migration of "Bantus".
2. The 12000 pages of /Xam baTwa historical Testimony collected by Dr Bleek and the Story depicted on the Linton Panel do not distinguish people into Khoi San and Bantu, it merely speaks of People, who lived together and whose history is centred around Southern Africa and Afrika at large who sought to live in harmony... Presumably as siblings. Nowhere in this 12000-page Testimony, do San baTwa recount a genocide of baTwa by abaNtu. Nor do they name them as foreigners or enemies.

3. Observation of similarities between Southern African "Bantus" and Central African "Bantus" does not qualify as an argument for the Southern "Bantus" to have Migrated Southward. Southern "Bantus" could as well have migrated Northward from the Cape Colony or they be rotationally using the Land to give it Rest every 7years or very 50 years as it was their custom.
4. Afrika of yore was crisscrossed with wide Highways (Mizwila/imiZila) that connected communities to each other as these people were and are related. Their visits to each other and the occasional fight did not signify Migration and/ or occupation

E: Verifiability, Neluvhalani argues that the Theory can't be demonstrated to be true, accurate, or verifiable (No Supporting evidence. Guthrie himself offered this theory tentatively and remarked that there was no Supporting evidence)

F: Replicability, Neluvhalani argues that the Migration Theory is not replicable

1. There is no other human history that Replicates it even though the continent's Landscape and the Farming style of "Bantus" is similar to what was practised in much of the world.
2. Harlan (1967) reminds us that "Centres of Agricultural origins are diffuse in time and space" It is not necessary, therefore for an expansion of an Agricultural civilisation to expand from one area to another as each area would be a centre of Agricultural origin. Harlan Favours the principle of diffuse origins of any particular plant or crop as well, which may explain the Agricultural revolution in Africa and the similarity of food species in Africa and America without it being a factor of importation.

Conclusion:

Scientifically, the Migration of "Black Bantu Farmers" from South-Eastern Nigeria or the Great Lakes into South Africa 1000 years ago, is Moot.

Moot, in that 60 000 years ago Homo Sapiens/Modern Human beings/Afrikan abaNtu, did Migrate Out of Africa to go and populate the whole Earth, whence they became European, Asiatic, Islandic, Australasian and Abya-Yalan (American), Moot in that, some of these Homo Sapiens/Modern Human beings/Afrikan abaNtu, remained in Afrika during that out of Africa Migration 60 000 years ago. Instead, they remained and Populated Afrika: East, West, Central, North and South. Their Population of these areas cannot be Classified as Migrations. They moved from place to place to satisfy their needs as Pastoralists, Hunters, Farmers and Traders, until they were disturbed by Colonisation which blocked their Trade routes, locking them into bounded Countries.

Khoe and San People, being Nomadic and Semi-Pastoralist Have Migrated the most, hardly spending decades in the same place, for them to say, this is my Country. For them, Afrika and indeed the World is their country.

It is Disingenuous and fallacious therefore, to Claim a Migration only of "Bantu" People from South-East Nigeria or the Great Lakes area into their Current Colonial Afrikan Countries in the 1500s or 1000 AD. The Bantu Migratory Theory is designed to render so called Sub-Saharan Black Bantu Afrikans foreign, to every Country in Afrika, whilst Claiming that Khoe and San People, who are the greatest Migrators are the first people of all Afrikan Countries.

Bantu, Khoe and San Nations Are Aboriginal, Autochthone and Native to all of Afrika. They are Pan Afrikanist in origin and Settlement. They are the first Nations of the entire Afrikan Continent: East, North, South and West. Pre-Colonially, Afrikans did not recognise Countries within the Continent. Various Empires exerted their Political Power over vast Nations who lived in various and vast geographic areas within the Continent.

Miller's Testimony of the Rocks (1980:201) puts it this way: "while all geologic history is full of the beginnings and the ends of species, it exhibits no genealogies of development." This observation speaks to the Scientific obsession of divorcing the presently living from their past, naming their Ancestors: Neolithic, Pleistocene and Iron Age Men; Australopethicus, Hominids, Neanderthals and Homo Sapiens, without linking these, to today's living breathing humans, who are their descendants.

Since Creation, Afrikans have identified themselves as People/Humans, which in their various languages is: abaNtu, baTwa, Antu, Wanhu, Wanu, Anhu, Vanhu, Batho, Vhathu, Bathu, Manhu, Watu, abaNtu.

abaNtu/baTwa and all the above words, are plural for **People.** Sons and daughters of Ntu. a(bantwana) ba(ka)Ntu. (Human Beings/Homo Sapiens/Sons of Ntu, the First Man, Known as Adam in the Quranic, Torah and Bible Traditions). umuNtu is, Singular for person. Son or daughter (Person) of Ntu (Breath of God/Spirit of God) = umu (ntwana ka) Ntu. baTwa/baRwa, is plural for Sons of People (Twa/Rwa = Son) (Human Beings, Homo Sapiens/Sons of Adam, the first Human Spirit Being)

The ba prefix, is a Nguni convention that identifies numerosity within a word. baShona for example means: Many people of the Shona Nation. It is used in place of the (vaShona instead of the Shona people or even Shonas) in other languages, this prefix is: a/vha/va/ma/wa.... In BaNtu, it is abaNtu; waTu; baTwa; aNtu; vaNhu; vhaThu; maNhu; xxx.

Thus baSan, baKhoe, amaNguni.... For the various San Nations, Khoe Nations, xxx

Afrikan Identity as abaNtu/baTwa is not an ethnic Identity, nor is it a Language Identity. it is an Identity of Humans as opposed to Animals. It is an Identity, of Homo Sapien, the son of Ntu, the first human being. It is an Identity, to which all Homo Sapiens belong, regardless of Phenotypic Characteristics, Birth Continent nor Language spoken.

All Humanity is thus: abaNtu/baTwa. Afrikan people are abaNtu/baTwa; European people are abaNtu/baTwa; Asian people are abaNtu/baTwa; Indian people are abaNtu/baTwa; Arabic people are abaNtu/baTwa; Abya-yalan (American) people are abaNtu/baTwa; Islandic people are abaNtu/baTwa. Because abaNtu/baTwa means: People/Humans. Full stop.

We, are **Afrikan** abaNtu/baTwa (African People), Countless in our Multitude and in our Union. Thus we reject the terminology: Bantu, as referred to us as a distinct ethnic group that differentiates us from our brethren in Afrika. We deem it derogatory and divisive. Its deployment has no other benefit but to Erase us from our Continent and Current Countries, as well as to expunge us from our History, leaving us unconnected and effaced. It is a term that should be retired from Scientific literature as Pygmy, Bushman and Hottentot were retired. What is the benefit of one being described as Bantu or not, if it is not to say: Egyptian Mummies Are Not Bantu, Pyramids were not built by Bantu, Bantus were not in South Afrika pre-colonially...? Yes, Bantu Philology has no other function but to deny and erase Afrikans from their Afrikan Heritage and Continent.

It is sufficient to identify us as Afrikan... Pan Afrikan, As Europeans are...Europeans, Full Stop.

For Expediency, in order to help readers to have a better grasp of the text, the 3000 plus Nations that Philology Classified as Bantu, will be Identified as Afrikan Farmer Nations with or without a bracketed (Bantu) for emphasis. This Description allows a Unification of all Afrikan Farming Communities, some of whom are excluded from the Bantu Classification because they have either protested to it or they do not use Ntu as an identifier for Human Beings (Sewochi, Setshaba, Buehyong, Arochukwu, Chimsindi... as examples). Khoisan which identifies the Hunter and Herder Afrikans will be rendered: Khoe Nations/baKhoe (Herders) and San Nations /baSan (Hunters), to emphasise that they are an Amalgamation of many Nations and not just one Nation. At times, People will be rendered abaNtu/baTwa with or without (People).

In South Afrika, where the Author is familiar with the descendants of the more than 1000 Farmer Nations, who Amalgamated into various "Nguni (N) and Sotho (S) Speakers" in the 1800s under the Pressure of Colonisation, these will be identified by Name. amaNguni in this Book, represents both "N and S" Speakers as vhaNgona (Amalgamated vhaVenda Nations); amaNguni (Amalgamated amaZulu, amaSwati, vaTsonga and amaXhosa "N" Speaker Nations) as well as baKone who represent the various Amalgamated baSotho or "S" Speaker Nations amongst whom are some: baRorolong, baKoena, baShoeshoe, baFokeng, baKgatla, baTswana, baPedi and many others who have been erased over time in Historical narratives, such as baLobedu, who are included in the Sotho Classification but who see themselves as more related to vhaVenda than baSotho. This is the same as the Kekana people who are Ndebele but are Classified as Sotho. These various Politically/Historically erased people, are still very cognizant of their Heritage and are sometimes represented in their various Chiefdoms. The N & S Speaker Philology traditionally excluded vaTsonga and vhaVenda as European Linguists failed to recognize these farmer Nations as one and to fulfill the Bantuist Theory which imagined vhaVenda entering South Africa from Zimbabwe in the 1850s as Trek Boere arrived in the North. The author rectifies this division. The Reader must remember that Modern Day Afrikan Countries are only 135 years old. Prior to this, Afrika was Borderless and Afrikans were just that: Afrikans, who Collaborated to initiate Ancient Civilisations and who Identified themselves by their Ancestry. Many Nations that are today deemed unrelated, are Brethren. Colonial Borders are responsible for Xenophobia; Ethnic Identities and Racism.

As Afrikan Farmers, Herders and Hunters, we are Afrikans.

We Identify as People/Human. **abaNtu/baTwa.** Homo Sapiens Our Land is **Afrika**

Our Way of Life of Life (Culture) is **isiNtu/kiNtu**

Our Spiritual Philosophy is **ubuNtu**

My daughter, Sharon Leith is fond of reminding me: "Africans must Remember that Africa is their Land and their Continent. We came here seeking Refuge and a better Life, but this, is your Land and we should be thankful to you for your generosity in showing us ubuNtu and sharing your land with us. We therefore should reciprocate this ubuNtu and be willing to share with you, that which we have gained from living in your land."

In spite of the African Identity being such a Painful and contentious one, needing 20 pages to explain, wherein Everything has been taken from the Afrikan: Land, Resources, Identity, Culture, History, xxx.

In the Spirit of ubuNtu, Afrikans choose to acknowledge that Some people of Indian, Chinese, European and other Descent, without any Afrikan Heritage in them, have lived in Africa for generations and contributed immensely to Africa, and that they, Identify as Afrikan. We ask that these people will treat this Identity, with the Magnanimity it inspires. They can do so, by acknowledging, truthfully, the History of how their Ancestry collided with Afrika. When they do that, they restitute Dignity and Identity to Afrikans, to Re-Humanise the Afrikan.

In Magnanimity, they too, can finally Claim their Space under the Afrikan sun. Unapologetically and Confidently, they can Identify as: as European Afrikans; Indian Afrikans; Chinese Afrikans; xxx; so that together with the Aboriginal, Autochthone and Native Afrikans, they can continue to build the Afrikan Continent, with revived Zeal, to Reconstruct Afrika, for Global Impact.

The Culture: kiNtu/isiNtu

"It was Natural for Europe to Conclude that the Africans had no History and no Written Language to Justify its Expansion into Africa, in terms of the civilizing mission of Uplifting the Heathens and savages of Africa." Harris, JE. (1972:18)

Unlike the Conclusions of Europe about Afrika, Afrikan people lived a Settled Lifestyle informed by Aeons of wisdom, millennia before Modern history.

A Settled Lifestyle, is a Lifestyle wherein the people endure in one place, living unsuspecting lives and at Peace with other Nations without constant threats of wars and because their Land and their Neighbors provide all they need in Mutual Symbiotic relations, there is no real need to go looking for Resources. People are at Peace and Unsuspecting of others.

They built Royal Citadels (Cities) and lived in them for thousands of years, only abandoning them because of War which usually broke out when one Kingdom is at conflict with itself, creating instability in the region as that conflict spills onto other Kingdoms. Wars were not about Resources. The other reasons for abandonment would be Pestilences or Natural Disasters. As Kingdoms enlarged, secondary Citadels would be built further away. The Grazing and Farmed lands would be Rotated. If Musanda wa ilwa (Royal Citadel is abandoned), it can be re-settled by descendants once the period of its Cleansing is determined to be complete. Sometimes, foreign (Foreign in the sense that they are not direct descendants) Nations may re- establish a Citadel that did not belong to them, leading to conflicting Material Cultures over different periods.

The Communities Were Established, with strong Political and a Cultural Systems. This is the Reason a Territory would be known by the Name of the Nation, Event, Belief of the people or some Natural Landscape (ka Ngwane, Kwa Zulu, ka Hasani, buLobedu, Phalaborwa, Ha Masia, Tshitandani), because the Nation would have endured in that Territory until even the Remotest Stranger would know the Place. Even Now, the older generation still refer to swathes of Farm lands by the name of the people who once lived there, precolonially.

The Communities Were Prosperous, living a long way away from each other as to allow room for expansion and because each community would be surrounded by Farming land, followed by Grazing land and then Preserved Wilderness Areas to allow Wild Animals Room to roam Freely. Khoe Nations lived a Semi Pastoral Lifestyle with Settled Kingdoms arranged in similar manner as Farmer Nations (Bantu), The difference being that they would Travel more frequently as they herded their livestock. Wide distances would be covered, leading to their Material Culture being widely dispersed in the entire Continent.

San Nations on the other hand, tended to live in the wilderness in small family groups that were Nomadic. These Nations (Nomadic; Semi Pastoralists and Farmers) lived Peacefully and Symbiotically with each other.

Each Afrikan Farmer Nation (Bantu) and Afrikan Hunter and Herder (Khoe & San) Nation has its own groups of Languages and therefore, its own words for different Terminology that will be used in this section. baKhoe and San Culture whilst exhibiting some of the generic cultural similarities also have their own emphasis, due to their Nomadic Lifestyles, that is not pursued here.

The Author will use the Luvenda Language, which belongs to the Nguni group of South African Farmer Nations, for most of the words and where other South African Language words are known, these will be used and where possible, Translated. The kiNtu/isiNtu way shared here is basic and generic and various families, Dynasties and Nations will exhibit various expressions for the same generic ways.

Pseudo-Cultures that were introduced through Colonisation, such as: Wearing Black for grief and those that became normalized as Culture when originally they were not, such as Slaughtering of Animals as a means of communing with Ancestors and wearing of isiphandla (Animal hide bracelet) versus slaughtering for propitiation for sin; Lighting Candles when someone dies and other funerary rituals; Proving Fertility prior to Marriage and many others, will not be Mentioned. Details of what happens in various Schools and Consultations will not be given as they vary from Nation to Nation as well as from Consultation to Consultation. This is just a broad strokes work. Each Family is encouraged to review its own Cultural Practices and adapt them to match the demanding times and the technological advances of the present age.

The Non-Afrikan and the acculturated Afrikan who reads this will gain a broader view into the generic kiNtu/isiNtu way that would assist them in Enculturating. The Enculturated Afrikan will be able to see similarities and differences with their own Culture.

kiNtu/isiNtu Sees Humanity as a Continual flow of the river of life from one Generation to another. The River has a Source and many Tributaries along the way. The River and its Tributaries eventually empty into the Sea and is offered back to the Rivers through Rains. In this way then, Ancestors are understood to belong to the great Ocean of the

Invisible dimension that imparts life to the Living in the various rivers of life. (Nevhutalu FS, Oral)

Ikenga-Metuh (1981:52) puts it this way: "The African World view sees Reality as a Unity of the visible and invisible Dimensions, in which Human beings dead or alive inhabit the same world with Invisible entities (spirits)."

For this reason, Genealogies are (were) Kept very Strictly. People are always referred to as: "Son of so and so..." to ensure that relatives are quickly and easily identifiable and one can see others in the context of the work of God in that lineage which started with Addamu and is continuing in that person: To be, the Image of God, to Multiply and Increase and fill the earth and to Subdue it as God's Steward. Surnames only Started with Colonialism. Precolonially, people were identified by their fathers and their Lands of origin.

The Bible, whose culture is very similar to and was influenced by kiNtu in Kanaan and Continental Afrika (referred to as Egypt in the Bible) attests to most of the Traditions shared here. When the reader reads the Bible, they must see if they are able to recognize the various customs for a richer experience of the Book.

A: The Invisible Dimension

The Invisible Dimension is Present, Real, Pervasive and Enduring. It is a Spiritual Dimension that cannot be seen with the naked eye. It is believed in by faith and Perceived and interacted with by those with Special Training.

The invisible Dimension is the senior Dimension and more Powerful Dimension. It is believed that the Invisible Dimension is a better Dimension and one that should be aspired to. The Invisible Dimension influences the visible Dimension. Everyone retires to this Dimension when they have completed their Purpose on Earth, to Rest with their Fathers. This is why amaZulu say when one passes away, *"uyadela wen'sulapho!"* (What a Joy that you have Attained to the Senior Dimension of Perfect Rest).

"In the Invisible Dimension, there is a Spiritual Hierarchy of entities that possess vital force or potency in varying degrees." (van Rheenen, 1991:208; Mbiti 1969:203)

The Hierarchy, sees, God who is Creator Source, at the top of this Hierarchy. God is the Supreme, All Present, All Powerful and All-knowing Being.

Invisible Dimension Hierarchy:

1. God
2. Lesser divinities/deities (gods)
3. Amathonga, Human Ancestral spirits (Ancestors)
4. Various Spirits for Life or death
   1.1. izithunywa (Angelic beings)
   1.2. Spirits that attach to Nature: Animals, Trees, Rocks...
   1.3. Anthropomorphous spirits (Shape shifting spirits)

God

Madiba (1996:271) as quoted by Khathide A.G (2007:321) says: "To Africans, God is the Supreme Power, and the whole of African belief is deeply entrenched in Him. God therefore is widely known and enjoys full support from Africans."

He is referred to as the Creator and Father of all creation, including both: man and heavenly bodies, the sky and oceans. He is strongly perceived as more than just a Parent or Guardian... He Represents Life, Hope, Love, Courage and Eternity."

God has Many names in all Afrikan Languages. Below is a sample of the names the Author is privy to from oral as well as written sources.

AmaZulu, amaSwati, amaNdebele

- *uZigi zakhe ziyezwakala* (The one whose footsteps are heard/evident)
- *o vela NqaNqi* (He who is from beginning to End/Alpha and Omega),
- *uMkhuluMkhulu, Mdala wezinsuku* (The Indescribably great one and who is older than Days)

vaTsonga

- *Xikwembu* (Supreme Deity)
- *Muvumbi* (Creator)

baYoruba

- *Olodumare* (King of Kings who is Permanent, Unchanging and Reliable)
- *Olorun* (Owner of Heaven)

baIgbo

- *Chiukwu/Chukwu* (Spiritual Being of great Size... The Source)

baEdo

- *Osanobwa* (Source of All Beings, Sustainer of the Universe)

baNupe

- *Soko/Suku* (Creator of Heaven and Earth)

baFon na baEwe of Dahomey

- *Nana Buluku* (Great Ancient one)

baGhana

- *Odamankoma* (One Full of Uninterrupted, Infinite Grace and who by Grace Created Heaven and Earth)
- *Nyame* (The One Who Satisfies)

AmaXhosa

- *uQamatha*, (The Supreme being who even the probing thoughts of man dare not defile...Man's knowledge is limited to the knowledge that *Qamatha* is the Protector, the Giver of Blessings and the Receiver of offerings (Dictionary of South African English)
- *Thixo* (Supreme Creator)

vhaVenda

- *Muhali/'nwali* (The Mighty one),
- *Thimudi* (Unknown/unknowable/unfathomable)
- *Mudzimu* (The Root/Source)
- *Yawe!* (The one who is Present when called upon in times of trouble),
- *Musiki wa litadulu na lifhasi* (Creator of All)

Zambia

- *Kalunga* (The Benevolent, The Vigilant and Watchful one),
- *Nzambi* (Amazing, Mighty and Good Creator God),

baKongo

- *Suku* (Originator),
- *aKongo* (God of Kongo)
- *Nzambi* (Amazing, Mighty and Good Creator God),

Basotho, Batswana, Bapedi

- *Modimo* (The Exalted),
- *Morena* (Lord)

baBamun and baRundi

- *Njinyi* (Who is He1? The Too High, Powerful and unFathomable),

vaKalanga

- *Mukuru* (The Great one)

Goam Khoe Nations

- *Thixo* (Supreme Creator)

vaShona:

- *Mwari, Weri* (The Great One)
- *NyaDenga* (of the Heavenlies),

baGanda

- *kaTonda* (Supreme Creator. Creator of all things and Lord of Creation)

And many more… that I am not Privy to. Please **Add your Language to the list…**

An analysis of these names shows that Afrikan baTwa/abaNtu experienced God in various ways and also felt that He was the unknowable knower of all (thus their keen interest for new revelation about Him). He is the Creator of all and Giver of all. He is the Root and the Source.

Missionaries being fearful of inadvertently using the names of gods for God, limited the Name of God in Bible Translations to names that conveyed the essence of either creator or Great one. In isiZulu, umKhulu ka khulu (The Indescribably great one, was rendered: unKulunkulu) making it seem as if Afrikans were being introduced to God for the first time by Missionaries.

According to *vhaNgona* (Nguni/Ngona) oral tradition: God is Creator of all and All things in the Universe Are Ordered by God. The various Names of God then speak to God's Character, Lordship, Abilities, Capacity and Relationship with Time, Space, Natural Forces, Supernatural Forces and Man

God is Perceived as Love and Light and loves Righteousness and Justice. When God created us, He gave us a deposit of His spirit which is our Light and Conscience and Love. This light teaches us God's Will and Teaches us to live benevolently (ubuNtu)

God is seen as Sovereign and thus Influences the Cosmos at Will. Humans are at the Mercy of Him as a Loving God who has ordered and Created all things for man to thrive.

God's Intentions for Humans are perceived as Good, and Goodwill Amongst Humans, is of the utmost importance in order to Promote Peace on Earth.

God intervenes in the affairs of Man if so entreated by the Ancestral Cloud of Witness Mediators who are closer to God by virtue of being in the Spiritual realm through death. In an Emergency however, the Name of God can be invoked directly for Intervention without first invoking the Ancestors. In Venda a Person would just Shout: "Yawe!" and call upon God for Assistance.

God is Worshipped and Connected to, through those one is familiar with and who through death are now Close to God as part of the Invisible Dimension in the Ocean of Life, thus the centricity of rivers and oceans in all spiritual rituals as well as the invocation of Ancestors in Prayer. isiNtu/kiNtu is very Hierarchical and one seeks the one immediately above themselves in hierarchy to entreat those greater than themselves. This is the role Ancestors are understood to play.

The everyday name for God in *LuVenda is: Mudzimu. Mudzi*(wa)Mu(thu). Mudzi = Root or Source. Muthu = Human Being. The Root Source of a Human Being.

This *Mudzi* (*Root/Life force, Ga!* In Xam) is both Natural and Supernatural. The Supernatural part of the Life Force is God:

The Natural part of the Life Force (Source) is occupied by: The King and Parents

The King as the ultimate earthly Mudzi who is in office on behalf of God (God in Flesh) and Parents being the Natural Mudzi (Root Source) through whom progeny finds bodily form through birth.

gods

These are Lesser divinities/deities (Male and Female). Most cultures name them as gods (zwidzimu, swikwembu, Medimo...) and sometimes adding the job description of that god (The god of Thunder, The god of fertility...). They are believed to have been created by God for the control of various aspects of the universe forming a type of counsel to God. The Female divinities mainly oversee Life Aspects of humans such as: The Weather, Fertility of Crops, Livestock and humans. They also attend to Birth, Rites of Passage and Death Life Events.

Awolalu (1979:20) writes that: "baYoruba hold the belief that as the Supreme Being created heaven and earth and all the inhabitants, so did He bring into being the divinities and spirits to serve his theocratic world."

De Villiers (2002) quoted in Khathide A.G (2007:324) claims that, based on records found in a 7000-year-old papyrus, the Queen of heaven mentioned 4500 years later in Jeremiah 7 & 44 is one such divinity.

Male divinities are concerned with Protection, Hunting, War and other aspects of safety.

Angelic beings

The next level is that of *izithunywa,* which are various spirits for life or death that aid humans. In some Cultures, Angels are perceived to be in the same league as gods.

Khathide, AG (2007) avers that: "These spirits help Humanity and can be contacted by those so gifted and trained in the Arts of the Invisible Dimension".

There are 2 types of Practitioners in the Arts of the Invisible Dimension:

Life Practitioners: Life Practitioners work to Heal, Bring Blessings and Restore Balance and they are: Priests (*Tshifhe*), Prophets/Seers (izanusi, izangoma), Medical Practitioners (*Izinyanga/abelaphi*);

***Occultic Practitioners*:** are practitioners for death as *abathakathi* (Witches, Wizards and Warlocks/Sorcerers). In kiNtu, witches and wizards practice the occult for their own gain or as requested by someone to do harm to another to retard their progress, to avenge themselves or gain advantage over another.

Practitioners are not limited only to Angelic interaction; they can interact with all spirits in this dimension. All Practitioners are able to manipulate spirits for life or death and to learn secrets from the invisible dimension (spiritual realm). They also get guidance about the type of medicines to use for various treatments or to cause pain, sickness and disease.

All Life Practitioners can bring healing. But each practitioner is a specialist in their field.

- Priests (*Tshifhe, Abathandazi*) are concerned primarily with Matters of Worship and would preside over family or National ceremonies;
- Prophets/Seers (izanusi, izangoma) specialized in divination and were responsible for interpreting the signs of the times and warning the Nation of future events as well as Prescribing Measures for preventing disaster;
- Medical Practitioners (*Izinyanga/abelaphi*) Specialised in healing and were consulted by the individual or family that needed healing.

Diseases were understood to be Spiritual with direct spiritual causes and indirect spiritual causes manifesting as germs, objects, accidents, tumours, malfunctioning organs, mental ill health etc.). Serious disease is usually perceived as a sign of Ancestral spirits seeking the attention of an errant descendant.

Management of disease is therefore Holistic: Spiritual, Physical and Emotional. Treatments are: Herbal Medical treatments, Surgical extractions and Spiritual exorcisms of undesirable spirits as well as spiritual re-alignments or acceptance of a spiritual call wherein the person might have to be initiated into their call (ukuThwasa). Treatments are always followed with preventive and protective treatments which again may be Herbal, surgical or spiritual, including wearing of Amulets and performance of rituals to appease the unhappy ancestor who wishes to get the errant descendant's attention where this is deemed to be the cause of ill health. The Medical Practitioner who does not have the other gifts might then refer to the Seer or the Priest for specialized treatments. These, in turn, may Refer back to the Medical Practitioner for further treatments.

What distinguishes practitioners ***is the intention***... Is it to give Life or to bring death? Missionaries who did not persist to understand this minefield of practitioners properly ***just classified all of them as Witch Doctors***, because they recognized that they had the power to kill (Witch) or give Life (Doctor). However, in authentic kiNtu, Practitioners for life never indulge in the dark side, whilst practitioners for death usually play in both spaces. The same way that a European trained doctor has the capacity to kill or heal but prefers not to kill even in compliance to the Hippocratic oath.

The **AD245** version according to https://en.wikipedia.org/wiki/Hippocratic_Oath went as follows:

"I swear by Apollo Healer, by Asclepius, by Hygeia, by Panacea and by all the gods and goddesses, making them my witnesses, that I will carry out, according to my ability and judgment, this oath and this indenture. To hold my teacher in this art equal to my own parents; to make him partner in my livelihood; when he is in need of money to share mine with him; to consider his family as my own brothers, and to teach them this art, if they want to learn it, without fee or indenture; to impart precept, oral instruction, and all other instruction to my own sons, the sons of my teacher, and to indentured pupils who have taken the Healer's oath, but to nobody else. I will use those dietary regimens which will benefit my patients according to my greatest ability and judgment, and I will do no harm or injustice to them. Neither will I administer a poison to anybody when asked to do so, nor will I suggest such a course. Similarly, I will not give to a woman a pessary to cause abortion. But I will keep pure and holy both my life and my art. I will not use the knife, not even, verily, on sufferers from stone, but I will give place to such as are craftsmen therein. Into whatsoever houses I enter, I will enter to help the sick, and I will abstain from all intentional wrongdoing and harm, especially from abusing the bodies of man or woman, bond or free. And whatsoever I shall see or hear in the course of my profession, as well as outside my profession in my intercourse with men, if it be what should not be published abroad, I will never divulge, holding such things to be holy secrets.

Now if I carry out this oath, and break it not, may I gain for ever reputation among all men for my life and for my art; but if I break it and forswear myself, may the opposite befall me." ***Translation from Greek by: W.H.S. Jones.***

Abelaphi ba se Mandulo (Ancient Healers) in Afrika also had their Oaths which were kept secret and known only to Practitioners that guided their Arts, so that they can be recognized as Practitioners for Life. Today, African Traditional Health Practitioners as of 2009 are Regulated by the Allied Health Professions Council of South Africa and they hold a similar oath to the current version of the Hippocratic Oath.

Ancestral spirits

The next level is occupied by: Human Ancestral spirits (Ancestors): *amathongo, badimo, vhadzimu, izinyanya…*

Connectedness to Ancestors/those who came before and are now dead and have joined the great sea of the invisible dimension is through the Blood (Genetic/Birth) which transmits Genealogical Purpose (***Calling***). Each Family Lineage is believed to be created with a ***Specific purpose/Calling*** to fulfill in the service of humanity and worship of God. This ***Purpose/Calling*** is Attended by "Gifts" that the family is imbued with to enable them to fulfill their Calling.

Respect in kiNtu does not permit a younger positioned person (Age and Status) to approach an elder directly. When one needs something from an elder, they approach someone older than them but younger than the person intended for that elder to intercede or mediate on their behalf.

In this Ancestral Spirits Paradigm, Ancestors are understood to be the "younger positioned person "nearest to the Creator" in the invisible Dimension and are therefore approached to Intercede for and Mediate on behalf of the Progeny instead of the people going directly to God. Pleasing the Ancestors therefore becomes of utmost importance to Afrikan abaNtu/baTwa who wish to have someone willing to obtain favor and Blessing from the Creator on their behalf.

Neluvhalani MC & Nevhutalu (Oral) explain that Parents are the *Natural Mudzi (Root/ Source)* who give birth to the Child and pass onto the Child their physical Attributes and *Life Call*. They are Responsible for raising their Children up in reverence for God, Knowledge of the Will of God and the Genealogical Call and Inheritance of the Family in the Earth.

When the Parent Passes on to the Invisible Dimension, if they have:

- Lived a full life span,
- Lived Righteously
- Accumulated Wisdom in this world and had
- Led the family well as an Elder and then
- Died Peacefully of Natural causes, they qualify to join the Cloud of Ancestral Witnesses: *amathongo, badimo, vhadzimu, izinyanya*. In some cultures, Ancestors are believed to be in a position to watch over the affairs of their Descendants and to have influence on what happens to their progeny. They are believed to be able to Intercede with God on behalf of their progeny. They can influence the guardian Angels of their progeny, so that, if the Progeny is delinquent, they would not be protected and misfortune would befall them, forcing them to remedy their errant ways. This is done to keep the descendants on track with their *Life Call/Purpose,* Bringing them good fortune.

Ancestors are therefore not Worshipped because they are not the ultimate Source. They are: Honored when the Descendants fulfill their Life's call and live out ubuNtu.

Natural spirits

The Next level is that of Natural spirits or forces of Animals, Trees and Rocks. This is why there are Holy Forests, Rivers, Lakes. It is also why Families Named themselves after Animals whose "spirit" they identify with and whose "spirit" they believe brings them good fortune and guidance.

Anthropomorphous spirits

Anthropomorphous spirits are ogre-like and often with sexual and/or malicious connotations. In South Africa, these spirits are referred to as *Tikoloshe, Maduhwane, imikhovu*... According to Khathide, AG (2007), *Anthropormophous spirits can shape shift, taking the form of anyone person or thing they wish to impersonate...* These spirits are therefore reportedly employed in witchcraft.

Witchcraft

Witchcraft is not part of Afrikan Culture. The same way that murder and stealing are not part of Culture. These are evil deeds that some people in their waywardness did as they still do everywhere and in every society. The Craft of witchcraft and wizardry is covert and known only by the practitioners. Since this is the domain of a few rather than the whole and it is not part of our culture, the author will not dwell further on the subject.

B: The Visible Dimension

The Visible Dimension is the *Physical world* (*The Seen and Tangible World*).

The Visible world is also ordered Hierarchically with the Supreme being of the Visible world being the ***King or Queen (Monarch)*** and the Royal Council. The *Monarch is Royal by birth* (Royal Lineage). The Next Level of Authority is the Tribal *Elders*, Followed by the *Parents*. Amongst the *Children*, there is also a Sibling *Hierarchy based on birth order which comes with Responsibilities.*

The Monarch is therefore the National Parent *Mudzi (Root Source*) and is Responsible for National Welfare on behalf of God *(Khotsi- pfareli/Pharaoh/Muwene/Khandake/iSilo/Shiri....*)

The Monarch

The Responsibility of the Monarch is dual: Spiritual and Political The Royal Lineage.

The Royal Lineage is from the first Man (Adamu/Hamo Sapiens) through to date. All Afrikan abaNtu/baTwa therefore are members of Royal Households. The Elder son/ daughter Succeeds the Monarch. If the Child is still too young to succeed the Parent, the other parent succeeds the spouse. In the event both parents are dead, the younger brother of the Monarch Succeeds the Monarch. If there is no younger brother or sister, the next level of genealogic relation would be next in line... Most Succession disputes arose secondary to these in Stead Monarchs refusing to abdicate the throne to the rightful successor or wanting their children to succeed them.

Each time an Elder son's house becomes too large, the Nation Would Multiply by coronating elder sons to Chieftaincy of Federated States that pay homage to their father's Monarchy.

The Hierarchy is thus: King, Paramount Chiefs, Chiefs, Lords, each with their own Counsel of Elders forming an executive council.

These Kings and their Dynasties lived Symbiotically and their borders were/are not in straight line boundaries and could not be neatly delineated as Today's borders seem to suggest. As alluded to earlier, The Responsibility of the King is that of Custodian of the People of God (*Khosi Pfareli*).

Monarchs are Responsible for Strategy, Vision and Mission as well as Values and Ethos that will ensure National and International Peace and Sustainable development of the Nation.

They are Custodians of Law and Justice as well as Culture, Customs and Traditions that enable the people to live out the Values of the Nation.

Monarchs According to Neluvhalani M.C (2017:368), wield immense Power and Influence as God's representative on earth as attested to by this luVenda adage: "*Iwe ane wa ri, ifai, ndafa!*" (You – in reference to the Monarch - who can Command me to die, and I die). The Monarch, like God, had many titles that were used depending on the attribute the subject wanted to address or invoke within the Authority of the King.

In luVenda, these are some of the names of a reigning Monarch: *Thovhele, Tabu, Mambo, Vhafuwi, Mavu, Muhali, Khosi...*

The Executive Council

The Monarch is Assisted by an Executive Council in his/her Reign which consists as follows:

- King's Deputy (*Ndumi*);
- Members of the Royal Council: Paramount Chiefs and the Chiefs
- *Khadzi* (The King's Sisters)
- Knights, who are the King's Brothers
- *Magota*, Counsellors of the Junior Chiefdoms
- The Priests (*Tshifhe*); Prophets/Seers (*Izanusi; Zangoma*) who Counsel the King on Matters of the Invisible Dimension. These are independent of the Royal Hierarchy and are not necessarily members of the Royal lineage. They counsel the King directly independent of the Bureaucracy of the Council.
- Community Elders: These are the next Level of Influence, determining ethical behavior and sanctioning minor misdemeanors that do not require a Court hearing. They Function Predominantly as Family Counselors, offering Arbitration, Reconciliation and Psychological Support.

Political Leadership Role of the Monarch

Politically, Afrika Practiced Communalism with Power Vested in Monarchs who were entrusted with Power by God to be Benevolent over the people on God's behalf. Thus, the Positions of the Seers and Priests were very influential on the Throne. The Monarch is supported by their Councils and Community Elders. There are Patriarchal, Matriarchal and Combined Leadership systems.

These Dynastical Genealogic Royal Leaders lead a Community of several hundred to several Thousands of people, assisted by Local and Regional Leaders wherein power is at times, Federated. The Regional Polity's influence extends over several Nations with Millions of people as the indirect subjects of the Regional Polity.

There was a Total of 26 or more Identifiable Regional Polities that reigned over Afrika at the time of the Scramble for Afrika. The Southern Polity was under a Monarch whose reignal Title was: Muwene (Similar to the Reignal titles: Khandake; Pharaoh; Morena; Thovhele; Kumkani; iSilo; xxx). The Domain of the Muwene was known as a Mutapa. Muwene we Mutapa (Reignal Monarch of the Southern Dominion). This Included today's Namibia, Botswana, Zimbabwe, Mozambique and South Africa. The Portuguese thought of this Dominion as a Country and named the Dominion Mono Motapa on their Maps.

The King Controlled Trade. The Monarchy is Responsible for Law and Justice and local Judges (Magota) were responsible for hearing Legal Matters. Land was Held in Trust by the King for Posterity. The Monarch Allocated Land to the people. The Monarch is also the leader of the Army and the Army serves at the monarch's behest. It was the Responsibility of the King to Protect and provide for the Poor in the Monarch's Territory. The King Ruled by Consensus, often guided by the Khadzi and Ndumi who formed part of the executive Counsel.

Spiritual Leadership Role of the Monarch

The Monarch, as Leader, also led the Nation Spiritually under special Circumstances, such as: National Thanksgiving; National Repentance; Rain Making or any other Events that are deemed to require God's intervention.

The Balance of Spiritual matters were handled by the Priests (*Tshifhe in LuVenda*) and by the Makhadzi (Elder Sister of the Family head) in individual Families.

Afrikan Traditional Religion/Spirituality will therefore be discussed at length here.

Spirituality in Afrika according to vhaNgona Tribal Authority (Oral Account) is seen as the driver for all Existence. It is Cosmic in nature and It Consists in a set of Laws, Principles, Regulations and Practices developed to embody the beliefs of Afrikan *abaNtu/baTwa*.

Afrikan *abaNtu/baTwa* believe that the Universe has a Creator Source who owns it and all in it and that everything in it is for the Creator's Glory.

The Creator Source has given *abaNtu* (People/Humans) a set of Laws, Principles, Regulations and Practices by which they should live as Stewards of the Creator's Creation. The Custodians of these Laws, Principles, Regulations and Practices are: The King *(Inkosi)*, Priests *(Tshifhe)*, Prophets *(Izangoma)*, Healers *(izinyanga), vho Makhadzi* (Family Spiritual Custodian) and the Parents (dead or alive) who weave these into the Culture, Traditions and Customs of the people to enable people to practice them easily and transmit them to posterity.

This *Cosmic Religion/Spirituality* (kiNtu belief System) is based on the following foundational Principles and Practices, using the *Tshivenda Experience* as a cross sectional representation of Afrikan Society.

1. ***The Relationship Continuum:***

   The Relationship between God, Human Beings, their Environment and the Universe exists in a Continuum. Some see this continuum as linear, whilst others see it as cyclical in a re-incarnate manner.

   According to Ukpong (1995:9), The entire Universe is seen as Participating in the one life of God with the Human being at the center of focus, such that the actions of human beings affect not only their Relationship with one another, but that of themselves with God and that of themselves with the Environment (Nature). Theron (1963:3) puts it this way "Nature, Human Beings and the supernatural, form a cosmic unity, a total community in which all are involved reciprocally", Thus the Source or Life force manifests itself in people, animals and objects" (Affecting the environment positively or negatively as seen with Droughts and deluges that follow human injustice)

2. ***Balance:***

   Harmony, Rhythm and balance between the visible and invisible dimensions is of the utmost import. When Harmony and Rhythm are disturbed, People Experience Misfortune, ill health and sometimes untimely death. The Disturbance of the Harmony, rhythm and balance between the visible and invisible dimensions is believed to be brought about through:

   - Dishonor of Authority
   - Transgression of Laws, Regulations and Principles of God as embodied in ubuNtu
   - Vengeance for wrongs done to others
   - Jealousy and Envy which often lead to abaNtu resorting to consulting those who are able to practice witchcraft: *baloyi, valoi, vhaloi, abathakathi* to bewitch another.

When an imbalance is recognized, diviners (*izanusi, inyanga, zangoma, Tshifhe...*) are called upon, by the person experiencing the disturbance or the King if the disturbance is National, to investigate the reason for the loss of balance and rhythm and for them to bring Reconciliation and restoration to this disturbance through various rituals or sacrificial offerings for Propitiation/Atonement/Cleansing. (Khathide 1999:72-73) bracketed and italicized words are the author's, to expand the characters recognized as diviners in kiNtu. Witches can also divine...

3. ***Practice:***

   Spiritual Practice is in the form of Worship. There are 3 types of Worship Services hosted by abaNtu

3.1. Nduvho: u Luvha, To Worship or offer Adoration to God:

Hosted as often as one feels the need. According to Nevhutalu, (Oral Account), *u Luvha ndi u losha nga muya* (To Worship is to bow in our spirit in Submission to the Spirit of God)

U Losha nga zwanda: When we use our hands (by lifting them up or Clapping them or putting them together) to Losha, we are saying: "I Recognise your Value" amaZulu say: izandla zedlula ikhanda (My Hands are raised high above my head as I recognize and honor your Value).

U Losha nga Mbilu ndi u Wa Mashuwo (ngaLurumbu): When we lie down in Prostration, we are saying: we are in Agreement with one to whom we surrender our lives to.

The above ways of Honor are also offered to fellow human beings.

U Losha nga Muya: When we bow our spirit, this is Unceasing Prayer. Worship in Actions. Total Surrender, offered only to God.

To breathe is to Worship, as we Mindfully recognize the Life-giving force each breath brings into our Nostrils and recognize that we have no control in any part of that whole cycle: The Provision of the Oxygen in the Air, The Ability of the Nose to take a breath and exhale it, The Lung for gaseous exchange, the Brain for automating the breathing cycle...! Our Recognition of that and Thankfulness for it, is Worship.

U Luvha therefore is to Worship and Give Thank Offerings and it is undertaken any time by anyone as they have the need and desire. It is a Lifestyle of Afrikan abaNtu. God is perceived as All Seeing and All Knowing and the rewarder of righteous Acts. All people therefore wish to live righteously in order to attract the favor of God... Worship is thus an attitude of willingness to live righteously.

3.2. Vhurereli: Hosted Annually

U Rera Ndavha is to Narrate a story... This is an opportunity for Supplication, Intercession and Consecration. it is an Annual Family and/or National Festival hosted by an individual family unit or by the Community at large or even nationally. This type of Session is mainly a Report Session (Praise/Thanksgiving Session) wherein the family, Community or Nation Reports back to the Life Source about life and makes Requests for what the People and Nature may require.

Vhurereli is an opportunity for one to confirm their faith in God. Gifts (*Misumo*), are usually presented as Testimony of the Love, especially from the Harvest to acknowledge that "All we have is from God" says Dube E.V. The Festival becomes an opportunity to Share and exchange ideas about all matters that are designed to shape the direction of a people in order to ascertain guidance in Solidifying their values and ethos.

As people *"Rera"*, they may come into Agreement about the Values and Ethos Thus Produced and decide to Practice these in a systematic way, thus allowing the evolution of Culture and Tradition, which would then be Solidified in Language so that the system becomes the Practice of all related parties to keep them as a united entity...

3.3. Muphaso: Atonement, Propitiation or Cleansing:

Hosted as Needed, this is a means of Communing with those in the Spiritual/ Invisible Dimension: God, Ancestors, spirits. It is done in order for one to gain Blessings. Muphaso requires the presence of a Cleansed and Designated *Makhadzi* (Eldest Daughter) whose responsibility is to Acknowledge the erring of the family. *Makhadzi* is responsible for Training and Teaching, therefore if a family or community errs, it is her responsibility to go to God and acknowledge this so that people can be cleansed and restored into right relationship.

A Goat may be slaughtered for this atonement.

Muphaso is only for the immediate family. It is Done any time as the family pleases or requires to Appease God or the Ancestors for wrongdoing and restoration of balance, or to Make Requests especially for Blessings and the strengthening of family ties. When this Service is required by the extended family, it is known as *Thevhula,* and when it is for the Community, it is known as *Bando*. In times of National Crisis, *Makhadzi* is Replaced by the Monarch, (*Thovhele/Khosi*) who is Regarded as the Kho(t)si (Father) of all.

In this instance, The Nation gathers together and presents itself before God in Prayer and Fasting in order to confess sin, repent and be forgiven.

Khosi (Monarch), (Standing in the stead of all *vhoKhotsi* (Fathers) receives all Repentance from all Children and Sacrifices an Animal for the Atonement of the sin of all. Religious Services Are Hosted at Altars (umsamo)... be they at home, at *Musanda* (Royal Palace) or Holy Forests and Lakes. Each home has an *Umsamo* (Altar), where the family Worships/Prays whenever they so wish.

The Altar constitutes a variation of the following Artefacts:

- Igneous Rocks collected from a River: Mboho (Pointed) and 2x Ngwane (Rounded) These are arranged in a Triangular format around a Bulbous tuber known as *Luhome/Thidingwane*, Symbolizing God at the top of the Triangle, abaNtu on the bottom right side of the Triangle and Earth on the bottom Left side of the triangle to acknowledge this Continuum. The bulbuous tuber is chosen for its Nutritious and Medicinal Value and its central position speaks of God's Provision of everything needed for the preservation of abaNtu.
- Items of value are placed on the right side of the Triangle as Acknowledgement of God's Provision to abaNtu: Something to symbolize the technological advancement of the Family or Nation (Weapons, Beads, Bangles... whatever is of value)
- Ludo, a gold plated Staff, to symbolize submission of man's wisdom to the wisdom of God

At a Prayer session,

- Seeds are presented. These may or may not be planted to symbolize Potential and Hope.
- Snuff is sprinkled as a symbol of Communion (smoking a pipe together) and also used as repellent to unwanted animals and insects;
- Incense is burnt as an invitation to the spirit(s) being summoned and as a representation of prayer;
- Mpambo, an unfermented sorghum beverage, made only for purposes of worship is poured to the ground as a Thank offering;
- Water, as a precious commodity that sustains life, is also poured out as an offering and to sow a seed representing God's Love, Grace and Generosity in affording abaNtu a new beginning.

The Prayer session sees the Worshipper calling out (Invoking) the names of his/her Ancestors who qualified to join the Cloud of Ancestral Witnesses using a Relic, passed down generationally on which are commemorated those Ancestors in the form of beads or however a family deems fit.

The Ancestors are called upon to entreat the great unknowable Creator Source (*Mudzimu/Thimudi*) for Blessings or Forgiveness and/or Thanksgiving. The Session is concluded with the sowing of a seed to symbolize rebirth in Newness. Singing and Dancing form a very prominent and central part of the Ceremony especially where the prayer is conducted communally as a family or community. People may then go into Trances wherein they receive answers to prayers in the form of instructions etc.

They may also become possessed by spirits if these were invoked (*u wa mudzimu*), this usually happens where the person has consulted Practitioners for treatment or when they are being initiated into a particular practice.

All religious ceremonies are undertaken to Solidify Identity and to Unite People, in the Advancement of the Purpose of those People in fulfilling the Will of God in the Earth through Equity, Righteousness and Justice.

Nevhutalu says, to the Afrikan, Life is about pleasing God. The more our Hearts; Minds; Bodies and Spirit are attuned to God, the more we become like God and are in God and are godly... It is then that...sin diminishes and the relevance of Hell and Heaven diminish, thus these concepts are generally not found in Afrikan Traditional Religion.

The Next Level of Authority in the Visible Dimension is the Authority of the parent. The Parenting Role will be explained further in the broader context of the Afrikan Societal Construct below.

Afrikan Social Construct:

Homesteads

The Architectural style of houses differed from area to area but all tended to be Circular (Rondavels) with Thatch roofs. Baked Earthen Bricks (called mud bricks in some literature) were employed in building the houses and women were expert at building the body of the house whilst the men specialized in roofing.

Either gender could start and complete a house by themselves. The Precision of building a circular Structure is remarkable and the thatching technique very elaborate. The Round house technology had been proven over millennia to be the most effective shelter against natural elements. This type of building has the lowest risk of causing injury if destroyed by inclement weather.

Some Communities used Grass for the Body of the House also. In Desert Areas where Grass is not available, Houses tended to be fully Earthen or Rock. The Musgum, an ethnic group in the far north province of cameroon, created their homes from compressed sun-dried mud to form, tall conical dwellings, in the shape of a shell (artillery), to allow Water Drainage.

Visit the Design Indaba electronic issue of June 2019 to see Mali's 3000 seater Mosque built completely in this Earthen manner as well as the Conical Musgum Homes at https://www.designboom.com/architecture/musgum-earth-architecture/

This development at eCabazini, Pietermaritzburg offers authentic Zulu Cultural experience and features both styles of Rondavels. Accommodation is reasonable. Used with Permission, Courtesy: https://www.afristay.com/p/31929

Different Houses were erected for different purposes: Cooking; Living Space and Sleeping quarters. In other Communities, a large house would be erected and then partitioned into various areas. Visit above link to get an idea...

Typically, a family unit would possess a Homestead with different and separated Rondavels for: Cooking; a Guest House; Children's shared sleeping Quarters separate for the genders: Male/Female, and where possible, also by age. The Main Parental bedroom would be the largest and most elaborate. If it is a polygamous union, each wife would have her own *umuzi* within the homestead with all the rooms already described. These houses were arranged around an open Lapa which was the Main Meeting Place of the Family for Meals, Meetings and Entertainment.

The Houses would be Interlinked by a *Guvha* (sitting pedestal) which served as a hedge and for sitting. The sitting pedestal would also surround each house, meaning one Homestead with 5 houses could comfortably seat 100 people and more if others sat on the Lapa floor itself.

Used with Permission, Courtesy: Lesedi Cultural Village. Ndebele Homestead https://www.gauteng.net/attractions/lesedi_cultural_village

Daily bathing took place in the Sleeping quarters but children could bathe outside (Since they normally shared sleeping quarters). For a proper Grooming Bath, People went to rivers to spend the Day, Bathing, Doing Laundry and Drawing Water. A Bushy nearby area would be cultivated with Trees that have leaves that can be used for wiping and designated as a Toilet. Defecation was into a hole. These were replaced with Pit Latrines. abaNtu ensured bodily excrement and hair were disposed of in such a manner that their "aura" would not be "stolen" for witchcraft.

The Cooking Room (So-called Hut in other Literature) Housed Food and Water Storage Jars; Meat Hanging Skewers; Stools for Sitting; Shelves for storage of Food; Pots; Plates and Cooking Utensils. The Cooking area would be built in the center of the room. (An Outside Cooking area would also be built).

The Bedrooms Consisted of: Sleeping Mats Rolled to the side; Shelves for Blankets and Clothing as well as Hanging pegs for Clothing. The Main Bedroom might feature a permanently built Sleeping platform that is used as a bed to the side of the room.

Afrikan abaNtu possessed Clothing for everyday wear and for Special occasions. These were different for the genders and for different age groups.

They were different for summer and winter and from culture to culture. Zwienda (Sandals) were made of Cowhides and were not worn every day.

In some Cultures, the Cattle and other animal Kraals and the Chicken Coups would be located in the Centre of these houses whilst in others they would be behind the house designated for cooking. Near the Kraal would be the vegetable patch for convenient everyday Herbs. The Hedge Forming Shrubs and sometimes Trees, would be cultivated around the Compound to protect against wild animals. Within the Compound there would often be several Fruit Trees. The Location of the Family Altar varied from family to family but would usually be in an area not easily accessible by someone who does not know the homestead but not far from the cattle Kraal so that worship can be private.

See https://www.afristay.com/p/31929 to get an idea of a homestead with the different areas.

A Typical Day

This entailed waking up at dawn to attend to various chores before the sun becomes prohibitively hot. They would take Food left over from the previous day to eat as Breakfast in the fields. They also used to forage snacks in the fields, gathering Fruit, Insects, and Water for refreshment. Women would work the Land; Men either went to Hunt or worked the Land with their wives. Young Men and sometimes Women took cattle for grazing.

Those who Remain at Home Clean the Common areas (Everyone generally Keeps their areas Clean); Take care of the younger Children and Prepare the afternoon Meals. The Grandparents and the young wife and some sisters are usually the ones who remain at home with the younger children. These help the young wife and train her in the lifestyle of this family, whilst supporting her with raising Children.

Children

- New Parents are surrounded by the extended family to help with Resources; Caregiving and Emotional support;
- Children are raised Communally. As the saying goes: It takes a village to raise a child, what this means is that the whole village is available both to Celebrate Support, Correct, Rebuke and Train a child as their own. It is for this reason that there are no Orphans where kiNtu and ubuNtu is well practiced.
- Children consider all parents as their parents and are willing to be guided by them
- When conflict between parents and children arise, the next of kin are available to act as mediators and conciliators and to offer an objective perspective and corrective adjustments to both parties.

Children Play all sorts of games and Learn Local Games; Dances and Sports. They Attend Various Initiation Schools that Train them in the various Stages of Life: Such as Ages: 5 – 7 (*Thungamamu*); Menarche and Semnarche with or without Circumcision (*Mula*)10 – 15 years; ulmbelwa: 12 – 18; Domba: 15 - 20

Khomba dzi a imbelwa dza Tshina Domba (Vogue Dance) and *vhaThannga vhaya Musevhethoni* 15 – 18 years, The Curriculum in these Schools is focused on:

- Hierarchical Authority and Respect
- Resilience: Commitment; Dedication; Determination; Perseverance; Faith
- Self-Control
- Environmental care
- ubuNtu
- Marriage and Family
- Culture and Traditions
- History and Philosophy
- Communities would hold Competitions against each other on the Dances, Songs, Art, Music, Sports and Academics learnt at these Schools.

Life Calling Schools were done as an "Apprenticeship" as one Trains under someone with the Skills for that Life Calling/Purpose.

When everyone comes back in the afternoon, The Family gathers around to Partake of Meals and to share the day's stories and learnings. Family History is shared. Various Life Lessons are shared through idioms, proverbs, folklore, riddles, songs and dances.

Cleaning was done as one went by their business of the day. As you used a space, you also cleaned it. Spring Cleaning would be undertaken only on certain days when Cow dung was applied on Floor Surfaces and houses were painted with various multicolored Clay (u shula, uku Sinda). Laundry would be Accumulated and young women would go out on a particular day in the week to do the Laundry by the riverside or at home if the family is able to harvest enough water. Water was Stored in meter high *Muvhelo* (Jars).

Excess Food was preserved for storage through Drying Processes: *Mikusule* (Dry Vegetables) na *Mikoki* (Dry Meat) and *Vhukhopfu* processed Sorghum and Mealies using a skill called usinda, ukugxusha and stored in *Madulu* (Silos) that can keep food fresh for years. Madulu also stored unprocessed food.

Marriage:

Marriage was largely arranged. It could even be arranged on behalf of the young and unborn children, especially where a family was indebted (*ufara Tshikukwana*). Normally the marriage would be between families that know each other and Respect each other with similar backgrounds. The young men however could also find wives for themselves. Once the potential wife is identified, *Makhadzi* (Father's sister) would go with a contingent of other qualifying members called *vho-Nendila* to visit the family and let them know that they hold the home in high esteem and wish for there to be a Relationship between the families (*u fhata vhushaka/ ukwakha ubudlelwane)*. Eloping occurred with the consent of the girl, If the girl's family was being unreasonable or the couple's love was considered forbidden. Another form of eloping was "forced" also called *ukuthwala,* where the young man would kidnap a girl and run away with her. This was not part of culture. The girl may or may never be rescued, this is also regarded as a criminal offense... but as it is with Stockholm syndrome, some girls would then consent to the marriage and the ukuthwala would be ratified and the marriage accepted.

Once the Girl's family Accepts the request for marriage, several elaborate visits ensue between the families to create a relationship between the families. These take the form of several feasts that take place, such as: *u ambisa*, ukucela (The Proposal); *u Shavhedza* (Family Visit of Acquaintance and payment of *lumalo also known as ilobolo*); *u Seliwa* (The Engagement); *u Kwasha vhengele*, uMembeso (Gift Sharing); *u Vhingwa/ u maliwa* (The Wedding), which lasts 7 days with various Celebrations in various locations daily. Each day various rituals are performed to welcome the *Muselwa* (young bride) into her new family. In each Ceremony, the new couple are given gifts suitable for them to begin a family. The ilobolo was elaborately calculated taking into consideration the social status of Muselwa (Bride) and gifts for the Parents. Traditionally 11 Cows of both gender and at various ages are given as ilobolo. Today, this is estimated based on the price of Cattle in Monetary terms. Ilobolo is meant to help the new Family begin a Family (ukuqala isibaya) and provide food for the Celebrations.

The Veiled young bride, *Muselwa*, together with her Bridesmaids, phelekedzi, would be left at the groom's home on the last day of the celebrations in the dead of night. This was meant to deter the groom from Claiming his bride before she is officially presented to him. The Bridal Party would remain in that family for a week or so, to help the bride to acclimatize into the new home and her role as *Muselwa*, bride in this family.

In this time, they would help her clean the home (u swiela na u shula), gather sufficient water (uka madi mulamboni) and wood (u reda khuni). They would have also brought some groceries. The Phelekedzi gather intel about the family and help the bride figure her way around. They would have been with her since the first time of ukuCela and through all the celebrations that have helped the two families come together over a period of about two years.

On the last Night that the bridesmaids leave, the Bride is taken to her Groom's Room by her mother-in-law. She would have been informed that she would be going into her husband's room and reminded of the premarital lessons she was given on how to enjoy the marital bed. From that night on, this is where she will dwell. Once she misses her period, she sends word to her Mother that she has missed her period. Her mother, in turn, will visit the Mother-in-law, to inform her of these developments and request that she informs her son and the father-in-law. Once the Pregnancy is deemed safe (12 weeks), she is taken to her parents' home so that her mother would be able to support her empathetically throughout her pregnancy and ensure she is not overworked.

She would give birth at home attended by the local midwife and/or grandmother. Makhadzi from the paternal side has the duty to name the child and once a contingent is sent to the Groom's home to inform them of the birth of the child, The Groom will respond by giving the visiting contingent some Clothes; provisions for the Baby and the Name of the baby as given by Makhadzi. After a few weeks of having been informed about the birth of the baby and having sent back the contingent with the provisions for the baby, the grooms family would visit their bride's family in order to: see the child, bless him/her and give the child a name. They would come bearing gifts necessary for the baby, the mother and the family of their in-laws. The new mother (muselwa) would then remain at her home until the baby is deemed mature enough to travel and safe from *infantile* death and weaned from exclusive breastfeeding, which would be a period of six months (6 months or so).

Breastfeeding is usually continued as a supplement for two more years until the baby has teethed, their bones strong and they are walking. Once the new bride/muselwa has borne her *Tanzhe* (1st born), She is now called: *Mufumakadzi/Musadzi* (Wife) and everyone now addresses her as "*Mme anyi- nnyi*" (*Mother of "so-and so"*). Each family has their own Rituals of welcoming and acknowledging a New baby that vary from family to family. The couple remains with the husband's /man's family until the marriage has gone through all its "teething problems" where the young family can receive support and the young wife can learn the culture and tradition of the family and completely bonded with the family of her husband. Once they are Strong enough as a Family, they leave the husband's/ man's father's house to begin their own Homestead as the founders of their own Dynasty. The Families help them set this home up from building their houses to owning Livestock and to ploughing their land/ grounds. The last born son in each family is expected to remain and live in his father's home together with his new bride and children to keep his father's Dynasty alive and take care of the elderly parents.

<u>*General Philosophy about Marriage*</u>

- Marriage creates Relations *(ubudlelwane/ vhushaka)* for families both in the visible and invisible Dimensions, thus various families will perform various rituals to bring the two families together.
- Dowry, *ilobolo/ lumalo* is paid to Assist the new family to start their home and to take care of the Wedding expenses;
- When a Man dies, his brother must take responsibility of his brother's household and if need be, marry his sister-in-law, so that she is well taken care of (ukungena) and protected and the brother's children remain in the same family lineage;
- Polygamy is a consensual open arrangement for the benefit of all parties involved;
- Marriage should be blessed with children for the perpetuation of the family name. Childlessness is managed through Polygamy if the wife is childless. If the husband is childless, the husband's mother arranges quietly for his brother to impregnate the wife;
- There are no children born out of wedlock. All children are acknowledged no matter how they come to exist. They are Named and given the dignity of a surname and a home;
- Families live near each other and form an extended support system for each other so that no one goes to bed hungry;
- Every one of the same Lineage is a Family Member and there are systems to inform who is responsible to care for whom. The eldest son takes the position of the father of the family once they become of a certain age or upon the passing of the father. If the eldest is a daughter, she takes the position of advisor to the brother and her voice is the ultimate voice
- If there are disagreements, Makhadzi is brought in to arbitrate, teach and counsel. Her Counsel is final and should be accepted by the couple.
- Wives are groomed to submit to their husbands. Submission is the Choice to allow someone to be the leader… the one who has the final say. In kiNtu, this position of honor is given to the husband, that he may have the last say. Wives

believe that their husbands are God's representative in their families and therefore, they are willing to trust their husband's leadership and submit to it.

- The family submits one to another according to age and the Children as well as the wife show this honor by Curtseying (Kneeling) when they address the elders (Parents/husband) or when they bring something to them. This is the highest form of honor for those one loves and holds in high esteem. Those who do it, do so voluntarily and believe it is a blessing to have someone greater than themselves that they can honor. This type of honor is training ground for us to learn Honor for God.

Gender

kiNtu is Non-Binary

People are just that… People. Pronoun them, rather than she or he, are used to refer to a person if the person is senior. No pronoun is used for peers. The Language permits for one to speak about a person or Deity without allocation of gender.

Although Gender roles are Strictly observed, Cross-over roles are permitted. There are no Gender Specific jobs. People Train for the Job that answers their Calling.

Sexuality

It was difficult to be able to see Sexual orientation of people because sex was not an everyday subject. It was experienced privately and usually within a Marriage relationship. People hardly ever shared the details of their escapades.

Close friendly Relations were possible amongst men and amongst women since the genders tended to socialise that way, thus it would be difficult to say such and such men or women were a couple because of the closeness of their Relationship as this was within "normalcy". If there were same sex couples, this would not be common knowledge.

Transgender needs did not surface because the Clothing was predominantly non-gender specific. If a man was effeminate or a woman masculine, they would not be treated any differently and thus would not be seen as outliers and they would have no need to assert themselves.

Economy

International, National and regional Trade occurred with use of *Tshelede/ imali* (Money) in some societies. Aksumite bronze, silver and gold coins that are older than 1500 years, West Afrikan Kissie Coins and Brass rods and Southern African copper ingots were used, however bartering was the greater medium of exchange. Across Afrika, a wide range of objects generally referred to as "currencies" were used as mediums of exchange. Excavations by de Maret and colleagues at Sanga and other places in the Democratic Republic of Congo identified different types of copper ingots that were traded over wide areas from 900 AD onward.

Archaeological work outside of trading centres has also identified objects that are known to indicate consumption of materials, commodities, and ideas originating from different areas. For example, excavations at Igbo Ukwu (c. 800–900 AD) in Nigeria produced a significant amount of glass beads that are like those produced in regions such as southern Afrika at the time. In addition, Igbo Ukwu yielded spectacular bronzes that were produced using tin and copper from widely separated areas of Nigeria. Furthermore, Igbo Ukwu yielded thousands of glass beads that were imported from North Afrika and the Middle East. The similarity between Igbo Ukwu beads and Zhizo types in southern Afrika suggests chronologically overlapping connections between, on the one hand, West Afrika, North Afrika, and the Middle East and, on the other, southern Africa and the Middle East via East Afrika. This attests to the fact that from 700 AD onward most Afrikan regions were networked through the emerging trading system that with time intensively connected Afro-Eurasia.

People owned their own Means of Production: Law, Land, Labour and Capital and they produced all that they needed for Life. Trade was only for the things that could not be locally produced. According to Bohannan and Dalton, *Markets in Africa* (1996) Afrikan Economies were embedded in reciprocity, redistribution, and administered exchange. They Traded in iron, gold, ivory, and possibly slaves in exchange for glass beads, cowries, and cloth.

Trade also occurred amongst baKhoe, baSan and the various Farmer Nations and where exotic wilderness foods, ivory, medicines, and honey from the bush were exchanged for Sheep, cattle, salt and Copper for Spears. This type of Trade also occurred within Communities where one family needed something and bartered it for what the other family needed. While trade and exchange may have been localized, various distribution mechanisms such as direct contact at individual or market levels were employed. Alternatively, a subsequent relay from producer to consumers was employed (Merchants). "Taxes" were paid in the form of Tributes to the King and as Tithes to God and to the King. (*Misumo/umkhosi wokweshwama*)

Food Production

The Settled Lifestyle of Afrikan abaNtu was made possible largely due to their Farming Expertise. Irrigation Channels (*Migero*) were created from undammed

Perennial Springs, fountains and rivers to irrigate the farms. Soil Cultivation was done by Individuals or Community in Madzunde, using personal Implements such as hoes or ox drawn implements. Farming entailed both Animal Husbandry and Crop Production. Various Cattle, Sheep, Goats and Fowls were farmed.

Various crops and types of Maize and sorghum and Millet with various names and various uses were harvested and formed a Staple for most Communities.

Maize did not come from America with the Portuguese as per the Migratory Theory. (See later on debunking the Migratory Theory). Some West Afrikan Countries even cultivated Wild Rice. Hundreds of Herb Greens; Some Tubers such as Sweet Potato and Afrikan Potato; Pumpkins were staple vegetables.

Orchards of Fruit were also cultivated. Food was also gathered from the wild: Over 300 edible food plants and fruit that grew wildly; More than 10 types of Super food edible Insects; Game was also hunted and various animals were eaten, Both Fresh water and salt water fish were also consumed.

Resource Values: Time, People and Money

Time

Although Africans were amongst the first to Measure Time at Nzalo ye Langa 200 000 years ago, and refined it into a 24h day and 60 minute an hour scale at Sumer and Time dials Created in Egypt as the first Clocks, Afrikans do not seem to have used Time as a factor of Production and Wealth Creation. Tshifhinga/Isikhathi/ixesha/Nkarhi... (Time), is seen as an unlimited Resource. It is available from when we are born until we die. It is inexhaustible and can only be invested, it can't be saved or wasted... It is available throughout the Span of life that we have been blessed with and nobody knows what their lifespan will be. We can only Invest our Time in Good Deeds. This is Afrikan Time.

Time is enjoyed in 3 hourly periods. In Tshivenda (Tshivenda is the Venda Culture and luVenda is the language used to Transmit that Culture, Lulimi lwa Tshivenda) These are:

Matsheloni	06h01 to 09h00 and 09h01 to 12 h00
Vhukati ha duvha (Middle of the day)	12h00
Masiari	12h01 to 15h00
Mathabama	15h01 to 18h00
Madekwana	18h01 to 21h00

Vhusiku	21h01 to 23h59
Vhukati ha vhusiku (midnight)	24h01 to 03h00
Madautsha	03h01 to 06h00

Thus, if one said: "I will see you in the Morning", this could be any time from 06h00 to 09H00 and even 11h00.

When Europe began its Global Naval expeditions in earnest, in search of the New World in the 15th Century, GMT was created to Aid Naval Navigation. Mean Time was calculated as the time each day when the Sun Crosses the Prime Meridian at the Royal Observatory Greenwich, so that, Mean time is Clock time rather than Astronomical solar time. GMT was then used to create Time Zones, which groups areas that observe a uniform standard time for legal, commercial and social purposes. These tend to follow Countries instead of Longitude for convenience. This is why if you are in a certain country with the same longitude as yours but that is in a different Time Zone, you can feel it is 08h00 but, the clock there says it is 06h00 am (This is the experience between Kenya and South Africa. South Africa uses SAST (South Africa Standard Time) GMT + 2h. and Kenya follows East Africa Time, which is GMT + 3h)

The Lunar Calendar is followed in Afrika. Months and Seasons are determined by the Position of the moon. There are 13 Months of the year which are named according to the type of weather experienced in those months. Afrikan Countries that were colonized had to drop their 13th month to align their Calendar to the Gregorian Calendar (Which had been instituted by the Catholic Pope, Papal bull inter gravissimas dated 24 February 1582 in Europe. This was done to Align the Celebration of Easter to the time of year in which it was celebrated when it was introduced to Europe by the early Church). The Names of the 12 months are still known in Vernacular and describe the prevailing Climatic Conditions of each month.

January	Masingana	Phando
February	Nhlolanja	Luhuhi
March	Ndasa	Thafamuhwe
April	Mbasa	Shundunthule
May	Nhlaba	Lambamai
June	Nhlangulana	Fulwi
July	Ntulikazi	Fulwana

August	Ncwaba	Thangule
September	Mandulo	Khubvumedzi
October	Mfumfu	Tshimedzi
November	Lwezi	Lara
December	Zibandlela	Nyendavhusiku
English	isiZulu	luVenda

Time was neither connected to Money nor Efficiency, it was just a measure of the day and used as a means of estimating when to do certain chores. It being Perennially sunny in Afrika, Chores were done in the early hours of the morning: 04h00 to 09h00 and 12h00 latest. The Afternoon was for Lunch and Siestas (u netulusa mirado which means "to relax the body parts"/u awela, which means "to rest"). The Evening was used for Teaching in the form of: Entertainment, games and telling of (Hi)stories; Sharing Wisdom through Fables, Idioms, Proverbs as well as Song and Dance around the fire. Sleep would be from around 21h00 (u isa marambo manweni).

- Einstein's Theory of Relativity has proven that time is relative. The rate at which time passes depends on your frame of reference.
- Afrikan time is therefore a real thing and Afrikans do well to respect it as it nurtures their biological Clocks, enabling them to age slowly as their immune system is not under a constant onslaught of Stress, created by the expectations of other people who demand that their pace be followed without any concern for the pace of those from whom they demand the pace.
- New Human Resource practices are beginning to recognize this need for people to work at their own pace and from their preferred locations. Covid 19 and the need to Social distance has fast tracked this transformation.
- The kiNtu worldview on time is therefore, that Although we do not know the Day nor the hour of our departure from Earth, there will always be this time whilst we are still alive... this Moment. This Moment is therefore recognized, acknowledged and savored. AmaZulu capture it this way: *"kujahwe'phi!?"* which is a question meant to root you or ground you in this Time and Moment by asking you "where are you rushing off to?... Stay, Smell the flowers, Eat, Drink and make a Friendship. Be, Present to this Moment. This is the only Moment you are assured of... Nobody knows what the unsearchable Past and the unknown future holds nor how long this life will be and what it holds in the next moment.

- *Vhathu ndi mapfura, vha a doliwa,* a LuVenda saying which means that "People are wealth, to be wealthy, one must immerse oneself in others." meaning that "you are as good as the people whose lives you impact" Your significance is in the number of lives you impact.... as opposed to the Assets You Amass.

- Time and Money are different values that are neither equal nor related. This is why the concept of selling Time, Talents and Skill for a Salary is difficult in Afrika. It is the reason Europeans struggled to get Afrikan labor until it was conscripted and Tax payment was demanded in Western Monetary values. The loss of ability to eke out a living from the Land and the entrance of Western convenient goods that were made mandatory and that needed to be purchased in western monetary terms converted Self-sustaining Farmer Traders, Hunters and Pastoralists into labourers and entrenched the dependency paradigm in the Afrikan mind, Wherein Afrikans could no longer produce the goods they consume and instead had to buy everything that they now needed but had no clue how to produce. The Law in place was foreign, The Land was estranged, Funding Capital was foreign and the Afrikans only owned Labor with little bargaining power on the worth of that labor.

- Impact is created by the gift of Time, Talent and Skill Resources. These gifts, it is believed will be reciprocated by the universe somehow. In Afrika, these Resources were not for sale. Afrikans understand their work to be a gift that they have the power/choice to bestow upon those they love or withhold from those they deem unworthy of the Gift. This becomes tricky in an Employment situation, where the employees understand themselves to be bestowers of the gift of Time, Talent and Skill Resources to the Employer. The Employees then expect the Employer to Reciprocate these gifts justly as it is believed in isiZulu, *izandla zi ya gezana* and in luVenda: "*ani tusi mathuthu kana thoro ya mbeu nga munwe muthihi", which loosely translated means, One hand can't wash itself and one cannot take a seed of maize with one finger"*, thus, it is expected that the Employer will thoughtfully consider the value of the Employee' Skill, Time and Labor, to the advancement of the Employer's ideals and compensate the Employee accordingly. The Strikes for wages that we see so rampantly in South Afrika are due principally because a scale for compensation of labor has been created unilaterally by the employer. The Employees are therefore left to figure out what their Time, Talents and Skills are worth and they demand this level of compensation without due regard for the Employer's liabilities as the Employment environment is foreign and legalistic, devoid of the usual Reciprocity ubuNtu spirit. Further, the Employees are perpetual workers, with no chance at Ownership, which creates Responsibility. This disconnect is also responsible for high Abseeintism, low Productivity and the reluctance of Afrikans to Price goods and services except for those who are Western encultured or have been given Measuring Standards for the value of these Resources.

- Money was a utility that people acquired when they needed it. The Worldview of Saving money was not known because the Measure of wealth was not in monetary terms but in terms of Relationships with: God; fellow Human beings; Availability of Land and its Potential; The Rule of Law; One's Ability to Work (Physical and Mental Health and Strength) and the Livestock that one owned. Money was literally useless and only necessary for some trades. Local Trade was in Kind or bartering.

<u>Language</u>

- Language transmits concepts, feelings and spirit;
- Language allows users to share ideas and thoughts;
- Language anchors one in one's identity;
- Language builds community, safety and confidence as everyone is confident of communication;
- Language builds and cements bonds of Relationships;
- Language fosters unity as people "read and sing from the same Hymn Book"
- Language is both Verbal and Non-Verbal. Non-Verbal Language is keenly sought and responded to...

Afrikans believe there is No need for a multitude of words. A Look, a Touch and a Presence is all that is required most times. It is also believed that there is no need to answer every comment.

- Words being understood to be creative were chosen very carefully
- In formal Communications, (where people are not just talking and making jokes) all Speech is permitted and allowed to be released fully without interruption, Ascription or Judgement. Listening is Valued and one is always allowed a pause before one answers and sometimes, it is common practice, for one to ask whether one could respond before they do so and to offer back what they believe is being said before they respond. Agreement is valued and always sought in Communication, thus neutral words are employed to acknowledge the other without committing to a Yes or No answer. The Person who begins the conversation owns the conversation and they should lead it whilst the listeners encourage them to keep speaking until they find themselves or the answers

they are seeking. The Listener does not proffer their opinions unless these are actively sought by the speaker, in which case, the Listener may give a parable, idiom or proverb in response that may help the speaker to find their solution.

- Silence is an important part of Speech in Afrikan Communication, with different types of Silence(s) being deciphered as:
- Silence of being Present;
- Silence of Contemplation;
- Silence of Acceptance;
- Silence of Agreement;
- Silence of disapproval;
- Silence of belligerence;
- Silence of Refusal...

When Communicating with someone in Authority, one shows their respect and humility by lowering themselves to that person either by:

- Curtseying, or sitting down. One does not stand whilst in Communication with someone older than themselves or of greater Authority. Standing is an act of defiance or belligerence. (Standing is Authority, Equality or Preparedness to do war on behalf of the elder and Kneeling/Sitting is Submission)
- Avoiding direct eye Contact if the person being addressed is not considered a threat and rather looking to the side or down;
- Because eye contact is not used in a friendly and respectful encounter, to ensure that the Addressor knows that the addressee is present, the addressee will respond to whatever is being said with family praise names for the addressor or a simple Yes (Yebo, Ndaa, Aaa). This Yes, does not imply agreement, it simply acknowledges that the addressee is aware that they are being spoken to and are actively listening.
- Eye Contact is maintained only where one is Asserting themselves or challenging the authority of whomever one is in communication with.

The Environment and Technology

People are understood to be Stewards of the environment and are eternally connected to it as their bodies return to it in death. The section on Religion explains this Relationship Continuum. Afrikans understand that all they need for Life is available in the environment and that the plant and animal kingdom have a legitimate right to the earth and that there is an interdependency between themselves, the plants and the animals. When Afrikans take out anything from the environment, they do so in such a way that they do not deplete that thing and they ensured that their Carbon footprint is minimal. From Building Material to Clothing to Food, there would be zero waste and recycling would be employed. Although Afrika is Archaeologically one of the richest Continents, most of our Material culture has decayed because Natural materials were used. Of all the Mining and Metallurgy that took place in Afrika precolonially, there is very little evidence of disturbance to the environment.

Afrikan Architecture from Antiquity showcases this relationship in that Afrikans use Natural materials (Earth; Stone; Grass; Trees and Animal hides) to build their cities and homes in a way that least disturbs the environment, employing rather very sophisticated engineering precision to ensure durability against all natural deluges.

Rivers were never fully Dammed to avoid them dying off. For irrigation, side migero (trenches) were dug to re-direct a flow toward Crops.

Fauna: Afrikan Farmer abaNtu consumed mainly domesticated animals that were allowed to live a full lifespan before being devoured. If hunting was required and also for San baTwa who did not domesticate animals, the animal was consumed for a long time and every part of the animal was consumed and/or utilized.

Flora: Responsible farming was employed and everything farmed was used. The Land was always Rotated and Rested from Farming and Grazing every seven years. This contributed to the fallacy of Terra Nullius amongst the Colonialists when they would see no clear evidence of habitation of an area and assume that it was devoid of owners. Grass and Trees were only harvested when need for building and only Mature Plants were used.

<u>Legal</u>

ubuNtu forms the basis of the Law of the Land. The Currently available decipherable written evidence is that of Egypt. In Egypt, ubuNtu Legal System Consisted in what is known as Maát. Maát is an example of the recorded and deciphered Legal Code of Afrikan Farmer abaNtu: The 77 Commandments of and the 42 Affirmations encompass some of the most representative of Afrikan Law. Together, they were considered the Divine Code of Human Behavior. They are the world's oldest recorded moral and ethical code for human conduct. Maát encompasses: Truth, Justice, Harmony, Order, Reciprocity, and Balance.

The Legal principle as addressed by Maát and ubuNtu with its Proverbs and Idioms create the backdrop against which Laws were based. The Afrikan Justice system is steeped in Justice and Righteousness, than in Law. Law is created to Support Justice and Righteousness. If a Law is deemed unjust, it ceases to be Law. This Paradigm is what creates conflict between Afrikans and Colonial Law, which does not always represent Righteousness and Justice (Apartheid Law as an example).

Justice is understood to be a State in which there is equity (Equal opportunity and Access) for all persons, creatures and the Planet. A state of balance wherein everything is aligned with the Divine and new possibilities emerge.

Law takes into consideration the Precepts and Regulations of God.

The Laws concerned themselves with Relationship to God; Relationship to fellow Human Beings and Relationship to Nature.

Sanctions were Restitutive, as an Application of balance, in order to restore Harmony to Society and the universe enabling the concerned parties on their journey of ubu(mu)Ntu.

Courts were presided over by local Judges who were advised by a counsel of elders. The Complainant produced the evidence and could draw upon community members to bear witness. The perpetrator would be cross-examined as well and given an opportunity to defend themselves.

In some cases, where the perpetrator is known for repeat infractions of the law, Mob justice might prevail as the Community takes matters in their own hands and run the perpetrator out of town, declared them a pariah and destroy their homestead. Those suspected of witchcraft would also be similarly treated.

This type of behavior occurred outside of the parameters and provisions of the Justice system.

The Philosophy: ubuNtu

"Europe assumed a position that the history of Africans and the Language of Africans were not worthy of serious study, because such would amount to European Retrogression rather than Progression. It was understood that one of the greatest contributions Europe made to the new world was the expansion and entrenchment of the concept of Black inferiority." Harris, JE. (1972:18)

Afrika, however, is the home to one of the world's prominent Life Philosophy of ubuNtu which is becoming world renowned as a Progressive Life Philosophy that was instrumental in the Bloodless Transition of the Apartheid Government of South Africa into a Democracy. Through the Application of this Philosophy, Mandela was hailed as a Peacemaker and honoured with the Nobel Peace Prize.

Benevolent Love, Purpose, Joy, Gratitude, Peace, Faith, Respect, Contentment, Acceptance, Justice, Balance, Reciprocity, Mercy, Community and Responsibility... These are the fundamental aspects of ubuNtu, which is an Ancient and enduring Spiritual Philosophy of Afrika that emerged organically as people studied themselves in relation to their Maker, Themselves, the Land they lived in and fellow beings they shared the Planet with. It influenced the Afrikan Way of living, whilst in itself being influenced by the Afrikan Continent.

It is this Philosophy that made it possible for a Feared Nation to be subdued in "one fell swoop" ... as it hoped against hope that its new visitors were benevolent. It is also ubuNtu that has ensured that Reade's Prophecy (1864) that "England and France will rule Africa. Africans will dig the ditches and water the deserts. It will be hard work and the Africans will probably become extinct. We must learn to look at the result with composure. It illustrates the beneficent law of nature, that the weak must be devoured by the strong." did not come to Pass in full (we did not become extinct) and it is ubuNtu which will restore Afrika's fortunes.

ubuNtu Being the fundamental nature of Knowledge in the Reality and Existence of Afrikan abaNtu, is ingrained in the genetic and psychological makeup of Afrikan people. For those who are not fully Western Enculturated, we instinctively know what an ubuNtu Response to any given scenario is. It is what makes us behave unpredictably in various situations. If ubuNtu is genetically ingrained in Afrikan abaNtu, why then, is it no longer practiced and seems to be least understood by most Afrikans and have to be explained?

Racial Classification of the dark skins of Afrikan abaNtu as "Black", made Afrikans internalize the negative connotations of the colour Black which is often, if not always, associated with: Darkness; Devil and Demons; Sleep; Aggression; Violence; Fear; Mystery; Barbarism; Uncouthness; Rebellion; Hunger; Poverty; Dirt; Ugly; Witchcraft and Sorcery (Black Magic); Bad Luck; Disease; Black listing; Discrimination; Disenfranchisement; Lack of Education; Backwardness; Lies; Dark Secrets; Sickness and Disease; Unreliableness; Black Market; Cheating; Macabre; Depression (Black hole)... This has contributed to a large extent to Self-loathing and distrust of everything Afrikan (as Black), leaving us Aspiring to become the opposite of Black.

The opposite of Black is White, which is associated with Purity; God; Light; Power; Innocence; Civilisation; Education; Financial Freedom; Enfranchisement; Safety; Cleanliness; Enlightment; Truth; Prosperity; Privilege; Freedom; Peace; Goodness; Happiness and being European. Being European, therefore, became proxy for Privilege and Afrikan children grew up Aspiring to become part of this privilege embodied in being "white" with the ambition of most youngsters in the oppressed generation being: *"I want to be white when I grow up"* as if being White was an accomplishment or an achievement.

Education in the Western Schooling System and Political Enfranchisement became the Passport to this "Whiteness" for Afrikans, so that they can live in "White" suburbs; Send their Children to "white" schools; Participate in "white" governments and gain positions of influence in "white" Institutions.

There were even "Blacks" who became exempted from being Black and who were given limited access to white privilege by virtue of Education in the 1800s. This is why to some extent, the legacy of the "Educated Black" who is suspected of being the white man's deputy still exists in South Africa. In this quest, Afrikans sacrificed their communal cognition of ubuNtu in preference for the western Individualised Cognition, making it impossible for them to be kiNtu enculturated and assimilate ubuNtu. This Westernisation and Loss of Communal Cognition over a period of 10 to 14 generations of Colonialism meant that the Cultural and Linguistic space within which ubuNtu could be transmitted was lost.

Today, although most Afrikans, especially Southern Afrikan are familiar with the Spiritual Philosophy of ubuNtu, Vhuthu, Botho, Unhu, Buthu, Vunhu... few can say with confidence what it means. It has become a catch phrase without commensurate power as the Creative Life-giving Spirit (Force/Energy) contained in the words has been lost. It is what is referred to by Shlomo (Solomon), the writer of Ecclesiastes in Chapter 7:7 "Oppression maketh a wise man mad".

ubuNtu Defined

ubuNtu, literally means: u(ku)b(a)u(mu)Ntu (ubumuNtu) The process of becoming Ntu, by being able to Recognise Ntu in another (Being able to recognize that the other is just as spirit (Ntu) as you are, encased in a different body and that both of you share the same Ntu and are the same Ntu. Recognising a member of the Pack...One who has the breath of Life (Ntu) in them. My Dad puts it this way: "People of the Heart that throbs because of the breath of life: duNtu, duNtu, duNtu...as it Pumps Blood through the Cardiovascular system, 80beats per minute, to keep us alive, reminding us that we are human (umuNtu) and that we did nothing to exist and that we are just like all others whose hearts throb: duNtu, duNtu, duNtu... powered by Ntu (spirit)"

Mboneni Matidza says: *"Taki, vhuthu ndi uvha muya muthihi na vhanwe thiri..." "Ndi uri, arali inwi ni tshikona u di vhona kha munwe muthu, ni muthu... ndi hone vhuthu hovho. Zwi ni ita uri ni kone umupfela vhutungu ngauri ni a kona u di humbulela uri zwino zwo tourani, ndo vha ndi tshi do tou toda munwe muthi atshi nthusisa hani? Hoyu thu, ndi ene muya... hoyu ane vheiwe na ri ovhudzulelwa kha Adamu, Adamu ambo vha mini? Avha muthu. Esina muya, ovha esi muthu..."*

Summary explanation of Mboneni Matidza's explanation of ubuNtu:

Ntu is spirit...the Spirit God breathed into his first son, in your Bible you call him Adam. That one, is Ntu. the first of the spirit sons. That is what we call him." If you are able to see Ntu, in someone or see yourself as that Ntu in someone, then you have become umuNtu." It is Being spirit. Being Human. A Human Being therefore is one in whom the Spirit of God dwells, and who shows attributes of the presence of God in their daily life interactions with others, as they recognize themselves (Ntu) and God's Spirit in the next person (Ntu).

Life is perceived as an experience through which the human being "evolves" into their full potential by learning what it means to be human and part of humanity, as apart from animals. "One is Deemed Human (umuNtu), when that one begins to locate God and themselves in the next person." Says Professor Nevhutanda.

I am, because you are, is the nearest explanation given to the adage: "umuNtu ngu muNtu ngabaNtu" which is the embodiment of ubuNtu. The full wording says: "umuNtu ngumuNtu ngabaNtu, itshe kalina ndlebe (yokulalela)". The Essence of this translates loosely to "I become human when I am Understood and Accepted by other Humans who can hear me and validate me as equal, worthy and meaningful. In turn, they are human when they develop the empathy to hear, understand, Accept and validate another as Created in the image of God and God's True Representative". This is why all invalidation of Black People is experienced by Black People as Racism rather than just rudeness or uncouthness. We understand that white people are choosing to "window" us and "unhear" us because of the colour of our skin, which they designated as evil, inferior and unworthy of privilege and access and further Institutionalised barriers of entry to enforce this unworthiness, meaning that Black people are subhuman and devoid of God.

When one begins to ask themselves: "How would I (as located within this person) like to be seen, heard and validated in this situation? How would God like me to see, hear and validate this person and how would He like me to obey His precepts regarding this person" and then proceeds to do that, then that one, has become umuNtu, Displaying ubumuNtu (ubuNtu). As long as our focus is on ourselves in a self-seeking and self-interested manner that is blinded to ourselves and God in the other, we have not matured to ubumuNtu.

Studying the Customs and Traditions of Afrikan abaNtu as well as Interviews with several Elders and Afrikan Wisdom Custodians (The Elderly), has allowed us to recover the Four Postures that Mature one into umuNtu. We have distilled them into a System of Practice in which Humans, can critically observe themselves as to measure their own Progress on the Path of ubumuNtu that will enable them to practice ubuNtu.

The 4 Postures toward ubu(mu)Ntu:

1. Upward Posture toward the Source of Life
2. Inward Posture Toward Self
3. Outward Posture Toward others
4. Downward Posture toward the Environment

In all these Postures, one Aspect or another or all of the Attributes of ubuNtu is emphasised. Benevolent Love, Purpose, Joy, Gratitude, Peace, Faith, Respect, Contentment, Acceptance, Justice, Balance, Reciprocity, Mercy, Community (Communalism, Communality and Communion) and Responsibility (Stewardship and Enterprise)

The **Four Postures Assume** neither hierarchy nor position. They are all essential to the Spiritual Growth of an individual in their Recovery of their ubu(mu)Ntu. Recognising that we are **Spirit**s, living in Bodies and connected through the Soul.

UpWard Posture: The Posture of Connection to Source

According to Nevhutalu F.S, One of the Beliefs that enable Afrikans to practice ubuNtu is the belief that abaNtu (People/humans) are not Self-Existent. They are created beings who have a creator and as such belong to that Creator who deposited Ntu (Spirit) in them. The Creator Automated His Creation by enabling the first created beings to be able to reproduce after themselves. There is therefore a continuum of creation from the first created beings to those presently living today. This continuum of existence should be revered and accorded: Respect and Gratitude.

The Eternal Invisible and Visible Creative Continuum as elaborated on in Part 1 (The Culture: kiNtu/isiNtu) is made up of a Hierarchy that sees:

- God as Creator of all and giver of purpose;
- Ancestors as the Carriers of Genetic Material and Relayers of Purpose;
- The King as Steward of God's People, Resources, Culture and Tradition
- Living Parents as the Living Guardians of the future generations;
- Peers as the Contemporaries and Mirror of the self.

***God is Respected and shown Gratitude* by abaNtu (People) through:**

- Observing various Religious (Worship) Ceremonies;
- Living Just and Moral lives;
- Living Communally and in Communion with others;
- Living out one's purpose;
- Recognising that the Body is the vehicle through which life is preserved and taking decisions that will ensure the preservation of one's life
- Honouring Parents;

These Acts of Honour toward God attract Positive Energy, Protection and Blessing. When one Honours God, God exacts vengeance on one's behalf, thus unrepentant injustice is left to God to avenge. ubuNtu does not have space for grudges and revenge.

***Ancestors are Respected* and shown Gratitude by:**

- Fulfilling one's Purpose/Calling;
- Recognising that the Body is the vehicle through which life is preserved and taking decisions that will ensure the preservation of one's life;

- Honouring Parents;
- Living Communally and in Communion with others;
- Knowing and Keeping One's Genealogy

The King as the Nation's Parent is honoured through:

- Payment of Tithes;
- Regard for the Rule of Law.
- Living Communally and in Communion with others.

Living Parents Are Respected and shown Gratitude through:

- Loving them and acknowledging them through gift-giving and Fellowship
- Supporting them especially in their Old age;
- Obeying them, generally being agreeable toward them and respecting their wisdom and counsel;
- Fulfilling one's Purpose;
- Recognising that the Body is the vehicle through which life is preserved and taking decisions that will ensure the preservation of one's life;
- Living Communally and in Communion with others by Being Generous to fellow human beings, starting with one's Siblings (their other children) ...

The upward posture is a source of Refreshment and infilling with Love for the inward work.

Inward Posture

In this Posture, abaNtu (People) draw on the Universal love of God to strengthen them for their interaction with others and themselves, so that they are able to see their faces and the face of God in the faces of others. Knowledge of/Faith in God's Justice as well as Respect of others, which is the belief in their Self-Efficacy, creates Skills, Values and Attitudes of Benevolent Goodwill. Benevolent Goodwill is when one wills good toward others in a way that is not self-profiting or self- promoting.

Whilst it is impossible to articulate the entirety of Benevolent Goodwill, in ubuNtu it is perceived in these broad subjects:

- Trust that God is in Charge of All and that He is Just to Avenge all injustices;
- Trust that People Are Self-Efficacious. This worldview avoids Patriarchal attitudes, preferring a Learning Attitude wherein one Listens and Learns to walk with others in an evolving Relationship rather than Transactionally;
- Trust that people mean well;
- Belief that all people have value and add value and exist for a reason. They do that which one is unable to do. They can think and see around the bends that one is blinded to. (In Afrika, even the opinion of those deemed mentally unwell is sought. It is believed that they may be perceived as unwell because they have an ability to see unusual perspectives);
- Non-Judgmental (Not imposing one's viewpoint and opinion on the circumstances of others);
- Offering Dignity in circumstances of Shame;
- Generosity;
- Hearing with ears of Innocence... believing that no Harm is intended;
- Recognizing oneself in others and sharing in their Sufferings and their Successes... "Their suffering is my suffering. Their Success is my success" Literally, one can boast about someone's achievement as if it were their own... because it is! This cleanses the soul of envy and jealousy;
- Believing the best of others and treating them with Kindness, Goodness, Mercy, Patience, Generosity, Compassion, Forgiveness and Fellowship.
- Respect of others as valuable and whose boundaries should be acknowledged;
- Not Critical and overly demanding of others;
- Recognizing that one is but a Part of the whole and not the Whole itself;
- Recognizing that one can't be all things to all men but can be something to someone and that someone no matter how insignificantly they are considered in society (for there is no such thing as an insignificant person) can be something to one. This attitude fosters Recognition, Validation and Compromise;
- Recognizing that one occupies a tiny portion of time in eternity and is part of a Relay to fulfill purpose in one's generation and pass it on to the next generation. One is meant to complete only their portion and allow the next generation to do theirs until the end of time.

This Paradigm of Benevolent Goodwill, creates an Atmosphere of Inner Peace. When one is at Peace, one is:

- Joyful in all Circumstances of Life;
- Free of Fear;

- Free of the Need for Approval;
- Content;
- Positively disposed toward others and Inoffensible.

When one lives life out of the Heart of Benevolent Goodwill, one is able to Mature in one's path toward ubu(mu)Ntu and is better able to reflect ubuNtu toward oneself and others, obviating the need for Actions of Spite. Actions of Spite encourage the desire to Control and Manipulate Other People and Circumstances for one's own ends. This creates an Atmosphere of Internal turmoil where in: Anger/Wrath/Rage; Malice; Bitterness; Comparison and Competition; Envy and Jealousy; Discord; Dissensions; Factions; Hatred and Resentment simmer, making it impossible for one to Mature in their path toward ubu(mu)Ntu and remaining incapable of reflecting ubuNtu toward oneself or others.

ubuNtu toward oneself is known as Personal ubuNtu.

This is the ability to understand that Charity begins at home. "What would I do for someone experiencing what I am experiencing?" then go ahead and do that for yourself. It is the ability to be Modest and Forgiving toward oneself.

It is also the Wisdom to keep oneself safe as to preserve one's life through the life choices one makes

Personal ubuNtu empowers one toward ubu(mu)Ntu

Recognize that every little way in which one exists, matters... it fulfills something in the Universe and covers a gap left by others. Learning to be Content with that contribution is the ultimate Personal ubuNtu.

Imagine the Waves of the Ocean...

From Inception of the World, all they ever do is: Ebb and Flow... Each day they do so with more vigor and self-admiration, clapping hands for themselves for repeating the same action because they know that their Ebb and Flow literally holds the world and earth together, in ways that scientists today still can't put their fingers on, Maintaining the Gravitational force, Influencing the Seasons, Creating the Hydrological cycle and Sustaining an entire Ecosystem.... Just by: Ebbing and Flowing!

The Waves Are Content to ebb and flow.

Like them, Ebb... and Flow by doing what you do, how you do it, on a daily basis, creating an enabling environment of myriads of things that matter in the grand scheme of the universe and that you may never fathom!

Your ebb and Flow is holding things together, making you a Gift to the World...

You are Necessary. Never STOP.

Personal ubuNtu is recognizing that in just one's ebb and flow, one Matters.

Outward Posture

Outward Posture is a Posture of Connectedness to all Life (Human and Non-Human) in Communion, Communalism and Communality.

Communal(ism) is having things in Common. It is the participation of everyone in Ownership, Responsibility and Profit. According to Neluvhalani, MC (2017:230) in this posture Afrikan thought is: "You are a person, I am a person, let us share in each other's fortunes in order for both of us to Enjoy Life together." amaZulu athi: *"Yiba nenhliziyo"* (Have a Heart! Be Compassionate and involved).

Communality is the Spirit of co-operation and belonging arising from common Ancestry (Humanity), Interests and Goals.

In this respect, Afrikans are willing to lend a hand to anyone who needs it. Let us work together to accomplish a Task. Izandla ziya gezana (You need both hands in order to wash them, each hand can't wash itself) Afrikan Cognition is that I will always need people (person) to accomplish any task efficiently and effectively. Thus Madzunde would be called for people to help each other plough their fields.

Communion is fellowship... it is the Interchange or sharing of thoughts or emotions through Authentic and Intimate communication and sharing.

This outward Posture is what allows Afrikans to always be willing to hear another... No matter whom they may be. "*itshe ka li na ndlebe*" (The stone has no ears.)

The Outward Posture, therefore, is the understanding that we all have a right and a Share in the Land that God has given to us to eke out a living from and that we, in turn, have the Responsibility to do so, in a sustainable manner that safeguards the interests of all and empowers all (People, Animals, Vegetation and the Land alike). This is so, because of "a feeling or spirit of co-operation and belonging" that arises from common interests and goals. Relationships therefore, take place in an Atmosphere of

Profound intimate interchange of thoughts and feelings, where everything is listened to and rested every 7 years, creating an atmosphere that enables the Community to hold things together in common and in Trust for Posterity.

In this Paradigm. God is Source of all Resources, Kings are the Custodians of the resources in Trust for the people and Posterity. Each person is expected to eke out a living from the Land in a responsible and sustainable manner, to support themselves and the Stranger who may pass by or come to live among them.

In his Doctoral Thesis, Neluvhalani MC (2017) avers that, ubuNtu is the intellectual quality of being Cognisant that one is trusted with the Privilege and Capacity to amass wealth (Financial, Spiritual, Social and otherwise) for the purpose of helping those less privileged. The Wealthy person shares their wealth with those who do not share the same privilege, not out of a superiority or patriarchal attitude, but from the attitude of understanding that one is but a conduit through which God's resources can be distributed. The Philosophy is: "That you may Enjoy Life as I do, for it is in your enjoyment that my wealth finds its purpose. If I have plenty and you have none, I will not be able to enjoy." It is this Cognition that makes it difficult for Afrikan people to eat in the presence of other people who are not eating and why it is rude to refuse food that one is offered.

Nevhutalu FS (oral) puts it this way: "ubuNtu is a sober-minded way of instilling Life and Hope in People, to live out their lives from a Morally Sound and Grounded Motive, that is Postured toward the Needs of others and not just their own."

The Communnalism, Communality and Communion of ubuNtu is seen in the following Traditions: -

Welcome: Karibu!

- Stranger and Kindred are alike. There is always food and Room for the "unknown" guest who might drop by. Literally, when Afrikans Cook, they always cook a surplus of food to ensure there is enough food for any unannounced visitors. (Ndilo ya Mueni)
- Living in a Tame but Wild world, Neluvhalani, M.C (oral) states that, People expected that a Passerby may travel longer than expected and find themselves stranded away from familiar territory without sufficient supplies and a place to sleep.
- The philosophy of the unknown guest assured one of Safety, Warmth, Refreshments and a place to sleep wherever they saw a light in the dark

or saw a Homestead. This person would then be hosted for as long as they needed and would become family going forth.

Greeting/Recognition and Inclusivity

- Greeting in Afrika is a Ritual. A Greeting may take as long as half an hour;
- It is important to greet every person, known and unknown. The Stranger is greeted to ascertain who the stranger is, in order to see if they are related and what their business in the region so as to ensure that they are well oriented to the area and safe.
- The duty to make the first greeting falls on the new entrant or on the Passerby;
- For strangers, Greetings are Introductions, wherein one enquires about the one being met, their parents, siblings and Children;
- An Attempt is made by one to find some connection with the person being met/greeted. Whose son/daughter are you? What are your Lineage Names? What is your totem? Where do you come from? What is the nearest Landmark to you?
- For acquaintances and related parties, Greeting Sessions are a Media Session; a Weather Report and Forecast as well as a Business Forecast;
- Greetings are an opportunity to Encourage one another.

Peaceful Co-Existence

- Every Person has a Right to Exist and needs space to Exist; Their Existence is Meaningful and Necessary and therefore, must be supported;
- The question is always: How can we make room for others?
- In co-existing with others, it is recognized that offense is likely to occur… The attitude of ubuNtu is that, No Offense is intended and None is taken... Presume that Nothing is ill-intended;
- Because of the attitude of Peaceful co-existence, Afrikans readily express their feeling of sadness or distress, and sympathy for someone else's misfortune. *Nxese!* (Sorry!) is readily uttered when someone experiences any mishap, even if the person commiserating is not responsible for the other person's misfortune. It is an expression that says: "I know how painful that must be and I want you to know that your pain is not imagined. It is real and Your pain is my pain. Be Comforted" (It is not an Admission of guilt or Responsibility for the misfortune of another). The Response to this expression of Shared pain is: Ngiyabonga

(Thank you). The person commiserating knows that they are not at fault and do not need to be reminded: "It is not your fault."

For Peaceful Co-existence, one has to learn to:

- Control their thoughts and their Passions;
- Trust the ability of one's Teacher(s) and the ability of one to assimilate what is being taught;
- Be free from Resentment under the experience of being wronged and Persecuted;
- Cultivate the ability to distinguish a path of peace and a path of war.
- Always Choose the Path of Peace as far as it depends on you. How can I resolve this peacefully? Not, who is right and who is wrong? Not, what are my rights that are being violated? It is not about asserting oneself or one's rights, but about being the Peace-maker. This attitude is what makes Afrikans to be considered docile, and mistaken for fools.

Togetherness, Co-operation and Reciprocation

- Afrikans believe that No person can be all things;
- All members of the Community are of value and add value;
- Give what you are able to give and leave room for others to supply the balance;
- *Izandla ziyagezana* (One hand can't wash itself... you need both hands for proper handwashing) is the Proverb that best encapsulates this philosophy and it is best demonstrated in the *following practices and shared resources*:

Practices and Shared Resources:

Grief:

- Afrikans do not allow anyone to grieve alone;
- Your grief is my grief;
- Funerals are attended by the whole village (related and unrelated);
- Afrikans will only miss a funeral under very extenuating circumstances, because this event does not repeat itself. Attending a funeral is the ultimate show of solidarity and compassion, thus the struggle to stop people attending funerals during the Covid 19 pandemic. In spite of people being aware that funerals

were super-spreaders, it had to take persistent education by Government and the very negative experience of Losing entire families, to discourage Afrikans to stay away from funerals. Thankfully, the availability of technology to Live Stream the funerals, enabled Afrikans to continue to show ubuNtu in a safe environment.

Celebration

- Afrikans Celebrate the wins of others as their own because they identify with their bretheren. I am Located in you...

Shared Resources

- Time: ubuNtu is about the willingness to pay the price of time to ensure someone's success;
- Capital: Those who have more Material resources share with those who are less privileged;
- Human: *Madzunde* concept is where people will take turns ploughing each other's fields (or whatever big project). Mutingati... (Picture billions of Ants attacking an elephant... it is possible for them to prevail);
- Land is not sold; it is held in Trust by the Living for the progeny

Socio-Econo-Political: Relationships

- Recognition of Social Hierarchy is of the utmost importance in the practice of ubuNtu as it fosters humility and confidence;
- When one knows that they are not the only person answerable on any matter, they feel safe, strong and bold. They can explore the world and interact with it boldly. Scientific research is beginning to understand the importance of being part of a pack in the evolution of the Human Species and the impact of this on Mental Health;
- As discussed earlier, ubuNtu Economics is not based on Scarcity for competing needs, but on Abundance. "There will always be sufficient resources for everyone." Is the central Economic Philosophy...This understanding fosters the willingness to share and to live communally.
- *Politically*, the Political head governs on behalf of God and with a broad executive council that ensures that they do not Lord it over the people. Therefore, in ubuNtu, one does not shy away from Politics but participates boldly, knowing that one's views are valid, valued and necessary. It is a duty to participate and

bring in one's gifts to the table for the advancement of society. "It is the ubuNtu thing to do" Ensuring that every Perspective is known.

- *Technological advancements* are for the good of the Nation and not for individual Competitive Advantage, thus intellectual property is shared openly. Gains from technological advances are shared communally. Afrikans will not easily repeat someone's business model as this is believed to be the calling of that person and repeating their business model is usually frowned upon and not regarded as Market research. Since No one person amasses wealth for themselves, Afrikans are confident that when this person (whose Business model they choose not to copy) becomes wealthy, they will share the profits with all in the Community.

Equality, Truth and Justice

- In terms of Justice, the Monarchy and Tribal Council Were Accepted as Just because they represented God and had the best interest of the people at heart;
- Their ability to arbitrate on all matters was Accepted especially because the sentiment of the Community was always sought in difficult cases;
- ubuNtu is willingness to subject oneself to the Council of the Elders and Trust their jurisprudence;
- God is believed to be all-powerful and all-knowing with eternal resources and therefore, best placed to avenge wrongdoing. Revenge is left to God.
- Equality, Truth and Justice are based on the Balance Applied in order to restore Harmony to Society and the universe.

Willingness to Forgive

Balance: Balance is a Central Tenet of kiNtu/siNtu. It is understood that unforgiveness and anger carry with them tremendous negative energy. Afrikans understand that hurt people, hurt other people... thus, regardless of the Pain one has been caused, one is willing to understand that the other person does not mean ill, they are blinded to goodness and possessed by selfish or other negative energy. They have not evolved well in their path of ubu(mu)Ntu.

vhaVenda would say: *hu na tshi itisi...* (Although the direct translation is: There is a reason, the spirit of the phrase is that, it is impossible for one who is a person, one who has evolved through the basic fundamentals of ubuNtu to behave in this manner. For them to commit this atrocity means they are blinded, self-absorbed and/or possessed of some negative energy) Afrikans are therefore empathetic toward even the Aggressor and are always seeking to restore balance by Apologising, Repenting, Forgiving and Releasing Amagqubu (Grudges).

Apology: To express regret for something that one has done/said that has affronted someone whether it is wrong or not. One apologises to restore relationships. Afrikans apologise readily because relationships are more important than pride. They do not believe that apologizing makes them look weak, rather a person who is able to apologise is a confident person who does not need to make themselves greater than another by asserting rightness.

Repentance: To express regret for wrongdoing especially where it relates to moral codes. It represents a desire to go back to the place of right standing with the one who was violated. Repentance is offered to the Stakeholder that is wronged by the violation of that moral code from the invisible to the visible dimension. The shedding of blood (goat or chicken) is usually required for the cleansing of the one who is repentant.

Forgiveness: To separate the offender from the offense. Being offended is a state of being held captive by hurt. It allows the Process of death and decay to come in. Physically, it manifests as various illnesses, from Hypertension to Diabetes to Cancer to Headaches to Depression and Anxiety. Forgiveness allows us to be unburdened of this hurt and to be released from Captivity, whilst allowing God to deal with the offender.

Whilst the offense does not go away because of forgiveness, those offended do not have to live in pain whenever they see the offender because they separated the offender from the offense. The offense can therefore be dealt with outside of emotions.

Afrikans believe that even if they are not avenged in their lifetime, God will not leave the guilty unpunished, unless they Repent.

Sometimes, we feel hurt by the most unthinkable entities... Ourselves, God, our Ancestors, Our Parents and even Nature. It is important to locate the source of one's hurt and forgive it, otherwise it dwells in different parts of the body as seeds of death which manifests in various diseases..., because unforgiveness is stagnation... a refusal to go past.

Faith, Love and Respect: Afrikans Approach others from a perspective of Safety rather than of Fear and Suspicion, believing in the good of everyone.

People are seen as bretheren... *Mfowethu*! My Brother, I know you mean no harm.

When one introspects one's Inward Posture frequently and ensures that it is always in Alignment (*U di thetshelesa which means to "self-introspect/ reflect"*), one is able to approach others in Faith and offer them Love and Respect. One whose inward posture is misaligned is said to be *in* bitterness (u ku ba muncu).

Afrikans understand that there is no correct way of being... There is just being.

We are NOT Human Correct-beings. We are Human Beings.

If there is no Correct way of being, it would mean that All ways of being are legitimate and subject only to the judgement of their Creator who created them that way for His own good Pleasure. ubuNtu is to Respect every expression of Humanity: Physical Appearance; Gender; Mannerisms; Sexuality; Beliefs; Clothing; Culture etc... every expression of being is just what it is... Being. Right and Wrong are not Attributed as only God is Privy to such matters. All expressions of being are respected as they are. Beautiful Flowers...

Our Response to people similar or different from us is Love and Admiration of the beauty of their being, because *muthu ndi muthu nga vhathu, tombo a li na ndevhe* (I am because you are). In this posture, I am humbled, to see that my expression of humanity is neither the only one nor the only correct or legitimate expression of humanity. It is just my expression...

When Afrikans enquire: "How are you?" they expect a genuine and authentic response and are available to Listen actively until the speaker is fully unburdened, if this becomes necessary.

4. DownWard Posture: The Posture of Stewardship and Enterprise

Connectedness to the Environment, at all Levels:

Physical: Earth, Fire, Water and Air/Wind

ubuNtu is to understand that one is intrinsically linked to one's environment in an eternal *Dance of Changes of Matter into Energy and Energy into Matter* and that no one state supersedes the other and therefore, each state is to be loved, honoured and respected.

The same Principles of Love; Balance; Justice and Reciprocity are applied to the environment.

The Contribution

Africa has Contributed much to the Civilisation, Industrialisation and Progress of the World.

The below-mentioned, are reasons why these Innovations are unknown.

Media is Led by the West and has a Bias for the West and its Colonial Agenda;

Mostly, Western Progress and Innovation has been Credited and Celebrated at the expense of Innovation from other People;

Some Artistc Licenses have been applied to various Historical facts about Afrika and Afrikan People, wherein Afrikan history and people are whitewashed or assigned ambiguous appearances in portraits, especially where their names are not indigenous Afrikan names. Artistic License refers to deviation from fact or form for artistic purposes and can include alteration of the appearance of historical figures for Artistic Aesthetics;

The Patenting of Innovations is a Western Concept and historically, Patenters would not register patents by Afrikans;

Most Afrikans who invented things, did so whilst under the employ of Western Companies. These companies would take the glory for the Innovation and the Innovator would never get to be known due to them being African;

Arabisation and Europeanisation of North Afrika, divorced Afrikan abaNtu/ baTwa from their pre-Arabic and Afro-Euro-Arabic North Afrikan Civilisations and Achievements;

European and Arabic Names of Afrikan abaNtu/baTwa make it difficult to recognise an innovation by an Afrikan, where no pictures are available or where whitewashed pictures are provided.

Simmering "divide and rule" sentiments have made Continental and Diaspora Afrikans to "Disown" each other, such that they do not celebrate each other's Innovations nor support them. It was an interesting phenomenon to experience, when Barack Obama was elected the first Black African American President of the United States and there were those who did not want Africa to celebrate his victory as he is regarded by some as not being "Black" but "Coloured". The same sentiments have been shared about Meghan Markel...there are those who want to insist that Prince Harry is not married to a Black Afrikan woman but to an American mixed descent daughter of a white man, as if her very Black Mother is insignificant. This Colonial Legacy makes our Afrikan Presidents fail to see the opportunity for Investment into Afrika by Diaspora Afrikans. Diaspora Afrikans are descendants of Continental Afrikans. They represent the Massive 14th - 17th Century Brain Drain of Afrika. There is hope however, as the Inaugural SA-USA Black Business Summit was held on 23/03/2021...

The Scientific and Academic Sectors remain predominantly Colonial and uninterested in Promoting Afrika. Very little has been done in these sectors to align known and verifiable evidence of Afrika's contribution to Humanity in the Mainstream Education Curricula and Media to make it Accessible to people to whom it would matter most to know the Truth.

Nor you ye Proud, impute to these the blame
If Afric's sons to genius are unknown,
For Banneker has prov'd
they may acquire a name,
As bright, as lasting, as your own
Thomas Gray, 1751 appearing in Banneker (1795:2)

Some of the well-known Contributions

General

- Afrikans are the Progenitors of Humanity. There is no Human being living today who has not descended from Afrikans;
- Being the Ancestors of Humanity, Afrikans seeded Wisdom, Knowledge and Understanding that would give birth to all Civilisation;
- Progenitors of European Civilisation: The Settlement of the Iberian Coast from 3000 BC by Afrikans and Phoenicians (Damascan and Lebanese Kanaanitic people - Afrikans) who also occupied Turkey influenced the Maritime Beaker culture through their Iron Metallurgy, followed by the later Silver Metallurgy;
- This was later followed by the 800 (711-1492 interrupted) year rule of the Peninsula by Afrikan and Afro-Arabic Maouri people (Moors/berbers) from today's Morocco who through their Turkic Islamic influence, Revolutionised Spanish Civilisation with: Chemistry; Physics; Philosophy; Mathematics; Astrology; Architecture; the Arts; Grooming; Cuisine and Street Lighting, leading to Europe's Renaissance. They built many Mosques, Palaces and Universities. The Alhambra Moorish Palace that was built by this civilisation is now a UNESCO world heritage site. The Moorish reign over what is Modern day Spain and

Portugal, Andorra, Southern France and British Crown Colony of Gibraltar (Iberian Peninsula) is what intensified the Trade Relationship between Afrika and Europe, leading to Portugal's Establishment of Trading Posts along the Afrikan Coast in the 1400s;

- The Hellenistic Literature of 300 BC which included The Wisdom and History of Egypt (being the whole of Afrika) was studied and learnt by the Greeks and Romans who incorporated it to their own wisdom that transformed the civilisation of Europe.

Calculation of Time

- First Calendar: At Mpumalanga, South Africa, our Ancestors used Dolomite Stones to Build inzalo yeLanga, the world's first Calendar in what is now named Waterval Boven. When Michael Tellinger came to know about it and studied it, he named it Adam's Calendar. The Associated Stone-walled Ruins that must have been settled by Bakone Ancestors then, were re-settled by their Progeny in the 1500s. This Calendar was used to tell time and understand the rhythm and cycles of nature which led to the changes in seasons informing time to till, plant and harvest the land, revolutionising Farming.
- Clocks: The oldest clocks are Egyptian sun clocks and water clocks.

Arts:

- As early as 70 000 years ago, Afrikan baTwa were documenting Life on Rock, The First form of Art and Writing;
- Classical Oral Literature is as ancient as the people themselves;
- Sculpting: Monumental Benin Ife Sculptures which were a refined and highly naturalistic sculptural Tradition in Stone, Terracotta, brass and copper as well as other Monoliths in Iron ore were common from the 1200s;
- Music and Dance, which have always been part of Worship, were innovated in Afrika as early as when we started building the iNzalo ye Langa Calendar and later, the Pyramids;
- Archaeology into Music is fairly recent and so, many artefacts that are Musical were incorrectly assigned. The earliest archaeological evidence of Music in Afrika thus far is 10 000 years old, which is younger than the Wind Instruments of Germany that are 35 000 years old.

Mathematics:

- The Lebombo bone discovered in Lebombo, South Africa is a baboon fibula that is said to be between 35 000 and 43 000 years old and which has Counting notches/incisions marked on it. Another bone with counting Incisions, is the Ishango Bone, which was discovered in the DRC, dating back to 20 000 BC;
- it is This Bone Incision Numerical system, according to de Heinzelin (1962:11), that would later influence Egyptian Mathematics. Egyptian Mathematics, in turn influenced world Mathematics.
- Lebombo is a mispronunciation of Luvhombo Mountains which are an 800 km long (500 mi), narrow range of mountains stretching from Hluhluwe in KwaZulu-Natal in the south to Punda Maria (Phando Vhuria) in Venda, Limpopo, South Africa in the north.
- The Bone Incision Mathematical Instrument in this area (Limpopo) was Replaced by Mufuvha (Tsoro in Shona), which allows for Multiplication, Addition, Division and subtraction; One of the oldest Mufuvha was carved onto a rock surface, on Mapungubwe Mountain. The same exists in Dzimbabwe at the Khami Citadel. (900 to 1400 AD)
- The earliest uses of mathematics were in trading, land measurement, painting and weaving patterns and the recording of time.
- More complex mathematics did not appear until around 3000 BC, when the Egyptians and Babylonians, began using arithmetic, algebra and geometry for taxation, other financial calculations, building and construction and for astronomy.

Metallurgy:

The oldest known mines in archaeological record are known as the 'Lion Cave' Mines are in Swaziland and date back 43 000 years. Making Afrikan abaNtu/baTwa, the oldest Iron Smelters. In addition, Afrika still leads in Mining roughly 46% percent of the world's diamonds, 62% of the world's platinum/palladium (of which South Afrika has about 97%) and 21% of the world's gold. This is the reason the Bible records them as Feared in the whole Ancient world, because of their Iron Spears, Stature and Wisdom (Budge, 1976:538-571 and Isaiah 18:1-2)

Writing: www.dailyhistory.org/how did writing evolve in ancient Egypt?

- Archaeology Magazine reported that the earliest Egyptian hieroglyphs date back to 3400 BC the oldest in the world;

- The Palermo Stone was written: 2393 BC to 2283 BC;
- The Egyptian Stela with the Hymn of Osiris was written in 1850 BC;
- This evolved to Writing on Papyri (Water Plant based paper) in demotic and hieratic scripts, which were cursive and used for religious and political needs. These persist in Coptic liturgical texts.
- 400 BC, Meroe had its own Meroetic Script (which has yet to be deciphered).
- For Context, according to: zmescience.com in their article by Tibi Puiu, (17/10/2017) The Earliest writing by the European Greeks based on the position and time frame of the artefact (not carbon dating) dates to 1450 BC (2000 years after Afrika had been writing.)

Philosophy and Religion:

- In Afrika, these have a rich and varied history, dating from pre-dynastic Egypt, continuing through the birth of Christianity and Islam. Arguably, central to the ancients was the conception of ubuNtu which is based on: Love; Justice and Truth, or simply: doing "that which is Humane and being Human". The idioms and Proverbs of Afrika are exhaustive. One of the earliest recorded works of political philosophy was the Maxims of Ptah-Hotep from around 2375 BC which are part of ubuNtu proverbs and idioms. They were written during the time of the Black Pharaohs, namely, Djedkare Isesi.
- In West, Central, East and Southern Afrika, Ideograms and logograms were used on Pottery and Rocks to confer Idioms, Fables, Riddles, Parables and Proverbs, which themselves were also used to convey deeper Wisdom. These were also used to Transmit History. Recently, Afrikan Authors are writing collections of these proverbs and idioms and unpacking their Wisdom to help impart Afrikan Wisdom, Law and Spirit.

Formal Education

Whilst Afrika boasts some of the oldest Family and Social Schools for all stages of life, Life Call and Trade Skills, it also boasts Some of the oldest Formal Universities in the world.

- Ez-Zitouna in Mount Fleury, Tunisia. Founded: 737 AD
- University of al-Qarawinyy in Fez, Morocco was founded in 859 AD
- Timbuktu in Mali, holds the Title for Most Universities in one Nation in the 12th Century. Leo Africanus is said to have exclaimed: "There is a great demand for books and more profit is made from the trade of books than from any other line of business in Timbuktu..."

Medicine:

Amenhotep and many Izanusi, inyanga and abelaphi who were named witchdoctors by European people as they tried to understand them, have innovated treatments from Antiquity:

- The earliest known evidence of Trepanation (drilling of Skull to relieve pressure) is in Egyptian mummies 6500 BC. Egyptian Surgical Instruments are found in Western Museums;
- The Ebbers papyrus (1550 BC) is full of incantations and foul applications meant to turn away disease-causing demons, and also includes 877 prescriptions. It may also contain the earliest documented awareness of tumours. The Bible alludes to the Tumours of Egypt, Deuteronomy 28:27;
- Homer (800 BC) remarked in the Odyssey: "In Egypt, the men are more skilled in medicine than any of human kind" and "the Egyptians were skilled in medicine more than any other art";
- The Greek historian, Herodotus, visited Egypt around 440 BC and wrote extensively of his observations of their medicinal practices. Pliny the Elder also wrote favourably of them in his historical reviews. Hippocrates (the "father of medicine") Herophilos, Erasistratus and later, Galen studied at the temple of Amenhotep, and acknowledged the contribution of ancient Egyptian medicine to Greek medicine;
- Many Traditional doctors in Southern Afrika have been treating Migraine and Cluster Headaches using "Acupuncture". They also did Craniotomies to remove tumours (Having realised long ago that the Brain has no pain receptors (nociceptors). They used fascia of cows for sutures;
- Each village had several Obstetricians who could turn Breech babies and deliver Breech babies as well as being able to handle most obstetric emergencies.

Architecture

- The Great Pyramid of Giza, which was probably completed in 2580 BC, during the reign of Black Pharaohs is the oldest and largest of the pyramids, and is the only surviving monument of the Seven Wonders of the Ancient World. The Architectural wonders of Egypt and the Nile basin are too numerous to mention them all.
- The various Stone-walled citadels scattered all over Afrika are even more impressive as they have survived thousands of years only because of Engineering Precision (No Mortar to hold the stones together).

- Cave Architecture is also very prominent throughout the Afrikan Continent and it takes serious engineering to carve out Room-sized cavities inside a Mountain wherein one can cook, bathe and have ablutions.
- The Grass Houses in their diverse and unassuming ways are remarkable in that they are some of the most advanced eco-friendly structures, leaving no Carbon Footprint. They are resilient against all types of weather and Protective in every environment. As if that is not enough... some of them were Mobile, and could be moved from one place to another. They are durable, lasting the family years as long as they are Maintained. The Architectural and Engineering Precision to build a Round Structure is more rigorous than that required for a square structure.

Scientific Record Keeping: Almanacs and Astrology

- Benjamin Banneker produced one of the first Almanacs. He was a self- taught: Mathematician, Astronomer & Naturalist. By 1797, he had authored 6 publications of the Almanac containing amongst other things: Calculations that predict the Solar Eclipse and Planetary Conjunctions; The Motions of the earth around the Sun and the Moon around the earth; True Places and Aspects of the Planets; Place and Age of the Moon; Calculations for Weather Forecasts as well as Methods of Calculating the Water Tides. His Almanacs also contained: Essays on Slavery and Equality which most likely influenced the Constitution of America, since James McHenry, a 1787 Signatory to the Constitution of the USA, wrote commendations for Banneker's 1792 and 1793 Almanacs.
- Alcorn George Edward Jnr created the X-Ray Spectrometer for Distant Galaxies. This earned him the NASA Goddard Space Flight Centre Inventor of the Year in 1984. Alcorn has around 20 other inventions to his name too.

Hair Dressing

- Afrikan Hair couture is best seen in the wigs of the pharaohs and izicholo of amaZulu and the various braiding and shaving styles so robust in the entire Afrikan Continent from antiquity. These various Hairstyles that were a form of writing were used extensively by the Slaves who used them to communicate to each other, Convey Messages and Transport various commodities, especially seeds that ensured the survival of slaves wherever they may find themselves. Teslim Opemipo omipidam records how the Cornrow hairstyle was used as an escape map from slavery across America and saved the lives of many. (oldnaija.com);

- Madame CJ Walker, in 1867, is the First woman to produce the African Modern Hair Straightening Comb and later, Modern African Hair Products and Beauty Salons at a Commercial Level;
- "Be it known that I, CHARLES ORREN BAI- LIFF, a citizen of the United States, residing at Kalamazoo, in the county of Kalamazoo, State of Michigan, have invented a new and useful Shampoo Head-Rest".

Catering

- Perryman F.R, in 1892, patented the first Caterer's Table;
- Alfred L. Cralle, was an African American inventor and businessman who is best known for his invention of the ice cream scoop.

Advertising

- John F Pickering invented the first airship (blimp) powered by an electric motor and directional controls. Blimps are now used for Advertisements.

Warfare

- "Those who survived either of the World Wars because of the gas mask, have Garrett Morgan to thank. Morgan first created the "safety hood" to help firefighters navigate Smokey buildings, later modifying it to carry its own air supply, making it the world's first effective gas mask."
  Morgan is also responsible for the Amber position in the Traffic lights, reducing Road Accidents;
- Dr Betty Harris, a leading expert in explosives, environmental remediation, and hazardous waste treatment, was awarded a patent for her TATB spot test, which identifies explosives in a field environment.

Gardening

- In 1897, J.W Smith innovated the Lawn Sprinkler;
- Beckett G.E invented the Letter Box for Mail Delivery Mounted in front of houses.

Farming and Food Processing

- JM Mitchell contributed to Farming Efficiency by Inventing a Check Row Planter which is drawn behind a Tractor to Sow Seeds;

- Peanut Industry: George Washington Carver, An Agriculturalist, received the 1923 Spingarn Medal and was posthumously inducted into the National Inventors Hall of Fame. He is credited as the father of the Peanut Industry, having developed more than 300 uses of peanuts;
- Ethiopian-born Gebisa Ejeta Developed a drought and parasite-resistant sorghum which saw him receive the World Food Prize in 2009.
- These inventions have significantly contributed to Global Food Security.

Technology

- Thomas Jennings Invented a process called "Dry Scouring", a forerunner of modern dry cleaning. He patented the process in 1821, making him likely the first black person in America to receive a patent;
- Rachid Yazami of Morocco invented Rechargeable Lithium ion batteries in 1980;
- Lewis Latimer invented The carbon filament, a vital component of the light bulb, making Thomas Edison's invention of the Light Bulb possible;
- Elijah McCoy, in an effort to improve efficiency and eliminate the frequent stopping necessary for lubrication of trains, devised a method of automating the task. In 1872, McCoy developed a "lubricating cup" that could automatically drip oil when and where needed. The lubricating cup met with enormous success and orders for it came in from railroad companies all over the country (USA). It was so popular that when other inventors attempted to steal his idea and sell their own versions of the device, companies were not fooled. They insisted on the authentic device, calling it "the Real McCoy." Often regarded as one of the most famous black inventors ever, McCoy was credited for 50 inventions over the span of his career.
- Granville T. Woods Created a device that combines the Telephone and Telegraph. This Patent was bought by Alexander Graham Bell. According to Biography.com: Woods's most important invention was the multiplex telegraph, also known as the "induction telegraph," or block system, in 1887. The device allowed men to communicate by voice over telegraph wires, ultimately helping to speed up important communications and, subsequently, preventing crucial errors such as train accidents. Woods defeated Edison's lawsuit that challenged his patent, and turned down Edison's offer to make him a partner. Thereafter, Woods was often known as "Black Edison."
- Dr Shirley Jackson invented the Touch Tone Telephone; Portable Fax (Wireless Fax, scanner and copier and printer); Caller Id and Call Waiting; as well as Fibre-optic Cable used for Computer networks and Cable TV Networks

- Marie van Britten Brown's patent laid the groundwork for the modern closed-circuit television system that is widely used for surveillance, home security systems, push-button alarm triggers, crime prevention, and traffic monitoring;
- Marian Croak holds over 135 patents, primarily in voice-over Internet protocol (VoIP). This is responsible for Phone services over the Internet such as Skype, WhatsApp calls etc. She has another 100 patents currently under review. She was inducted into Women in Technology International's Hall of Fame in 2013;
- Henry T Sampson and George H Miley co-invented The Gamma Electric Cell which converts High Radiation Energy to Electricity;
- Lisa Gelobter was integrally involved with the advent of Shockwave, a technology that formed the beginning of web animation. She also played a major role in the emergence of online video, later serving on the senior management team at Hulu. She is currently serving as the Chief Digital Service Officer with the US Department of Education at the White House in the USA
- Philip Emeagwali, Winner of 1989 Gordon Bell Prize for: "Price Performance in High Performance Computing Applications," Invented the world's first super computer able to perform 3.1 billion calculations per second. His Simulation was the first program to Apply a Pseudo-Time Approach to reservoir modelling;
- Jesse Ernest Wilkins, Jr. is one of America's most important contemporary mathematicians. At 13, he became the University of Chicago's youngest student. Wilkins continued his studies there, earning a bachelor, masters, and eventually, his doctorate in mathematics at the age of 19. Wilkins worked with future Nobel laureate, Eugene Wigner, and made significant contributions to nuclear-reactor physics, now known as the Wilkins effect and the Wigner-Wilkins spectrum. His greatest contribution to scholarship was the development of mathematical models to explain gamma radiation and his work on developing a shielding against gamma radiation;
- Afate Gnikou of Togo, invented the E-waste 3-D printer built entirely from discarded electronics. The invention is also aimed at controlling the massive electronic waste issue in Afrika through repurposing discarded computer and industrial materials;
- Frederick McKinley Jones, Founded the "Thermo King", a Cooling Systems Company. He is the Winner of the National Medal of Technology (America). He designed a Portable Air Cooling Unit for Trucks carrying Perishable Food to Maintain the now indispensable Cold Chain. It was Patented in 1940;
- Marc Hannah, Special Effects Creator. This computer scientist is one of the founders of the software firm, Silicon Graphics (SGI), where the special- effects genius developed 3-D graphics technology that is now used in many Hollywood movies.

Motoring

- Richard B Spikes, invented Automatic Gear Shift for cars, patented on 06/12/1932 and which is now used in all Automatic Cars;
- Bisi Ezerioha of Nigeria, a professional racing driver, engine builder, engineer and industrialist has been credited with Honda engines like the D16A6, D15B7, F22A, F18A and D16Z6. The work from his Bisimoto Engineering firm has further expanded to the turbo-charged Honda market as well as the Porche 911s and his accomplishments have been credited worldwide in the auto industry.

Modern Medicine

- According to Dr B.M Mayosi SAMJ, (S. Afr. med.j.vol.105 n.8 Pretoria Aug/15) "William Anderson Soga was the first black medical doctor in South Africa. He was the son of Tiyo Soga from Tamarha near Butterworth in Transkei, who was ordained as the first black SA minister of religion in the United Presbyterian Church of Scotland on 10 December 1856.
  Soga qualified in medicine from Glasgow in 1883 - about 30 years before the creation of the medical school in Cape Town, and 60 years before UCT and Wits considered black people fit for admission to their "hallowed halls". Soga's example was followed by John Mavuma Nembula, who graduated with the degree Doctor of Medicine from Chicago in 1887, and Abdullah Abdurrahman, who earned the Scottish Triple in 1893." Dr James McCune Smith was the first African American Medically qualified doctor: 1813.
- In 1880, Powell Johnson invented the first eye protectors (patent no. 234,039), which improved upon the eye-protection that would be used by firemen, furnace-men, as well as others who are often exposed to intense light, and for those with poor eyesight;
- Otis Boykin is credited with making circuit improvements to pacemakers after losing his mother to heart failure. But this single improvement was among a long list of achievements. Boykin had 26 patents in his name and is famed for the development of IBM computers, burglar-proof cash register, chemical air filters, and an electronic resistor used in controlled missiles and other devices;
- Dr Charles Drew, In World War II, played a major role in developing the first large-scale blood and Plasma banks as well as Blood Mobiles;
- Percy L. Julian discovered A New Process of Synthesis. His synthesis process is critical to the medical industry, as it allows scientists to create chemicals that are rare in nature. The chemist's work led to the production of Synthetic

Hormones such as, the birth control pill and improvements in the production of cortisone, a synthetic steroid.

- Dr Osei Hyiamani of Ghana is the first person in the world to establish the role of endocannabinoids in fatty acid synthesis and oxidation in liver disease, obesity and diabetes. This is important in the Management of Obesity and Diabetes
- Dr Seyi Oyesola of Nigeria has invented the "Hospital – in – a – Box" Concept wherein a self-powered, off-the-grid, handheld hospital which helps doctors perform quick and easy medical examinations anywhere in the world with the help of wireless technology. The handheld 'box' contains a spirometer, ECG electrocardiogram, nebuliser, otoscope, thermometer, cuff, pulse-oximetry, wireless transmitter and can be powered by solar, AC/DC, battery or vehicular power.
- South African Sandile Ngcobo discovered that laser beams can be digitally controlled. This discovery will significantly change the healthcare, manufacturing and communications industries. Essentially, the laser's 'beams' can be digitally modified before it exits spatial light modulators, meaning you only need one laser for whatever you want to do;
- Dr Patricia Bath invented the Cataract Laserphaco Laser Probe for the removal of eye Cataracts;
- Dr Oviemo Oadje of Nigeria Invented the EAT-SET which recovers the patient's own blood from internal bleeding and safely reinfuses it into the patient's system within 24 hours after a haemorrhage. The system aspirates blood which is haemorrhaging from the patient and reinfuses it into the patient's bloodstream through the use of gravity. The invention has seen Dr Oviemo receive several awards from, among others, the African Union and the World Intellectual Property Organisation.
- In 2015, Ludwick Marishane of South Africa Patented a Formula for Dry Bath. Using Gel in a Sachet Allows one to take a Bath without water. This addresses challenges of Water Scarcity and Water Borne diseases;
- In 2019, Professor Mashudu Tshifularo and his team at the University of Pretoria performed the world's first middle-ear surgery using 3D technology! They effectively replaced the hammer, anvil, stirrup and the ossicles, that make up the middle ear. The surgery, which can be performed on everyone including new-borns, has benefitted two patients already (2020). The 3D Printing technology is used to print the bones and also used during surgery to reconstruct the ossicles

eColonial Political and Philosophical Afridentity & African Renaissance

- Amongst Luminary Pioneers are: Patrice Lumumba; Haile Selassie; Kwame Nkrumah; Ahmed Sekou Toure'; Rolihlahla Nelson Mandela; Nnamdi Azikiwe; Steve Biko; Robert Sobukwe; Martin Luther King; Malcolm X; Marcus Garvey; Sam Nujoma; Uhuru Kenyatta; Paul Kagame, xxx...

deColonial Economics and Philanthropy:

- To give the Correct perspective on the deColonial Aspect, we need to look at the Precolonial examples of Wealth. Afrika had a thriving Economy and Monarchs who controlled it were Spectacularly Wealthy. Of those whose documentation is currently known, two stand out:
  Solomon, King of the United Kingdom of Israel, Kanaan (Present day Israel) 970 – 931 BC
  Nett Worth based on the estimate of the 25 Tons (666 Talents) of Gold he received from Ophir Annually for 39 years is estimated in today's value to be: 2 Trillion USD (Number of Tons over 39 years' x Gold Value today). This excludes all other sources of his wealth from Trading and his 1000 Fleet of Ships.
  Mansa (Emperor) Musa of Mali (North West Afrika), 1312 AD
  Mansa Musa had so much Gold, on his Hajj Pilgrimage to Mecca he gave away so much Gold that the Value of Gold Crashed for 10 years. His Wealth is estimated in Today's Terms by bbc.co.uk at about 400 Billion USD. Jeff Bezos in 2021 tops the list of the wealthiest at 190 Billion USD (210 billion poorer than Mansa Musa)
- Today, Mr Aliko Dangote of Nigeria (11.3 billion USD) and Mr Patrice Motsepe of South Africa (3.1 billion USD) Top the Charts. Ranking 195 and 1035 respectively in the world on the Forbes Richest List. In 2013, persuaded by their Faith and Culture of ubuNtu, they joined the "Giving Pledge", committing to give away half their wealth to Charitable Causes. Mr Motsepe made his Wealth in Mining whilst Mr Dangote is in Cement. They made their wealth against the odds of the Colonial and for Motsepe, Apartheid Legacy that saw their people dispossessed of their mineral rich Land with all evidence of their Mining History since Antiquity.
- Richard Maponya, another South African Business Innovator, died at age 99, still active as a Businessman. He started in Business when it was illegal for Afrikans to be in Business in South Afrika and there was no enabling legislation. Beating all the odds to become the First South African Afrikan to develop one

of the largest Malls in South Africa and within South Africa's oldest Township, SOWETO.

- Other Afrikans who have broken the Western Economic Barriers and become billionnaires against all odds and in a Foreign Economic System are: Mike Adenuga(Nigerian) – $9.1 bn; Robert Smith (American) – $5bn; David Steward (American) – $3bn; Oprah Winfrey: First Female Black billionaire (American) – $2.5bn; Strive Masiyiwa (Zimbabwean) $ 2.4bn; Michael Jordan (American Sports) – $2.1bn; Michael Lee Chin (Canada) – $ 1.9bn; Abdul Samad Rabiu (Nigeria) – $ 1.6bn; Folorunsho Alakija (Nigeria) – $1.1bn; Mo Ibrahim (Sudanese British) – $1.1bn

Christian and Spiritual Perspectives

- Since 60 AD when Christianity first came to Continental Afrika from Israel, Afrikans have strived to reclaim God's Narrative about them in the Bible. The same can be said about Muslims.
- Among Organisations and People who have pioneered this Move are: the indigenous Zionist Christian Movements in the variety famous for their Starched Green, Blue or White Linen;
- Missionary Organisations such as CAPRO Missions are starting to focus on the unreached people of the world in a Culturally sensitive manner.
- Afrikans Recognise that the Gospel of Jesus Christ and Islam can be preached within the Context of any Culture. Jesus Himself chose to be born into a Culture, the Jewish Culture and He began to help people to see God's way within their culture;
- In the Mature Man Reformation Era, my husband, Bishop Emmanuel Vusumuzi Dube of Ethekwini Community Church, a church that he established in 2005 is amongst many who are striving to restore the Way of Yeshua ha Mashiach (Rendered Jesus Christ in English) within the Afrikan Way of Life, kiNtu and its Spiritual Philosophy of ubuNtu.

This Work of Historical review seeks to Reconcile the Afrikan Nation Family within itself and the Rest of the Human family who when they left Afrika, populated the emerging continents of Europe, Eurasia, the Americas, Australasia and some of the Islands.

It is the intention of the Author, to Provoke a deep unquenchable Thirst, within the reader, to dig deeper into their own: Personal, Family, National and "Country" History. It is deliberately crafted so as to provoke Research and Mobilise Individuals,

Governments and the African Union to the Action of Restoring ubuNtu kubaNtu. This will contribute to Dismantling embedded negative and damaging identities and perceptions deep in the Afrikan abaNtu/baTwa psyche, that have kept us enslaved, 403 years after Slavery was dismantled and 27 years after the last Afrikan Country became Democratic.

The Afrikan Renaissance

In 1910, at the tender age of 25, Pixley ka Isaka Seme became South Africa's first "Black" Advocate. In 1912, he became the founder, and later President of the African National Congress.

Seme was born the fourth son of Sinono & Kuwana Seme in Inanda, Durban. They were based at the Inanda mission station of the American Zulu Mission, a Mission of the American Board of Commissioners for Foreign Missions. His mother was a sister to John Langaibalele Dube (who is a Ngcobo descendant).

He Studied at the Mission's High School, Adams College and at 17, Seme left to study in the U.S at Mount Hermon School, Columbia University, where he earned the Curtis Medal: Columbia's highest oratorical honour. He Studied further at Oxford University. Whilst at Oxford, he became a member of the Jesus College. He was called to the Bar on 8 June 1910. Seme returned to South Africa that same year, and began to practice as a lawyer in Johannesburg. This is the Speech he gave on the Occasion of his Graduation from Columbia University, USA on 05 April 1906. It is extracted Verbatim from the Website of the African National Congress.

I have chosen to speak to you on this occasion upon "The Regeneration of Africa."

I am an African.
and I set my pride in my race over against a hostile public opinion. Men have tried to compare races on the basis of some equality.
In all the works of nature, equality, if by it we mean identity, is an impossible dream!

Search the universe! You will find no two units alike.

The scientists tell us there are no two cells, no two atoms, identical.

Nature has bestowed upon each a peculiar individuality, an exclusive patent from the great giants of the forest to the tenderest blade.

Catch in your hand, if you please, the gentle flakes of snow.

Each is a perfect gem, a new creation; it shines in its own glory - a work of art different from all of its aerial companions.

Man, the crowning achievement of nature, defies analysis. He is a mystery through all ages and for all time.

The races of mankind are composed of free and unique individuals.

An attempt to compare them on the basis of equality can never be finally satisfactory.

Each is self. My thesis stands on this truth; time has proved it.

In all races, genius is like a spark, which, concealed in the bosom of a flint, bursts forth at the summoning stroke. It may arise anywhere and in any race.

I would ask you not to compare Africa to Europe or to any other continent. I make this request not from any fear that such comparison might bring humiliation upon Africa. The reason I have stated; -a common standard is impossible!

Come with me to the ancient capital of Egypt, Thebes, the city of one hundred gates. The grandeur of its venerable ruins and the gigantic proportions of its architecture reduce to insignificance the boasted monuments of other nations. The pyramids of Egypt are structures to which the world presents nothing comparable. The mighty monuments seem to look with disdain on every other work of human art and to vie with nature herself.

All the glory of Egypt belongs to Africa and her people.

These monuments are the indestructible memorials of their great and original genius. It is not through Egypt alone that Africa claims such unrivalled historic achievements. I could have spoken of the pyramids of Ethiopia, which, though inferior in size to those of Egypt, far surpass them in architectural beauty; their sepulchres which evince the highest purity of taste, and of many prehistoric ruins in other parts of Africa. In such ruins Africa is like the golden sun, that, having sunk beneath the western horizon, still plays upon the world which he sustained and enlightened in his career. Justly the world now demands- "Whither is fled the visionary gleam, where is it now, the glory and the dream?"

Oh, for that historian who, with the open pen of truth, will bring to Africa`s claim the strength of written proof. He will tell of a race whose onward tide was often swelled with tears, but in whose heart bondage has not quenched the fire of former years. He will write that in these later days when Earth`s noble ones are named, she has a roll of honour too, of whom she is not ashamed.

The giant is awakening! From the four corners of the earth Africa`s sons, who have been proved through fire and sword, are marching to the future`s golden door bearing the records of deeds of valor done.

Mr. Calhoun, I believe, was the most philosophical of all the slaveholders.

He said once that if he could find a black man who could understand the Greek syntax, he would then consider their race human, and his attitude toward enslaving them would therefore change. What might have been the sensation kindled by the Greek syntax in the mind of the famous Southerner, I have so far been unable to discover; but oh, I envy the moment that was lost! And woe to the tongues that refused to tell the truth!

If any such were among the now living, I could show him among black men of pure African blood those who could repeat the Koran from memory, skilled in Latin, Greek and Hebrew, Arabic and Chaldaic – men great in wisdom and profound knowledge - one professor of philosophy in a celebrated German university; one corresponding member of the French Academy of Sciences, who regularly transmitted to that society meteorological observations, and hydrographical journals and papers on botany and geology; another whom many ages call "The Wise," whose authority Mahomet himself frequently appealed to in the Koran in support of his own opinion-men of wealth and active benevolence, those whose distinguished talents and reputation have made them famous in the cabinet and in the field, officers of artillery in the great armies of Europe, generals and lieutenant generals in the armies of Peter the Great in Russia and Napoleon in France, presidents of free republics, kings of independent nations which have burst their way to liberty by their own vigor.

There are many other Africans who have shown marks of genius and high character sufficient to redeem their race from the charges which I am now considering.

Ladies and gentlemen, the day of great exploring expeditions in Africa is over! Man knows his home now in a sense never known before.

Many great and holy men have evinced a passion for the day you are now witnessing their prophetic vision shot through many unborn centuries to this very hour.

"Men shall run to and fro," said Daniel, "and knowledge shall increase upon the earth." Oh, how true! See the triumph of human genius to-day! Science has searched out the deep things of nature, surprised the secrets of the most distant stars, disentombed the memorials of everlasting hills, taught the lightning to speak, the vapors to toil and the winds to worship-spanned the sweeping rivers, tunneled (sic) the longest mountain range-made the world a vast whispering gallery, and has brought foreign nations into one civilized family.

This all-powerful contact says even to the most backward race, you cannot remain where you are, you cannot fall back, you must advance! A great century has come upon us.

No race possessing the inherent capacity to survive can resist and remain unaffected by this influence of contact and intercourse, the backward with the advanced.

This influence constitutes the very essence of efficient progress and of civilization. From these heights of the twentieth century I again ask you to cast your eyes south of the Desert of Sahara. If you could go with me to the oppressed Congos and ask, What does it mean, that now, for liberty, they fight like men and die like martyrs; if you would go with me to Bechuanaland, face their council of headmen and ask what motives caused them recently to decree so emphatically that alcoholic drinks shall not enter their country - visit their king, Khama, ask for what cause he leaves the gold and ivory palace of his ancestors, its mountain strongholds and all its august ceremony, to wander daily from village to village through all his kingdom, without a guard or any decoration of his rank - a preacher of industry and education, and an apostle of the new order of things; if you would ask Menelik what means this that Abyssinia is now looking across the ocean - oh, if you could read the letters that come to us from Zululand - you too would be convinced that the elevation of the African race is evidently a part of the new order of things that belong to this new and powerful period.

The African already recognizes his anomalous position and desires a change. The brighter day is rising upon Africa. Already I seem to see her chains dissolved, her desert plains red with harvest, her Abyssinia and her Zululand the seats of science and religion, reflecting the glory of the rising sun from the spires of their churches and universities. Her Congo and her Gambia whitened with commerce, her crowded cities sending forth the hum of business, and all her sons employed in advancing the victories of peace-greater and more abiding than the spoils of war.

Yes, the regeneration of Africa belongs to this new and powerful period! By this term regeneration I wish to be understood to mean the entrance into a new life, embracing the diverse phases of a higher, complex existence. The basic factor which assures their regeneration resides in the awakened race- consciousness. This gives them a clear perception of their elemental needs and of their undeveloped powers. It therefore must lead them to the attainment of that higher and advanced standard of life.

The African people, although not a strictly homogeneous race, possess a common fundamental sentiment which is everywhere manifest, crystallizing itself into one common controlling idea. Conflicts and strife are rapidly disappearing before the fusing force of this enlightened perception of the true intertribal relation, which relation should subsist among a people with a common destiny. Agencies of a social, economic and religious advance tell of a new spirit which, acting as a leavening ferment, shall raise the anxious and aspiring mass to the level of their ancient glory. The ancestral greatness, the unimpaired genius, and the recuperative power of the race, its irrepressibility, which assures its permanence, constitute the African`s greatest source of inspiration. He has refused to camp forever on the borders of the industrial world; having learned that knowledge is power, he is educating his children. You find them in Edinburgh, in Cambridge, and in the great schools of Germany. These return to their country like arrows, to drive darkness from the land. I hold that his industrial and educational initiative, and his untiring devotion to these activities, must be regarded as positive evidences of this process of his regeneration.

The regeneration of Africa means that a new and unique civilization is soon to be added to the world. The African is not a proletarian in the world of science and art. He has precious creations of his own, of ivory, of copper and of gold, fine, plated willow-ware and weapons of superior workmanship. Civilization resembles an organic being in its development-it is born, it perishes, and it can propagate itself. More particularly, it resembles a plant, it takes root in the teeming earth, and when the seeds fall in other soils new varieties sprout up. The most essential departure of this new civilization is that it shall be thoroughly spiritual and humanistic -indeed a regeneration moral and eternal!

O Africa!
Like some great century plant that shall bloom In ages hence,
we watch thee; in our dream
See in thy swamps the Prospero of our stream;
Thy doors unlocked,
where knowledge in her tomb Hath lain innumerable years in gloom.
Then shalt thou, walking with that morning gleam, Shine as thy sister lands
with equal beam.

Salungano

Are you an Afrikan?

What does it mean for you to be Afrikan?

How will you Honor your Heritage?

What Cultural Practices will you Espouse and Incorporate into your family?

What will your Legacy be?

In what way will you Practice ubuNtu? Create 10 Practices

UpWard Posture

InWard Posture

OutWard Posture

DownWard Posture

If you are Afrikan but not Afro-descendant, how will you Honor Afrikans?

If you Afrikan in the Diaspora, How will you, Honor Afrika

Part 2: The unTold (Hi)Story

"The Line of ill-intentional Egyptologist, equipped with a ferocious erudition, have committed their well-known Crime against Science, by becoming guilty of a deliberate falsification of the history of humanity."
Cheikh Anta Diop

Origins

This, is a Synoptic synthesis and distillation of well recorded History with other usually disregarded sources of History, in order to create one seamless Afrikan Historical Narrative from Creation. It identifies the personalities of Scientific History in today's living descendants, who are usually veiled and or erased in Scientific Nomenclature.

The Author being a Person of Faith, and Most Afrikans being people of faith, Scriptures and Oral evidence from various faith traditions are quoted extensively as evidence, in the same way that scientific evidence is quoted. For most Afrikans, Oral and written Scripture are as authoritative as the scientifically derived evidence.

This Seamless, flowing and comprehensive Narrative, is given in the format of a Time line. Details are limited to highlights without much of a discursive narrative, except for topics that are known to be of concern for Afrikan People.

I would have loved to be able to identify all 10 000 and more, surviving Afrikan Nations in their Lands; Languages and Histories by Name. However, the Vastness of the Continent; The Time span involved and the Lack of corroborative written data for Afrikan Oral and indigenous knowledge, as well as the length of the book that would be required are prohibitive. 10 000 books are required for each Nation and these will be written by the descendants of each of these Nations, Inshallah. (#AfricanHistoriesProject is a Multidisciplinary Team that will be set up in each country to work on this and GlobuNtu Publishing is interested in helping writers publish such books).

I therefore encourage Afrikans to Note the Gaps in my Narrative, and Accept my deepest Apology to them. The gaps are not meant to Silence or deliberately "unhear" them yet again, they just represent my ignorance. This is my First Fruits offering unto the Many Books that shall be born henceforth, in every Nation. It gives the Skeleton of our History, and surely, as each one of us Calls on the Breath of God to enter the bones: The Muscles; Sinews; Nerves; Blood vessels and organs will attach, to make it, a Mighty Hunter before God.

<u>The Big Bang and the Birth of a Planet</u>

According to **Scientific** Calculations, the earth was born 13.8bn years ago, following the Big Bang (Single Singularity expansion). www.space.com

Hubble, after observing that galaxies were moving apart from each other, Theorised, that at some point, they must have been together. Based on this Assumption, Over the past seventy years, Physicists and Cosmologists Have Mathematically concluded that the Universe began at a Single Singularity (Moment) called the "Big Bang" which has Expanded to form the Universe over Billions of years, estimated to be 13.8 billion years. The fallout of energy from this "Big Bang", is theorised to have caused the birth of Planet earth 4.5 billion years ago at the periphery of the Universe. Earth is thought of as a Molten Larva of gasses and water that boiled and simmered for about 500 million years.

It is further surmised that the Big Bang established Laws such as the Law of Gravity, Reproduction and others, that would Govern, Regulate and Sustain the Planet.

New Scientific evidence however, seems to suggest that the Earth and the Universe, may have formed much quicker than earlier thought, in a matter of 5 million years. (Science Daily, 2020)

According to the **Quran:** The Earth was formed about 305 000 years more or less ago: Surah Al Maáriji (70:4) – The Quran. "The Angels and the Spirit will ascend to Him during a Day the extent of which is 50 000 years" (50 000 years' x 7 creative days plus the 7000 years or since then = 357 000 years ago)

According to the **Byzantine Belief (Old Roman Empire)**: Panodorus, a Monk of Alexandria, calculated that Creation must have taken place 5493 BC (7513 years ago)

According to **Afrikan Cultural thought**: Creation of earth as part of the creation of the Universe, occurred in the Eternal Past when time was irrelevant, thus the age of earth is accepted as incalculable, suffice it to say it is, "Zwigidi zwa zwigidi zwa zwigidi zwa minwaha" (Thousands upon thousands upon Thousands of years ago). This is considered as The unknowable past. "Zwine ra zwidivha, ndi zwa vho khotsi ashu, zwi na zwigidi zwatahe" (What we know is the time that belongs to our fathers, it spans 9000 years) (Nguni Tradition)

According to **Mayan Tradition**: Creation took Place in 3114 BC (5134 years ago)

(www.historymuseum.ca)

According to **Hindu Tradition**, which Recognises cycles of time that may be as long as trillions in number, the earth is thought to have been created 4.3 billion years ago because, the Puranic Texts say: 1 day of Brahma is 1000 x the sum of 4 yugas (4 320 000 in years) = 4.3 bn years.

Christian Tradition holds 2 Schools of thought:

Young Earth School: This Tradition holds that the Earth was Created 6024 years ago, based on the literal reading of Genesis 1 (1 day = 1 day) and the Historical Span of the events recorded in the Bible = 4004 years + 2020 since then.

Older Earth School: This Tradition holds that the Earth was Created 13024 years ago or billions of years ago, based on the reading of Genesis 1 in the light of 2 Peter 3:8 – The Bible, which reads: "But, Do NOT Forget this one thing, dear friends, With the LORD a day is like a thousand years, and a Thousand years are like a day. It is therefore believed that each creative day and 1 rest day (7days) are equal to Thousand(s) of years. Thus, Creation Date is calculated to be 7000 years or more plus 4004 Biblical History Span + 2020 years AD = Billions or 13024 years ago.

Scientific Dates and the Dates of other Traditions, begin to **Correspond** from around 3900 BC (Bronze Age), thence, only 1 date will be captured. The Age of Historical Events in this section will therefore be summarised as follows: Oldest dates represented by the Scientific dates (13.8bn years ago) and Youngest dates represented by the oldest of the younger dates. (13004 years ago).

Homo Sapiens: The First Upright, Wise Human Being

There are predominantly two Schools of thought (Conventions) and more recently a third, regarding The origins of the first Upright, Wise Human Being/Homo Sapiens/ Human Beings/Mankind/People/abaNtu: Evolution; Intelligent Design and Creationism.

1. Evolution (Darwin's Theory of Evolution/Darwinism)

This area of study is undertaken by a wide section of Scientists, including Anthropologists, Paleontologists, Archaeologists and Geneticists.

The Theory of Evolution holds that Species change over time, through Natural Selection and environmental Input, so that only the fittest survive. Over time, as Species adapt to their environment through small adaptations, these add up to create a new species that has evolved from what it was like, earlier and which is better suited to survive in the future. The Theory was arrived at by Alfred Russel Wallace and Charles Darwin. The Backbone of this Theory is DNA Sequencing which shows that All life shares a Last Universal Common Ancestor (LUCA).

According to Cosmological Theory, Highly Energetic Chemistry from the "Big Bang" fallout, produced a self-replicating Molecule around 4 billion years ago, when the Planet Cooled down. This is the Molecule that produced LUCA 500 million years later (3.5 billion years ago)

LUCA's Genetic Material, is found in all Living things today. From 3.5 billion years ago, LUCA began replicating and forming groups of cells until eventually, these grouped to form various living things. 800 million to 500 million years ago, the first animals emerged from LUCA. Dinosaurs were the largest animals in this era.

65 million years ago, an Asteroid collided with earth at the Yucatan Peninsula in Mexico, causing the extinction of Dinosaurs and the subsequent flourishing of mammals.

4 to 2 Million years ago, *Australopithecine hominids* "made their appearance" some are thought to be as old as of 9 million years ago.

Several species, of Australopithecines, including: Garhi, Sediba, Africanus and Afarensis, have been proposed as the ancestor or sister of the *Homo* lineage. The first fossils were discovered, in the Afar Triangle of Afrika (Ethiopia), hence the name "Afarensis". It was nicknamed "Lucy" (From LUCA?) These species have morphological features that align them with *Homo genus*, but there is no consensus as to which gave rise to *Homo*. The other hominids were discovered in the Koobi Fora of Kenya as well as Sediba and Taung in South Africa. Some of the famous Paleoanthropologists to make these discoveries are: Raymond Dart and Richard Leaky.

Australopithecus Hominids, were succeeded by various Classes of Homo Species: Neanderthalensis; Naledi; Luzonensis; Heidelbergensis; Habilis; Florensis; xxx; Erectus and maybe, in its own Class, Homo Ergaster. These were all Hunter gatherers, capable of making fire. They seem to have Started in Afrika and then Migrated out into other continents with Homo erectus migrating out 1.8 million years ago (the 1st out of Afrika Exodus).

Homo Ergaster remained in Afrika. Homo Ergaster evolved into Homo Sapiens 200 000 years ago. Homo Sapiens is also referred to as Modern Humans (Erect Wise Man) who cultivated crops and domesticated animals. Their Skull remains were first found in Ethiopia at the Omro River in 1926.

In 2017, however, this view has shifted to Morocco, as older Homo Sapiens (315 000 years old) Jaw Remains has been identified and the view is now a Pan Afrikan origin of Homo Sapiens. Afrika as a whole, is therefore, is now considered to be the Cradle of Mankind. (This area of study is not static. It is ever-evolving and every country is combing their lands in search for the oldest Human remains, in the bid to be the site of the origins of Humankind)

The Age of Human remains, is determined by using Radiometric dating of the decay of isotopes of fossils and their surrounding environment. Radiometric dating can be affected by Environmental changes such as Floods and Volcanoes making material culture seem younger or older than they are.

2. Intelligent Design

Intelligent Design is relatively new in the Origins Debate and it holds that: "The Complexity of Life demands an Intelligent Designer". It refutes Darwin's Self-Replicating and Natural Selection Mechanism. It Bases its Theory on Irreducible complexity, which states that: "It is impossible for Certain biological systems to have evolved through successive small modifications, to pre-existing functional systems, through natural selection, because no less **complex** system would function."

It therefore Claims "God's hand" to explain the perceived gaps of Science. This area of study is done by a wide section of Scientists who also follow a Spiritual Faith Conviction, including among them, Anthropologists, Paleontologists, Archaeologists and Geneticists. In his book, A Brief History of Time, Hawking, S. (1989) states: "It would be very difficult to explain why the universe should have begun in just this way, except as the act of a God who intended to create beings like us." Collins FS (2006) Remarks: "The existence of the Big Bang, begs the questions: What came before the Big Bang and who or what caused that? Did Nature create itself or does it have a creator who caused the Big Bang?"

3. Creationism

This Convention is held by most Cultures as well as Religions/Faiths. Creationism Credits God and his divinities or other Deities as the Creator(s) of the Heavens and the Earth and everything in them. The History of Mankind is then followed in greater detail within the written or oral Scriptures of the Adherents.

The History of Mankind can readily be deciphered from these Scriptures that name a "Birthplace" for Humankind as either "Here" or Eden and goes on to further explain how humanity became dispersed in the whole Earth.

According to most *Afrkcan Traditional Religions,* In the beginning, God created people using these elements: Earth; Water; Fire and Air/Wind individually or in combination, with or without the aid of divinities. Generally, in most of these Narratives, In the creative process, People emerge from the Marshes (Umhlanga). God then gives people laws on how to live on earth. People wanted a say in how things should be and invariably, this always created distance between God and people. In some versions, the other deities come to the defense or support of human beings. (various versions of these narratives exist).

Egyptian Written narratives show that, Afrikans believed that prior to the creation of humans, there was only Dark Matter. In the beginning was the Dark matter and the world was an expanse of dark and chaotic water. Atum the creator God emerged from these chaotic waters by uttering his own name. He carries the ankh, a symbol of life and Royal authority. Atum created twins: a son and a daughter who symbolize Life and Justice, these two separated the sky from the waters and produced Dry land. More gods were created, amongst whom was Re, the sun god. Humans were created from the tears of (Re) the Sun god's eye that became dislodged from his head, when other gods fought over the eye. Humans dwelt on the dry land where they co-existed with the gods on earth. When Re was old, some gods and humans sought to oust him. This Rebellion caused Re, to disappear below the earth but Thoth, the Moon god, knowing that the sinking of the sun would destroy human life, had mercy on the humans, and he was given a spell to protect them. The Saving spell resulted in earth separating from the heavens and gods from humans. Khosi Pfareli (Pharaohs), those who reign on God's behalf, then became the custodians of Life and Justice on earth. (Adapted from www.historymuseum.ca) This Egyptian Narrative is similar to that of the baLobedu ba ga Modjadji, in South Africa as well as the Akan people of Ghana.

Scientists now have evidence of the existence of Dark Matter because of the gravitational effects it appears to have on galaxies and galaxy clusters. Dark matter accounts for 85% of matter in the universe. There are no Instruments currently that can directly observe Dark Matter, which is completely invisible to light and other forms of electromagnetic radiation, therefore it is invisible. The Bible records: "Now the earth was formless and empty, Darkness was over the surface of the Deep, and the Spirit of God was hovering over the waters... and God said..."

In one of the isiZulu versions advanced by the foremost *iSanusi uCredo Vusamazulu Mutwa*, after God Created Humans in Afrika from the Marshes, People were "*Ngcukubili*" (Both Male and Female in one). Humans used Telepathic/Mind Communication. They had no words. One Day, "Them" or "Chitauri" (Speakers) came out of the Sky in huge "ships", promising humans great gifts if humans would worship them. They drove human beings into a choice of 2 caves that transformed them into male or female, then they gave them the gift of language, which made them lose their Telepathic Communication abilities, creating confusion and disagreements amongst the people. Chitauri were cruel to humans and exploited them. They taught humans technological advances, predominantly for the benefit of the Chitauri, amongst which were Mining and Architecture. This narrative is reminiscent of the Genesis 6 Biblical Narrative and that of the Book of Enoch, which is Apocryphal, which speak of "the sons of God" who came on earth and had relations with human daughters, bringing forth Giants, Mighty men of Renown who seem to have seeded Technological advances on earth.

In the Quran, the Story of Creation is recorded in various places throughout the Quran 21:30 says: The heavens and the earth were joined together as one unit, before we clove them asunder and 41:11, Allah said to it and the earth: "Come together, willingly or unwillingly." They said: "We come together in willing obedience" 21:33 says: "It is He who created the night and the day and the sun and the Moon; all swim along, each in its rounded course. 51:47 "The heavens we have built them with power. And verily, we are expanding it" 50:38 "We created the heavens and the earth and all that is between them in six days, nor did any sense of weariness touch us"

57:4 "He it is who created the heavens and the earth in six days, then established Himself upon the throne. He knows what enters within the heart of the earth, and what comes forth out of it, what comes down from heaven, and what mounts up to it. And He is with you wherever you may be. And Allah sees well all that you do" 15:26 "We created man from sounding Clay, from mud molded into shape" 7:189 "It is He who created you from a single person and made his mate of like nature, in order that he might dwell with her in love. The Quran also narrates about Giants of 'Ad and Thamud, who were huge and powerful and could uproot a Tree with their hands. These Giants were Civilised and Skillful, but because of this, they became arrogant and according to Surah 41:15, "They turned arrogant on earth and opposed the Truth..." so, they were wiped from the surface of the Earth.

In the Bible, the story of Creation and early History is narrated in Genesis1-12. These Chapters, give a narration of the Creation of the Universe; the Earth and everything in them. It also narrates the first part of the History of Mankind (Human Beings/Wise Erect Man/Homo Sapiens/People/abaNtu) until people were scattered abroad the earth, then narrows down to the History of predominantly the Israelites, with other Nations mentioned only as far as their History intersects that of the Israelites. Biblically, the area of Man's Origin is named Eden. The Bible does not say where Eden is, rather, it describes its Locality by means of 4 Rivers that bounded this area. Genesis 2: 7-14: "Now, a river went out of Eden to water the Garden, and from there it parted into four water heads."

<u>The Location of Eden based on the Names of the four water-heads</u>

1. <u>Pishon</u>

"The Name of the First is Pishon, which winds through the entire land of Havilah, where there is gold. The Gold of that Land is good. Bdellium and the onyx stones are there.

There are two schools of thought about the identity of this River:

School 1: This School of thought sees Havilah as the Middle East because one of the sons of Shem is Havilah. The Pishon is believed to be a fossilized river that starts in Turkey and encompassed the entire Middle East into the Gulf of Aden in Yemen. The Middle East has both Gold and Bdellium.

School 2: This School of thought sees Havilah as Afrika because Havilah is also the name of one of the sons of Kush (Cush). Afrika is also the home of the world's best Gold; In this scenario, the Pishon is understood to be the Rift Valley System which also begins in Turkey and the Jordan River through East Afrika, Kenya and ends in Mozambique, winding through the entire Land of Havilah.

According to the Webster Dictionary, Bdellium is: Reddish Tree Gum Resin used in Myrrh found in the Middle East, India and Afrika. Some sources see it as a precious stone or pearls.)

2. ***The Gihon***

The Name of the second river is the Gihon (Giyon, which is the Blue Nile), It is the one which goes around the land of Kush (East Afrika). Early Chinese Maps show the Nile starting in Mozambique and draining into the Mediterranean Sea. (The Nile empties Northward into the Mediterranean Sea).

3. ***Hiddekel***

The name of the third river Hiddekel which goes toward the East of Asshur. Asshur is in the Middle East. This river is postulated to be the Tigris in the Middle East.

4. ***Euphrates***

The fourth river is the Euphrates. This is the only river that is still called by the same name today and it is found in the Middle East. River Course: Turkish Mountains to the Iraq/Kuwait border

The Location of Eden is therefore: Middle East/Arabia (2 of the 4 Rivers) and East Afrika, (2 of the 4 Rivers). Prior to the Scramble for Africa, the Middle East/Arabia was known as North East Afrika. Thus *The Bible Places the birthplace of Mankind in Afrika: The Garden of Eden*. This is the same location advanced by Scientific evidence for the emergence of Modern Man/Homo Sapiens.

Ancient History

In this portion of History, The Author Transposes the three Creation Schools of thought, onto each other, to tease out common thoughts, so that one seamless Narrative can emerge that is coherent for any adherent to any School of thought.

13.8bn years ago or 1304 BC

The Heavens and the Earth (Universe) were created or came into being following the "Big Bang" Singularity of God's Creative "Let there be" Call.

Genesis 1: 1- 31 TLV

1 In the beginning God created the heavens and the earth (The Heavens speaks of the Universe with its Planetary System and the Earth Speaks of Planet Earth)

2 Now the earth was chaos and waste, darkness (Egyptian texts call this, Dark matter) was on the surface of the deep, and the *Ruach Elohim* was hovering upon the surface of the water/deep. (Pre-Singularity State)

4.6bn years ago or 9000 BC

3 Then God said, "Let there be light!" and there was light. **The first day** - (The Singularity/ Big Bang energy and space-time of the universe may have appeared as Light in the otherwise Dark Space, but this could also speak to the Creation of the Light-giving bodies of the Universe: Sun, Moon and Stars)

6 Then God said, "Let there be an expanse in the midst of the water! Let it be for separating water from water." **the second day**. Separation of Earth from the Heavens as attested to by Most Traditions.

9 Then God said, "Let the water below the sky be gathered to one place. Let the dry ground appear, and it was so, and God called the dry land Earth, and the gathering together of the Waters he called Seas" And God saw that it was good. Scientifically, 4.5bn years ago, the Earth formed at the periphery of the Universe when Gravity pulled swirling Gas and Dust from the Bing Bang, in, to become a Planet, with 1 Super-Continent, surrounded by water. The Super-Continent was named Pangea.

4bn years ago or 9000 BC

Highly Energetic Chemistry from the "Big Bang" fallout fog becomes elementary particles necessary for the support of Life on Earth.

3.5bn years ago or 9000 BC

LUCA (Last Universal Common Ancestor) is "Born" from this Highly Energetic Chemistry and it gives rise to processes that create various Life forms in Response to every "Let there be" Command of God.

11 Then God said, "Let the land sprout grass, green plants yielding seed, fruit trees making fruit, each according to its species with seed in it, upon the land." And it happened so. **The third day** – The Scientific Evidence for Earliest Grass and Trees is: 60-55 Million years ago though... instead of 3.5bn years ago (is this a dating issue or did green plants and grass really appear after the extinction of Dinosaurs? How did Gaseous exchange happen if there was no Photosynthesis? The Scientific Time line also shows an Oxygen Crisis at about 2.5bn years ago, Making the Bible Chronology of early Grass appearance more plausible. The reason for the lack of evidence of grass can be myriad, including being highly biodegradable).

14 Then God said, "Let lights in the expanse of the sky be for separating the day from the night. They will be for signs and for seasons and for days and years. **the fourth day**

20 Then God said, "Let the waters swarm with swarms of living creatures! Let flying creatures fly above the land across the expanse of the sky." **the fifth day.** (These again took their genetic Material from LUCA. Earliest evidence of Fish species is 530 million years ago and birds, 60 million years ago.)

250 Million years ago or 8000 BC

Pangea Drifts apart into Gondwana and Laurasia and Over millions of years, the Continents drift (Techtonic plate movement) to current positions. This date for Continental drift is irreconcilable to the Biblical date, which is much younger... around 2200s BC.

60 Million years ago or 8000 BC

An Asteroid Collides with Earth at Yucatan in what is today, Brazil, leaving one of the world's largest Craters, the Chicxulub Crater as Testimony. This impact is believed to have caused the Extinction of 1/3 of all Animal Living Species (Predominantly Dinosaurs). The Bible and the Quran do not record this Event as having taken place, but then again, these books do not record every detail of everything. They write broad strokes of it. Since Remains of several Dinosaur Species have been re-discovered in Egypt in 1999 (Nortdurft, W), It is possible that some Egyptian Scroll may turn up with Accounts of these.

4.4 – 2 Million years ago or 8000 BC

Australopithecus Hominids make their appearance.

The Bible does not mention this Pre-Human Ancestor. The Mayan Creation Story however, shows the Deities creating man 3 times… Is it a narration of Hominids, Homo Non-Sapiens and finally Homo Sapiens?

400 000 years ago or 8000 BC

24 Then God said, "Let the land (enriched with LUCA) bring forth living creatures according to their species—livestock, crawling creatures and wild animals, according to their species." And it happened so, **the sixth day.** The Earliest evidence for lions: 350 000 years ago and Livestock: 8000 to 12 000 years ago

300 or 200 000 years ago or 8000 BC

Homo Sapiens is said to have appeared in Afrika, during this time. Their Skeletal Remains have been found in Kassies River and the Border cave in South Africa; Laetoli in Dodoma, Tanzania; Omo and Herto in Ethiopia and recently Morocco.

Biblically,

Still on the 6th Day of Creation,

26 Then God said, "Let Us make man in Our image, after Our likeness! Let them rule over the fish of the sea, over the flying creatures of the sky, over the livestock, over the whole earth, and over every crawling creature that crawls on the land."

27 God created humankind in His image, in the image of God He created him, male and female He created them (Adam and Eve/Addamu-Ntu and Efe)

28 God blessed them and God said to them, "Be fruitful and multiply, fill the land, and subdue it. Rule over the fish of the sea, the flying creatures of the sky, and over every animal that crawls on the land." And Genesis 2:15, Then the LORD God took the man and placed him in the Garden of Eden, which as we have explained earlier is Anywhere from Arabia/Middle East - usually thought of as Iraq - to the Eastern Afrikan Coastal area (This area coincides with the Scientific findings: Kassies River and the Border cave in South Africa; Laetoli in Dodoma, Tanzania; Omo and Herto in Ethiopia).

200 000 years ago or 5000 BC

The Bible in Genesis 10, is the only Book that Identifies the various people of the world and Identifies their Lands in Ancient times. Although this Text has been abused for Racist agendas, it is still the most relevant and only Clear Narrative that Identifies people in their lands, in a way that is credible and is still provable today in the enduring descendants of the Lands. Interestingly, this Narrative Identifies all the 4 descendants of Ham, who was Dark skinned very Clearly, locating each of them in the Identifiable Kanaan (Canaan) and Afrika (Africa). The Bible also gives a clear record of the Relationship of Afrikans with the Neighbouring Nations of Arabia, Turkey, Iran, India and Iberia. These are corroborated by Ancient Sumerian Texts, later Arabic and Roman Historical Narratives as well as Archeaological findings. Valuable as Genetics are, sometimes the reading of their results can be biased as they are read against the backdrop of a standard that may be erroneous in its Assumptions. For Example, if my Assumption is that: Afrikans are White and Indo-European. Genetic Material from Afrikan people would become my Standard for White Indo-European genes. When I study the genes of people from Europe, their genes would not match my Standard and I would conclude that they are neither white nor Indo-European. For Genetics to be of True value, the Standard needs to be correct.

In the absence of detailed Ancient Records of who is who and where they come from, the Author uses the Biblical Narrative to Identify Afrikans and other Nations in their Lands. Material Culture of Afrika is then treated as the Material Culture of Afrikans and where Genetics seems to have difficulty in explaining presence or absence of Afrikan genetic material, the reasons for this are extended.

The Biblical Narrative is woven to the Scientific findings to give Identity to Scientific Nomenclature and make sense of the Gaps in each Narrative.

According to the Bible, from 200 000 years ago (5000 BC), The first Couple Walked with God, whom they named *uZigi zakhe zi ye zwakala* (one whose footsteps are heard), *o vela NqaNqi* (Alpha and Omega), *uQamatha* (Omnipresent), *Muhali/'nwali* (Mighty one), *Kalunga* (The one who welcomes you at the thresholds of death), *Thimudi* (Unknowable), *Modimo* (Supreme Source), *Zakazim* (He whose ways are unknown), *Imana* (Creator), *Maita zwitoma* (He who does good things) *Akongo (God of Kongo), Yere, Mungu, Mulungu, Mukuru, Yatta, Thixo, Rugaga, Ori, Wari, Weri, NyaDenga, Enkai, kaTonda....* According to their experiences of Him in the Garden as He visited them, "In the cool of Day" (Genesis 3:8) and helped them Navigate the Earth. This is Communion, a Relationship between Man and God. Spirituality, not yet packaged into a religion.

One day, they were tempted by a snake, that they apparently could communicate (maybe telepathically) with. The snake tempted them to put their Trust in themselves, their ability and knowledge, rather than in God. This Temptation is followed by a visitation from Angelic beings who intermarry with the daughters born to the first couple. Genesis 6:1-5, Now it came to pass that when men began to multiply on the face of the earth and daughters were born to them, that the Angels interfered with humanity and had children with Human Daughters, and to them, "Mighty Men of Old/Men of Renown" were born, The Annunaki/Anakim/Nephilim. These Annunaki seem to have influenced the Progressive Technological Advances of this era and also contributed to wickedness which increased during this time, leading to God reducing Human Lifespan on earth to 120 years and vowing to wipe out this wickedness through a Flood. (This is corroborated by the Quran, Book of Enoch and Afrikan Tradition as alluded to earlier)

Nukhu (Noah), the 9th descendant of Adam, finds Grace in the eyes of God and God tells him that everything on Earth was going to be destroyed, but that if he followed God's instructions, he and a representation of every animal on earth as well as his family, would be saved. Nukhu follows God's Instructions and he and his family are protected from the flood which takes place during his time. The earth was flooded and all living things perished but God saved Nukhu (Noah), his wife, his three sons and their wives and representatives of every animal. Afrikan Nursery rhymes to date still speak of the Flood of Noah as for example: *vhaVenda: Mvula I ya na milobilo kolongonya, vho mmane mbebeni, kolongonya, Ninnyise Muragani, kolongonya kolongonya, Nndukhulu i na biko, kolongonya kolongonya... baSotho: Mmangwane Mpulele, kenelwa ke pula...*

Not everyone in the Scientific Community corroborates this world-wide Flood. Montgomery, DR in his book: Rocks don't lie: A Geologist investigates Noah's Flood proves that such a deluge did occur, however.

The Sumerian story told in the Enmerkar and the Lord of Aratta texts around 2500 BC speaks of similar events. The Quran attests to this deluge in Sura 71. Once the Flood subsided and the Ark settled on Mount Ararat in Turkey, Nukhu, his wife and their sons and their wives and the animals came out of the Ark and Travelled Eastward toward Shinnar/Sennar (Southern Mesopotamia/Middle East). Nukhu seems to have suffered a Depressive episode after the Flood that killed all his relatives (and possibly post-traumatic Stress from hearing their wails of "Mmangwane Mpulele ke nelwa ke pula and Mvula iyana milobilo kolongonya kolongonya"). He consoled himself with Alcohol that he fermented from Grapes that he had cultivated.

One Day, whilst drunk Nukhu lay naked in his Tent, where Khami (Ham) finds him and goes out to inform his brethren Shem and Japheth. His older siblings come in walking backwards and covered their father's nakedness. This possibly precipitated the first Human Sibling Rivalry, when the two elder brothers, informed their father of the incident once he was roused from the intoxication. The Bible records that when Nukhu *heard* about this incident, he became angry and cursed (K)Hami's son, Kanaan (Canaan) declaring him a slave to both Japheth and Shem. He then Declares that Japheth would dwell in the Tents of Shem.

The Blessing of God However Stands. In Genesis 1:28 and Genesis 9, God Blessed Nukhu and all three of his descendants, including their descendants in their loins (Kanaan) and also: "What God has blessed, no man can curse". Numbers 23:8&20. It is for this reason that God sent descendants of Shem (Abram and Jesus) to Kanaan years later to break Noah's curse over his grandson because although it did not reverse God's Blessing, it did affect Balance in Kanaan's life.

Genesis 12:3, God Addressing Abram: "Through you, all the families of the earth shall be blessed." Jesus was later sent to die for the sins of all men (curses) in Kanaan and thus restore Balance for Kanaan and all of humanity. The Curse of Ham (in fact, Kanaan) was used to justify the oppression and slavery of Afrikan people, by people who held the Bible or Torah as their Holy Scriptures.

During this time, the Human Family is said to have spoken one Language, possibly Proto-kiNtu (Proto Afro-Asiatic or Syriac). These people are said to have journeyed from the Ark which settled on Mount Ararat in Turkey toward Shinnar (Sumeria and or Mesopotamia).

It is here in Sumer, that according to Genesis 11 and the Book of Jubilees 10:20 – 21, and as attested by Enmerkar and the Lord of Aratta texts, people united to erect the Tower of Babel at Shinnar (Ancient Babylonia). This was done possibly under the leadership of Nimurut (Nimrod), son of Kush (Cush), son of Khami (Ham Spelt in this book as (K)Ham to accommodate both spellings... with or without i), son of Nukhu (Noah). The Pseudo-Philo text attributes the building to Nimrod prince of Ham, Joktan prince of Shem and Phenech son of Dodanim and prince of Japheth. It is also here that God confused the tongues of the people, so that they could no longer understand each other. This interruption in language flow, caused people to stop building the Tower and to be dispersed thence. Scientifically, the Human Family originated in Southern Afrika and journeyed North-Easterly to Tanganyika, Kenya and Ethiopia, whence they dispersed to other Continents, because of a change in Climatic conditions as will be elaborated later.

Biblically, the dispersal to populate the whole earth, followed family groups, since each family spoke a common language. The Families were of the three sons of Nukhu (Noah): Japheth; Shem and (K)Ham.

The family of Japheth whose descendants according to Genesis 10: 1-5 KJV are:

"The sons of Japheth are: Gomer, and Magog, and Madai, and Javan, and Tubal, and Meshech, and Tiras·[3] And the sons of Gomer; Ashkenaz, and Riphath, and Togarmah·[4] And the sons of Javan; Elishah, and Tarshish, Kittim, and Dodanim·[5] By these were the isles of the Gentiles divided in their lands; every one after his tongue, after their families, in their nations. They reached the "Coastlands" of Europe and Asia (40 000 and 80 000 years ago respectively).

The family of Shem (S(h)emitic/Semitic People) Genesis 10:22

[22] The children of Shem: Elam, and Asshur, and Arphaxad, and Lud, and Aram. (5 S(h) emetic Nations) [23] And the children of Aram; Uz, and Hul, and Gether, and Mash. [24] And Arphaxad begat Salah; and Salah begat Eber. [25] And unto Eber were born two sons: the name of one was Peleg; for in his days was the earth divided (Continental Drift, Scientific date dates this event much earlier); and his brother's name was Joktan. Joktan begot Almodad, Sheleph, Hazarmaveth, Jerah, Hadoram, Uzal, Diklah, Obal, Abimael, Sheba, Ohir, Havilah and Jobab. Joktan's Nations according to Genesis 10:30 dwelt as follows: "[30] And their dwelling was from Mesha, as thou goest unto Sephar a mount of the east. Elam, and Asshur and Lud, and Aram lived in the Middle East as follows: Aram, present day Syria; Elam, Present day South western Iran and, Present day Assyria; Lud, Present day Turkey". [31] These are the sons of Shem, after their families, after their tongues, in their lands, after their nations.

They are the S(h)emetic Arameans, Elamites, Assyrians, Hebrew, Israelites, Jews, Arab Bedouins of these Current Nations: Saudi Arabia; Kuwait; Oman; Qatar; United Arab Emirates; Yemen; Bahrain; Jordan; Syria; Iraq. These are all related S(h)emetic People, who shared the Peninsula with Kanaanitic Nations on the Levant and who were later joined by Afrikan baKushi and Persian Indo- Europeans in Sumer and Mesopotamia.

Hebrews are all the S(h)emetic people whose fathers are: Joktan or Peleg. From these, the descendants of Abraham are either Afro-S(h)emetic Ishmaelite (descendents of the 12 sons of Ishmael whose mother was Hajra, the Egyptian), Afro-S(h)emetic Edomite or Afro-S(h)emetic Israelite (descendants of the 12 sons of Jacob, who gained their Afrikan heritage when they were slaved in Egypt and whose descendants there and afterward married Egyptian and Kanaanitic women).

The Iraelites became scattered in the world, but some of them are today's Afro-S(h)emetic Samaritans and Palestinians, whilst others are Afro-S(h)emetic Jews (who are the descendants of Judah and his descendants, David and Solomon married Kanaanitic and other international women are very mixed heritage with a spectrum of phenotypic features). Then there is a Multitude of Converted Jews of Afrikan, Indian, Asian and European descent, who have been Jewish for 2500 years and are not aware that ethnically, they are not Jews.

According to today's Racial Classification, therefore, it is True, that there are: Black Ethnic Jews, White Ethnic Jews, Asian Ethnic Jews, Arabic Ethnic Jews, as well as Black Convert Jews, White Convert Jews, Asian Convert Jews.

The family of Khami (Kem/Kmt Ham)

Kmt, means: Dark as in burnt earth/Alluveal Soil.

Khami's Descendants are: Kush (Cush); Misraim (Mizraim); Phuti (Put) and Kanaan (Canaan). These are Nations that have been derogated/Classified as: Black, Bantu, Sub-Saharan, Negroid, Negro, Kaffir, Caffer, pygmy, Hottentot and Coloured. They settled Kanaan, Continental Afrika and the Afrikan Islands, according to their families and later, some were carried to Slavery in other Continents, becoming the Afrikan Diaspora.

Eldest son: Kushi: Kushi means, of a dark skin and also means Wisdom. Genesis 10:7-20

Kush beget: Seba; Havilah; Sabutah; Sabuteka, Nimurut & Raama, whose sons are Sheba & Dedan.

baKush descendants created The World's first Political Kingdom: Ta-Seti Kingdom in 5900 BC, which is expressly described by Ezekiel as lying to the south of Egypt (Misraimi) beyond and Its limits on the west and south were undefined... basically: from Today's Sudan, Eastward and Southward to to the Horn of Afrika and to South Eastern parts of Afrika in what is today KwaZulu-Natal.

This first Continental Civilisation was centred around the Nile River. The Nile River (in Luvenda: *Munavhawaile*, which means, River that winds throughout) is North- flowing and is among the world's longest water-ways (6650 km) and is called the Father of Afrikan Rivers. It rises South of the Equator around Tanzania, Burundi (Kagera River and Lake Tanganyika), Rwanda, Democratic Republic of the Congo, Kenya,

Uganda, South Sudan, Ethiopia and Sudan as the Blue Nile (Gihon, whose source is the Abay River) and the White Nile whose sources are Lake Namlolwe/Nnalubaale (Lake Victoria) in Tanzania and Lake Nyanza (Lake Albert) (in Uganda. The 2 rivers meet up at Khartoum to run through Egypt so that at latitude: 30° 15', the Nile divides into two principal streams, which, in conjunction with a third that springs somewhat higher up, forms the Delta, the principal stream thence pours itself into the Mediterranean Sea. Old Chinese Maps show it Starting in Present day Mozambique and joining Lake Victoria (Literally winding through the entire Land of Cush/Havilah). The Pyramids are built along the River. It is responsible for the Fertile Land around it, as it supplies irrigation schemes and the fertile black soil. it was the major Transport System connecting Northern Afrikan to Southern Afrikan Resources which were used in Contribution to the Sumerian and later Mesopotamian Civilisations of the Arabian Peninsula, where Nimrod built the cities of Akkad, Erech, Calneh and Babel.

In common with the other baKushi (Cushite) tribes of Africa, their skin was black, to which there is an obvious allusion in Jer 13:23: "Can the Cushite change his skin?" Cush (Heb. *Kush*) Genesis 10:6 -8; 1Chronicles 1:8-10; Psalm 7; Isaiah 11:11 and Appearing as Ethiopia in: Genesis 2:13; 2 Kings 19:9; Esther 1:1 & 8:9; Job 28:19; Psalm 78:31 & 87:4; Isaiah 18:1, 20:3-5, 37:9, 45:14 and Ezekiel 29:10, 30:4- 5, 38:5 and Zephaniah 3:10, Acts 8:27, Psalm 48:14; Isaiah 18:1; Jeremiah 46:9 Isaiah 11:11 & Ezekiel 38:5. Job 28:19; Pliny, *Hist. Nat.* 6:29; 37:8 and Strabo, 16:4, Isaiah 18:1-2; Zephaniah 3:11

- baKushi today, speak kiNtu dialects that have been designated: Austronesian, Afro-Asiatic; Nilo-Saharan KhoiSan and Bantu A, B &C by Comparative Linguists, for most: KiSwahili, English and Portuguese are now Lingua Franca with Vernacular being used in the various parts.
- Their descendants Today are some Afrikan abaNtu (People) whose Lands are:

- *The Horn of Afrika,* as the Post-colonial countries of: North and South Sudan; Djibouti; Eritrea; Ethiopia and Somalia; with descendants spread Westward as well as far as Ghana and Nigeria and possibly other West Afrikan Nations;
- *Parts of Arabia,* living amongst the Shemitic Arabs in the cities established by Nimurut (Nimrod) in today's Iraq. Today, Afro Iraqis account for 17.48% of the population of Iraq. There is also a Population of about 2 million indigenous Black Iraqis in South Iraq who are probably some of these descendants but whom historical narratives assume to have come into Iraq as Migrants or Slaves. www.minorityrights.org/Black-iraqis;

- *East Afrika,* as the Post-colonial countries of: Tanzania; Kenya; Uganda; Rwanda; Burundi; Malawi and the Islands of Comoros, Mauritius; Seychelles; Reunion and Madagascar
- Southern Afrika, as the Post-Colonial Countries of: Namibia; Botswana; Zambia; South Africa; Lesotho; Swaziland

With regard to the Worship of God, they are of these Persuasions: Christianity, Islam, Judaism, Afrikan Religion, Rastafari, other Religions and None. Some have become Linguistically and Culturally Arabic through Islamic influence, whilst those who are indigenous to Arabia have been Arabic without necessarily being Muslims.

Misraimi (Mizraim)

Misraim beget Ludim, Anamim, Lehabim, Naphtuhim, Pathrusim, Caphtorim and Casluhim, (out of whom came Philistim/Philistines/Filistina/some of the Palestinians of the Gaza Strip). Khami's second son is Misraimi *who dwelt in Egypt.* Josephus *(Ant.* 1:6, 2) says that all those who inhabit the country call it Mestre (Misr), the natives of Modern Egypt invariably still designate it by the same name: Misr. The Kingdom of Misraimi (Egypt) Extended is bounded by Palestine (Kanaan), Idumaea, Arabia, Petraea, and the Arabian Gulf. On the West, the moving sands of the wide Libyan desert obliterate the traces of all political or physical limits and in the South, the Southernmost parts, Ezekiel 29:10 and Ezekiel 30:6, to what is today South Africa and Westward to Central and West Afrika. It is Bordered by Kushi on the East.

Egypt is also called in the Bible, "the land of Ham", which speaks of the entire Afrikan Continent. Psalm 105:23&27; Psalm 78:51; Psalm 87:4, 89:10 and Isaiah 51:9. The common ancient Egyptian name of the country is written in hieroglyphics (Medutu) as Kmt. This name signifies, alike in the ancient language and in Coptic, "black," *sun-burnt,* as a characteristic of Afrikan Nations.

The description of Misraim's skin tone by name, Kem/Kmt (dark), and the pattern of his settlements of the Afrikan Continent, to multiply, increase and fill it, is self-explanatory as to whose ancestor he is.

The Kemitic people Speak kiNtu dialects designated Afro-Asiatic, Niger Congo, Nilo-Saharan, KhoiSan, Bantu A&B and Austronesian by Comparative Linguists

- With regard to the Worship of God, they are of these Persuasions: Christianity, Islam, Judaism, Afrikan Religion, Rastafari, other Religions and None. Some have become Linguistically and Culturally Arabic through Islamic influence.

- Their descendants Today are some Afrikan abaNtu of:
- North Afrika as the Post-Colonial Egypt
- West Afrika as the Post-colonial countries of:
- Benin; Burkina Faso; The Gambia; Ghana; Guinea; Guinea-Bissau; Gabon; Ivory Coast; Liberia; Mali; Mauritania; Niger; Nigeria; Senegal; Sierra Leone; Togo; Western Sahara; Mauritania and the Associated Islands of: Sao Tome & Principe and Cape Verde.
- Central Afrika as the Post-colonial countries of:
- Angola; Central Afrikan Republic; Chad; Cameroon; Congo Brazzaville and Democratic Republic of Congo; Equitorial Guinea; Gabon; Sao Tome and Principe;
- Southern Afrika as the Post-Colonial countries of: Namibia; Botswana; Zambia; South Africa; Lesotho; Swaziland

Phuti:

Phuti is third among the descendants of Khami, Genesis 10:6; 1 Chronicles 1:8; Jeremiah 46:9; Ezekiel 27:36, 30:5 & 38:5; Judges 2:23. baPhuti Descendants are not Mentioned in the Genesis 10 Account in the Bible. It is possible that they were Women? Or that Phut was Childless or omitted for some other reason. However, Libya and the lands West to it are associated with Phut. The Countries West of Egypt: Morocco, Libya, Tunisia and Algeria were known as Phut in the Septuagint, indicating that he may have had descendants. They served in the Egyptian army (Jeremiah & Ezekiel 30:5 and the Navy of Tyre. Helped Egypt together with Ludim, Nahum 3:9 and Jeremiah 46:9). baSuki (The Sukkiim), who, along with baKushi (the Cushites) and baLubi (Lubim or Libyans), formed part of the host of Shishak (2Ch 12:3), are in the Septugiant, designated as Troglodytes, i.e. cave-dwellers, and were, no doubt, the people known to the Greeks by the same name, as inhabiting the mountain caverns on the west coast of the Red Sea (Diodorus. Siculus. 3, 32; Strabo, 17, p. 785), possibly where the city of Petra was later built. The evidence of this Cave Dwelling Practice, is known all over Afrika.

In South Africa, some of these caves have been preserved, like the Cango caves; Blombos cave; Boesmansgat; Bomplaas cave; Cooper's cave; Sibudu Cave; Border Caves of KZN; Diepkloof Rock Shelter; Echo Caves; Gondolin Cave; Makapansgat; Motsetsi Cave; Nelson Bay Cave; Pinnacle Point; Sterkfontein; Sibudu Cave in Tongaat; Sudwala Caves; Wonder Cave; and many more.

- baPhuti Speak kiNtu dialects designated: Afro-Asiatic; KhoiSan and Bantu A&B by Comparative Linguists
- Their descendants Today are:

- The mixed Heriatge ((K)Hamito-S(h)emito-Iberian) descendants of the Maure (Moors), Imazinghen and other Afrikan Nations, who have been derogated as Berber.
- Some Afrikan abaNtu of the Sahel, as the Post-colonial countries of: Senegal, Mauretania, Western Sahara, Mali, Burkina Faso, Niger, Nigeria, Sudan, Eritrea, and North Afrikan Nations of: Morocco, Algeria, Tunisia and Libya
- They are some of baSan; baSahrawi, baFula, baTuareng; baMozabi, baAmazigh, baSandawe, baHadza, baNama, baOwambo, baHerero, baMaasai and others, who were displaced Eastward and Southward by the Islamic Trade and conquests after 600AD.

Some of these people remain Landless in the entire Afrikan Continent and whilst some persist in their lands of origin, they are oppressed, with very little access to economic and political franchise. Most are displaced to the Post-Colonial Countries of: Nigeria, Niger, Ghana, Senegal, Burkina Faso, Tanzania; Namibia; Botswana; South Africa; Rwanda; Burundi; Equatorial Guinea; Gabon; Angola; Kenya; Madagascar; Zambia Uganda; Democratic Republic of Congo; Guinea where they are also marginalized.

These wars started during the worldwide Covid 19 Pandemic Lockdown, to show how disgruntled these communities are and how deep their wounds run. In Western Sahara, in 2020, some have been living in Refugee Camps for 2 generations and have never been to school.

They are predominantly Nomadic hunters and Pastoralists; Some have Assimilated into the other Dynasties. With regard to the Worship of God, they are of these Persuasions: Afrikan Religion, Judaism, Christianity, Islam, Rastafari, other Religions and None.

Most identify as Arabic Lingo-Culturally whilst others Identify as Berber,

Kanaan: (Ca'naän),

Genesis 10:15, Canaan was the father of Sidon his firstborn, and of the Hittites, 16
Jebusites, Amorites, Girgashites, 17 Hivites, Arkites, Sinites, 18 Arvadites, Zemarites and
Hamathites.

Later the Canaanite clans scattered [19] and the borders of Canaan reached from Sidon toward Gerar as far as Gaza, and then toward Sodom, Gomorrah, Admah and Zeboyim, as far as Lasha.

Kanaan is the name of the 4th son of (K)Ham and the country peopled by his descendants, Kanaan (Canaan) "the Land of Milk and Honey", the Levant, which is the part of the Arabian Peninsula on the Mediterranean Coast.

According to Zephaniah 2:5, 1 Chronicles 1:1& Genesis 10:6, Kanaan is the Land known Today as Israel and Syria and includes Bethlehem Genesis 48:7, Bethel Genesis 35:6, Hebron Genesis 23:19, Shechem Genesis 33:18, Shiloh Judges 21:12 as well as Jebus (Jerusalem) Judges 2.

The Kingdom of Kanaan Extended as follows: On the west the Mediterranean Sea is its border from Sidon to Gaza Genesis 10:19. On the south it is bounded by Egypt in a line running from Gaza to the southern end of the Dead Sea, including the Judean hills, but excluding the country of the Amalekites. The Jordan was the eastern boundary; no part of Kanaan lay beyond that river according to Numbers 33:5. On the north, Kanaan extends as far as Hamath, Genesis 17:8 The coast from Sidon northward to Arvad, and' the ridge of Lebanon, were also inhabited by baKanaan (Canaanites.)

Sidon, one of the other 10 sons of Kanaan is the father of the Sidonians and Phoenicians of Damascus and Lebanon and his city was Sidon.

In several passages baKanaan (the Canaanites) are mentioned with baHiti (the Hittites), baAmori (Amorite), baJebusi (Jebusites), baGirgashi (Girgashites); baPerisi (Perizzites) and baHifi (Hivites) as in Deuteronomy 7, as if they constituted a special portion of the population, however many accept that all these are Canaanites. It is still the custom amongst Afrikan abaNtu, that some descendants retain for their territories the name of their common ancestor, in this case Kanaan, whilst others prefer taking, as a distinctive appellation, the name of some subsequent head or chief of the tribe and thus: Amori, Hivi... baKanaan (The Canaanites) have a Language, the Language of Kanaan (Isaiah 19:18). They are the Palestinian Arabic Bedouins (baBadawi) who are Nomadic and still Merchants to this day. Zephaniah 1:1; Hosea 12:2; Isaiah 23:8. They are the sons of (K)Ham and Brethren to their Continental Afrikan sons of (K)Ham (Kush, Misraim and Phut).

The Sidonians (Phoenicians) Collaborated much with the Continental Afrikans especially in Trade. Literature tends to want to Classify Phoenicians as Superior and Non-Afrikan. Wherever they dwelt in Continental Afrika or Collaborated with Continental Afrikans, their Identity is magnified over that of the Continental Afrikans. It is not uncommon also to find them Classified as Romans, Greeks, Anatolians, that is to say: Caucasian or White. Phoenicians were Black Afrikan sons of Kanaan, The sons of (K)Ham. The one whose Grandfather cursed. Their Prowess is proof that the father's curse could not overturn God's Blessing which pre-dated this Curse. There is no reason to Imagine the Phoenicians to have looked different from their brethren. Even if they did look different, they probably looked like the Bedouin Arabs that they were/are. If they looked Greek or Middle Eastern, it still does not change that they were Kanaanitic, descendants of (K)Ham, Whose Afrikan Continental siblings were/are Misraim, Kush and Phut. In Collaborations, they were not the superior Nation, they were an equal sibling Nation who brought into the mix, their gift as Tradesmen. I emphasise this here, because Phoenicians have been caucasified and are classified white. A battle the American Phoenician migrants fought hard for, just so that they may have rights in America. Khater, Akram (November 20, 2014): How the Lebanese became white? unfortunately this victory of an oppressed minority served to divorce them even more from their true heritage and identity. This has entrenched the superiority complex that continues to strip Afrikans of any sense of achievement... so that, Yes, you did that, but it was because you worked or were supervised by Caucasoid Phoenicians or Caucasoid Arabs or Caucasoid Egyptians or because of the Romans and the Greeks. The Afrikan must understand that the History of Afrika and the early civilisations are their History. The time for tip toeing around this matter is over. We are grateful that the Bible, prior to Racial Classifications and the demeaning of Afrikan people, had already Categorically defined who the Afrikan is and what they looked like as well as where they lived. Were it not for this simple Clear tabulation in Genesis 10, we would have no way of knowing our History and our Greatness as Genetics would simply be given an incorrect standard that we would never fit into. We are also grateful that the field of Genetics is evolving and it can also tell us physical traits.

The description of Kanaan by Lifestyle, and the pattern of his settlements of North-East Afrikan Arabian Peninsula, to multiply, increase and fill it, is self-explanatory as to whose Ancestor he is. They Speak Kanaanitic kiNtu dialects designated Afro-Asiatic by Comparative Linguists.

Their descendants Today are some Arab abaNtu of:

- The Middle East, as the Post-Colonial Countries of: Israel, Westbank and Gaza Strip. Some autochthone Palestinians/Samaritans and Ethnic Jews/Israelites who are culturally and Linguistically Samaritan, Palestinian, Arabic, Hebrew and or Jewish.

- With regard to the Worship of God, they are of these Persuasions: Samaritanism, Christianity, Judaism, Islam, Baha'I, Druze, Kanaanitic religions, Rastafari, other Religions and None.

Continental Mixed Heritage Descendants: 20 000 000 or more people

- With the advent of Colonialism, mixed heritage Afrikan abaNtu were born whom in other countries were raised Afrikan and speaking the Vernacular or Colonial language of that Country. In South Africa, most were raised separately and designated: White Afrikaner or Coloured depending on the depth of their Melanin and the Curl of their Hair. Most Speak a Colonial language or an Indo-European dialect of kiNtu known as Afrikaans.
- With regard to the Worship of God, they are of these Persuasions: Christianity, Judaism, Islam, Afrikan Religion, Rastafari, other Religions and None.

Islandic Afrikan People: 20 000 000 people

- Autochthone Native Islandic People, designated by Philologists as Austronesian are descendants of all Noah's Children Japheth, Shem and (K)Ham's 4 sons: Kushi, Kanaan, Phut and Misraim.
- They populated the 220 Afrikan Islands whose Population now stands at 20 000 000 people from the time of the dispersion of the sons of (K)Ham or Out of Afrika Dispersion and who did not lose their "Sub-Saharan features".
- Most are of Mixed descent from the first dispersal and with the various settlers who settled in their Islands.
- Some are of Slave legacy from the Afrikan East and west Coasts, brought into the islands as slave labour from the 15th Century.

With regard to the Worship of God, they are of these Persuasions: Christianity, Judaism, Islam, Afrikan Religion, Islandic Religion, Rastafari, other Religions and None

Diaspora Afrikans: 190 000 000 people

Diaspora Afrikan abaNtu (People) in other Continents are descendants of all the 4 (four) Ancestors of Afrikan ((K)Hamitic) people, as well as Afro-S(h)emetic and S(h)

emetic People who lived in Afrika. They Speak Languages of their Diaspora Lands, sometimes with a heavy Afrikan influenced dialect. These are the:

- Sons and Daughters of the more than 12 000 000 to 20 000 000 people affected by Chattel Slavery and who were traded in the Americas, Europe, India and Arabia;
- Autochthone Afrikans who reached the Americas and Europe from the time of the Out of Afrika Dispersion as well as later due to Trade and Kingdom expansion to Mesopotamia, Indus Valley (The Siddi and Dravidian Africans, 2600 BC), China (The Yueng, who are Founders of the Shang Dynasty) Iberia (The Mauri) and America. Winters, C.A (1986). "Dravidian Settlements in Ancient Polynesia", India Past and Present 3, no2:225-241
- Those who reached the Americas through Early Naval Explorations to America from predominantly West Afrika (http://kalamu.com)

With regard to the Worship of God, they are of these Persuasions: Christianity, Judaism, Islam, Afrikan Religion, Islandic Religion, Rastafari, other Religions and None

Thus the 4 sons of (K)Ham populated the Afrikan Continent, The Islands; what is today named the Middle East (Arabian Peninsula), Europe, Asia and the Americas as follows:

- Kush settled Central Afrika; Sudan; The Horn of Afrika; Sumer and Mesopotamia; the South Eastern Arabian Peninsula Yemen and Oman; The entire East Coast of Afrika down to South Africa as Today's 9 Provinces of South Africa and the East Coast Islands.
- Misraimi settled Present day Egypt; Central Afrika; West Afrika and the entire West Coast to the Southern tip of Afrika in South Africa as today's nine Provinces of South Africa as well as the African Islands on the West Coast.
- Phut (Libya) settled North Afrika, West of Egypt, known as the Maghreb as well as what is today named the Sahel and possibly Central Afrika.
- Kanaan settled Present day Israel and Palestine, Syria, Bethlehem, Bethel, Hebron, Shechem, Shiloh, as well as Jebus (Jerusalem).
- All 4 Descendants settled 220 Afrikan Islands and the Diaspora of Europe; Arabia and the Americas and their islands.

Scientifically, the Out of Africa Migration of Modern Humans into all the Continents was due to a Climatic shift from Wet to Dry (Post Fall, Desertification of Arabia and North Afrika).

According to Science daily (07/05/2010) Cambridge University, New research confirms the "Out of Africa" hypothesis, that all modern humans stem from a single group of (Afrikan) Homo sapiens (Modern Human Beings), who emigrated out of Afrika 2,000 generations ago, to spread throughout Eurasia, over thousands of years. Homo Sapiens then replaced Homo Neanderthalensis and others in Eurasia as a result of Assimilation and extinction of the latter. The European, Asian and American Afrikan abaNtu then lost their Melanin, becoming light skinned and their eyes becoming Blue, Green and Grey and their hair lost its curl becoming longer as they adapted to the Colder weather.

According to: https://www.smithsonianmag.com/smart-news/heres-how- europeans-quickly-evolved-lighter-skin-180954874/ Recent evidence supports the late appearance of the light complexion in Europeans, meaning that Ancient Indo Europeans were "Black". They Spoke Proto-Indo-European language.

Some "Black" Farmer Modern Humans (Bantus) did not emigrate, they remained in Afrika and populated the entire Afrikan continent together with their Hunter-Gatherer and Herder (Khoisan) brethren who did not emigrate. These are Today's Afrikan People.

According to Rito T, Viera D, Silva M, Conde-Sousa E, Pereira L, Mellars P, et al. (March 2019). "A dispersal of Homo Sapiens from Southern to Eastern Afrika immediately precedes the out-of-Africa Migration." Kassies River and the Border cave in South Africa; Laetoli in Dodoma, Tanzania; Omo and Herto in Ethiopia. From here, the people Migrated to West Afrika, North Afrika and the World through Egypt and possibly the Strait of Gibraltar.

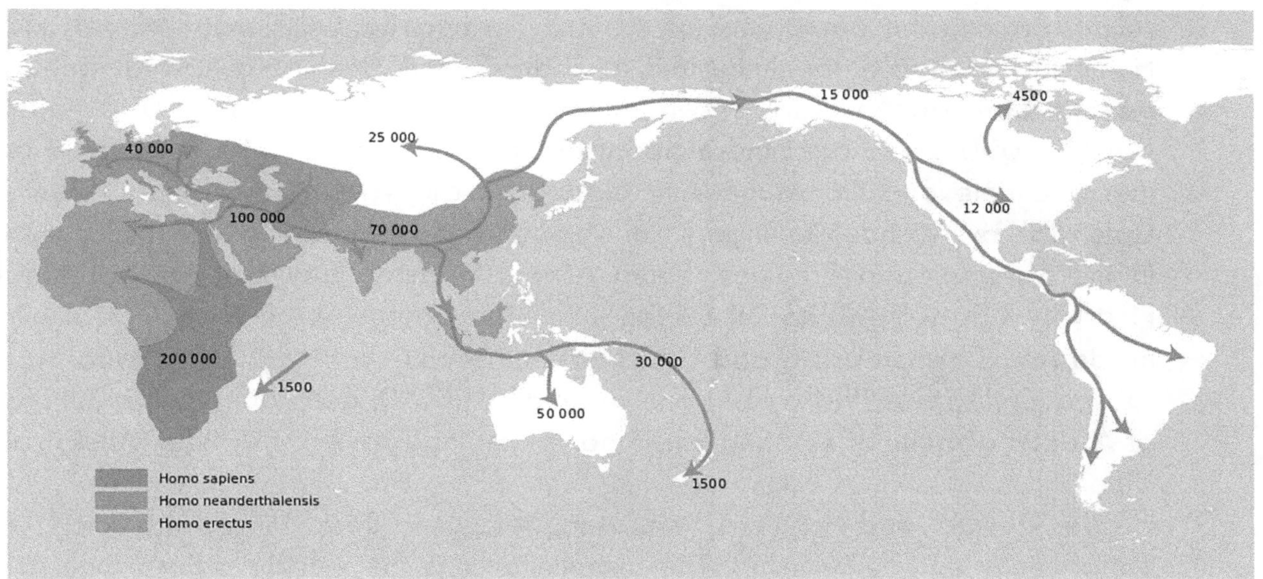

Credit: By NordNordWest - Spreading homo sapiens ru.svg by Urutseg which based on Spreading homo sapiens.jpg by Altaileopard, Public Domain, https://commons.wikimedia.org/w/index.php?curid=34697001

- Evidence that proves the Persistence of Farmer Afrikans (Bantus) in Southern Afrika after other Farmer (Bantu), Hunter (San) and Herder (Khoe) Afrikans, left the Continent to populate other continents is as follows:
- When the land was still Volcanic, some stepped on the hot larva and left their foot prints. The Foot Prints on Igneous Rock are identified as possibly belonging to Farmer and or Herder Afrikans because of the Stature (deduced from the size of the foot print) and the fact that the Human prints are accompanied by Cow's Hooves. These are found at a place aptly named: Mulenzhe (Foot) in Nzhelele, Limpopo Province. This site is undated, and not Protected by UNESCO, nor by the local Arts and Culture Department. (courtesy: Neluvhalani M.C (2017) Doctoral Thesis). According to SAHO, Huffman, T.N (2010) Wits: "Human footprints have also been found at Nahoon Point up the Coast from Port Elizabeth and they are important ancient evidence of Modern Human Anatomy", these 3 sets were dated to 125 000 years ago;
- The Multitude of Middens (Dung and Refuse Heaps) along the entire Southern Afrikan Coast confirm a settled Lifestyle of people who domesticated cattle and lived in one place for a long enough time to create a Dumping site.
- The Multitudes of Caves that were listed earlier in relation to the Troglodytes, the oldest of which are the Sibudu Caves and the border caves in of KwaZulu-Natal, dated at about 77 000 years ago, in which Human Skeletons were

found, Proving the persistence of Afrikan Farmer (Bantu), Herder (Khoe) and Hunter(San) people, the Ancestors of Today's N & S amaNguni/vhaNgona/ Bakone Speakers in today's KwaZulu-Natal from as early as 77 000 years ago. 75 000 years ago, these people built their first Dolomite Rock circle to measure time and Commune with God at Inzalo ye Langa (named Adam's Calendar by Michael Tellinger), at what is now known as Watervaal Boven in the Mpumalanga Province, South Africa. Nearby, they built one of their First City Citadel with Rocks. Evidence for The Houses which were most likely made from Earthen bricks and Grass has not been excavated. The Citadel was subsequently re-settled by baKone around 1500 AD, according to the Culture of Afrikan abaNtu of rotating land and re-settling previous Mashubi (Ancestral Cities).

- Herder, Farmer and Hunter Afrikan Ancestors, used Rock Art to Chronicle Life Experiences and to Worship. The Lynton Panel is the world's oldest Rock Art dated at 50 000 years old. It was found in what became known as the Maclear Farm in the Eastern Cape, South Africa in 1917. It is currently housed in the *iZiko* Museum in Cape Town.
- The Stone Walled Citadels Scattered all over South Africa whose earliest evidence according to Sampson (1974:250) are at Zeekoegat 27 in the Northern Cape, and dated to 200 000 years ago and whose youngest are The Stone Walls at Simon se Klip on the West Coast of South Africa that are dated to around 500 AD, show progressive development. Some of the most Well-known Citadels are: Moor Park in the KwaZulu-Natal Midlands; Ntsuanatsatsi in the Free State; Kliprivíersburg; South of the Vaal River; Badfontein and Watervaal Boven in Mpumalanga; Dzata in Venda, Thulamela in Venda, Mapungubwe on the Confluence of the Shashe and Vhembe rivers and later, the Dzimbabwe Citadel and Khami Citadels. The Suikerbosrand Nature Reserve near Johannesburg shows changes in settlement patterns from dispersed homesteads to nucleated towns by the 1300s AD comparative with West Afrikan and European Settlements. The Sadr Laden Paper by Karim Sadr (05/04/12) suggests that the distribution and Chronology of these Stone-walled Structures may represent the fusion of indigenous LSA herding Cultures (Khoe Nations) with Bantu-Speaking (S and N: Sotho and Nguni) Agricultural Cultures, proving the Symbiotic nature of their Settlements."
- The earliest Pottery can only be dated to 7000 BC. Considering that these were made of Clay, it is possible that they existed earlier, however, but disintegrated over time.

- Although Evidence of Iron Tools is only dated to 500 BC in East Afrika, this is still 1300 years earlier than Europe. Metallurgy in Afrika is definitely much older since The oldest mine in the World is the Ngwenya Mine in Northwest Mbabane, Swaziland (43 000 years old). Its Iron Ore deposits constitute one of the oldest geological formations in the world. The Mapungubwe golden Rhinoceros proves that Afrikan abaNtu were already proficient in mining and Smelting Gold by 1000 AD. Biblically, this evidence is even older. When the Israelites left Egypt, they were given Gold articles by the Egyptians in 1876 BC (Close to 4000 years ago). There was so much Gold that the Israelites were able to melt some of it and create a Golden Calf, that they proceeded to worship in the Desert, when Moses was on the Mountain for 40 days. Thus Gold was also produced in Afrika much earlier than the date allocated to the Mapungubwe Golden Rhinoceros. Nandoni Mines that are undated and Flooded under the Nandoni Dam (Nandoni means Place of Smelting) in Limpopo, Venda, are evidence of some of the places where Metallurgy took place. Pottery found when the Dam's Wall was constructed are undated and kept at the University of Venda. Many Gold and Iron Mines are scattered throughout East, Central and Southern Afrika dated at these early dates. In Zambia, investigations carried out in the 1960s by Dart & Beaumont (1969) showed that both Iron ore and Manganese, which are used to make Steel, were being mined in Southern Afrika during the Pleistocene age (12 000 years ago). The Iron Tools and Cities are evidence of a Sedentary Settled Lifestyle, which was Agrarian compared to Hunting and gathering. Which means by 10 000 BC, the Southern Afrikan Lifestyle of amaNguni/Bakone/vhaNgona (N&S Speakers) was a Settled Lifestyle and the progress of their Settlements show their Symbiotic Lifestyle with Khoe Nations and San Nations.
- In Science Daily, retrieved 20/10/20: Stone Age Pantry, Archaeologist unearths earliest evidence of modern humans using wild grains and tuber food, It is reported that: "in 2007 Julio Mercader, of the University of Calgary, recovered dozens of 100,000-year-old stone tools from a deep limestone cave near Lake Nyasa (Niassa) in Mozambique showing that wild sorghum, the ancestor of the chief cereal consumed today in sub-Saharan Black Bantu Afrikans as flours, breads, porridges and alcoholic beverages, was being consumed by them (Homo Sapiens), along with African wine palm, the false banana, pigeon peas, wild oranges and the African potato. This is the earliest direct evidence of humans using pre-domesticated cereals anywhere in the world. San Diet does not include processed Starch. Processed Starch is a Staple diet of Bantus, as well as the beers made from it. According to Peregrine Nutrition: What did the

Bushman actually eat, retrieved 20/10/20, San Diet is predominantly Meat (40%) eaten with vegetables. Bantu diet on the other hand is Predominantly Starch (Processed Sorghum and Maize) eaten with Vegetables and/or Meat. Julio Mercader's findings thus confirm the co- existence of San, Khoe and Bantu and their symbiotic relationship.

- Ancestors of Modern Afrikan baSan, baKhoe and amaNguni (Bantu) Nations started Trading with each other (as well as internationally). To Calculate and keep Accounting Records, they developed a Numerical system, by making notations on bone as Mathematical Instruments: The Lebombo bone is 35 000 years old, whilst the Ishango bone is 22 000 years old. These instruments were followed by Mufuvha on Rocks which allow Multiplication, division, addition and subtraction. There is a Mufuvha carved on Rock at Mapungubwe, possibly where the international Market traded...? This may very well be regarded as South Africa's first Stock Exchange.
- Weaving of Baskets, Mats and Masila/indwangu (Cloths) is evident from 9000 BC. Bark Cloth was made from bark of the Mutavha tree (Ficus Natalensis) to make Mashedo (Loin Cloths), Minwenda in LuVenda and amabhai in isiZulu (Sarong like Cloths) and Blankets. Western Afrika was more advanced with Cloths, weaving them from Cotton as well from 9000 BC. VhaNgona Cultural Movement (oral) and Rwawiire, S. &Tmkova, B. (2014).

From about 10 000 BC, Afrikan Farming Communites settled around Rivers and Lakes in a symbiotic relationship with their Herder (Semi-Pastoralist) and Hunter brethren. The Nile and Kongo River systems provided a Transport System from South to North. Civilisations around the Nile and the Lakes Flourished, with the first Continental Political System led by (K)Ham's first son, Kush, according to the Afrikan Culture of Seniority in leadership.

Kush became King over what is today South, West, Central and East Afrika as well as Sumer. Members of this Dynasty, from South, East and Central Afrika established the City of Ta-Seti in what is today Sudan (Kush) around 5900 BC. This City was contemporaneous with other civilisations in the Continent. According to New Light on the Archaeology of Sungbo Eredo, South-Western Nigeria, August (2016) by Olanrewaju Lasisi, most Mashubi Royal Citadels (Archaeological Stone Ruins sites) in Afrika such as the Sungbo Eredo, Mapungubwe, Dzimbabwe, Watervaal Boven etc, were occupied cyclically over various periods and the early dates of occupation go as far back as 5000 years ago.

Misraim became King of Misraim, Present day: North, West, Central and South Afrika.

Kanaan became King of present day Israel, Lebanon, Damascus and Syria and Phuti became King of Present day West and North Afrika Punt.

Using Kush (Cush) as an example, King Kush's sons: Seba, Havilah, Sabita, Raama, Sabiteka and Nimrut (Nimrod) became paramount chiefs with responsibility of leading their families and extending their father's rule, king Kush, through their descendants. Raama's sons: Sheba and Dedani became Chiefs under their father. Nimrut's Kingdom Expansion into Shinar (Sumer) to Establish the Cities Babel, Uruk (Erek), Akad (Accad) and Calneh were viewed as Expansions of King Kush's Kingdom as Nimrut was a Paramount Chief in his Father's Kingdom. King Kush would have been Succeeded by Seba. Whilst the Chiefs and Paramount Chiefs were succeeded by their respective Eldest Children... to today's current monarchies. Each time an Elder son's house became too large, the Nation Would Multiply by coronating elder sons to Chieftaincy. The Hierarchy is thus: King, Paramount Chiefs, Chiefs, Lords... each with their own Counsels, forming. These Kings lived Symbiotically and their borders were not in straight line boundaries and could not be as neatly delineated as I have made it seem.

The Regional throne would rotate amongst the various Nations as decided by many factors such as: Resource Wealth; Trade Agreements with international Nations; Military Strength; Purpose/Calling of the Nation as Priests, Kings, Traders, Industrialists etc. Succession battles within a certain nation, rendering that nation weak and giving opportunity to a Robust Monarchy to take the lead.

Around 4500 BC, Nimurut, in collaboration with the Autochthonous, Aboriginal, Indigenous and Native S(h)emetic people of Arabia and other Nations who later joined, established Sumer. This corresponds with the Biblical narrative of the Tower of Babel in Shinar. This Civilisation was followed by Civilisations in the Indus Valley (India) led by the Misraim Dravidian people of North and West Afrika around 4000 BC. The Phutites (baPhuti) Sukiim and Lubim (Native Moroccans, Algerians, Tunisians and Libyans), who are Imazighen and Mauri People of North Afrika as well as various West Afrikan baMisraim, established the Iberian Peninsula Civilisation, circa 3500 BC (Portugal, Spain, Gibraltar, Andorra and Southern France). Phoenician Bedouin Tradesmen who are the ancestors of today's Lebanese and Damascan Arabs thrived "running" the Trans-Saharan Trade Routes and establishing Ports in Iberia and the North Afrikan Coast, in Tunisia (Kart- hadasht/Carthage).

Hwt-Ka-Pta (Egypt) was established around 3100 BC as a Tribal Confederation of the (K)Hamitic Siblings, to be a "Gateway" Trade Centre and Religious Centre for the Continent. It was recognised as the City of All (K)Hamitic people. Thus its name, Kemet, Kmt (Of Kham). Pharaoh Narmer (Nemes) was the first Pharaoh of the Confederate (United) Hwt-ka-Ptah, being lord of two lands, Upper and Lower Egypt.

Goods moved from the South to the East and through the Lakes and the Nile to Egypt and then to Sumer and Indus Valley. Goods also moved from the South to the West through the Kongo River system and through the Trans-Saharan Trade Routes to the Iberian Coast through Today's Morocco and the Strait of Gibraltar. Egypt became rich from all the Tributes it received for the Trade and Huge Temples were built in honor of God from all the collaborators.

The Unity of the Material Culture of the people of Afrika as well as their cultures and belief system testify to their Ancient Connections which were interrupted by Colonialism and Imperialism. The Headgear of the Pharaohs can be seen in their various expressions in North, West and South Afrika's isiCholo; Their Bow and Arrows in all corners of Afrika; Their Dances; Cuisine; burial rituals and many others bear Testimony. It is seen in the Centricity of the Falcon, Vulture and Birds as well as the colours of the Country Flags Today: Red, Green, Gold and Black.

The most recent discovery by Michael Tellinger and Johan Heine of the possibly 200 000-year-old City Spanning 10 000 km in Southern Afrika (Maputo), proves the extent of the Kushitic civilization, that it was from Southern Afrika to North Afrika. The Ankh discovered on one of the walls proves that Afrikans had faith in God from the time they walked with God in the Cool of day after Creation. Sumerian tablets of the Kings list successive kings from 224 000 years ago. Bradfield, L (29/04/2019), Opinion article on the South African.com: 200 000- year-old city found in Southern Afrika may rewrite history.

As recorded in these scriptures: 2 Chronicles 12:3, 16:8; Jeremiah 46:7; Daniel 11:43) "Libyans and Ethiopians and Nations of Afrika, who belonged to the vast army with which Shishak, king of Egypt, came out of that country against Rehoboam, king of Judah." This shows that all Afrikan abaNtu (People) were united, lived together, collaborated and enlisted on the Continental Army. They knew each other and were not divided by the Forests or the Desert nor the new artificial Political borders. Philological and ethnological data lead to the same conclusion.

In, Poole, *Genesis of the Earth*, (p. 214) Sir H. Rawlinson brings forth evidence that trace the early Babylonians to Ethiopia, particularly the similarity of their mode of writing to the Egyptian, and the indication in the traditions of Babylonia and Assyria of "a connection in very early times between Ethiopia, Southern Arabia and the cities on the Lower Euphrates," (Rawlinson's *Herod.* 1:353 n.)

According to https://www.biblicalcyclopedia.com/C/Cush.html, "There are strong reasons for deriving the non-S(h)emitic language of Babylonia, variously called by scholars Kushitic and Scythic, from an ante-Shemitic dialect of Ethiopia." It is because the Kushitic people contributed to that civilisation.

In his book 'Egypt', British scholar Sir E.A. Wallis Budge states that: "The prehistoric native of Egypt, both in the old and in the new Stone Ages, was Afrikan and there is every reason for saying that the earliest settlers came from the South." (What is today Classified as Sub-Saharan Africa). He further states: "There are many things in the manners and customs and religions of the historic Egyptians that suggests that the original home of their prehistoric ancestors was in a country in the neighbourhood of Uganda and Punt [present day Somalia]."

"The Greek historian Diodorus Siculus devoted an entire chapter of his world history, the Bibliotheke Historica, Universal History Book III. 2. 4-3.3, to the Kushites "Aethiopians" of Meroe. Here he repeats the story of their great piety, their high favour with the gods, and adds the fascinating legend, that they were the founders of Egyptian civilization, invented writing, and had given the Egyptians their religion and culture." (K)Hamitic

The Terms: Aethiopian, Kushite, Nubian were universally used to apply to all Afrikan abaNtu who later became known as Black, Negro, Kaffir and Bantu in the whole Continent and the Diaspora.

Herodotus who described the Egyptians as being very black with woolly hair. (Herodotus, 2003: 103,119,134-135), is considered to be "the father of comparative anthropology and ethnography, and is said to be, more modern than any other ancient historian in his approach to the ideal of total history. Many scholars (Aubin, Heeren, Davidson, Diop, Poe, Welsby, Celenko, Volney, Montet, Bernal, Jackson, DuBois, Strabo), ancient and modern, routinely cite Herodotus in their works on the Nile Valley. Some of these scholars (Welsby, Heeren, Aubin, Diop, etc.) explicitly mention the reliability of Herodotus' work on the Nile Valley and demonstrate corroboration of Herodotus' writings by modern scholars. Despite Controversy, Herodotus has long served and still serves as the primary, often only, source for events in the Greek world, Persian Empire, and the broader region in the two centuries leading up to his own days. Even if the Histories (by Herodotus) were criticized in some regards since antiquity, modern historians and philosophers generally take a more positive view as to their source and epistemological value.

Welsby, Derek (1996:40) said that "archaeology graphically confirms some of Herodotus' observations". Snowden mentions that Greeks and Romans knew of "negroes of a red, copper-coloured complexion...among Afrikan tribes" and proponents of the Black theory believe that the Black racial grouping is comprehensive enough to absorb the red and black skinned images in ancient Egyptian iconography. Basotho and vhaVenda of Southern Afrika attest to this as they have names for the entire spectrum of abaNtu skin tones that include red: Motho o mo Khwibidu (red person in SePedi) Muthu Mutswuku (red person in Luvenda) and in isiZulu and isiXhosa amaMbovu (Red people)

The British Africanist Basil Davidson, stated that "Whether the Ancient Egyptians were as black or as brown in skin colour as other Afrikans, may remain an issue of emotive dispute; probably, they were both. Their own artistic conventions painted them as pink, but pictures on their tombs show they often married queens shown as entirely black, being from the south: while the Greek writers reported that they were much like all the other Afrikans whom the Greeks knew." Davidson, Basil (1991).

While at the University of Dakar, Cheikh Anta Diop, used microscopic laboratory analysis to measure the melanin content of skin samples from several Egyptian mummies. The melanin levels found in the dermis and epidermis of these mummies led Diop to classify ancient Egyptians as "unquestionably among the Black races". At a UNESCO Symposium in 1974 where Diop was the only Afrikan, he invited other scholars to examine the skin samples. Diop also asserted that Egyptians shared the "B" blood type with black Afrikans. The other scholars at the symposium however rejected Diop's Black-Egyptian theory, preferring that the Population of Egypt has Always Been Multi-hued. Diop, Cheikh Anta (1974:236-243).

Around 1785, Volney stated, "When I visited the sphinx... on seeing that head, typically Negro in all its features, I remembered...Herodotus says: "...the Egyptians are black with woolly hair." Virtually all Egyptologists and scholars currently believe that the face of the Sphinx represents the likeness of the Pharaoh Khafra (Cheophs).

Misraimi (Egypt) is a descendant of Afrikan (K)Ham and the original inhabitants of Hwt-Ka-Pta (Egypt). Like His father, Misraimi was "Black".

Some People Ask: "If Ancient Egypt was "Black" why is it that very few "Blacks" remain? The answer to that is this: Firstly, the now Arabic people of Egypt are "Black" in the strictest American Racial definition of Racial Classification, in which having one drop of Black Blood makes one Black. Today's Egyptian shows the entire Spectrum of Humanity as a Genetic Melting pot of the Ancient world's 6000- year span to date. However, according to CNBC news article: The 2020 Census continues the whitewashing of Middle Eastern Americans at nbcnews.com, North Afrikans and Middle Eastern People are made to Classify themselves as White in America. This Classification is based on the Racist 19th century Caucasoid, Negro and Mongoloid Classification that was created by Europe in order for it to Appropriate North Afrika.

One only has to look at America and the plight of Native Americans to understand how this works. The People of Abya-Yalan (Ancient America), were and are Native Americans, who at one stage were named Red Indians. Today, only 530 years after its colonization, the population of Native Americans is only 6.8 million (1.6% of the Total American Population). The reason for this is Genocide; Settlement of foreigners; Assimilation of Native populations by Foreigners through mixed descent and Displacement of Natives into enclaves and Reserves that have left them with about 8% land held in Trust for them. The same was repeated in Australia and South Africa amongst the Khoe and the San People.

Using this scenario, how many Afrikan (Sub Saharan Bantu) people, do we expect to still be physically recognizable in Egypt and the rest of North Afrika 2600 years after their major conquests and displacements?

Does it matter if Ancient Egyptian History is the History of Black Sub-Saharan Farmer, Hunter and Herder Afrikans? Does it matter if Black Sub-Saharan Farmer, Herder and Hunter Afrikans initiated the Sumerian, Indus Valley and Iberian Civilisations? Does it matter if Britons 7000 years ago were Black with curly hair and blue eyes? My friend Dumile would say an Emphatic: "Absolutely!" in her Private School English Accent. If it did not matter, why the Copious Research to negate, veil, unhear and erase Sub-

Saharan Black Afrikan History from Ancient civilisations? Knowing the certainty of this history serves to Motivate Afrikans to their Greatness by reviving Hope through Validation. It rebuilds their Dignity. It restores their Magnanimous Spirit of ubuNtu.

Whether those who worked hard to Erase, Unhear and Silence this knowledge try harder to continue on that trajectory or not, as in this Most Recent Research done on Mummies in 2012, wherein the Mitochondrial DNA from 151 mummified Egyptians was analysed illustrates. Scientists looked at DNA excavated in the early 20th century. Radiocarbon dating showed that they were entombed 1388 BCE to 426 CE. These 1,300 years of ancient Egyptian history includes many foreign conquests, Egypt's incorporation into the Hellenistic world and then the Roman Empire.

n Keeping with the History of the Conquest of the era, the new genetic analysis of the mummies showed that these mummies were of people who originated to the greatest extent, from the countries around the eastern Mediterranean and specifically Anatolia in modern day Turkey. This is the first time DNA has been isolated from Egyptian Mummies. Mummies from older Time periods (3000 to 1500 BC), have not been Tested. Scientifically, the Logical sequence of Testing, should have been to try and Test these older Mummies, because the Testing of Mummies for their Ethnicity was initiated by Cheikh Anta Diop when he proved by using a simple Melanin Test, that Ancient Egyptian Mummies Were Black. His findings were dismissed. This Genetic Study, should have Tested the older Mummies to disprove or corroborate Diop's earlier evidence. But Alas, we Test Mummies that History already tells us would be white, to prove that they were white. Why? Is it not to unhear, silence and deny? Today, you have heard the Truth or the Truth you knew has been confirmed. Rise up and be #NoLongerSilent. Let Hope anchor your Soul, settle your Heart and reduce the Anxiety and Depression spawned by effacement and which have reached Pandemic proportions in Afrika.

The Most well documented Chronicle of Afrikan Kings of the time are Kemetic (Egyptian). They were Recorded by the Egyptian Priest, Manetho in the 3rd Century BC. As a Priest in the Temple at Heliopolis, he had access to Original Sources. He is responsible for Tabulating the 30 dynasties of Egypt that are recognized in Historical Records today. A great site to visit to see the features and Names of the Khosi pfareli (those who rule on behalf of God/Pharaohs) is: https://Pharaoh.se

Part 3: The Glory and the former Days

The Latter Glory of this House Shall be greater than the Glory of the Former
Haggai 2:9 Bible

Bronze, Iron Age & Classical History

6000 BC – 900 AD

The Bronze Age Dates Correspond for all Historical Narratives. Most of the History here onward focuses on parts of Afrika, where written records have been found and decrypted. Southern Afrikan writings on pottery have been largely dismissed as Decorative and its written history is unknown, however, where Indigenous knowledge is known to the author and can be verified by some written body of knowledge, this will be narrated.

This Period saw increased Technology, Formal Religion, Travel, Farming and the development of a Sedentary lifestyle for the Farmer and Semi-Pastoralist Afrikans who established Polities and Cities for their Rulers.

Travel introduced Trading and The Interpolation of Cultures. This necessitated complex mathematical formulation and Writing, to aid communication and keep Records.

The Sumerian Script has been termed Cuneiform, whilst the Egyptian script is termed hieroglyphs (Medutu) and Tartessian of Iberia. Ancient writings have now been identified in East Afrika as Meroetic (Sudanese), which is thought to be from 2000 BC. Ge'ez Script is accepted to be from 800 BC and is still used in Ethiopia for Amharic, Tigrinya and several other languages. Nsibidi idiographic and logographic Writings of South East Nigeria have been found on pottery dating from 400 AD and may be older. Many others that need further study are writing systems of baAkan of Ghana called Adinkra, Lusona of what has come to be known as: Angola, Zambia and Democratic Republic of Congo. vhaVenda as part of the Nguni Nations of Southern Afrika maintain that their writings on Pottery were ideographic and logographic, used for Mathematics as well as to Record History and Transmit Cultural Wisdom.

The earliest writing in Europe is a Clay tablet fragment (2.5cm tall and 4cm wide). It is thought to be an Economic record as it lists Names against numbers. found in Greece dated at 1450 BC, it is 2000 years younger than writing evidence in Afrika.

Archaeological evidence of the Trade between Afrika with Sumer (Mesopotamia), China, India and Iberia is evident in the entire Afrikan continent wherever archaeological finds are made, and as far afield as Southern Afrika at Phalaborwa, Watervaal Boven, Mapungubwe, Dzimbabwe, KwaZulu. This is why when Afrikans are Silenced, Erased and unheard in History Books, our History is attributed to "unknown Black civilisation which is Not Bantu but may be by Chinese, Indians, Phoenicians or Aliens".

Further, the Archaeological digs are limited to the first few layers, revealing the latest civilisations for Sub-Saharan Afrika, dating from 500 AD only. These findings are then Communicated in isolation from the broader 200 000-year Sub-Saharan Material Culture, so that when one reads a typical Sub-Saharan Historical Account, one is left confused by the sudden appearance of "Bantus" with no Past. Europe's earliest Stone Ruins are from 400 BC. The only other older Stone Ruins Are Stone Henge (5000 BC), The Megalithic Temples of Malta are on the Mediterranean Sea

Trade and Religion, brought exchange of ideas and the unique Expansionist ideas of Domination of one Society by another, for the sake of their Raw Materials and for their Proselytization.

The two Predominant Modern Proselytising Religions in Afrika are: Christianity and Islam. At first, Christianity spread organically and was considered a Heresy, with Christians being persecuted and suppressed. However, once Nations made Christianity a State Religion, the Church and the State used each other to achieve their goals. Islam would later follow the same trend and the two Religions would be pitted against each other as they both Claimed to represent the only True and Final Word of God. Through their Political Connection, both tied Religion to Trade, Slavery and Imperialism. Recognising themselves as the bearers of Light, invariably meant they held the opinion that those they Proselytised were inferior and in Darkness, Enabling the development of a Superiority Complex in themselves. This Cognition would later be Instrumental in the development of Racial thought from 500 AD onward.

The Chronological History in this Section will thus be dealt with, in a manner that follows the Developments of the early Civilisations that Afrika Contributed to as well as the impact of Trade and Religion on Afrika.

It is organised in a manner that follows the 4 sons of (K)Ham as: Kanaan, Phut, Misraim and Kush.

For ease of reference, the Map of Afrika with its relation to the Middle East and Iberia is reproduced. The Author recommends that the Reader Prints this map, so that the Narrative can be followed with ease.

The Lighter Unnamed Portion of the Map is the Middle East (Arabian Peninsula) at the Top Right hand corner and the Iberian Peninsula on the Top Left Hand corner. Kanaan is the part that is connected to Egypt and on the Coast of the Mediterranean Sea (Levant). Sumeria (Mesopotamia/Persia) is the fertile Crescent of the Tigris and Euphrates. The Indus Valley is the area separated from the Arabian Peninsula by the Red Sea, above Oman. Saudi Arabia is the Middle part of the Arabian Peninsula. The bottom parts of the Peninsula are Yemen, Oman and United Arab Emirates.

Civilisation, Trade and Religion and how they Shaped Afrika

It is possible that Afrikan people have been Migrating in and out of the Iberian Peninsula since the first Out of Africa Migration, participating in the 9000-year- old Balkan Civilisation that is buried under the sea. Certainly, they Migrated in and out of the Arabian Peninsula and the Indus Valley from antiquity. As elaborated earlier, Afrikans participated in the Sumerian Civilisation followed by the Indus Valley and Iberian Civilisations.

In the Iberian Peninsula (Modern day Spain and Portugal, Andorra, Southern France and British Crown Colony of Gibraltar), their civilization, together with their Kanaanitic Phoenician Brethren (Lebanese and Damascan) produced the Beaker Civilisation as well as the Tartessian Script (Writing). The Phoenicians further Established Trading Posts on the Mediterranean Coasts of North Afrika in what is today Tunisia, Libya and Algeria, together with the indigenous Amazigh and Fulani as well as other indigenous Nations of these areas. In Tunisia, they established Kart-hadasht (Carthage).

In the Meantime, From Ta-Seti, the people of the Sudan, a Name given later by Arabs to describe Black Sub-Saharan people that the Arabs had not conquered, the descendants of Kush and Misraim, collaborated to establish Hwt-Ka-Pta (Egypt), as a Gateway Trade and Religious Centre. The Northern (Lower) Kingdoms were ruled by Kings, whilst the Southern (Upper) Kingdoms were ruled by Priests. Pharaoh Narmer is the first Pharaoh to unify the Southern and Northern Kingdoms into one, around 3100 BC until 1800 BC, a Period termed the Old Kingdom and Middle Kingdom Periods of Egypt, by Historians.

It was during this time, that the Hieroglyphic Script was developed and later the first Hymn Books of Praise for God were imprinted on Papyri by Pharaoh Khufu. The 80 Egyptian Pyramids and the Sphinx were also built during this time.

As a Religious and Trade Centre, Hwt-Ka-Pta (Egypt) was not militarily Formidable. Its Army was not geared for War and its Government was more Religious than Political and therefore weak.

2000 BC The Nubian Dynasty succeeded Kush and it persisted until, 1504 AD when it was divided between Egypt and the Sennar sultanate.

1830 to 1750 BC, the S(h)emetic Hebrew Joseph whose family sojourned in Kanaan and whom his brothers had sold into slavery because of jealousy, successfully

Explained, Interpreted and gave a solution to a Dream about Drought that God had showed the Pharaoh and that had troubled the Pharaoh gravely. As a result of this, Joseph (a foreigner) was made Grand vizier of all of Egypt by the Pharaoh. When the Drought came, it also affected Kanaan, which was ill prepared for it. Joseph had his family move to Egypt to escape the Drought and be close to him, Genesis 37-46. Many Nations were also attracted to settlement in Egypt during this time including the Neighbouring Kanaanites and from as far as India and China according to some scholars. The 12th Dynasty seems to have failed to manage the chaos created by these settling Nations and ultimately the "foreign settlers" took control of the Political reigns of Egypt and became the 13th to 15th Dynasties of Egypt, in the Second Intermediate period (1600 BC). They are known in History as the Hekau Khasut (Hyskos), which means Foreigners. The Hekau Khasut introduced Horse drawn Chariots to Egypt and Militarised it, strengthening it as an Economic Power-house but losing its Religious Ethos. It is during this Period that the Israelites become slaves in Egypt, which explains why the New King did not know Joseph. Exodus 1:8, Then a new King, who did not know Joseph (To whom Joseph meant nothing) came to power in Egypt. And he said to his people, "Look, the people of the Children of Israel are more and mightier than we; come, let us deal shrewdly with them, lest they multiply, and it happen, in the event of war, that they also join our enemies and fight against us, and so go up out of the land." The Israelites were then enslaved for 400 years in Egypt. Upon release, they would wander forty years in the desert before returning to Kanaan and eventually arriving there in1399 BC.

They had become a Heterogeneous Hebrew Israelite Nation because of the admixture with Egyptians during their stay in Egypt. Moreover, they were followed by a mixed multitudes of people, who left Hwt-Ka-Pta (Egypt) with them in the great Exodus (Exodus 12:38). After sojourning in the wilderness for 40 years, they Conquer Kanaan (Palestine) and inhabit it, Each Nation (son of Jacob), appropriating land in Kanaan, by conquering and/or displacing the Kanaanites who move into Modern day: Turkey, Iraq and Saudi Arabia, whilst some remained in the Land, for not all Kanaanite Cities were fully conquered however, and Jebus (Jerusalem) is one of those Cities that is not fully conquered. Judges 1:21, "The Benjamites however, did not drive out the Jebusites, who were living in Jerusalem. To this day the Jebusites live there with the Benjamites." This is why Jerusalem has Jewish and Palestinian quarters to this day. King David finally captured Jebus in 1041 BC and his son, King Solomon, built the first first Temple there in 957 BC.

Egypt Flourished during the Hekau Khasut period and this period, (1600-343 BC), has been termed the Golden Age of Egypt.

1075 – 927 BC, the Southern Kingdoms began to assert independence from Northern Kingdoms and from 744 BC, the 6 pharaohs of the 25th Dynasty were from the Norther Kingdom of Nubia (Kush): Piye (Usimare); Shebitku (Djedkare); Shabaka (Nefer-ka-re); Taharqa (Khune-fer-tum) and Tantamani. They ruled Egypt from Napata (Modern day Karima (Kerma) Sudan, which had succeeded Ta-Seti. They served to restore Religious order in Egypt. During this time, Egypt became Allied with Syria, which was related to the Ancient Kushitic cities of Nimrod.

In Iberia and North Afrika, around 1000 BC, several waves of Celtic and Visigoth People migrated from Central Europe and Settled in the Iberian Peninsula, joining the Afrikan people who lived there. The Communities co-existed peacefully, Intermarrying and making Iberia Cosmopolitan. This Civilisation was expanded when in 800 BC and in response to increasing demands for Silver from the Assyrian Empire that succeeded Sumer, Khathago nova was established at what is today Cadiz (Gadir) by the Phoenician Kart-hadashians/Carthagians. Slavery, which was predominantly supplied from captives of war from all over the world increased and Athens (Attica) used as many as 30 000 slaves in the silver mines to satisfy this Demand. Hasdrubal, the Carthaginian General who is believed by some scholars to have been black (since North Afrika was still Black Afrikan and Black Kanaanitc/Phoenician), established another Port in today's Cartagena, Spain. The Greeks are responsible for naming the Peninsula: Iberia, after the river Ebro.

The Process of inward migration of Communities from central Europe and North Afrika into the Iberian Peninsula would continue for generations. Making Portugal, Southern France, Gibraltar, Andorra and Spain as well as North Afrika: Morocco; Algeria; Tunisia and Libya a very Cosmopolitan (mixed heritage) community. Genetic Testing proves that the Iberian Peninsula has the highest Sub-Saharan "Bantu" African admixture. The Canary Islands show a larger North African "Bantu" footprint, because of the Native North Afrikan Ancestors, who were the first to arrive on the islands about 3000 BC. In Afrika the Romans would later refer to these mixed heritage people as Berbers (Barbary)... a Term most are starting to distance themselves from as they re-affirm that they are descendants of: Lubi; Sukiim, Imazinghen, Rifian; Shilah; Numidian; Mauri; xxx Ancestors.

965 BC, Kushitic Khandake (Queen) of Sheba who lived on the Afrikan East Coast (Ethiopia) visits Solomon. Some scholars believe she was from Mesopotamia (Sumer). (Shem also had a descendant known as Sheba). Whether she marries Solomon or not, is not explicit in the Bible. Solomon did marry Kushitic wives amongst his many consorts (300 wives and 1000 Concubines), Probably for Political and Strategic purposes. Solomon's International wives are another reason for the mixed heritage of Jews. He, himself was of mixed descent, being the son of David (Shemitic) and "she who was the wife of Uriah" (The Hittite, a Kanaanite descendant of (K)Ham, 2 Samuel 11-12 and 1 Kings 1- 2. The Solomonids of Ethiopia are the descendants of this Sheba Khandake and King Solomon. Their Christian Dynasty which has persisted since the 1st century AD are responsible for the rich Christian Heritage in Ethiopia. This Solomonid Dynasty is the one that would later succeed the Aksumite Kingdom as the Abbyssinian (Ethiopian) Empire. it has never been fully Colonised. It repelled the Ottoman, Egyptian and 1st Italian attempts to subdue it. The Scramble for Afrika determined its borders and also created for it, the Problems of Tribalism that came with the boundaries and evolution from Monarchies to Democratic leadership which would manifest themselves during the 2020, Covid 19 Global Lock-down. Ethiopia thrived as a Monarchy, and from in 1930 to 1974, Tafari Makonnen, whose Reignal Title became Haile Selassie I (Power of the Trinity), was its Emperor. Although Tafari was a Ras (Prince) and a Regent in parts of Ethiopia, he was not in the Lineage for the Monarchy. His Marriage to a daughter in the Royal household, as well as his progressive leadership style, saw him become the Emperor of Ethiopia. He brought Ethiopia into the League of Nations and the United Nations and made Addis Abbaba the major centre for the organization of African Unity (Now, the African Union). It was his Speech to the United Nations that would help him get back on the throne when Italy deposed him for 5 years. The Progressive leadership style of Ras Tafari (Haile Selasse) is what inspired the Rastafarian Movement which was developed in Jamaica during his early reign in the 1930s. Famine, worsening unemployment, and the political stagnation of Haille Selasse prompted segments of the army to Mutiny and they deposed him in 1974. He was kept under house Arrest until he died, and the Monarchy was abolished, by the Dergue (Council) which held Marxist ideologies, became the Provisional Military Government of Ethiopia. The Dergue, ruled Ethiopia from 1974 to 1987. At this time, the Military leadership civilianized the administration and Colonel Mengistu Haile Mariam, head of the Communist junta, became its interim President. Power changed hands several times until 1991 when the Transitional Government of Ethiopia (TGE) was formed and took over power in 1991 until 1995. The Federal Democratic Republic of Ethiopia was then proclaimed in August 1995. It is led by a Ceremonial President and an Executive Prime Minister. Meles Zenawi became Ethiopia's first prime

minister. He introduced Ethnic Federalism which benefits Tigrinyans disproportionately. In 2012, Meles dies in office and is succeeded by Abiy Ahmed (born 1976), of the Oromo tribe. He gains Acclaim worldwide for opening up the restrictive Ethiopian Economy. On October 2019, he is awarded the Nobel Peace Prize for his peace-making efforts, which ended two decades of hostility with Eritrea. In November, the ruling coalition agrees to form a single party, but the Tigrinya party refuses. In 2020 when the regional elections are delayed because of Covid 19, Tigray State defies the delay and holds their regional elections, which the Federal Government does not recognise. On the 4th of November 2020, President Abiy sends troops into Tigray, accusing the Tigranyan Party of attacking federal troops based in the region and a conflict ensues. The TPLF however Claims that Abiy is doing it to punish the region for the September vote. By the end of 2020, 50 000 people had become displaced to Sudan, women were being violated and family separated due to this conflict, which is quickly becoming a genocide of the Tigranyan people... As will be seen later, this is a Legacy of the division of Afrikan people into Ethnic Tribes and the creation of borders during the Scramble for afrika. The Population of Ethiopia is 112 million people.

In 930 BC, the United Kingdom of Israel Split into Judah (Southern) and Israel Northern Kingdoms.

927 BC: Jerusalem becomes the capital of the (southern) kingdom of Judah.

800 – 600 BC, The Iberian Civilisation flourishes and People from this Civilisation and the people of the Afrikan North & West Coasts continue to trade with each other, getting various goods from Southern and Western Afrika and transporting them through the Trans-Saharan Trade routes. This Trade system is responsible for the establishment of the many powerful and rich Empires of North, Western, South and Central Afrika.

World Dominion Cognitions begin. The Persians were the first to Dominate the Arabian Peninsula and North Afrika. They were followed by the Greeks, the Romans and the Muslim Caliphates.

The Battle of Megiddo, in 609 BC, is a battle wherein Pharaoh Necho II of Egypt was denied passage through Israel by King Josiah when Necho was on his way to help the Assyrians in their fight against the emerging Babylonian empire. King Josiah was defeated and Judah became annexed to Egypt, 2 Kings 23:26-37; Josephus and 1 Esdras. The Bible seems to suggest that this type of battle will be fought again in Meggido by the whole world against the Returning Christ, Revelation 16:16. The Quran also mentions an End Times battle at Meggido. Megiddo is where the Via

Maris Trade Route was guarded. This may allude to the end Times war being about Economic and Spiritual matters.

750 BC Meroe became the southern administrative centre for the kingdom of Kush at a time when Napata was still its capital. After the sack of Napata in about 590 by the Egyptian pharaoh Psamtik II, Meroe became the capital of the kingdom and developed into a wide and prosperous area, Eastward to what is horn of Afrika today and the South-Eastern border of Arabia, today's Yemen and Oman, as well as Southward on the Afrikan East Coast.

605 BC: Battle of Carchemish is a follow-up battle on Megiddo which completed the establishment of the Middle East and Egypt as allied forces, isolating Israel.

597 BC: King Nebuchadnezzar II of Babylon Captured Jerusalem and 10 years later destroyed Solomon's Temple. The destruction of the Temple dispersed Israelites & Jews into Afrika and other Nations, whilst others were taken captive/exiled to Babylon (2Kings 24; 2 Chronicles 36; Ezra 2-6; Nehemiah 7; Jeremiah 27-39 and Daniel 1-5). 538 – 142 BC. In 535 BC some Babylonian exiles are returned by Cyrus the Great as he orders the rebuilding of the Temple in Jerusalem (Isaiah 45, Daniel 1-6) in 527 – 516 BC based on the instructions that he received from God (Ezra 1-6). This period also signifies the start of Judaism as an organized religion. The Term Jews would later replace the Hebraic Children of Israel. The dispersal of Jews continued under Persian and Hellenistic (Greek) Rule. Persian Rule was in 486 BC under King Ahasures/Artexerxes of Persia (Queen Esther's time), when his kingdom stretched all the way to India on the East, Egypt (11 years) as the 31st Dynasty, and Horn of Afrika, bringing Judaism to the Horn of Afrika and West Afrika. Some of these fugitives migrated as far south as Southern Afrika and West to West Afrika.

The Persians were replaced by the Greeks in the "World Dominion" Games, under Alexandra the Great, whose Empire stretched from Greece to North Afrika and North Western India from 332 until 309 BC. Alexandra was replaced by the Ptolemies, who were also Greek from 305 BC to 30 BC.

During his reign, Ptolemy Soter assigned Demetrius Phaleon an Athenian Politician who had fallen from power and who had sought Asylum in Egypt, to Create the Alexandrian Library of the 9 Muses. This Hellenistic Library housed the History and Wisdom of the Mediterranean; Afrika and India. 200 000 to 700 000 books on many topics including Mathematics, Law, Drama, Egyptian Traditions and History, detailing the 30 Afrikan, pre-Persian Ancient Egyptian Dynasties, the first Translation of the Torah Hebrew Bible, known as the Septuagint, Philosophy, Medicine and Natural

Science and much more. The Books were written in both Greek and Kemitic. Egypt became the premier destination for "University" Studies in the thenworld. (It followed in the footsteps of the Platonic Academy established by Plato in Athens, also referred to as Athens University, in 387 BC).

The Growing Roman Empire sought to displace the Phoenicians from the Afro- Iberia Trade, and in 264-146 BC, a series of Wars that have been named the Punic Wars (Wars of those who speak Punic, a Phoenician language), were fought between the various States of Rome and Kart-hadasht (Carthage), Tunisia. At this time, Carthage was the dominant power in the Mediterranean Sea. Carthage's Trading on the Iberian Peninsula was booming, whilst Italy was rapidly expanding and requiring more raw material and for which they wanted to "go direct" to source for. The two Nations fought over this Trade, in wars that took place on the Sicilian Island and surrounding waters as well as in Corsica, Sardinia and Tunisia. In the second of these wars, Hannibal, Hasdrubal's younger brother, led a successful offense by Crossing the Alps, a feat that had thus far been considered impossible. Carthage was finally subdued in the third Punic war. In 146 BC, the Romans stormed the city, sacked it, slaughtered most of its population and completely demolished it, taking over its territories, which became the Roman Province of Africa (Present day Morocco, Algeria, Tunisia, Libya and Egypt, as well as Israel (Kanaan) and Iberian Peninsula (which became Province of Hispania). North Afrika became increasingly Mixed heritage and Cosmopolitan. Iberia then became the source of Silver, Food, Olive oil, wine and metal for Rome, without the Middle man (Phoenicia). Rome occupied North Afrika until 600 AD, almost 700 years. During this time, they introduced Latin, which influenced many of the Afrikan languages in these areas. Most Afrikan people took up Greek and Roman Names, so that their identities as Afrikans can't be deciphered from their names today.

In a bid to establish the legitimacy of the rule of the Ptolemic Kings over Egypt, Ptolemy V, gave an offering of Grain and silver to the temples on Mekhir (March) 196 BC, the 8th year of his reign. That year, there was particularly high flooding of the Nile. He had the excess waters dammed, for the benefit of the farmers. In return, the priests pledged that the king's birthday and coronation days would be celebrated annually and that all priests in Egypt would serve him alongside the other gods. This pledge was recorded as a Decree on a Stella (Rock), whose copies were to be placed in every temple in the land. The Stele was recorded in 3 scripts: Ancient Greek (Government language), Kemitic hieroglyphic Language of the gods and Kemitic demotic Language of documents. It is this Decree that would enable linguists later to decipher Ancient Kemitic (original Egyptian Language) because the Greek

Script on the Stele Translated the Ancient Egyptian Scripts and by the time the Stella was discovered, Ancient Greek was still known. The Stele would later be removed possibly during some Egyptian invasion and was used to build a Fort in the town of Rashid (Rosetta) which is 56km East of Alexandria in Egypt. The Stella was later discovered by French officer Pierre Francois Bouchard during the Napoleonic war of 1798-1801 in Egypt.

Cleopatra was the last Ptolamaic Pharaoh. Upon the death of her father, Ptolemy Xii, Cleopatra and her brother ruled Egypt together. This Power-share was not very smooth however, and she and her brother Ptolemy Xiii contested the throne. In a bid to establish the power of Cleopatra, Julius Ceasar, who was her lover, set fire on the harbour in 48 BC, and Ptolemy Viii drowned whilst trying to escape. The fire destroyed the branch of the Alexandrian Library situated at the harbour. The Library, was one of the largest Libraries of the Ancient World. It contained a significant amount of written Afrikan History.

(27 BC: The Roman Empire emerges as a post Republican Roman Polity, when Augustus Caesar – Gaius Julius Caesar Octaviunus, the nephew of Julius Caesar, proclaimed himself the first Emperor of Rome. The Empire became the next "World" leader, displacing the Greeks whom it had conquered. The Roman "World" Rule persisted until 1453 AD with the fall of Constantinople. As a Polity, it included large territorial holdings around the Mediterranean Sea in Europe; Northern Afrika and Western Asia. This 1480-year Roman Imperialism further entrenched the Cosmopolitan nature of North Afrika, Thus the discovery in 2012, that the 151 Mummies from this era whose genes were tested proved that they were mummies of white people (Romans would be Classified as white or Caucasoid today). In 31 BC: The Roman empire made Israel a Roman Province until 619 AD.

25 BC: As the Roman Empire Swoops Southward, to expand Southward into Afrika. They are repelled by Khandakhe (Queen) Amanirenas, of Meroe in the Sudan. Khandake Amanirenas repels the Roman invasion and retaliates by capturing a series of Roman forts and concluding the campaign by decapitating the bronze Statue of Caesar Augustus, which she places at the footstool of her throne, declaring that Rome will never conquer Meroe. Rome has never conquered Meroe even according to the word of the Queen. Other famous Prominent Political figures/Warrior Queens in Afrikan History are: Queen Gudit; Queen Amina of Zazzau in what is now Northwest Nigeria; (Queen) Yaa Asantewaa the Queen mother of Ejisu in the Ashanti empire; Queen Yennenga of Burkina Faso; Queen Nzinga of Angola, Ndongo and Matamba, Queen Modjadji, umKabayi ka Jama wamaZulu; the Rain Maker Queen of baLobedu

in what is today South Africa, Khadzi dza vhaVenda and surely you know some in your culture. Their life stories are fascinating and Testimony to the Equal Society that was Afrika.

12 BC – 182 AD: Another Golden age of Kushitic Meroe culture under King Netekamani, without Roman Influence or conquest emerges

04 AD: Yeshua ha Mashiach (Jesus the Messiah/Christ) who is revered by Christians as their Saviour, is born in Bethlehem of Judea in Kanaan (Israel). Israel was under Roman Rule at this time. His Genealogy is Afro-Shemitic. Matthew 1. Judah (Shemitic) begot Perez and Zerah by Tamar, a Kanaanite woman; xxx; Salmon (Afro-Shemitic) begot Boaz by Rahab, a Kanaanite woman; Boaz (Afro-Shemitic), begot Obed by Ruth, a Shemitic Moabite Woman. (The Moabites are a dynasty descended from the Incestuous relations of Lot and his daughter when she and her sister, raped their father, in his drunken stupor; xxx; David (Afro-Shemitic) begot Solomon by her who had been the wife of Uriah the Hittite (a Kanaanite woman); xxx. Genesis 38 – Tamar; Book of Ruth – Ruth; 2 Samuel 11- 12 & 23 – Uriah & Matthew 1. This makes Jesus' Heritage Strongly Afro-Shemitic. Recent Scientific evidence points to a Jesus with a dark skin tone and curly hair, like that of a mixed heritage Afro-Arabian. The reason why Jesus is thought of as "White" is because of the later Artistic License of the 500 AD Roman Artists who were commissioned to make portraits of Jesus to Strengthen the new Christian Identity of the Roman Empire. It had been declared Christian by Emperor Constantine with the Edict of Milan in 313 AD (See later)

The Artists had never seen Jesus nor did they know him. They only followed the Brief: "This is a Heavenly King". So, they used what they knew. They borrowed from existing Portraits of Powerful Earthly Kings and gods, Using the Likeness of Zeus and the image of an enthroned Roman Emperor". Zeus was worshipped prior to the Romans Accepting Jesus Christ as their new heavenly emperor, as such, Jesus had to be portrayed looking like a younger version of Zeus.

Jesus Christ is also not his birth name. He was born Yeshua Emmanuel ben Joseph ha Mashiach. When the Bible was Translated to Greek from Aramaic, Yeshua was written out in Greek and Latin, instead of just being left in the Aramaic and it was rendered: Iesus. Iesus when written out in English became Jesus. Mashiach is Aramaic for Anointed. Anointed in Greek is Christos and this in English was rendered Christ. Ben is Aramaic for Son of or descendant of. Emmanuel, his other given name, was left unchanged and it means: God with us. Therefore, if you were to Translate his name it would be: Yeshua (Savior/Deliverer) Emmanuel (God with us), ben (son of) Joseph, ha (the) Mashiach (Anointed).

There are some who say it does not matter what skin color he was, and whether his name was translated or not, because God knows it and it has Authority no matter which language we use to call it.

Maybe it does not matter. If it did not matter, then why did the West keep quiet about their Artistic License of Jesus' portraits and his name for 1500 years? Was it not to make it easy for Europe to Accept a Messiah who does not look like them? Afrikans (and other Nations), Chose to believe in this Messiah in spite of having been made to believe that he does not look like them, because they truly believe that regardless of color, He was sent to save all Humanity. Now that they know, that he actually has the heritage of all mankind, they together with all of mankind can be bolder in their faith in his ability to "Seek and to Save that which was lost".

I am Takalani Mafhungo Vivian Dube, Mukololo wa Luvhalani. I am Happy to translate my Name for you, so that you can enjoy its meaning, as I do, for it bears the full meaning of my existence and purpose. Takalani (Rejoice) Mafhungo (Good News) Vivian (Life giving) Dube (Is my Surname by Marriage and it means Zebra, the Reconciler) Mukololo (Princess) wa (of) Luvhalani (Neluvhalani is my Maiden name and it means: God is the owner of the Flower on the prairie, He who plucks it, is in danger of God's vengeance (Flower, in this instance, speaks of people and the act of plucking the flower is murder).

As much as I love you understanding my name, I do not appreciate you calling me: Rejoice Vivian, the Princess of Heaven. If you do that, the meaning of my name stays the same, and perhaps you enjoy it better, because it is suddenly understandable to you. The power and purpose of my Name remains the same regardless of the Translation, But, you deny me my heritage and History. My parents gave me a Name in Vernacular and another one in the colonial language, that I needed, in order for me, to be legitimate, at the time of the registration of my birth. This, is my Heritage, which should be preserved for my posterity, for them to be able to better understand themselves in the context of their lineage. If I don't, 1000 generations from now, people will be confused as to whether I was muVenda or Latin/English, as is the case, today, with Jesus whom most of us grew up believing to be White and English, Fair-skinned with long Blonde Hair and Blue eyes. Coincidentally, I also thought Egypt and Israel were mythical lands in heaven when I was 9 years old... I did not know that the History of the Bible was real, verifiable and Historically Predominantly Afro-S(h)emitic.

After 1500 years of saying Jesus Christ, (37 years for me) it is taking time for me to just say Yeshua ha Mashiach, and not feel like I have to explain myself, so, for the purpose of this book, I will use both names together or separately. I hope you will follow and make up your mind which name you will use in your personal prayers, if you do use His Name in prayer. Heaven knows and is not confused...

30 AD: Yeshua ha Mashiach is Crucified. He rises on the third day. He appears to many people as a Testament of his Resurrection. He himself had raised a number of people from the dead during his ministry even as the Old Testament Scriptures had prophesied. Matthew 17:22-23; Hosea 6:1-2; Psalm 16:10 as quoted in 1 Peter 3:18-22; Mark 16:7; John 20:16-30; Luke 24:13-53; 1 Corinthians 15:7. Quran 3:55 & 5:75

30 AD: All Nations Worship in Jerusalem: Acts 2: 1-10: "Now there were staying in Jerusalem God-fearing Jews from every nation under heaven, both Jews and converts to Judaism" The Bible Records in this verse some of those Nations as:

- Parthians, Elamites and Medes: Iranians;
- Residents of Mesopotamia (Iraq; Kuwait; Syria; Turkey);
- Judea (Kanaan, Palestine);
- Cappadocia, Phrygia and Pamphylia (Turkey);
- Pontus (Greece) and Cretans (Greece);
- Asia (Asia);
- Land of the Hittites (Kanaanitic);
- Egypt (represented the whole of Afrika) and the parts of Libya near Cyrene (North Afrika);
- visitors from Rome (Europe);
- Arabs (Arabs).

All 3 sons of Nukhu (Noah) are recorded here as Jewish. Some are Ethnic Jews whilst others are Jewish by Conversion to Judaism. All would go to Israel to Worship as they still do today as Jews, Christians, Moslems, Baha'i and other Religions.

60 AD: The Disciple of Jesus Christ, Mark, Brings the Gospel of Jesus Christ (The Way: Acts 19:23), to Egypt, establishing one of the earliest Christian Communities in the world outside of Israel, The Coptic Church. Acts 8:26 however, records that Phillip Baptised an Ethiopian Eunuch who was an official to the Queen. Later in Acts 19, this Ethiopian Eunuch is identified as Simeon the Niger, who is among those who were recognized as Prophets and Teachers in Antioch. It follows that as a Teacher, He may have established a Community of believers in Ethiopia around this time. There was also Lucius of Cyrene (Libya). In the first century AD therefore, there were already several communities of Christian believers in Afrika.

70AD: Fall of the 2nd Temple in Jerusalem. This is followed by the dispersal of the Jews and their Persecution. The Coptic Church in Egypt is established. The first Complete Bible is compiled in Coptic (Kemito-Greco-Roman language). The Church Spreads to Libya and Tunisia as well as West and East Afrika, especially Ethiopia and syncretically down the East Coast to Southern Afrika. At the Khami Ruins, there is a Cross carved on a Rock (Since Khami is only dated at 1460 AD to 1650, the cross could also be from the contact with Portuguese Missionaries at this later date).

180 AD: In Kart-hadasht (Carthage), Tunisia, 12 - Christians are executed for their Christian beliefs (Refusing to swear by the genius of the Roman Emperor). They are sent to the lions, a "Sport" that was already in place during Daniel's time (620 BC)

182 AD: Roman Emperor Diocletian, launches great persecution against Christianity. Christianity was still perceived as a Heresy in Rome during this period.

7 March 203 AD: In Kart-hadasht (Carthage), a 21-year-old young mother, Vibia Perpetua together with her highly pregnant helper, Felicitas and others, were executed by being gouged by bulls, for Lese' Majeste (Harming the ruler) when they refused to acknowledge him as a deity. Both the women are now acknowledged as Saints by the Roman Catholic Church.

The Afrikan Church grew very rapidly in North Afrika to: Libya, Tunisia, Morocco, Algeria as well as Mauretania and Numidia. Judaism, Being Similar to what is now referred to as Afrikan Traditional Religion and, some "Black" ethnic Jews and "Black" Converted Jews, having fled to these areas earlier, it was easy for Afrikans to Accept the Message of the Messiah. They quickly Assimilated Christian beliefs into their own religion (Syncretic Christianity) whilst some Converted Fully.

184 – 253 AD, The Afrikan Mystic, Origen of Alexandria, Egypt, is one of the early Christian scholar, Ascetic and Theologian. He was a prolific writer who wrote roughly 2,000 treatises in multiple branches of theology, including textual Criticism, Biblical Exegesis, Homiletics, Hermeneutics and Spirituality. He has been described as "the greatest genius the early church ever produced" McGukin (2004:25). He influenced much of European Theology and He is Considered one of the Church Fathers.

311 AD: Church experiences its first Split, called the Donatist split. Donatism is a philosophical take on Christianity by the Afrikan Church who claim Donatism to be the Authentic Christian Church; It espoused Willingness to be Martyred and Doctrinal Conservatism. Donatists' famous statement is: "What has the Emperor to do with the Church?" When a Bishop who had "Denied" Christ in the face of Persecution is made

Bishop of Kart-hadasht, a Split of the Afrikan and Roman Church occurs. Afrikan Christianity is still to date more conservative than the European Church with more emphasis on right and wrong rather than on Relationship and Grace.

328 AD: The Ethiopian Tawahedo Church begins. It is Aligned to the Coptic, Armenian and Syrian Eastern Orthodox Church

380 AD, Christianity becomes the Religion of the Roman Empire by the decree of the Eastern Roman Emperor, Theodosius I. This had the effect of tying Christianity to Greco-Roman Culture. (Much like Islam became tied to Arabic culture). 391AD: in his quest to destroy pagan Temples from all Roman territories, Emperor Theodosius orders the destruction of the Temple of Serapes, which housed the second Branch of the Library of Alexandria. Thankfully, in 2002, The Egyptian Government established the Bibliotheca Alexandrina, which houses the world's largest digital repository of all surviving Ancient Manuscripts.

400 AD: King Ezana of Ethiopia makes Christianity Ethiopia's official religion (This too, ties Christianity to the Ethiopic culture). The Christian Scriptures are translated to the Ge'ez language of Ethiopia, 1000 years before it is Translated into English. English, the Language of Anglo Saxon Migrants who migrated from what is now: South Germany, Denmark and Netherlands became a language between 500 and 700 AD.... One of the world's younger language and true to its youthfulness, the most influential language today.

451 AD: The Egyptian Coptic Church and the Roman Churches differ on the Nature of Jesus Christ at the council of Chalcedon and Split. The Coptic Church is now a Non-Chalcedonian Eastern Orthodox Church. The Copts, hold that Christ is both human and divine, mystically united in one. The opposing view is that Christ is perfect both in deity and humanness... (The One Person, One Nature Position)

On 22 April 571AD: In Mecca, Saudi Arabia, Muhammad ibn Ábdullah PBUH is born. At Age 40, in 610 AD, Muhammad ibn Ábdullah PBUH, began to have revelations from Allah that become the basis for the Quran and the foundation of Islam. He Condemned idol worship and polytheism which had become rampant in Arabia. He begins to share his Revelation and Doctrines.

600 AD:

Christianity spreads to Nubia (Present Day Sudan) and a very strong Christian community thrives, Building one of the largest Cathedrals at Dongola.

622 AD:

Prophet Muhammad moves to Medina, as he is resisted in Mecca. 622 AD, now marks the beginning of the Muslim Calendar. Some of the Prophet's followers crossed current Djibouti and Somalia to seek refuge in present-day Eritrea and Ethiopia during this Hijrah as was common for people from the Arabian Peninsula to do so for Trade. The Indigenous Worshippers of Ethiopia as well as the Christian Community that was already established here, welcomed the Muslim worshippers in true ubuNtu and to this day, Muslims and Christians live peacefully in Ethiopia.

By 630 AD: 20 years from founding Islam, the Prophet, Muhammad ibn Ábdullah PBUH, had unified most of Arabia under a single religion, Strengthening the Arabic Identity through Religion. Islam becomes influential in the Iberian Peninsula, the Mediterranean and North Afrikan Coasts as well as India.

On 08 June 632 AD: Prophet Muhammad ibn Ábdullah PBUH, dies and is buried at al-Masjid an-Nabawi.

639 AD, the beginning of Arab Islamic conquest of the Nations. In Afrika, Islamic rule persisted until 1798 AD (1159 years). Most Nations that had become Islamic during Islamic rule continued to practice Islam, making Islam and Lingo-Cultural Arabic Identity amongst Afrikans 1382 years old. Christianity in North Afrika thrived for about 500 years and died except in small enclaves like Ethiopia where it has persisted since then to date: 1961 years. Christianity was re-introduced in the Continent first by the Portuguese in 1490, a total of 530 years and in some areas, it is only 200 years old. Christianity has not managed in these 200 years to establish a strong Scholastic Tradition in Afrika. This has created deep problems with syncretism and false prophets. Moreover, just like Islam, it has been associated with Political Establishments of foreign Governments on Afrikan Soil. This has left people suspicious of the Motives of organised Religion and unwilling to be fully committed to any religion even if they might check a certain religious box when asked to do so in a census. In the absence of the Afrikan belief system of ubuNtu, people have become effaced and lacking a Moral compass in spite of being aligned to a Religion, more so because very few Afrikans remember what their forefather's Spirituality and or Religion entailed.

This Period Represents a Time of increased Political Organisation at Regional level in Afrika, as the Persian, Greek, Roman and Islamic invasions undermined Continental Structures. Regional Polities emerge formed by related Nations that maintain Local Political Autonomy whilst paying Homage to the Regional Leading Polity. The Rise and fall of Afrikan Dynasties and Kingdoms amongst themselves, are not the Conquest of one Nation by another foreign one nor of displacement of one by another, but rather expansion of Kingdoms of Related people who came together for a Common good, often times with poorer Kingdoms surrendering their sovereignty to the more powerful Dynasties. Seniority, Trade and Military prowess contributed to the decision as to which Dynasty would become the Regional Polity/Empire. Older Empires of the initial Ancient Phutic, Misraimic, Kushitic and Kanaanitic people were, Succeeded, rather than Replaced (as often portrayed in History Books) by the Empires of their descendants. Some of them would have a greater sphere of influence or less and sometimes merged with other empires whilst at times breaking ranks with others... To understand it better, Visualise a Waning and Waxing pattern on one spot, with different centers of influence at different times... These new Empires would or would not, carry the same name as their predecessors, as they named themselves by the name of the father, Land Marks, Natural Events, Animals they prized (Totems) and Historical Events, as for example: Kush, Nubia, Meroe, Aksum, Ethiopia and Sudan... (are the same people through different ages, whose presence was not bounded by the current Colonial borders but was widespread to the South as far as today's South Africa and to the North and West coalescing with Misraim and Phut.) It is also possible that these Northern Civilisations that are more famous, because of Archaeology, are actually extensions of the Southern Empires, whose evidence is older. Think South-North evolution rather than North South. An Inverted Afrkan Map so to say... Foreign Invaders then renamed the various Afrikan people and their territories, according to their perceptions of them, as for example, the Arabs named all the Southern Lands to which the Northern Afrikans were displaced to, as Alkebulan and bilad Al-Sudan (Land of the Blacks). Presumably, these would be the Cosmopolitan Arabs who had Indo-European (P admixture and were lighter skinned than the S(h)emetic Arabs who were darker and had associated with afrika since the dawn of time. When Europe later Scrambled for Afrika, Sudan became a Country that represented only the extents of the Meroetic Civilisation and even less, whilst Ethiopia became confined to the Aksumite influence.

Each Empire represented hundreds of Nation States. To Name them all is an impossible Task for any one Historian. Trying to do so, will always leave a bitter Taste, of the Dominions kind. Even my attempt below at Naming a few of the better known (acknowledged in Literature) Empires and Kingdoms is bound to leave many feeling riled. I Ask you to see yourself as an Afrikan and understand that the mention of one is an Acknowledgement of all. I also ask that this be the impetus you need to research and write about your people. The Little mound that seems inconsequential probably hosts a wealth of History. Any old city already Investigated in Afrika is probably just the tip of the Iceberg, as the recent new discoveries of cities in the over researched Egypt prove.

Do not ignore that seventy-year-old Koko le Nkgolo (Grandma and Grandpa in seSotho), they are the Wisdom Custodians.

They can tell you about the Mound, the forgotten Language, The Meanings of the various Customs and Traditions, your Genealogy and History... Ask the Questions... Don't be frustrated when at first it seems mythological and confusing... your Lingo-culture is no longer aligned. Gradually over time, the scales will fall off your eyes and you will see as you become enculturated

The Statement which will follow much later and quoted from https://theculturetrip.com/africa/nigeria/articles/history-rediscovered-sungbos- eredo-nigerias-lost-yoruba-kingdom-2/ encapsulates how our History has been Researched and narrated, to ensure that whatever archaeological evidence is found in Sub-Saharan Africa is confined to a period of 500 – 1300 AD, in order for it to tie in with the Bantu Southward Migration Theory. if new Archeological digs at Mapungubwe and Dzimbabwe and Sibudu and others, were to be dated earlier, the Migratory Theory would fall flat on its face as indeed it already has, when we take into consideration the continuous evidence of the presence of Farmer (Bantu) communities in Southern Afrika from as long ago as 200 000 years ago.

I think the important thing is to remember that Bantu Migration is a Theory... It is okay to ditch it, Nobody will die if we abandoned it, as we did the multi- regional Theory of the origins of mankind (But then again, there are those who are still pursuing it...) It is imperative therefore that Afrikans also know the Afrikan Truth, and stick to it, in order for them to be able to make sense of their world.

This is the Afrikan Truth which is well Corroborated by many suppressed Scientists and erased or unheard in acknowledged scientific evidence:

Life began in Afrika, When some of us left Afrika to Populate the World, Some of us remained and populated the whole of the Afrikan Continent from South to East, the Islands and Arabia as well as to West and North Afrika. Our Material Culture is similar because we are one people, sons and daughters of 4 sons of K(H)am, son of Nukhu (Noah), Son of many others to AddamuNtu, the firs spirit son of of God to be Human. Over Millenia, we have admixed with our Sons and daughters who returned to the Continent, so that some of us have become, Berber, Arab and Coloured, whilst others of our Children were carried off to the Diaspora. We are Farmers, Pastoralists and Herders. We have always roamed the Continent freely, undeterred by any artificial or natural boundary. There is neither a North Arabic Afrika nor a South Bantu Afrika. East, West, North, Central and South are just but Cardinal Points. They are not Confines, nor are they determinants of Relationships. We can't be packaged into neat boxes through Philology. There is one Afrika. Afrika, Know this, thy Truth and be set Free. Refuse to be indoctrinated and brainwashed with Theories of Foreigners.

If you hold to Quranic or Biblical Scriptures, they do not conflict with this Truth. Read them with open eyes and you will be illuminated. I spent a considerable time synthesizing Scriptural evidence with Scientific evidence on the section on Origins. Feel free to re-read it and have a better picture. It is the same picture being viewed through different Lenses and sometimes different orientations of the Map perhaps? But be assured, it is the same picture. Open your eyes and see!

Finally, here is that Statement from the Culture trip...

"At one time, scholars used to divide the three thousand-year history of southern Nigeria (which other scholars date to 8000 BC, Oriju, J.N (2011) into four great cultural periods. They used to speak of the Nok Culture, the Igbo-Ukwu Culture, the Yoruba Kingdoms and the Benin Empire as if they are divorced from each other and unrelated and represent diverse unrelated people... This view, was boldly challenged by the findings of a team of Bournemouth University scholars led by archaeologist Dr Patrick Darling. Since 1994, the team discovered and mapped the remains of yet another Nigerian kingdom, this time covered by centuries of forest overgrowth: The Sungbo Eredo. Barnaby Phillips of the BBC described the discoveries as possibly Africa's largest single monument." The Walls of Benin as they are also known are larger than the Wall of China. They are 160km wide and 20m high (That is the same as a 20 storey skyscraper building!). Darling estimated that they "cover 2,500 square miles (6,475 Square kilometres) and consist of more than 500 interconnected communal enclosures."

If one takes this example on the West, and Tellinger's 200 000 year old city on the East and the Southern Kingdoms of Mapungubwe, Dzimbabwe, Khami, Barolong and Bakone as well as the Ancient Northern Cities of Egypt, Libya, Tunisia, a picture begins to emerge of an interconnected Continental Metropolis of Farmers, Traders, Hunters and Pastoralists, Collaborating and living Symbiotically, albeit maintaining different Lingo-Cultural Identities that are steeped in the same Politico-Econo-Religious order.

Whatever Afrikan Kingdoms we know... They Represent Successive Monarchies who are the descendants of the original Biblical 4 Afrikan fathers: Kushi, Misraimi, Phuti and Kanaan. For those who do not subscribe to this History, These Empires represent the fathers of all the first amongst Homo Sapiens who emerged in Afrika and who are the progenitors of Modern Human Beings that went on to populate the whole world and the Afrikan Continent. What is dated at 500 to 1500 AD therefore is the last Precolonial Empire and is an extension of its predecessors since Creation of man or the emergence of man on earth, 6000 BC Biblically and 300 000 BC or more, Scientifically.

Some of the Precolonial Continental Empires that have evolved since creation and are better known to the West and recorded in Literature are:

Kanaan, North Afrika, what is now the Sahel, Central and West Afrika: The sons of: Misraim, Kanaan, Phut and Kush

Kanaan Empires: The 10 Nations of Kanaan: Hittite, Hivites, Girgashites, Arvazites, Perrzites, Jebusites, Sidonians (Damascan and Lebanese) Phoenicians who are in parts of today's Israel, Palestine, Lebanon, Syria. Kingdom of Marrakesh (Today's Morocco) was the Capital of 3 Moro/Mauri Imazighen Dynasties (rendered Moor in English); Kart-hadasht Empire (Carthage in Tunisia), This empire was a collaboration between Kanaanitic Phoenicians and Phutitic or Misraimi Imazinghen and Tuareng people together with Khoe and San Nations in their roles as Pastoralists and Hunters who lived symbiotically; Kemet (K(ha)mit) or Copt (Coptic) and Misri (Misraimi) Empire in what is today Egypt. Various Misraimi Nations; Tuareng Empire; Amazigh Empire; Fulani Empire; Haratin Empire; Lubim, Sukiim, Mande Empire; Wolof Empire; Soninke Empire in today's Mauritania and Western Sahara, Numidia Empire; Biafra Empire; Mossi Kingdom; Loropeni Kingdom; Jolof Kingdom; Barra Kingdom/Niumi Kingdom; Fulo Empire; Soninke Empire; Serer Empire; Mandinka Empire: Mende Empire; Jola Empire; Kaabu Empire; Keita Empire of Mali; Ghana Empire (Wagadu) with its largest city, Koumbi Saleh which traded in Kola Nuts that became the secret ingredient in Coca Cola, Mali Empire, Wolof Empire (Koumbi Saleh); Jenne-jeno; Timbuktu; Kangaba Kingdom; Akan Empire; Igbo Empire which established Nri city for the outcasts of society where they were rehabilitated and restored to their fortunes (Similar to Jewish Cities of Refuge); Hausa Empire and the Nok Culture; Ife Kingdom; Benin Empire which built the Sungbo Eredo; Ife Empire; Nupe Empire; Bake Empire; Aro Empire; Mandara Empire; xxx.

Central, East and Southern Afrika:

Duguwa (later Sayfuwa) Empire succeeded by Sao Empire which was succeeded by Kanembu who first established Kanem City in Chad, with its many fortified walls and the origin of the Trans-Saharan Trade Route; Bagurimi Empire; Waddai Empire; Bulala Empire; Tubu Empire; Mubu Empire; Kush Dynasty evolved to Nubia Meroe and Aksum which later became Sudan and Ethiopia. These extended further South on the East Coast and Centrally beyond the Current extents of the Countries by these Names and covered: Somalia, Djibouti, Eritrea and Ethiopia. with various Chiefdoms and cities including Kerma; Kanem Empire; Bachwezi Empire which succeeded the BateMbuzi Dynasty and was located in Kitara covered Present Day: Kenya, Uganda, Tanganyika (Tanzania), Rwanda, Burundi, East DRC; Zambia and Malawi; Present day: Angola; Botswana; Lesotho; Mozambique; Namibia; South Africa; Swaziland; Zambia; Zimbabwe were led by various Empires including: Kongo Kingdom which stretched from present day Angola to present day Kongo and was led by Luken Lua Nimi. The Kongo Kingdom controlled the Trade Routes along its Waterways (The 6990 km long Kongo River and the Atlantic Ocean); Lunda State; Luba State; Mapungubwe which was succeeded by Dzimbabwe and Khami Controlled the Trade on the South Eastern Seaboard of present day Mozambique and KwaZulu. It was imagined to be a Country by the Portuguese who called it Mono Motapa afer the Reignal Title of the Monarchy of a Territory: Muwene we Mutapa. This Connection through Regional Polities is the reason why surnames of people from different countries are similar and can be found to be similar as from South Africa to as far as Malawi and with sprinkles throughout the Continent and sometimes as unimaginably far as India. As an example, the Dube Surname. There are Dubes in South Africa, Mozambique, Zimbabwe, Malawi, Botswana, Nigeria, Canada and India as part of the Dravidian Brahmans. The Predominant Dialect in Southern Afrika was Kalanga (Galanga/ Karanga) (Most Current Nguni Languages in South Africa: Different Sotho Dialects (seSotho, sePedi, kiLobedu, seTswana, seKgatla) as well as luVenda, xiTsonga, isiZulu, isiXhosa, isNdebele, isiSwati, Tonga, carry Kalanga words, it was the predominant dialect during the Mutapa Empire.

The Arabic Cultures/Civilisations in Continental Afrika, are Cultures/Civilisations of Continental Afrikan (Black people) who became Muslim and collaborated with their Arabic brethren to advance their People. They do not represent the Civilisation only of "invaders or conquerors". Just because a Civilisation and Name is Arabic does not mean it is the Civilisation of Islamic Arabs. It was a collaboration of the existing (Black) Afrikan Nations with the incomers or the civilization of the (Black) Afrikans who converted to Islam and became Arabised. Much like Spain and Portugal were before the Arabs were expelled. They built their own civilization in collaboration with the

Muslims and sometimes by themselves as Muslims. The Almurabutin (later) demonstrate this point very well.

Within each of these Regional Polities, are Hundreds of Nations, Represented in Today's surviving 10 000 or more Nations of Continental, Islandic and Diaspora Afrikan abaNtu. baTwa (Khoe and San) as Nomadic and Semi Nomadic Cultures tended to keep their Political Systems small and they did not generally rule over large areas. However they were very integral to the aba(ka)Ntu (Bantu) Farmers brethren, each Society bringing their skill to bear for the survival of the whole.

Some of the baTwa Nations still known are: baHerero; Okavambo Nama; N; Gorinchukwa (Goringacona) misspelt as Griqua in Literature; Xam!; IIXengwi; NIlnle; Khomani; Haillom; Namkhoe; OraKhoe; !Khuai-Seroa; Swara; Chokwancho; IIKxau; Tswanatsatsi; Khoekhogowab; Gonaqua; Hoengeniqua Inqua, Hadzabe; xxx. Most have Amalgamated under one Identity as for example the Khomani Nation in South Africa. BaTwa/baRwa KhoiSan People (baKhoe and baSan Nations) are NOT extinct, contrary to Historical narratives that fail to recognize the erasure of Nations through Population Classifications and that also fail to recognize the continuity of lineages in other nationalities. After all, we are all KhoiSan. They are the Progenitors of all Humanity.

In 640 AD, The Kingdom of Aksum (Spelt in Ge'ez: መንግሥተ አኵስም), succeeded Meroe, spanning what are now Eritrea, Northern Ethiopia, much of eastern Sudan and southern/eastern Yemen at its peak.

640-750 AD: Arabic Muslim Umayyad Caliphate takes over North Afrika and Contributes to North Afrika becoming more Arabic and Islamic.

It is during this Umayyad Caliphate, that in the 7th Century, Caliph Abd el-Malik, builds the Qubbat As-Sakhrah (Dome of the Rock) in Jerusalem, it was completed in 691 AD. It is built on the Place where the Jewish Temple stood earlier, and where the foundation Stone is. The Foundation Stone/Rock is believed to be where the Holy of Holies was in the Temple of Solomon and where the creation of the world began. Some believe the Tabernacle is still hidden under the Rock. In Islam, It Commemorates the Place Whence Prophet Muhammad commenced his Night journey and Ascended to heaven. It is believed that Angels visited this spot, 2000 years before the creation of Adam and that it is where the Trumpet will sound on Resurrection day. It is also believed to be the Spot where Abram prepared to Sacrifice Isaac (Ishmael for Islam).

700 – 1240 AD, Wagadu kingdom Spread across parts of what is now Mauritania, Senegal, and Mali. It was an important stop along the trans-Saharan trade route

which connected Western and Southern African Goods to the markets found along the North African coastlines of the Mediterranean Sea. One of its capital cities, Koumbi Saleh, was the biggest city south of the Sahara Desert. At its peak, it was home to between 15,000 and 20,000. They specialized in the trade of gold and kola nuts which became the secret ingredient in Coca-Cola centuries later. The Kingdom of Ghana was succeeded by Mali around 1240 AD.

711 AD: The Kanaanitic Damascan Phoenicians who had embraced Islam became the Umayyad Caliphate. They Named the Nations in which they had Trade centres: Afriqqiya: Morocco, Algeria, Tunisia and Libya. With a greater impetus from Islam, it was time to "Wrest" back the Iberian Peninsula which they had lost to the Greeks and the Romans earlier in the Punic wars. The Governor over Afriqqiya, Musa ibn Nusayr, instructed his Mawla (Guardian) and General of the army of Tangier, General Tariq ibn Ziyad, a Muslim Maori (Moor) to Wrest the Iberian Peninsula from the Germanic Visigoths and to re-establish Afrikan rule there.

Tariq and an army of 7000, crossed the Strait between Morocco and Spain, dismounting at a Mountain that would later be known as Mountain of Tariq (Gibraltar) and the strait also became known by that name. He successfully subdued the Visigoths and reigned there for a year, handing over to the Umayyad Governor thereafter and the Peninsula subsequently became known as Al Andalus – Land of the Vandals. This would successfully restore Afrikan and Kanaanitic (Damascan) Authority over the area for 800 (711-1492 interrupted) years and through its Islamic Influence, Revolutionised Spanish Civilisation with: Chemistry; Physics; Philosophy; Mathematics; Astrology; Architecture; the Arts; Grooming; Streets; Lighting...; leading to Spain's Renaissance. They built many Mosques, Palaces and Universities. This Afro-Arabic Civilisation further exposed Europe to Afrika and the East, allowing for further Mixed heritage populations of both Al Andalus and North Afrika, with a vibrant Cosmopolitan Religious, Cultural and Political heritage. The Alhambra Moorish Palace that was built by this civilisation is now a UNESCO world heritage site.

The Initial Conquest was strengthened by the later Al Murabitun (Almoravids) and Al Mohad Dynasties. This Moorish reign over what is Modern day Spain and Portugal, Andorra, Southern France and British Crown Colony of Gibraltar is what intensified the Trade Relationship between Afrika and Europe. Discrimination by Nationality and Religion created Strife in Al-Andalus (Iberian Peninsula), contributing to the enduring Christian – Islamic Strife. Arab Muslims from the Middle East were at the top of the Segregationist social hierarchy, whilst Afro Muslims occupied a lower level and Christians of all Nationalities as well as Jews were the bottom of the rung. Jews and

Christians became Allies against the Muslims. Christians however would sometimes independently fight both Muslims and Jews.

Islam's Influence in North Afrika, the Horn of Afrika and the East Coast of Afrika increased. Arabic became the new Culture and Language, which broke down ethnic loyalties further as everyone Muslim became "Arabic" culturally and Linguistically. Islam was instrumental in the following empires: Kanem; Idrisid; Mogadishu; Maghrawa; Kano; Almurabitun (Almoravids); Kilwa; Almohad; Marinid; Mali; Marinid; Ajuran; Ifat; Songhai; Bornu; Adal; Wattasid; Sennar; Saadi; Dendi; Darfur; Aloida; Kong; Majeerteen; Futa Toro and Jallon; Sokoto; Gomma; Jimma; Hobyo; Harar

800 AD The Walls of Benini are re-built during the reign of Queen Bilikisu Sungbo and they become known as the Sungbo Eredo

Between AD 900- 1300 The kingdom of Mapungubwe on the Confluence of the Shashe river in the now Limpopo Province of South Africa was still powerful due to the strong culture of gold and ivory trade that continued to prosper along the east coast of Afrika to India and China, when the Trans-Saharan Trade routes were taken over by the Muslim Caliphates and West Afrika became the Gold leader in the Continent. It is Considered the most influential and important Iron Age site in Southern Africa in this time period. The Musanda (Royal Citadel) was on the Hill, where the Priestly King and his Military kept watch over the Confluence to see any invaders and protect the flourishing community of over 5000 people living and working in the valleys below.

950 AD: The Ishmaili Shia Fatimid Caliphate gains control of Northern Tunisia and Algeria, its influence reaches the entire North West Afrika... Morocco to Nigeria...

969 AD: Fatimid dynasty takes Egypt from Turkish (Ottoman) Empire, they desecrate the Pyramids, taking some of the stones to build the City of Cairo. The Caliph, el-Hakim then went on to Persecute Coptic Christians for 25 years: 996- 1021AD leading to Christians converting to Islam, so that today, the first Afrikan Nation to receive Christianity is 99% Islamic. The Coptic Church however, still stands. After a devastating defeat, the Sudanese Christian State of Makuria signs the Baqt Treaty with the Muslim State of Egypt at Dongola. This Treaty sees the state of Makuria having to capture and deliver 350 slaves every year to Egypt. This Treaty lasts 700 years. To preserve their own population, Slaves were captured from other Dynasties all over the continent, as far South as Today's South Africa. This is the reason today it is believed that all the "Bantu/Sub-Saharan" genetic heritage of Egypt is attributable to Slavery.

1000 – 1591 AD, The Songhai Dynasty succeeded Mali and spanned today's: Benin, Burkina Faso, Guinea, Guinea-Bissau, Mali, Mauritania, Niger, Nigeria, Senegal, The Gambia, was one of the largest states in history on the continent. Its most prominent city was Timbuktu

1040 AD: Yahya ibn Ibrahim, who was a leader of the Amazigh, Gudala Tribe, converted to Islam. After his conversion, he went to Mecca for his Hajj (Pilgrimage). When he returned to his home, he tried to implement the things he had learnt there, which the locals found too rigorous and they ran him out of Town. His Teachings finally found root amongst the Lamtuna Empire of the Sahara in 1040 where he initiated the Al Murabitun (Almoravids) Dynasty. The Dynasty grew to Western Sahara, Mauretania and Morocco where They took over the Trans-Saharan Trade routes and established the City of Marrakesh as their new Capital. From there, the Dynasty spread as far South as Senegal and as far North as the Iberian Peninsula, Suppressing the Visigoth Empire again. The Al Murabitun set out to Convert all of Afrika and Iberia to Islam, starting in North Afrika. Thus in the first Century, Islam dominated North Afrika, East Afrika and the rest of the Mediterranean world. The Almohads took over from the Almurabitin to continue Islamic rule in Spain in the 12th Century. Spain reclaimed its sovereignty in 1212 AD. During the later Scramble for Africa, Spain "Picked" the Lands of their former Rulers as their Colonies. To Date Western Sahara, Mauritania and Morocco's Relationship with Spain is turbulent.

1095 – 1291, The Latin (Roman) Christians organized themselves Militarily to overthrow Islamic Rule of the Mediterranean and North Afrika. These were bloody wars that in Iberia were referred to as Reconquista wars. Islamic Rule would be Restored by the Mamluks in 1291 until 1516. This 400 years of Religious war created deep wounds between Islam and Christianity, so that there is simmering Animosity, Intolerance, fear and suspicion of one by the other.

In the start of the Crusade in Iberia (Al Andalus) the Muslim Moors were deposed, by the Christian Visigoths in 1492, in what was later termed the Reconquista wars. It is estimated that as many as 100 000 Moors perished and/or were enslaved. Both Moors and Jews who did not convert to Christianity were expelled from Spain. In a period of 117 years, between 1497 and 1614, 500 000 to 800 000 Moors were expelled in boats to North Afrika, forfeiting their Properties, whilst others died on the journey or whilst refusing to be expelled. This Expulsion, created deep generational wounds that still fuel talk of expulsion of "Settlers" in South Africa, whenever racial tensions amongst the indigenous Afrikan and the Settling Afrikaner and British simmer.

In Uganda, these expulsionist notions were acted upon, when 60 000 Asians who were British Subjects in Uganda, were expelled by Idi Amin on 08 November 1972.

The Crusades and expulsion of Afrikans from Iberia made Islam more attractive and it took root in North; West and Horn of Afrika. Islamic Conversion was also less upsetting than Christian Conversion, because it was more lenient to Afrikan Traditional beliefs such as Polygamy. Its Linguistic and Cultural Impact conferred Arabic Identity on Afrikans who followed Islam. Islam also created Trade and increased Formal Scholarship opportunities. This Scholarship was responsible for the beginnings of Afrikan Historical writings in Modern Scripts as found in Timbuktu. Heavy taxation of Christians in places like Egypt also forced further large numbers of Coptic Christians to convert to Islam.

Ṣalāḥ al-Dīn Yūsuf ibn Ayyūb (Saladin) of the Ottoman Empire, overthrows Mamluk Rule in Israel in 1187, This rule lasted until 1917 when It was overthrown by the British. British Rule lasted until 1948 when the last British troops withdrew from Israel and the State of Israel was declared.

In the same year of the Saladin's Conquest of Israel in 1187 AD, God appears to, King Gebre Mesqel Lalibela of Ethiopia of the Zagwe Dynasty, in a dream and commands him to build 7 Thekenu Churches in Aksum that would serve to symbolize: spirituality and humility (ubuNtu), as well as to represent the New Jerusalem in Ethiopia, since the "old" Jerusalem (in Kanaan) had been captured by the Muslim leader, Ṣalāḥ al-Dīn Yūsuf ibn Ayyūb (Saladin). These are Constructed between the 7th -13th Century AD, in Lalibela in the Amhara Region of Ethiopia. An Obelisk (Thekenu) is a tapered Monolithic Pillar hewn from a single piece of Rock, usually Granite. In this Tradition, each Thekenu Church, was built from a single piece of rock. These Churches, which are still functional, were declared as World Heritage sites by UNESCO in 1978. They are part of a long tradition of Ancient Egyptian Thekenus, built by the Pharaohs in honor of God. The Egyptians, placed them, in pairs at the entrance of temples. Most have been carried off to France, UK, USA (Central Park New York), Netherlands, Turkey, Poland and Italy (In the Vatican City), whilst, 11 are still standing in Egypt, including one at Cairo Airport. This Thekenu Tradition was taken over by the Western Church who build Obelisks as part of their Church Structures.

1200 AD the Regional Polity of Mapungubwe was succeeded by Dzimbabwe and the Regional King was known as the Muwene whilst the region of his influence was called Mutapa in Tshishona and Tshikalanga. Muwene we Mutapa (The King of the Mineral (Gold) producing Belt/Domain). Muwene reignal title much like the Khandake of East Afrika, Nana of West afrika and the Pharaoh (Pfareli) of North Afrika. We (of) Mutapa is a conjugation of Matope and u Tapa (u Tapa is to Flick, Matope is of Alluvial Gold mud). These Kings tended to be Mighty Militarily and got a Reputation of being Ravagers, especially in the Advent of the Portuguese whom they repulsed in War often.

The Muwene lived in the Dzimbabwe Citadel. Dzimbabwe (House of Stones...) is the largest single stone built structure in Southern Afrika. It is an Architectural marvel in the league of the Pyramids and the Sungbo eredo, in that it is circular, the stones that are built as high as 10m high, 6m wide and 244m long are held together by geometry. There is no mortar between them and almost a 1000 years later, they are still standing, not withstanding earthquakes, invasions and other calamities. It was a Metropolis of a population of between 18000 and 25000. The city which was 7square kilometers was organized around a lineage associated with the city itself and then the extension of Authority beyond in Southern Afrika.

When The Portuguese came into contact with Southern Afrikans at what is now Mozambique in the 13th Century and learnt of the Polity's area of influence, namely, the Present day Countires of: Namibia, Botswana, Zambia, Zimbabwe, Mozambique and South Afrika, they named the Polity's area of Domain: Mono Motapa as a Mispronunciation of Muwene we Mutapa

The People under the Domain were from different Dynastical families, speaking Dynastical Languages that were similar to each other but not the same. Due to Close similarities, people spoke their own language to each other. This practice is very clearly demonstrated today in places like what is now called Limpopo where in a group one person will speak KhiLobedu and the respondents will answer in SePedi, XiTsonga or LuVenda and Shona.

Dzimbabwe's Polity was succeeded by Zvongombe also in present day Zimbabwe. When Mwene Mutapa fell under Portuguese meddling in 1450, Khami Empire became the new regional Polity. Khami is famous it for holding the record for the longest decorated wall in the entire Sub-Sahara region. These are 6m high by 68m long retaining walls of the precipice platform which bear a checkerboard design along the entire length.

1230s AD: The Ancient Empire of Ghana declines and is Succeeded by Empire of Mali under Mansa (king) Sundiata Keita after he defeats Sosso ruler Sumanguru. Mali Monopolises the Trans-Saharan Gold Trade Route and produces 50% of the world's Gold. Mansa Musa of Mali becomes the world's Richest Ruler (even by today's Standards (See Part 1: Their Contributions). Timbuktu becomes one of the

Most important learning centers of this time, attracting students from the Continent, the Middle East and Spain.

The Iberian Connection is resurrected and Strong Trade relations between Benin and Portugal are re-instated, wherein Palm oil, Pepper and Ivory products are Traded for Manilla and Firearms, necessitating a visit to Lisbon by Benin's Ambassador.

1317 AD: Christianity Collapses fully in North and East Afrika and Dongola Cathedral is converted to a Mosque. Islam is established as the dominant Religion in North, West and East Afrika

This is the Time of Cities, Towns and Markets in Afrika, Comparable to those of Europe at this time. Interest in the Afrikan Continent as a whole increases in Europe.

14th century – Empire of Mali reaches its peak.

Queen Amina of Zazzau expands the Zaria emirate through a series of wars.

1471AD: The Portuguese arrive on the Gold Coast to establish a permanent Trading Port. In 1482 AD, they begin building Elmina Castle on the Gold Coast

1488 AD: Bartholomew Diaz goes round the Cape of Good Hope, He is the first in Modern European History of Navigation to go round the South African Cape to establish a direct route with India and he named it: Cape of Storms. As Many as 20 Ship wrecks have occurred in these waters

1490 AD: First missionaries come to Kongo from Portugal and the King converts to Christianity.

1492 AD: 03 August, The Italian, Christopher Columbus from Genoa, set sail from Spain to find an All Water Route to Asia (Asawu), 2 Months later on 12 October, he lands in the opposite direction... The Bahamian Island of Guanahani (San Salvador)

1497 AD: The Portuguese begin to Build Multiple Forts around the Coast of Afrika and Commission expeditions to search for "New Worlds".

Portugal Commissions Vasco da Gama and his Team, to investigate a Sea Route between Portugal and India. He departs from Lisbon on 08/07/1497 and anchors on 07/11/1497 at the Southern Part of Afrika (0°,0°) IIHui! gaeb, and Names It Cape of Good Hope. He barters for cattle with Khoe Nations and Passes. He then Anchors at Kwa Xhosa, what is Today called Mossel Bay, on the 25/11/1497. His interaction with the local people is not recorded.

Later, he Anchors at the Southern-East Coast of Afrika: Kwa Zulu and names it Natal: 16/12/1497 (some sources say 24/12/1497). There are no Records to say what the interaction with amaNgcobo (now a part of the Zulu Kingdom) who lived in the area was like, however, in their next Trade voyages between 1552 and 1689 (137 years), the Portuguese would experience a Series of Shipwrecks off this Coast of KwaZulu. The Noord became the first vessel to Moor at the Durban Bay. Unable to salvage it, The Crew of the Noord, settled with the Native amaZulu in the various Communities, becoming Assimilated in those communities.

Next he anchored at Inharrime, which he names: Terra da Boa Gente (Land of the good people), following the Hospitality vaTsonga show him and his Crew. At Mozambique Island however, the interaction with the locals was hostile, as Christian-Muslim Tensions surfaced. He Bombarded the Town to prevent the locals following after him, and sailed away. However, his Notoriety was to precede him at Mombassa where he was almost avenged for the Mozambique attack but he managed to foil the attack and moves on to Malindi. At Malindi, the Welcome was better and he was provided with an expert Pilot, who helped Steer the boat to India. He arrived in India, Calicut on 21/05/1498 and Exclaimed: "For Christ and for Spices". He then returned to Lisbon on 09/09/1499.

These expeditions and the Iberian Peninsula Exposure, gave Europe a better sense of the Afrikan Continent and Tales of Afrikan Wealth Spread in Europe. Afrikans continued their Settled Lifestyle in Peace, Happy, Well Nourished and Healthy. Producing and Consuming their own goods as well as Trading with their Trading Partners. They fell in love, Married, Had Children and Raised them within their Cultures and Traditions. Curing diseases and advancing Technologically. The Life of Afrikan abaNtu/baTwa, in Antiquity, was not in "black and white" as we so often see depicted in books. It was in color, as is seen in their Art. The sun shone then, fully and brightly, as it does Today. Afrikan abaNtu/baTwa, thought of themselves the same way that we do about ourselves, today. They thought of themselves as Equal to All Men and they did not perceive themselves as Black People. They described themselves as People: abaNtu/baTwa. Then they would use their Genealogic Praise to locate themselves within families and Nations. They had their own way of Worship, but were keen to learn new Spiritual Revelations as they are an open-minded Society.

At this time in History, the West had become aware of the Lucrative "Half Way" Station to India in the South of Afrika at IIHui! gaeb, which they named, the Cape of Good Hope. There are many Capes all over the world, a Cape is a Promontory or Projection of Land into the Sea. There are 10 Capes along the Afrikan Coast, including the 3 in South Africa: Eastern Cape; Western Cape and Northern Cape. Tales of the Beauty, Sophistication and Wealth of Afrika, gained traction in Europe especially amongst those with Iberian/Al Andalus Connection: Dutch, British, Spanish and Portuguese. An unspoken Competition for Afrikan Trade Agreements and Routes usherd in the Age of the Conquistadors. Anyone with any means, sought to Conquer the "New World" in search of a better life. These were either Merchants or People Commissioned by European Monarchies, who wished to increase their wealth and broaden their influence over world affairs.

The four Monarchies involved in the Iberian Coast: Britain, France, Visigoth Germanic People, Spain and Portugal began in the 15th Century to jostle for Power, looking for "The Gold of Ophir", for their Gold Bullion, with which they could safeguard their Investments against currency fluctuations. They also sought the Spices and Luxuries of the East. Being The Intervening Continent between East and West, and also having demonstrated Wealth, Afrika became the Playing field upon which the dreams of Europe would be realized. "A No Man's Land" (Terra Nullius) Ready to be conquered.

The Portuguese, Start the Competition, by gaining concessions to build Trading Posts along the Afrikan Coast. They build More than 60 Forts around the Afrikan Coast line for Trade. These would later be used to hold Slaves before being Transported to Portugal, France, Britain, Spain, America, Brazil, Haiti...They Displace the Arabs from the Trade Hegemony over Afrika.

The Below is a Table of the Forts and Castles that were built around Afrika for Trade:

Fort	**Host Country**	**Investor**
Elmina Castle, 1482	Ghana	Portugal. Taken over by Netherlands: 1637-1872 and Britain: 1872-1957
Sao Catano, 1505	Mozambique, Sofala	Portugal
Real Castelo, 1506	Morocco	Portugal
Mazagao, 1514	Morocco, El Jadida	Portugal. Taken over by Morocco: 1769-1912 and France: 1912-1956
Saint Anthony, 1515	Ghana	Portugal. Taken over by Netherlands: 1642-1872 and Britain: 1872-1957
San Sebastian, 1520	Ghana	Portugal, Taken over by Netherlands: 1642-1872 and Britain: 1872-1957
Sao Sebastiao, 1558	Mozambique Island	Portugal
Sao Sebastiao, 1575	Sao Tome and Principe	Portugal, Taken over by Netherlands: 1641-1644

Sao Miguel,1576	Angola, Luanda	Portugal. Taken over by Netherlands 1541-1648
Real de Sao Filipe,	Cape Verde	Portugal 1857
Cacheu, 1588	Guinea Bissau	Portugal
Jesus,1593	Kenya, Mombassa	Portugal. Also used by Oman and Britain
Muxima Fortress, 1599	Angola, Muxima	Portugal, Taken over by Netherlands: 1641-1648
Kambambe Fortress,	Angola, Kambambe	Portugal 1604
Fort James. 1663	Gambia	Britain

In a Span of 70 years, the Portuguese had Traversed Afrika West to East: Angola, Kongo, Zambia, Zimbabwe, Mozambique. Having converted the King of Kongo to Christianity in 1497, they Noticed that the Countries South of the Zambezi River paid homage to a Regional Polity, referred to as Muwene we Mutapa. Not understanding the Concept, they Thought the area of the King's Jurisdiction was to be perceived as one contiguous Country, thus naming Modern Day: Namibia, Botswana, Zimbabwe, Mozambique, South Africa, Lesotho and Swaziland: Mono Motapa.

1502 AD: Juan Cordoba, a Portuguese, is the first identifiable European Merchant

to send an Afrikan Slave to "The New World" (Americas) In South Afrika, amaNguni, baSan and baKhoe are part of the International Trade Routes through Maputo and Kongo. Now ships are beginning to make stops at the coast more often and they start Trading directly with these, affecting the Balance of Power as Monarchs lose their control over Trade Routes.

unregulated, these Trades are sometimes unjust and end up in fights between the Europeans and the Natives.

1503 AD: Antonio de Saldhana, Portuguese Fleet commander is injured in one such incident in IIHui! gaeb when he follows a stream from Table View to the foot of Table Mountain, and tries to do a deal with baSan. baSan considered the deal unfair and negotiations failed, leading to a "Scuffle" and Saldhana and his crew had to depart.

1510 AD: Francis de Almeida's Crew tries to Kidnap San Children and steal cattle. They are also driven back. Earlier that year on 22 January, King Ferdinand of Spain had authorized a shipment of 50 Afrikan slaves to be sent to Santo Domingo. This was the Start of the Systematic Transportation of Afrikan Slaves to the New World.

1513 AD: Leo Africanus visits Timbuktu in Mali, West Afrika. He came from Granada in Iberia, to see its famed Libraries and Universities. He would write: "More wealth is to be made here from the selling of books than from any other form of Trade". Every other house hold had a Library in Timbuktu and the people loved learning.

1519 AD: Fernando de Magalhas (Magellan), Portuguese, sailed for Spain with a fleet of 5 ships to Circumnavigate the Earth, Departing on: 20/09/1519. He anchored at IIHui! gaeb (what would later be named Cape of Good Hope) on: 27/04/1521, and Trades there... Some Scholars Claim that a battle ensued between him and an Alliance of baTwa and amaXhosa, however he was ultimately Killed in the Philippines by a Crew member because of his leadership style that disintegrated his Fleet. Only 1 Ship returned to Spain in 1522

1553 AD: Britain sends an expedition to Benin in Mali, and establishes a trade Relationship. In June 1580 Queen Elizabeth 1 Commissions Sir Francis Drake on a voyage around the world and whilst passing the Cape area he remarks: "This Cape is a stateliest thing and the fairest Cape we saw in the whole circumference of the Earth." He named it, Cape of Good Hope. 1600 – 31 December, The English join the Race for the Trade Route to the East and Establish the East India Company.

It was a Company Established for the Exploitation of Trade with East and South East Asia as well as India. The Company later became an Agent of British Imperialism in India and acted as a Catalyst for British influence in Asia.

1602 – Johan van Oldenbarnevelt founded the Dutch United East India Company (Verenigde Oostindische Compagnie – VOC), a chartered company, incorporated by Shareholders and granted exclusive rights by royal charter for the purpose of trade, exploration, and/or colonization by any means necessary. The Aim of the DEIC was to send ships (Built by the company) to East Asia to buy: Pepper; Cinnamon and other Spices and trade them on European Markets. It successfully eliminated the Portuguese competition who had been in the game a whole century before it.

1610 – The English East India Company Train a baTwa Intermediary at the Cape of Good Hope for Trade with locals whose name was "Coree". The Crew of the Hector kidnap "Coree" to England to Teach him more English so that he can further British interests upon his return. He is returned in June 1614. He uses his knowledge to further his own interests instead and was not very cooperative. "Coree" is killed by the Dutch in 1626 for refusing to give them food.

1626 – The British groom a Replacement intermediary, from amongst a different family of baTwa, who lived nearer the Beach and whom the Dutch named "Strandlopers". He was a Chief and his name was Autshumato. Autshumato was given an English name: Harry, and became known as Harry, the Strandloper.

1631-1632 Kumkani Autshumato is taken to Bantam to learn English and he gets to work as an Intermediary between the Dutch, the English and baTwa.

1647- On its return journey from India, in March 1647, the Dutch ship, the Haarlem, ran ashore in Table Bay. The Ship could not be salvaged and whilst some of the crew were able to return to the Netherlands with a ship that was on its return journey, sixty sailors had to stay behind. They had to wait a year for a fleet to take them home. During their time at the Cape of Good Hope, they were allowed by the Local baTwa Chief to Build Shelter, Plant Vegetable Gardens and hunt game as well as trade with the local baTwa (Khoe and San). This experience of Hospitality gave the Crew Confidence to Recommend the advantages of the occupation of the Cape as a Refreshment Station in 1649. The Recommendation was made to the Directors of the DEIC (VOC) to establish a Refreshment Station at the Cape of Good Hope.

1652 – The DEIC Commissioned Janze van Riebeeck to establish a Refreshment Station and a Layover Port for DEIC ships at llHui! gaeb, Cape of Good Hope in what is today, South Africa. This ensured that Crew would remain healthy, without the terrible scurvy, for the duration of the voyage. This Reduced the company's overheads and ensured a better Profit. Trade figures confirm the growth of the DEIC business after 1700, because of the Refreshment Station, According to: www.tanap.net/content/voc/organisation,

The land he came to establish a Layover station in, was not known as South Africa, which only came into existence in 1910. It was a land of various related Nations who lived symbiotically, as Settled Farmer amaNguni and baSotho with their now related vhaLemba and abaNgoni brethren together with the Pastoral bakhoe and the Hunter baSan Nations. Their Towns, Markets, Royal Citadels and Cities dotted the whole of Southern Afrika, interconnected by wide imZila (Roads) leading also to the Coast where they Traded Internationally and recently more exclusively with Portugal. The Various Nations had their own Royal Households, most of whom paid homage to the Muwene we Mutapa Mavura Mhande, who at the time of Janze van Riebeeck had just signed a treaty of vassalage with the Portuguese. This treaty also signaled and ending to the sphere of influence of Mutapa over Southern Afrika reducing it to present day Dzimbabwe only.

Some of the more well-known Dynastical thrones and cities (Yes South Africa's first City is not Cape Town...) of Southern Afrika at the time are: Danangombe (Dhlodhlo); Manyanga; Thulamela; Manyika; Bokone City in Watervaal Boven. Mpumalanga; baTswana City of Kweneng in Johannesburg; Taung; boTlokwa; Cango Caves; Manyanga (Intaba zika Mambo) in KwaZulu; Nhandare (Naletale); Phalaborwa

City in Phalaborwa; Dzata City in Venda; Fura (Aufur and later ophir) Butuwa; Torwa; Maravi; Merina; Rozvi; Ndwandwe; Mthethwa; Zulu; Xhosa; Bhaca; Thembu; Sekhukhune; Morolong; Mokwena; Mulobedu; and as many as the more than 821 426 surnames of South Africa (Those listed are so listed as an example, not because they are the only legitimate dynasties)...There are many Dynasties and their Stone walled Citadels are scattered all over Southern Afrika, of which close to 300 are known in all current 9 Provinces of South Africa in Private farms with Afrikaans or English names, making it almost impossible for the descendants to recognize their Ancestral homes. Suffice it to say, if you ever hear of an Archaeological site, that simply means: "Digging around your Ancestral Home to Study the Settled Lifestyle of your Ancestors".

Not surprisingly as per van Jaarsveld whose History of Afrikans had to be recorded by civilized Europeans on their behalf as well as the later Bantuist School of thought, the Narrative tends to associate the earlier Cave Towns and sometimes even the Stone-walled cities, with only baSan, whom they have erased by pushing out of South Afrika, Assimilating and designating Coloured, so that, these civilisations can be the civilisations of the extinct baSan or an unknown people. The very Historian's own words though, claim that baSan were Hunter gatherers who did not remain in the same geographic area for more than a few years, so how did they build cities? "Bantus" are negated, unheard and silenced all the time when they tell the histories of their citadels and caves. Dzimbabwe was only acknowledged to be the Legacy of "Bantus" as late as 1960. Now when you read the Tour Magazines, Plaques at Tourist sites and History Books on South Africa, you will have a better understanding as to why you can't find yourself until suddenly your Ancestors are either running away from Shaka or Stealing Cattle from Trek Boere... Those of you who are so, called, will use your callings/careers/skills to correct the Afrikan Legacy. I am just a voice in the Wilderness... "Hear ye the Word of the LORD". Use this Book as a Resource to drive your Idea for a Dissertation. Be rest Assured, whatever I have mentioned in this Book, is readily available in many volumes of books and journals.

In 1798 AD, Napoleon Bonaparte (French), invaded Egypt. In an Arabic Proclamation, he assured the Egyptians that he had come a s a Friend to Islam and the Ottoman Sultan, to Punish the usurping Mamluks and liberate the people. One of the first European Nations to "Intervene" in Afrikan and Arabian Politics whenever they had something to gain from it? When Napoleon died, his Successor entered into negotiations with the ottomans and the Convention of Al-Arish (January 24, 1800) agreed to evacuate Egypt. This did not work as Kleber who sponsored the Agreement was deemed to have exceeded his authority. In 1801 a Triple embargo ensued from the British, Ottomans and British Indian Forces. it was during this time, that the French found the Rosetta Stone. From this time, Modern day Travellers and explorers began uncovering the monuments of Ancient Egypt and in 1822 AD, using the Rosetta Stone, the Hieroglyphs were deciphered for the first time, by Modern Linguists, as this had been written in the Ancient Kemitic Language and interpreted into Greek. This is how the Ancient language of Egypt was revived and people today can read Ancient Egyptian. The Suez Canal was built 1859 to 1869, and during this time, Egyptologists began formal excavations in Egypt. French rule lasted until 1882.

These invasions on the North and the South of Afrika, attracted other speculators to Afrikan invasion which was becoming frenzied, thus a Conference was convened in Berlin to come up with a solution that would abate European War for afrikan Resources.

1885 – 1914 saw Afrika carved up by Europeans as Europe Scrambled for Afrikan Resources in what became known as the Scramble for Africa. The Scramble divided Nations into separate countries and created concepts of Ethnicity and Tribes, which divided Afrikans and stirred Mistrust and Xenophobic feelings as Afrikans are made to believe that they are unequal to each other and that some Nations (Ethnic Tribes) are more sophisticated than others, have more European Features or are more prestigious than others.

Egypt which was already under British rule during the scramble in 1885, continued under British rule. When the British defeated the French, they took the Rosetta Stele and it is on Display at the British Museum since 1802. Some of the other copies that Ptolemy had ordered to be placed in every Temple in the Land have apparently been found since and are housed in various Museums all over the world.

A year after Libya gained her independence as the first Country to do so, "At 07h30 on the Morning of July 23 1952, the voice of Anwar Sadat came over the Radio to Announce that, for the first time in **2000 years**, Egypt would be ruled by Egyptians. Egypt had gained her Independence from Britain and from a long line of Invaders since the Hekau Khasut.

Her Borders are now based on the Cartography of the Scramble for Africa. She is now separated from the Civilisations that helped build her as a Gateway City and the House of God. Hwt-ka-Ptah.

The People of the Land have now become fully Cosmopolitan with Genetic Heritage from: (K)Hamitic (Kushitic, Misraimic and Phutitic) "Bantu" or Nubian Afrikans; (K)

Hamitic Levantine Kanaanitic Arabs (some of today's Palestinians); Achaemenid/ Iranian Arabs; Greek; Roman; Turkish; Arabs; Indians, French and English. They have a 9-12% chance of showing genetic make-up from any of these Nation groups. They are Afrikans, Their Language is Afro-Asiatic (Afrikan and Asiatic Languages).

Although Egypt does not Classify People racially, she does struggle with Racial Intolerance, especially against those who are obviously Kushitic/Nubian or "Black". They are often derogated as slaves, the Legacy of the Baqt Treaty... Which has ensured that the only Memory of (K)Hamitic Afrikans in Egypt, is that of them being Slaves. The population of Egypt, currently stands at 101 Million people. Egypt, the Maghreb, Sahel and Horn of Afrika Countries are now part of the Arab League of Nations because they are Lingo-Culturally Arabic. There is now an Arab Afrika and a Sub-Saharan Afrika... In the beginning, it was Not so.

Salungano

Take Time and Summarise your Learnings from Part 2 of this Narrative. How will you allow what you have learnt to influence your life?

Part 4: Imperialism

**"Why should I be driven across the river?
I am an old woman, I have been here since I was a child,
I have brought children up here; and some of them have died before me,
and their graves are here. I have been living with my own people in my own country, and I have done nothing to make the governor
deal so harshly with me. What, have I done?"
Nonesi, Queen of abaTembu as quoted in Holden, W.C, The Past and the Future of the Kaffir Races (1886:440)**

Muwene we Mutapa falls

The Historical Narrative, will now Focus on South Afrika, as a sample Narrative of the Colonisation of the various parts of Afrika, which subsequently became packaged as Countries. The Scramble for Afrika which happens 233 years into the invasion of Southern Afrika, will be narrated in Isolation at the end and prior to the Conclusion of the Book.

Monomotapa, on Public Domain at: https://commons.wikimedia.org/w/index.php?curid=9029799

World Maps at this time Referred to Afrkca as Aethiopia and Africans were called Aethiopians in general. Thus the naming of Afrikan led churches in the 1800s as Ethiopian Churches (Amatopiya).

When Janze van Riebeeck arrived in Muno Mutapa, in 1652, to Establish a Refreshment and Layover Station for the Dutch East India Company, He found the First Nations of what was later named South Africa: The Native, Indigenous, Aboriginal, Autochthone Afrikan abaNtu/baTwa of Khoe, San and Nguni descent. These people, lived a settled Lifestyle, with Established Towns and Markets. They had established Religious, Political and Social systems as well as long-standing established International Routes with their Trading Partners from Arabia, India, China and Portugal. According to Oral Tradition and as Attested to by: Dobler, G (2009), baSan, amaNguni and Khoe Nations dwelt peacefully with each other in a mutually beneficial relationship coalescing seamlessly, so that it was not always possible to distinguish one Nation from another. The Empires were independent political entities and polities, held together by loose tribal lineages, that could be broken and reformed as necessary. They Traded with each other, Consulted each other on Spiritual and Political Matters and Intermarried and recognised each other as related Nations. It is from this Cognition that Queen Nonesi bewails the forced removals of her people, what was happening was unfamiliar to her. In her continent, when a Nation subdued another, it did not forcefully remove them from their father's land unless it was taking them as captives.

Kingdoms occupied well defined areas of Towns with dwellings surrounded by Farm land, followed by Grazing land and then large Stretches of Forested Nature Reserves that abutted on the Forested Nature Reserve of the next Kingdom. This would be followed by grazing land, Farm land and then the Town with dwellings of the next Community. The entire Coast was uninhabited in terms of there being settled Cities, as it was considered to be prone to Natural hazards and it was part of the wild Nature Reserve with well-defined Dumping sites (Middens). These Nature Reserves are the reason for the ease with which it has been for the Colonial Government to Fence off Nature Reserves All over South Afrika. Southern Afrika has a Total 506 Nature Parks. The Megafauna Conservation Index Assesses the Spatial, ecological and financial contributions of 152 different countries towards conservation of Megafauna. Afrika dominates the Top Results, with Botswana scoring 100%.

Animals were understood to be as Native and Autochthonous to the Land as everyone else, with a right to an undisturbed habitat. baSan, and to a lesser degree, Khoe Nations Were Watchers of the Woods and Trekkers (Able to follow/Track Animals or people for long distances). Their Skills helped to keep the Sedentary amaNguni, informed of what was going on outside the City gates. This is the reason why baTwa were easily cast in the role of Intermediary between the first Settlers and amaNguni and why they were the first people to be encountered by Janze van Riebeeck.

The Nature Reserves, helped to create a Natural barrier and Protection, against Invaders. The Inhabitants understood the habitat of the Animals, and knew where to Travel, and the Animals generally avoided the Mizwila (Highways) that humans used. The Invader would unfortunately not be familiar with the territory, and their disturbance of the ecosystem helped to alert the inhabitants of the possibility of an invasion.

A Stranger would be forgiven to believe the Stretches of Forest were "Empty" of people and available for Occupation. The Wild Nature Reserves are the first areas that the Colonialists Settled on, this is also part of the reason why they were not vehemently opposed the second they landed on what the Portuguese had termed Costa de Cafferaria (Coast of the Caffers, referring to the Southern Coast of Afrika. This would later become South Africa). abaNtu/baTwa did not expect anyone to Settle in these unpredictable and wild areas Permanently... They only opposed the settlers when they started expanding to the Grazing and Settled lands and when they erected fences that cut off Access for locals to their Holy Woods, Rivers and Seas.

According to Joyce, P (2007:8) "Contrary to the myth that became an accepted fact by later generations of Afrikaners, the earlier Afrikaners knew from their various earlier Treks inland, that the land was not "empty" of people, and that inland settlement would involve agreements with local tribal groupings and on occasion, outright war and conquest." The Voortrekkers who were smaller in number and were just looking for a better life, tended to intermarry and Assimilate into the indigenous Nations, producing some of the first heritage mixed descent people of Muwene we Mutapa.

South Africa, as a State, resulted from the appropriation of part of Muwene we Mutapa Lands that belonged to baSan, baKhoe and amaNguni Nations, after waging wars with them, that provoked wars amongst the various Afrikan Nations as they were thrust upon each other by the invading Settlers, which lasted close to 250 years. These wars were concluded with Conquered lands becoming the British Cape Colony; British Colony of Natal (which became Natalia Republik and again British Colony of Natal); Afrikaner Orange Free State Republik and the Transvaal Republik. The intervening unconquered parcels of land would always represent a conundrum. This was solved by pushing Afrikans out of these swathes of land, which were then handed out to Settling Europeans as Farms. The displaced Afrikans were then pushed together into pockets that the Apartheid government tried to convert into Independent Non-South African Countries. Of the current 40 000 or so farms in South Africa which are still predominantly owned by white people, most are larger than 16 square kilometres in size and the largest (about 85 farms, are 120 square kilometres in size: Durban to just before Mooi river). The average Afrikan person in South Afrika is still Landless. Those who own land in the form of a Township home, own 150 square metres, whilst their Suburban White Counterparts owns 1200 square metres. Afrikans who live in the "Tribal" lands, do not own Land as Afrikan land is Inalienable (Dissimilar Law Practices in one country, a legacy of Colonisation and Apartheid...)

After a series of brutal wars between the Boer and British Settling Nations, the two Republics and two Colonies, became united in 1910, to become the Union of South

Africa under British Rule. The Union of South Africa became Independent of British rule in 1960 under Afrikaner leadership, when it exited the British Common Wealth and became the Republic of South Africa. The Republic of South Africa became a Democracy in 1994 following a Negotiated Settlement which was followed by open Polls, wherein, the Majority "Black" African National Congress, became the Governing Party of the Republic of South Africa, with the former Ruling "White" Nationalist Party and its "White" Opposition, the now Democratic Party, as well as the predominantly Zulu iNkatha Freedom Party, becoming the Main Opposition Parties.

In 1994, Not Seeking to Polarise the population, and as part of the Codesa Negotiations, the young Democracy of South Afrika, opted to Keep the Afrikaner Name of Country unchanged, as the Republic of South Africa. It also elected to keep the Colonial and Apartheid Governing Administrative Apparatus intact with its Laws and Traditions, repealing blatantly Segregationist laws over time.

Basically the New Government took over, voetstoots:

- The Imperialist British Government and its Culture;
- Its Political Laws,
- Its Dutch-Roman Law,
- Its Western Economic Laws,
- Its endemically Corrupt systems, where the rule of law was designed to generally work in favour of the few settlers, the Ruling elites and White Men;
- The use of the English language and later Afrikaans as languages of the Court and the Economy, tacitly excluding non-Anglophone members of society from justice and global economic networks;
- Free Capitalist Market, which was only legal amongst Colonialists and Afrikaners, and which enriched them, creating a corrupt Relationship between State and Business; wherein Business people were politicians who influenced Government spending in favour of their business industries. Cecil John Rhodes being the most eminent example.
- Structural and Infrastructural bias and injustices;
- Bribery, Extortion, Cronyism, Nepotism, Parochialism, Patronage, Influence peddling, Graft, Embezzlement, Misuse of government power and State Capture by the Rich, wherein the Rich tended to also be the Politicians and whose companies traded with the State. The DEIC, a Company, was the First Government of South Africa, and the South African Government was later built on its Trade Charter Foundations, which enabled, Human Rights Violations.
- Police brutality;

- Repression of political opponents and Media as well as Capture of the Media;
- Unequal taxation;
- Withholding of Licensing and Permits for Natives, Indians and Chinese people;
- Inaccurate Asset registers which allowed for looting of State Assets when Government Handover was done in 1994-1998;
- European Electoral and Campaign Laws...

This Baggage, was taken over, by the Afrikan Ruling Party, "voetstoots", without guarantee or warranty, for them, to Govern the "New Democracy".

The "New" Government, Repealed some blatantly Discriminatory Laws. Whilst some Traditions Were Transformed to better Reflect the "Multiracial" Nature of the Society. The democratic Government and its organs are however, still largely Imperial British and Apartheid Afrikaner. (Much like waking up one Morning and finding a European Monarch on the Zulu Royal Throne, with some Zulu names changed to European Names. This can be compared to Exactly what happened in Egypt with the Ptolemaic Pharaohs).

The Democratic State, has not Managed to build a Nation from the heterogeneous Citizens of the New Democratic Society who are:

- Autochthone, Native amalgamated amaNguni Nations, who are now, so-called Black;
- Autochthone, Native amalgamated baSan, who are now, so-called Coloured and Black;
- Autochthone, Native amalgamated Khoe Nations, who are now, so-called Coloured and Black;
- Autochthone, Native amalgamated mixed heritage Nations, who are now, so-called Coloured and Black;
- Amalgamated Nations of Indian and other Asian descent, who are now, so-called Black and Indians;
- Amalgamated Nations of European and mixed heritage Afrikaner Nations, who are now, so-called White.
- Amalgamated Nations of Chinese and other Asian descent people, who are now, so-called Black and Chinese.

These Labels: Black, White, Indian, Coloured and Chinese, deny people their Identify, History and Heritage. Most people, younger than 70 years, do not know how they came to be: White, Chinese, Indian, Black, or Coloured, nor how that identity, confers upon them or denies them the privilege of being South African.

Indians, Chinese, Blacks and Coloureds on the one hand, are considered, just that: A Misplaced Skin Colour or a foreign Continent of Origin, full stop. Whites, on the other hand, are South Africans. Most whites, also understand why this country is known as South Africa. They also understand, the Governmental Legacy of South Africa and the significance of the "Three Ships". They are well versed, with the law of South Africa, and comfortable with the mechanisms of Lobbying for Changes in these laws... Because, South Africa: is "their Country" and the Law that Governs it, is theirs. Some, amongst them are even determined, to use these institutionalised laws, to get back into the Ruling Seat, regardless of the number of votes they get at the Polls, by using the Law, to: frustrate, hamstring and bog down the Ruling Party in courts, reversing every change made by the Ruling Party, that they dislike, through the courts.

The following Narrative, is the Narrative of the Events that led to the birth of this Democratic Republic of South Africa and its divided people who have yet to Norm into a Nation. Since this History has been extensively covered in History Books, and is readily accessible, I will highlight the Untold Narratives to help the Reader understand the "unsaid", which does, affect the current State of affairs. In order for the Reader to understand their world and the prevailing conditions that enable their particular experiences, so that the reader is Empowered to determine their own Future going forward. For Non-South Africans, the Narrative will help them get context to the Media Headlines.

In 1652, The Profit making DEIC did not expect to create a Settler Community in the Cape Colony. Unfortunately, as time went on, *European Politics* spilled over on to our shores creating the Perfect Storm that necessitated Settlement of the Cape Colony and later the rest of South Africa, De-stabilising Afrikan baSan, baKhoe and amaNguni Nations since then to date. The Destabilisation Waves are still in flux, as more than 80% of "Black" South Africa still does not understand what is this Democracy that now rules us, except that we have the right to Vote... (This is perfect vernacularized English....)

One can glean from van Jaarsveld (1975) that the Dutch and later the British who arrived on the shores of South Africa already knew the American Experience of how the few can Dispossess the many of their Land and when this became necessary, the Tactics were put to good use.

- They knew that the Local Inhabitants were not Violent and generally Welcoming (ubuNtu) and that concessions to build and Trade could be attained.
- They also knew that War with advanced Artillery would be sufficient to subdue a small Kingdom and that the other kingdoms were unlikely to interfere in the

fight, unless the threat was deemed National, as the Locals preferred dialogues to Confrontation.

- They Knew that there were enough Europeans who sought New Lands to Settle outside of Europe for Political and Religious asylum, as well as for Economic opportunity. They also knew that Bringing in these Settlers and Uniting them under one "White Race" would increase their Populations and fortify them. Settlement opportunities attracted Political and Religious refugees as well.
- They knew that Once Settled, they could use their Laws to Govern the New Territory using Proclamations, Forced Removals and Displacements to Non-Arable "Reservations" of the Natives and thus Creating Economic Dependency toward themselves.
- They knew that they could Create a Two State Nation, wherein there is a White State that supplies goods to a captive Native (Black) Market who have no means of production and have to pay Tax.
- They knew that Divide and Rule tactics work and they went about Teasing out Ethnic groups into separate identities and Nations and forcing them into Reservations for these Nations and subsequently creating Competition amongst them.
- They knew the Vulnerabilities of Local Nations to Foreign diseases and how these had wiped out Multitudes of the Natives in the Americas.
- They knew that to build Infrastructure in the New land they could use Indentured Labourers and Slave Labour, forcing Natives to accept Low wages and undermining their Resistance to the Invasion.
- They knew that there was Mineral and other wealth in the Land because of the North, East and West Afrikan experience, and they knew that these regions traded with the South (Gold of Ophir Notions).

Cape colony and the first Resistance Wars

06 April 1652 to 07 August 1795 DEIC (143 years) Rule

On 24 December 1651, Janze van Riebeeck, his wife, his son and a crew of 90 indentured labourers (Company Servants) and a Board of Directors for this Mission, Set Sail as a fleet of 3 ships: The Dromedaries, the Rejigger and the de Goede Hoop, from Texel, Netherlands for what had come to be known in Europe as Cape of Good Hope... the Most beautiful of all the Capes. This voyage was intended for the setting up of a Refreshment Station and Layover for the DEIC ships enroute to India. They Possessed a Royal charter which gave them Carte Blanche authority for purposes of trade, exploration, and/or colonization by any means necessary.

On 05 April 1652, IIHui! gaeb Land (as it is known to the Native Khoe and San) is sighted and on 06 April 1652, The 3 Ships dock at what is now known as Table Bay, Western Cape. Kumkani (King) Autshumato continues to be their Interpreter and Intermediary.

Within a week of Arrival, Construction work on the Fort of Good Hope had commenced in the Middle of what is today Adderley Street in IIHui! gaeb (Cape Town). It was constructed with Mud and would be reconstructed with Stone as the Military Grade Structure that it is, in 1666. It is the oldest Colonial Building in South Africa (354 years old in 2020). Older Afrikan Structures 200 000 years old and dated to only 1500 years ago have not been re-enforced, they remain unrecognised, unacknowledged and unprotected in Private farms and are regarded as Ruins, rather than buildings. In South Africa, all buildings older than 60 years are protected by the New Resources Act of 1999, but Not so, the Ruins...

The Castle has served as Living Quarters for the first Settlers; Local Headquarters for the South African Army in the Western Cape; Prison for slaves and high profile Resistance Prisoners from Inception and Seat of Government in 1811. In 1936, it was declared an historical monument and It is now a Military Museum. In 2018, Statues of some of the Early Resistance Leaders of South Africa were installed at the Castle of Good Hope as an acknowledgement of and to embrace our Past, toward Conciliating the people of South Africa. The Statues installed are of: Kumkani Doman wa maCoChonqua (Khoe Nation); iNkosi uCetshwayo wa maZulu; Kumkani Langalibalele wa maHlubi; Kgoshi Sekhukhune wa baPedi. In 2020, the first ever South African Muslim Heritage Museum opened at the Castle to showcase the rich Muslim Heritage and the contribution of Islam to South Africa.

Meanwhile, In Europe:10 July 1652 to 05 April 1654, the Dutch Republic and England became engaged in a Naval War, which Necessitated the Settlement of the Cape Colony by more Settlers in order for the Dutch to maintain their Naval Dominance in the Atlantic Ocean Waters. This necessitated more extensive Farming, which, in turn, necessitated more labour than what the 90 indentured labourers had capacity for.

The Native Khoe Nations, baSan and amaXhosa were unwilling to work farms, preferring to continue with their Herding and Hunting Lifestyles, wherein they, Produced and Consumed their own Food, Clothing and Utilities and Traded with the surpluses for whatever they could not produce. For the Land provided all that they needed and their Law created an enabling environment.

The Company thus forcefully enslaved Khoe and San Nations, empowered by the DEIC Charter. They also imported Slaves from Jakarta in Indonesia, Madagascar, Mauritius and the East Coast of Afrika at Delagoa Bay and Sofala to work the Farms. (Black Afrikan, Black Malagasy, Asian Indonesians from the various nation groups of Jakarta who are Malay speaking people, which in south Africa were just lumped as Indian)

The First Foreign Slave to arrive is: Abraham van Batavia (a man from Batavia in Jakarta whom they named Abraham. His birth name is unknown). He arrived in 1653.

The same year, King Autshumato is Accused of stealing Company cows and sent to Robben Island. His !Oroloas (Ward) spelled Krotoa in Dutch and used as her name and whom they further name Eva, worked for Janze van Riebeeck as Translator and Home Manager. She intervenes on behalf of King Autshumato and he is released after serving a 2-year banishment. He is re-instated in his former position as Fort interpreter. Eva later married Pieter van Meerhof, the first recorded Colonial-Native Mixed Marriage in the Colony.

Kumkani Autshumato becomes wealthy as he is in a position which allows him to Trade with various people. He empowers his community and his Military becomes strong and feared by the Company. This fear simmers to date in South Africa. It is responsible for the lack of Transformation in the Economy, wherein, Large White- led/owned Companies will not support nor skill small Afrikan (Black) led Companies for fear that these will one-day grow and become competitors to the White-led Companies. It is believed that if an Afrikan led company thrives, Afrikans will use their Majority numbers (49m vs 4m) to turn that Afrikan Company into a large company overnight and thus supplant the White-led Company. In severe cases, the small Black (Afrikan) led companies are sabotaged as Banking friends will not support the Afrikan-led companies with funding. If they survive and thrive, the Tax man will be at their door and has no problem pushing these small companies into liquidation or dissolution even though the law prohibits this. Taxation is a Specialty in the Bachelor of Commerce Training. Accountants are costly. Many people who start businesses, do not know when to start engaging the services of an Accountant and often times, they do not have Book Keeping Skills, nor do they know what source documents to keep and how to file them. This tempts many to contract Accounting Skills on an ad-hoc basis and sometimes fall prey to Tax officials who, for a fee, will produce Tax Certificates for them, filing erroneous information just to get a Tax Certificate printed. After 5 years, when the business is viable, these practices catch up with the small company and they are faced with a Tax Liability that they can't pay and they are deemed either negligent or evasive and as per the new Tax law, Tax Administration Laws Amendment Act of 2020 (promulgated during Covid 19 Lock down), they can even be imprisoned. All the Tax ignorance violations that small black-led Companies commit are deemed "Willful and without Just Cause". The decision as to the willfulness, is determined by someone who sits in the Tax office and interacts with data... Never having met nor seen the business owner or business in question and the impact of that business upon its community. The inability of the business owner to defend their actions makes their actions willful and without just cause. According to a Businesstech article of February 2020, "Henceforth, your intention does not matter – where you "negligently" fail to comply or make certain mistakes on your taxes, you commit an imprisonable criminal offence." In a Country where Unemployment is high and small businesses are encouraged, why is Tax not taught as the third Language? After all, it is a Language. It is supposed to be the language of ubuNtu. Contributing to the wellbeing of those who are unable to do so, through the entrepreneurial talents of those who can.

In South Africa in 2021, one can be imprisoned for:

- Failure to Register details with SARS or to notify them of any changes to one's details;
- Failure to Appoint a representative taxpayer or to notify SARS of such Appointment or change in representative taxpayer;
- You receive compensation for assisting someone with their taxes and you fail to Register with SARS as a Tax Practitioner;
- Failure to submit a Return when required to do so;
- Failure to Retain all substantiating records;
- Failure to provide any information as and when requested by SARS to do so;
- Failure to appear and comply when one is requested by SARS to attend a meeting or hearing in order to give evidence;
- You are issued a directive or instruction by SARS and you fail to comply;

- You fail to disclose any material information to SARS or you fail to provide SARS with any Notification as required under any Tax Act;
- You are notified by SARS to pay an Amount on another taxpayer's behalf in settlement of a Tax debt and you fail to do so;
- You have a withholding obligation and you fail to withhold or deduct the Tax correctly and pay it over to SARS.

Whilst these Steps are bold and necessary, the problem remains: "When did SARS do a Nation-wide Campaign to teach the hundreds of Thousands of enthusiastic businesses how to do all the above?" A visit to the nearest Tax Office is enough to discourage anyone... The queues are long. The Officials Busy and Impatient. An average young black South African changes their address 3 to 4 times a year due to the exhorbitant Rentals. The Act Assumes: Access to Phone, Email, Physical Address, Data and Taxation working knowledge... The very Taxes that enslaved and criminalized Afrikans as will be elaborated later, are being resurrected for the same purpose in the guise of protecting the fiscal purse and making Big Business Pay. The Truth is that Big Business wrote the Tax Laws. Big Business knows how to work the System. Big Business Pay their Accountants well and they make sure they are well versed with taxation, so that they are Squeaky Clean when it comes to taxes and in fact, they get big Tax Rebates Annually. It is the small black- led Business that will be shut up and the owner Imprisoned and remain with a Life- long Criminal Record. A simple exercise by SARS could see them never having to destroy any business and imprison anyone in their effort to help people Practice ubuNtu. SARS can run a Basic 1Week Tax Course for new Business owners at their offices. 52 Trainings in a year, for a Class of 40 people is 2080 people Trained at each SARS office x 100 branches = 208 000 people literate in Tax in 1 year.

In1655, two more Intermediaries Are Appointed to the Castle: Khaik Ana Makouka and Doman, in a bid to reduce Autshumato's power. Both men are Leaders in their Communities. They become his Protégés' but are unhappy with his approach to Resistance.

The increased Farming Demands saw the Company issuing Permits in 1657 to nine (9) of the 90 Company Indentured Labourers/Servants who had become Free from their Indentured Servitude to the Company and who named themselves Vryburghers. They were given permission to Settle and Farm along the Liesbeeck River in order to deal with a Wheat Shortage. They were given as much land as they could cultivate in three (3) years to sell the Harvest exclusively to the DEIC at prices determined by the DEIC. The 9 Vryeburghers established two Colonies. They Could select a piece of Land "as Long and broad as they wished".

Harman's Colony Amstel/Groene Veld): Herman Reemanjenne of Cologne, Spain, a Marine; Jan van Maartensz de Wacht of Vreland, a Marine; Jan van Passel of Geel, a Soldier; Warnaar Cornelisz of Nunspeet, a Boatman; Roelof Jansen of Dalen, a Soldier

Stephen's Colony (Rondebosch): Steven Jansz Botma of Wageningen, a sailor; Hendrik Elbertz of Ossenbrugge, a Cadet; Otto Jansen of Vreede, a Soldier and Jacob Corneliz of Rosendaal, a soldier.

These families and the balance of the 90 original Settlers who later joined suit, have kept these Farms in their families since then (350 years). Some have sold them for a profit, Creating unimaginable Generational Wealth. The Land that the Dutch East India Company (DEIC/VOC) gave them was the Appropriated Nature reserve, Grazing Lands and Dwelling Lands of baKhoe; baSan and amaXhosa Nations.

In 1658, some slaves that were under arrest escaped from the Fort. Janze Van Riebeeck takes King Autshumato hostage and transfers him to Robben Island in a bid to force his military to return the slaves in return for his release. King Autshumato becomes the first man to successfully escape Robben Island by rowing a boat back to the Mainland. He and the other Intermediaries continue to use their Positions to further their own Personal and National interests, often playing the Westerners against each other.

The Establishment of Farms, Injustices against baSan and baKhoe Nations, increased encroachment on baKhoe and baSan Land, Banishment from Sacred Sites and sources of Water and Medicinal Resources that left baTwa vulnerable, Application of DEIC Charter Law on baTwa (San and Khoe Nations) to disposes them of Cattle and Land as well as unfair Trade, lead to two (2) major Wars which were triggered by seemingly unrelated Incidents that provoked the deep seated wounds.

The first Khoe-Dutch War is led by Doman in 1659. This is followed by a series of What is referred to as "Skirmishes" in Literature but which are far from that. They were wars in which people lost their lives, fighting for their land, their rights and their livelihoods. These were the first Armed Struggles to liberate South Africa. King Autshumato helps to broker Peace and a Treaty is entered into, that lasts for a few years. King Autshumato dies in 1663.

Janze van Riebeeck remained Leader of the Cape Colony for 10 years, until 1662. He was Promoted to Secretary of the Governor of Jakarta (Batavia East Indies). When he left the Settlement for Jakarta, there were: 132 officials, 35 VryeBurgher Farmers, 15 Women, 22 Children and 180 Slaves. These are the only people that are listed in the population Census of South Africa for 1662, to date. The register shows the population in the Cape in 1658 as 360 (sic) people.

The Population of baSan, baKhoe and amaXhosa who lived in this area was never acknowledged and still isn't. Their number may not be known, but they can be acknowledged in population lists issued by the New Democratic Government that reflect Population of South Africa from 1652, to avoid perpetuating the myth of an empty land. Scientists are very clever at Estimating such numbers. The Population of Britain is boldly given as 2 million people in 100 AD by Mattingly, D. (2007), as for example. It should thus not be difficult taking into consideration all the factors, to estimate the population of baKhoe, baSan and amaXhosa in the Cape Colony area in 1658, unless of course we wish to erase them. It is not surprising then, that the population of South Africa and Southern Afrika in 2020 is still grossly under estimated.

The Statues of Janze van Riebieeck and his wife, Maria de la Queillerie, remain in Adderley Street, IIHui! gaeb. The Coat of Arms of the City of IIHui! gaeb (Cape Town), in 2020, is allegedly based on that of the van Riebeeck Family and the Western Cape Coat of arms now bears symbols from that Coat of Arms as well: A Cluster of Grapes, an Anchor, a Crown, a Quagga, a Bontebok and a Khoi Clay Pot with a conical base, with the Motto: Spes Bona (Good Hope).

In 1665, John van Arckel became the first Minister of a formalized Dutch Reformed Church in the Cape Colony. Although Bartholomeus Diaz, a Catholic, did hold Mass on the Island that would become known as the Island of the Holy Cross, which is found off the coast of today's Port Elizabethan Coast (Gqeberha) in December 1487 or January 1488, No other Churches were permitted in the Colony except later (1688). The Lutheran Church, however, had been permitted from 1665 as more Germans Settled in the Colony, followed by the Anglican in the 1795 as Chaplains to their Soldiers, the London Missionary Society in 1799 and the Catholic Church only in 1837.

The Second Khoe-DEIC war took place in 1672 when baTwa from King Gonemma's Nation ambushed and plundered an Afrikaner Hunting Party. This led to a series of battles in 1672, 1673, 1675, 1676 and 1677 when a Treaty was finally reached. baTwa had been at war for their Land since 1510 when their Children Were Kidnapped, a period of more than 150 years.

The colony rapidly expanded into a settler colony in the years after its founding. Segregation of South African people began. Segregation was a divide and Rule Policy of the Settlers to ensure their safety. The earliest of this was in the form of a Hedge that Janze Van Riebeeck planted in 1660, to prevent baKhoe and baSan interacting with the Colony. The Almond Hedge would cut baTwa off from their Sacred places and Resources. This Celebrated Hedged is now a National Monument and parts of it can be seen at the Kirstenbosch National Botanical Gardens. Although Van Riebeeck is celebrated as the the person who planted it, the Trauma it created on baKhoe and baSan is still not acknowledged on any write up about it. Further, people were Segregated legally and Scientifically through Classifications: Natives or Indigenous People and Settlers. Literature between 1652 and the 1800s and sporadically in the early 1900s Classified All Afrikans as Indigenous and Native but a perusal of Reports, as the years go by, will reveal that these terms became reserved for Khoe Nations and San Nations as the amaNguni family was divided into ethnic groups and Tribes and Classified as Bantu and Black, erasing them from South Africa.

Later, Some of the Vryburghers Named themselves indigenous Afrikander and later Afrikaners, completely severing their ties with their Native lands and Appropriating South Africa as their "Vaderland", They became the Afrikans whilst the Afrikans became Bantu and Black.

The Revocation of the Edict of Nantes sees French Protestant Worship become unprotected from Persecution from the Majority Catholic Church in France. This forces French Huguenots (Protestants) to flee to various countries including the Cape Colony. By 1692, a Total of 201 French Huguenots had settled at the Cape of Good Hope. Simon van der Stel (a mixed heritage Afrikaner whose mother, Maria Lievens was an Indian woman from the Coast of Goa) became a Governor of the Colony and he set aside land for them at a Settlement he named: The French Corner (Franschhoek) and Drakenstein (Paarl). They are later Assimilated into the Afrikaner Trek Boer population, ensuring, a "pure" European lineage in South Africa. The French were experienced Oenologists, thus they Farmed grapes. The Wine Route, and its wealth is their Legacy. These were later joined by close to 4000 German Males from all Germanic Speaking Nations of Europe: Germany, Sweden, Denmark and Belgium between 1652 and 1806. Today, 40 French Huguenot, Germanic Surnames and about 1020 Dutch surnames survive in South Africa. All these were given Land to settle on, upon their arrival in South Africa. This land was appropriated from the Native baSan, baKhoe and amaXhosa Nations of the now Western Cape. Since these First 4000 Germanic Settlers, were mainly Men and the French Huguenot Settlers did not have sufficient European women for them to marry, they married some of the Slaves, Khoe; baSan and amaXhosa women, whilst other just had Children with them without marrying them, creating a Mixed Heritage Nation that would later be classified as Coloured. This Nation would suffer some of the most gruesome atrocities

Consequent to the Settling of Muwene we Mutapa as they were divided by virtue of their phenotypic features into: Black, Coloured and White by virtue of the Judgement of an Inspector, who was sometimes assisted by his infamous Pencil... The Pencil Test, ruthlessly divided families and created generational trauma, colourism and insecurity. The precursor to this separation had been when the Afrikaners separated themselves from their amaGoringaicona (Griqua) mixed heritage descendants, who did not "look fully white". Afrikaners named these descendants Basters. Their famous Leader was Adam Kok. The "Basters" (amaGriqua) trekked with the Trekboere out of the Cape Colony into "Kafferaria" as a separate Nation. They would align themselves with each other against amaXhosa and later, other amaNguni Nations. This caused deep wounds between amaNguni and mixed heritage amaGoringaicona (Coloured people). That persist today.

The Cultural Mix of People developed a new language named: Afrikaans Kinderduitz (Kitchen Dutch. A Language created by those who worked in the Kitchens as they sought a way of communicating with each other and their Slave masters). It was first written in Arabic by the people who created it, the Slaves of East Afrika, Jakarta, India, baSan, baKhoe and amaXhosa. Afrikaans features, Afrikan, Arabic, French, Dutch and English words. (Cape Town Slave Museum documents). Today it is the Language of Afrikaners, Coloured people and Black people (especially in Orange Free State and Pretoria), about 7 million people. Another 13 million people speak Afrikaans from having learnt it at School.

Later, in a bid to reduce the amaNguni Afrikan population Statistics in the Cape Colony, when the Government took a Census, they would designate everyone who was not White in llHui! gaeb, as Coloured (Cape Town Slave Museum documents). This was done, so that the Population of the Cape Colony, would comprise only of: Coloured people and White people, Expunging and Erasing baKhoe Nations, baSan nations, amaXhosa Nations, Malay and East Afrikan people, from the Cape Colony and today's Western Cape Province. It is this Classification that is responsible for the wide spectrum of Cape Town's "Coloured" people from the very Dark with curly hair to very Indian to very Malayan and to very white with Blonde and Blue eyes.

It is also the reason why 300 years later we can have a Historical Narrative that says: "*Traditionally the Western Cape has not been inhabited by black people in large numbers. This is however changing at a rapid pace as a migration is currently underway. Black people from the Eastern Cape and other parts of South Africa are moving into Cape Town at a rate of about 50000 people per month and with no housing available for them, they are building shacks on any piece of open ground they can find. This influx is causing the local authorities major headaches as they strive to house the influx of people*" Cabanga, O! (exclamation of bewilderment)

The Dutch expanded their Occupation of the Cape serially, pushing baKhoe, baSan and amaXhosa out of the Cape Northward into today's Northern Cape, Free State Province and the countries of Namibia and Angola as well as Eastward to today's Eastern Cape and KwaZulu-Natal. This trend continued throughout what is now called South Africa, Afrikaner Free Burghers who also name themselves Trek Boers (migrant Farmers), trekked in-land into what they called Kafferaria. They disposess Afrikans of their Land, based on their Calvinistic Dutch Reformed Worldview and of their Reading of the Biblical Book of Joshua, where God tells Joshua and the Israelites in their quest to Possess Kanaan: "Every Place on which your foot Shall land I have given it to you", as God's Providence for the Trek Boer, to disposess the Southern Kanaanites. Some Afrikaners align themselves with Israel on this basis and believe that their "struggles" are the same. They do their best to establish Republics everywhere their feet landed. These Settlements were met with great upheaval and the abovementioned centuries' long wars as well as wars with the other amaNguni Nations later on.

The British later serially disposess the Afrikaners of these Republics that they had created until the Republic of South Africa is formed in 1910.

baTwa populations that were vulnerable due to their Nomadic Lifestyles were rapidly reduced through: The Small pox epidemic; Slavery, War and being hunted down like animals (on the strength of the DEIC Charter that gave the company carte blanche authority to do whatever was necessary to establish their Trade). They were also reduced through Assimilation into the Coloured, Afrikaner and amaNguni Populations. They were pushed further and further into the Desert North of the Cape, where they became trapped into Child Slavery (them voluntarily selling their children for survival), Cattle Thieving, Indentured Farm Labor and Alcoholism (10 Hot Tots Wages) as they fought to sustain themselves. Small Communities Who Still adhere to the Nomadic Lifestyle remain in isolated pockets of the Cape and are still trapped in the role of exploited Farm Laborers and the scourge of Alcoholism.

By 1824, according to Van der Merwe (1937:153), baTwa had been dispossessed of 80% of their land. This is still their Struggle today, where there is little recognition of their Land, Language and Heritage in South Afrika. They remain Land-less, Face-less, Language-less and Legacy-less.

Since 2017, Kumkani KhoiSan, his wife and six others have been on a Protest Camp at the Union Buildings Garden, Demanding to see the President to hand him a Memorandum with 4 demands (as at March 2021, they were still there):

- Recognition of Khoe and San as the First Nation of South Africa
- Recognition of all their Languages as official Languages
- Return of their Land
- Abolishment of the term: Coloured

In the Meantime, The Traditional and KhoiSan Leadership Act 3 of 2019 was Gazetted on 28 November 2019 by the President, without their input. Gazette 1550

The Traditional and KhoiSan Leadership Act Aims to:

- Provide *for the recognition* of traditional and KhoiSan communities, leadership positions *and for the withdrawal of such recognition;*
- *Provide for the functions and roles of traditional and KhoiSan leaders;*
- Provide for the recognition, establishment, functions, roles and administration of kingship or queenship councils, principal traditional councils, traditional councils, KhoiSan councils and traditional sub-councils, as well as the support to such councils;
- Provide for the establishment, composition and functioning of the National House of Traditional and KhoiSan Leaders;
- Provide for the establishment of provincial houses of traditional and KhoiSan leaders;
- Provide for the establishment and composition of local houses of traditional and Khoi-San leaders;
- Provide for the establishment and operation of the Commission on Khoi- San Matters;
- *Provide for a code of conduct* for members of the National House, provincial houses, local houses and all traditional and Khoi-San councils;
- Provide for regulatory powers of the Minister and Premiers;
- Provide for transitional arrangements;
- Provide for the Amendment of certain Acts;
- *Provide for the repeal of legislation*; and to provide for matters connected therewith.

These Provisions although promising, do not answer any of the (although needing refinement, none-the-less) Legitimate Demands made by King KhoiSan and his Compatriots.

For an in-depth look at Verbatim Journal entries of the Settlers in the 1600s, one can visit: e-family.co.za/ffy/surname_index.htm which hosts such Transcripts from the DEIC's First fifty years Journals. This is a good resource for the Day to Day happenings and the people involved in this Era in the Cape Colony, from the perspective of the Dutch Journal Keepers. The baTwa/abaNtu Version of the Story remains untold, even as this is an Attempt to tell the broad picture of that story with the hope that more Indigenous Authors, Scientists and Researchers will begin to write, and that their writings will be supported by our Government and the African Union and added to our School Carricula.

From the 1700s, Vryeburghers had been venturing out of the Colony into what was named Cafferraria, Seeking Freedom from DEIC Economic domination. Much Intel was gathered during this time that was freely shared amongst Vryburghers. At first, Families Trekked on their own usually joining Native Kingdoms and Assimilating into the Settled amaNguni Nations. Sometimes, they would be given Lands of their own by the Kings, so that some of the Trek Boers were enthroned as Chiefs by the Dynasties they joined, as part of the Custom of ukuSisela, as explained in the Prologue. Honors were conferred on them, Tracts of Land measured out for them and Royal Princesses given as wives, so that they could begin Dynasties and live amicably with the amalgamated amaNguni Nations of baSotho, baTswana, baPedi, baLobedu, vhaVenda, vaTsonga, baTonga, amaSwati, amaXhosa, amaZulu, amaNdebele, that they joined, as was the Custom. They would raise the Children in the Local manner of the people, with the added European Culture, whilst being Bilingual in Speech. The Apartheid Government later brutally separated these families as Some Were Classified Coloured whilst others are Classified Black and yet others, White, alienating them from each other, their Properties and Generational legacies whilst creating deep resentment and generational wounds that still simmer to date, in some families. There are Coloured families where the Grand Children have not seen their Grandparents and some still can't visit their fathers and are excluded from the generational wealth of their families.

Some of these Nations are known as abeLungu Nations. The Most well-known of these Dynasties are:

- Buys Dynasty: King Coenraad de Buys is the Ancestor of the Mixed Heritage Buys People who live in Buysdorp at the foothills of the Soutpansberg in Makhado. They speak Vernacular languages: LuVenda, Sepedi and xiTsonga.
- Henry Fynn Dynasty whose descendants have now been dispossessed of their land as they became designated coloured under the Apartheid regime.
- John Dunn Dynasty. John Dunn was given Land and wives by King Cetshwayo in the Tugela area. He had apparently had 49 wives (one of whom was white) and 171 children.

- Nathaniel Isaacs Dynasty was formed when he became stranded after being shipwrecked off the Coast of Natal. He was given Land by iNkosi uShaka

In 2016, I accompanied my Dad, Dr Matshikhiri Christopher Neluvhalani, to Mapungubwe, where he was invited to speak as an Autochthone descendant of Mapungubwe. He was one of those people who were instrumental in the Repatriation of the Remains of our Ancestors from the University of Pretoria for them to be reburied on Mapungubwe. During our visit, we slept at a certain Bed and Breakfast Establishment whose name I will not disclose, in order to respect and protect their right to privacy. As my companions (Pastor Nevhutalu and Ms Sharon Leith) and I waited for the Check in Team to attend to us, we sat in the pleasant Gardens of the establishment. A Feature in the Garden caught my attention and I went closer to investigate. I discovered that it was, in fact, an Altar, mounted atop a Rock. It was a 3 pole Altar encased at the top with Gold Sprayed animal hide. My eyes "opened" and I suddenly realised the entire mound was a shrine of some sort. I brought my observations to the attention of Pastor Nevhutalu as he is regarded as an expert in both Afrikan Traditional Religion, Judaism and Christianity. He was able to see the entire picture hidden in plain sight in a beautiful Garden... I Asked Sharon to take a picture.

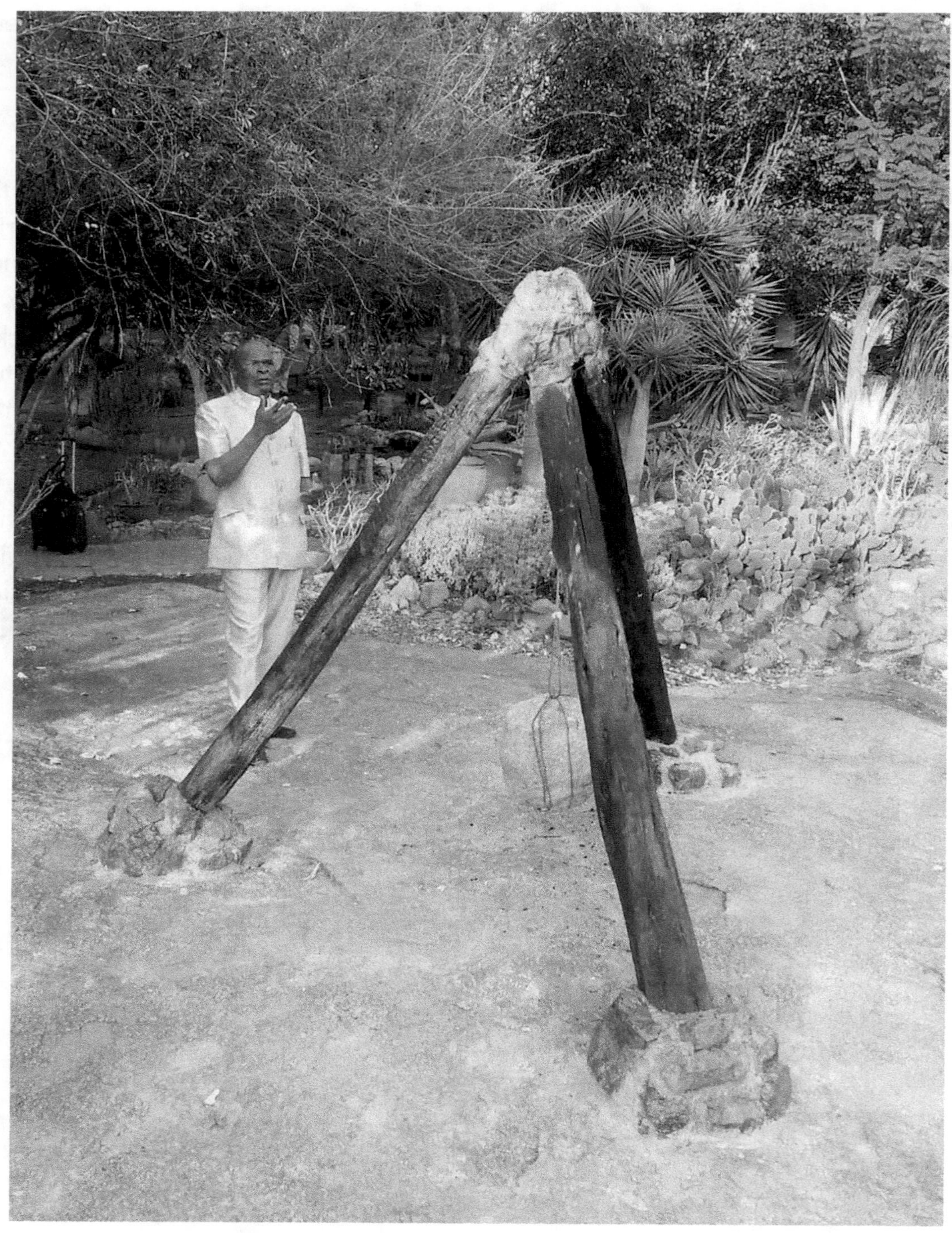

Picture Credit: Sharon Leith. Ps Nevhutalu in the Picture, Author's Personal Property

We were very shocked to find this Kanaanitic Altar in a "white" owned establishment. We were to be dumbfounded by the next revelation... As we waited for the Allocation of our rooms in the Reception area, we Noticed a beautiful Map of South Africa. It was the Portuguese Mono Motapa version of 1571... We wondered why the owners Cherished this Map so much? The answer was to be revealed to us by someone who mistook our identity.

At Dinner that evening as we were minding our own business, One of the Managers came to see if we were fine and "finding everything in order?" Pastor Nevhutalu took that as an invitation and began a conversation with the Manager, and asked: "Tell me about the altar you have in the Garden". I almost fell to the ground from the shock of hearing him ask the question so innocently and brazenly!

The young "White" manager became very excited and animated as he pulled up a chair to join us. He began to rattle off the Plans that "his" people have of Restoring "Mono Motapa". They were an Organisation of the descendants of the San people (sic) that sought to work with some amaNguni Chiefs to Claim back "Mono Motapa" from South Africa, leaving out KwaZulu-Natal as well as the Eastern Cape as those were traditionally English. Their Capital would be at Fhambananalo (a few kilometres from Mapungubwe) on the Mountain of the gods: TshaMavhudzi, where they planned to Build a Pyramid structure that would house the Parliament of "Mono Motapa". The Pyramid would be constructed in Glass and be encased in Gold at its pinnacle, just like the Pyramids in Egypt and they would be Aligned in longitude and latitude to the Egypt Pyramids... he trailed off as his guest, who was an umNguni Chief, arrived and he realised we were not together. He abruptly left us to join his guest and they started speaking in hushed tones.

I was flabbergasted and this is the first time I am sharing this incident...

A perusal of all the History written about South Africa, reflects that it is still written from the Migratory Theory Dominions position, in spite of the scanty and refutable evidence proffered for the Theory. It was deliberately so written and remains unchanged in spite of a "Black Government" being in power, to ensure that the ambitious plans that were accidentally shared with us above would one day come to pass...

Do not be surprised one day, when a White passing, mixed heritage Afrikaner, raises his hand to be recognised as the legitimate bona fide successor, to the baTwa Throne. This chief will then re-Claim the Cape Colony as the Land of baTwa, whist the indigenous and aboriginal baTwa descendants who are currently Classified as "Coloured" and who may not know their San Heriatge or even know that they are "coloured" because they were Classified as Black, remain Landless and without Identity. The long history of Marginalisation of baTwa as well as the unfortunate Afrikaner farm murders, could be used to create a perfect Legal cause for the new Afrikaner batwa Nations, represented by their organisation which is a Member of the United Nations, to lobby the United Nations for the Secession of the Western cape from South Africa. The well documented Genetic Studies that prove their KhoiSan heritage would be used to Justify a cause for the First Nations to be able to gain Independence. South Sudan separated from North Sudan in 2011 on these grounds... Further, a Co-alition can be formed between amaNguni Chiefs and the new baTwa (KhoiSan) Chiefs, to Claim: Orange Free State and the Transvaal to form the New Nation of Mono Motapa and then realise the above dream. Multitudes of Afrikans who no longer know the history of their ancestors will be left landless again.

All of us read the Historical Narrative of South Africa and wonder: "Really? Who wrote this? How Ludicrous? That is not True..."; "But we are also the first Nations..."; "How did they derive that from one Jaw?" We Speak out or complain in hushed tones hoping that the Historians will correct our History. Instead their voices become louder and they teach this history to our children as though it is verifiable Truth. When confronted, they say: "The History of the first Nations of South Africa has never been written, it remains for their Children to tell the Stories of their Ancestors. Maybe one day, they will write." Listening to this on my City Tour Bus in Cape Town as it meandered through the Wine farms, I almost gave myself Angina, then I realised... It is True. Why should they be interested to tell my Story? They do not know my story. They don't want to know my Story, they only know theirs and they are only interested in that. So, as a Descendant of some of the First Nations of South Africa, LET ME WRITE... and, here we are.

Let us be #NoLongerSilent.... Indian, White Afrikaner, White English, White other Nationalities, Chinese, Afrikan (So called: Black and Coloured) ... We can't afford to be divided any longer. We should work together, Acknowledge the Injustices; heal the wounds and build a South Afrikan Identity and Nationality that can create a Better Life for All, because Together We Can, in a South Africa That is Alive with possibility (Credit: Slogans of the ANC, DA and Brand South Africa)

Formation of Colonies and Republics

1737: The Moravian Brethren led by George Schmidt sets up a Mission Station in Genadendaal. It is the first Mission Station in the Land. Schmidt was sent to take care of the Dutch Reformed Church believers, but he also made it his ambition to share the Gospel with baSan. He experienced opposition from both sides and was expelled after converting five (5) baSan.

1741: Pope Benedict the XIVth promulgated the papal bull "Immensa Pastorum Principis" against the enslavement of the indigenous people of the Americas and other countries.

1760: Pass Laws begin to be Passed. Slaves were expected to carry a Pass when going from one place to another. Europeans were allowed to Stop Slaves and ask them to show this Pass. These were expanded in 1857 as the Kaffir Pass Act no. 23 to Control amaXhosa movement into the Cape and later, on a grand scale, by the Apartheid government. It wasn't until 1807 when Slavery was abolished in Britain and in 1834, when this was extended to slave trading throughout the British Empire. The Abolition of Slavery proved to be an important turning point for Vryeburgher boere and Christian Missions: For the Vryeburghers, they could no longer Farm Cheaply with Slave Labour and the compensation they were offered for the loss of their slaves did not satisfy them. For the Missionaries, Human compassion in Europe for the plight of slaves meant that money could be raised to fund the considerable expenses of setting up a mission, paving a way for Mission Stations to be set up all over the world. 1799: The London Missionary Society Arrives in South Africa. Their first work was amongst baSan who still did not respond very positively to the Gospel. However, the Gospel was not completely rejected by them... It was more their resistance to enculturation that made it seem as though they had not received the Gospel. The Christian Community had grown organically albeit syncretically from the first five (5) Converts. This became the trend amongst all Afrikans who went on to establish their own Churches after receiving the Gospel and refusing to practice it in a Eurocentric form, as they sought to see themselves in the Bible and interpret the scriptures for themselves, recognising them as the Scriptures of their Ancestors and abaNgoni or vhaLemba (so called Black Jews/Israelites) who lived amongst them. Some of the Narratives in the Bible felt farmiliar and the Bible was accepted as a Book of Consolation and the Revelation of the God of Afrika. Finding no expression in the "White" Churches however, pushed Afrikans to found their own Churches. The Catholic Missions began in 1837, at Marian hill, in KZN and together with others, was instrumental in offering the first formal Schools and later universities for Natives ("Blacks) in what would later be known as South Africa. Other Missions Also Started on the shores of South Africa in the 1800s, American, Swiss, Presbyterian, Methodist and many others. The Society for the Propagation of the Gospel was one of the late arrivals as it arrived in 1821 and was set up in Wynberg.

1780 – 1784 European Anglo-Dutch War spills over onto the Dutch Cape Colony of Mutapa (what would later be known as South Africa) when it leads to the DEIC losing its State Support and ultimately being dissolved as a Company. Dutch Nations amalgamate and form the Batavian Republic. In 1795, Britain, was again at war. This time, with the French, during the French Revolution. Britain thus took over the Dutch Cape Colony, (since it had subdued the Dutch in 1784), to fortify itself Navally against the French in the Atlantic Ocean. Thus Ended the Dutch's, DEIC, 143-year Rule of the Cape Colony. The Anglican Church which thus far had been denied entry into Southern Afrika, used this opportunity to send Chaplains to troops, in 1795 and 1806, gaining entrance to the Cape Colony for the first time. Britain occupied the Colony until the Peace of Amiens in Muizenberg in 1802, when the Colony was returned to the Dutch Republic, which had Consolidated its Nations to become the Batavian Republic. The Cape Colony and all other colonies of the Netherlands become part of the Batavian Republic: 1803 to 1806.

Several waves of Boer Frontiersmen (Vryeburgher Afrikaner Voortrekkers) who did not settle and become assimilated into amaNguni Nations, kept journeying out of the Cape Colony into the interior of Muwene we Mutapa. A Borderland area called a Frontier would then develop between the advancing Voortrekkers and the Resident amaXhosa, to create a buffer between the two Nations. Whenever the Frontier would migrate, War would break out. A series of 9 wars lasting 100 years were fought between amaXhosa and the Voortrekkers and Sometimes the Colonial Government with or without the support of the Imperial British Government (Britain). Most of the first wars were fought around the Fish river at Cacadu and later the Kei river (Nciba) as amaXhosa and baKhoe Nations repulsed the attempt to create this empty buffer zone. These wars saw the Voortrekker Boere take various routes to penetrate what they called Kafferaria Northward and Eastward, following the path of least resistance. The wars are recorded as the Bloodiest Wars in Africa in Modern History, as amaXhosa fought to retain their Land. The Nine Wars Later Co-incided with wars between The Settlers and the other Native amaNguni Nations, as well as Anglo-Boer Wars, toward the Formation of the Union of South Africa when Europe was Scrambling for Afrika.

1779 to July 1781, Frontier War: the first amaXhosa-Trekker War is triggered when Further Encroachment on amaXhosa Land by Boer Frontiersmen (Vryeburgher Afrikaner

Voortrekkers) now involves inhabited amaXhosa Towns at Cacadu (Zuurveld). The war is triggered when Boers Allege that amaXhosa stole their Cattle. amaXhosa are defeated and forced out of Cacadu

1789 - 1793: 2nd War, Frontier War: amaGqunukhwebe, Xhosa descendants of Gcaleka and Rharhabe who are later split into Pato and Kama Chiefdoms as well as the displaced Khoe Nations Chiefdoms of: Gonaqua; Hoengeniqua and Inqua, penetrate back into Cacadu (Zuurveld) and re-occupy the land.

1799 - 1803: 3rd War, Frontier war: again amaXhosa and Khoe Nations Re- occupy Cacadu (Zuurveld) and other Lands from which they had previously been displaced. baKhoe are allowed to re-occupy whilst amaXhosa are not allowed, in a divide and rule tactic that would prove worthwhile later.

1811 - 1812: 4th War, The British led by Colonel Graham join in the fight and there are Forced Removals of amaXhosa from Cacadu (Zuurveld) and Settling of the area with British Immigrants in what is today Grahamstown, in honour of Colonel Graham. The General John Cradock who was the Governor of the Cape Colony on Reporting on the war is quoted to have said: "no more bloodshed than was necessary to impress on the minds of these savages a proper degree of terror and respect was shed in this campaign." What he meant, was that he scorched their farms and homesteads, confiscated their Cattle and killed some of them.

1814 – Cape Colony is formally ceded to the British Crown by Netherlands. The British paid 6 million pounds to Netherlands for Land that did not belong to them. The Cape Colony Remained a British Colony until the establishment of the Union of South Africa in 1910. The first Governor is Lord Charles Somerset who immediately Lobbies Britain for more Settlers to be sent to the Colony and more so the Eastern Cape area.

1815: The Frontier wars, and the continued Trekking by Voortrekkers, into the interior of Muwene we Mutapa (What they named Kafferaria and would ultimately be named South Africa), causes a Reorganisation of the Settlements of amaNguni Nations as they Crush on to each other Eastward, Meeting with the Amalgamating Zulu Kingdom that is asserting itself as the next Southern Polity. This became known as Dimfecane (The Crushing), erroneously spelled Difaqane in literature. Both the British and the Boers would Align themselves with amaNguni, baKhoe or baSan Nations to fight each other or to fight amaNguni. This alignment would ensure that the Assisting Nation, is helped to Assert itself against their brethren as they fought each other over the now Scarce Resources: Cattle, Land and Trade Routes. The ensuing succession battles within Monarchies, made it easy for a Nation to be captured and converted into a Pawn for Alignment in these Boer-British Wars. The "Ethnic" generational wounds created by this betrayal of brethren caused divisions amongst Afrikans as they ceased to identify as abaNtu (People), but rather as this or the other group which is better than another... so called Tribalism has its roots here.

During this Crushing time, amaMfengu Nation was displaced Westward from the amalgamating amaZulu Kingdom coming to Rest amongst amaXhosa. They became the perfect pawns in the game as they would be pitted against their Hosts on the promise of power. They formed part of the Boer Commandos on the Frontier to fight against the British and/or amaXhosa. They are brilliant horse riders and Sharp shooters and the Voortrekker Commandos would send them out to fight in their battles. Today, amaMfengu descendants have not gained any land that either the Boers or the British gained in these wars. In true isiNtu/kiNtu, they have become part of amaXhosa Nations in spite of the earlier betrayal.

1817: Rharhabe amaXhosa Royal Household had become divided over relations with the Colony. In 1817, this disagreement became an all-out one-day war as Uncle (Kumkani Ndlambe) and Nephew (Kumkani Ngqika) battled in the bloodiest war in all amaXhosa History, weakening the Nation. On the defeat of the British aligned Kumkani Ngqika, The British Raid Ndlambe and take 25 000 head of Cattle. amaXhosa repatriate some of these and are forced by a court of law to restitute them. This leads to a full scale 5th war against the Cape Colony Wherein Prophet and chief advisor of Kumkani Ndlambe, Makhanda Nxele (the left handed one) whose name in literature is captured as Maqana/Makana Nxele, decides to lead a 10 000 amaXhosa Force on an attack of Grahamstown. baKhoe Nations who had remained in Grahamstown when amaXhosa were expelled, led by Jan Boesak enable a colonial garrison to repulse Makhanda, who suffers the loss of 1000 Soldiers. Makhanda Nxele is eventually captured and imprisoned on Robben Island. On June 2018, Grahamstown was re-named, Makhanda in his honour.

amaXhosa are pushed further East to the Keiskamma river and later in the same year, Large numbers of amaXhosa were again displaced across the Keiskamma, by Governor Harry Smith, causing overpopulation and hardship in the area. amaXhosa who remained in this colony are dispossessed of land through the infamous scorched earth tactics. In 1820, the long-awaited 10,000 British sponsored Settlers arrive, 5000 remain in the Cape Colony whilst 5000 are given farms in Zuurveld on the Eastern Cape Frontier, where amaXhosa had earlier been forcefully removed. They were intended to Anglicize the area, make it defensible, offset the Dutch population politically and take up Farming. Most of these settlers who were Merchants however did not want to farm, they retained the Farms but reverted instead to their Trades and built Towns. Some amaXhosa are returned here as indentured servants to the British.

In 1822, Captain William Owen was formally commissioned to survey the South Eastern Seaboard of Afrika, which was now KwaZulu, as the Zulu Nation had now fully Amalgamated after Dimfecane. They wanted to Concretise the Knowledge that they had gleaned from the many Travels to the area by the Portuguese since 1497 and some of whom had Naturalised to the area. They met the local amaZulu, who had returned to their Settled lifestyle in the area, Trading with the Portuguese at Delagoa Bay. Their Settlements were arranged with the Towns, followed by Grazing Land and then Nature Reserves. Durban and the surrounding areas were part of that Nature Reserve (The current CBD was a Swamp and Elephants and Jackals roamed what is today Umbilo, Glenmore, Berea, Resevoir Hills, KwaMashu, Inanda, Umlazi, Lamontville, Morningside, Westville...)

In 1823, the first European settlement arrived on the vessel, the Salisbury. Lieutenant James King and his crew, intended to establish a Trade Post on the South Coast. iNkosi, uShaka ka Senzangakhona, gave them Concession to Establish it. Unfortunately, Lieutenant James King, dies before he is able to use the Concession.

Following this, Francis Farewell, gets a party of 30 men together to leave the Cape Colony and go to kwaZulu, to establish a Trade Port. An advance party led by Henry Frances Fynn arrives on 10/05/1824.

Frances Fynn finds King Shaka in ill health having suffered a mortal wound from an attempt on his life. He Nurses him back to health and he becomes a Trusted Friend. As alluded to earlier, King Shaka honors him with him a piece of land and he gets married to a Zulu Princess uNdlunkulu Mavundlase, who succeeds him to the Throne upon his death. He wrote two books, the Diary of Henry Frances Fynn as well as Meeting Shaka. They are written through a Dominions Lens, but do give a good idea of Life in Muwene Mutapa of yore. Frances Fynn played a Crucial role in gaining King Shaka's tolerance for the settlement of the British Traders at what would become Port Natal. King Shaka thus gave the Merchants Concession to develop a Port at what is today the Durban CBD. The British would later Claim that they were given 6000 square kilometres of land, (Slightly larger than Northumberland, a sovereign state in the UK), bounded by the Indian Ocean on the East, the uThukela River on the North and Pietermaritzburg on the West. They begin work on the Port and Settle there.

In 1828, iNkosi, uShaka, is assassinated by his brothers: Dingane and Mhlangana. In his death throes, King Shaka gives his brothers this eerie prophecy: "Angeke ni li buse, li zo buswa amankengana" (You will not reign over this land, it shall be overrun by the foreigners). His brother Dingane, succeeds uShaka as King of amaZulu.

Intervening the Wars, The Criminal Procedures Act no. 40 of 1828 is enacted. This Act, is largely Accusatorial: "Guilty until Proven otherwise". Hence, the Accusations of Cattle thieving on whose balance a war would be waged, as the accused is deemed guilty until proven otherwise... This Act, and its Amendments, were Consolidated in the Criminal Procedure's Act, 56 of 1955, which is currently Law in South Africa. The Accusatorial Nature of our Law is Responsible for the way the South African Criminal Justice system works in Charging people, and the way the South African Media Reports its News on any Subject, wherein people are presumed guilty as long as they have been charged or served with a matter. The practical dilemma that face(s) 2020/21 the African National Congress with its "Step aside Rule" is created by the Accusatorial Nature of our Law: "guilty until proven otherwise" thus a member has to Step aside until the Criminal procedure is completed as they are presumed to be guilty.

1834 – 1836: 6th amaXhosa War, British governor, Sir Benjamin D'urban, believed that Kumkani Hintsa ka Khawuta, Paramount-Chief of amaGcaleka, commanded authority over all amaXhosa and therefore held him accountable for an attack on the Cape Colony, and for "looted cattle". D'urban goes to the frontier in December 1834, where he leads a large force across, the Kei River, to confront Kumkani Hintsa at his residence, and dictate terms, to him, which were as follows: That further amaXhosa land: Keiskamma to Kei River be annexed and become Queen Adelaide Province, with King William's Town as the seat of Government. The new province was declared to be for the settlement of: amaXhosa "Tribes" Loyal to the Cape Colony. The rulers of the amaXhosa "Tribes" deemed Rebellious were replaced with British approved rulers. Usually these would be from the amaMfengu Nation as it was hoped that they would gradually, with the help of missionaries, undermine amaXhosa tribal authority. Kumkani Hintsa Refuses and war ensues. On 17 September 1835, Kumkani Hintsa is Murdered and his body is brutally Mutilated. This Campaign destabilises the area, leaving 7000 people of all races homeless, and Prompting the Piet Retief Manifesto on 02/02/1837, at what is now known as Grahamstown. The Manifesto was followed by the Great Trek. Queen Adelaide Province was dis-annexed and D'urban repudiated. Stockenstrom became the new Governor of the Eastern Cape, and he managed to establish a workable treaty between the British and amaXhosa, Leading to a 10-year period of peace.

The Great Trek (Die Groot Trek), began in earnest after the publication of the Retief Manifesto, which listed the reasons for the Great Trek. There were several parties, the most prominent of whom were three, led by Andries Pretorius, Hendrik Potgieter and Piet Retief as the Prominent Leaders. There are Towns in South Africa that still bear their names: Pretoria; Potgietersrus and Piet Retief. The Commandant in Chief was Petrus Dirk Uys (Dirk Uys Street is off Umbilo Road in Durban). Adam Kok's amaGoringaicona (Griqua) also joined in the Trek. The Alignment of amaGoringaicona with Boers, Cemented the later Black-Coloured Suspicion and Tensions.

These were their Reasons for Trekking out of the Cape Colony enmasse: 1835 - 1846

- Dutch-British Bitterness:
- Dutch-British Bitterness and Anti-British sentiments were high amongst Afrikaners because of the various Wars they had experienced with the British in the Cape colony and in Europe. The Secession of the Dutch Colony to Britain in 1814 meant that Afrikaners would be under British Rule. This was unacceptable.
- The abolition of slavery:
- The abolition of slavery meant that Vryburghers could no longer own slaves. Firstly, this made farming life more difficult. Secondly, Although Britain allocated the sum of 1 200 000 British pounds, as reparation to the Dutch settlers for the "loss of slave labour", the Afrikaner farmers had to lodge their Claim for this Compensation in Britain. The Voortrekkers disputed both this requirement and the amount being offered.
- The Liberal view of Britain on the Status of Afrikans in their Native Land as equals, meant that, All Slaves: Native Khoe Nations, Native baSan, Native amaNguni, Colony Settlers and Afrikaners were now equal in the eye of the British Colony. This did not sit well with the former slave owners. The Liberal view had resulted in the hanging of 6 Afrikaner leaders, by the British Colony, when these (Afrikaners), killed some Khoe men for "Stealing" their Cattle, a matter that would have been inconsequential prior to the outlawing of slaves.
- 1820 Settler Competition:
  Britain supported the 1820 Napoleonic wars Financially. The wars negatively impacted Britain, leaving it with Serious unemployment problems. To alleviate the unemployment problem, the Cape Colony Government encouraged the unemployed Britons to come to the Cape Colony to settle the land of amaXhosa, that they had named British Cafferaria, in what is today, the Eastern Cape. The Importation of British Settlers was an attempt to strengthen the eastern frontier (KwaZulu) against the Trek Boere, providing a boost to the English-speaking population of South Africa, so that the English population would be more than the Afrikaner Dutch. The settlement policy led to the establishment of Albany, a centre of the British Diaspora. 4000 of the approved Applicants arrived in

the Cape in 60 different parties between April and June 1820. They were granted farms around Bathurst in what is toady Eastern Cape but most did not have farming experience, So, they kept the Land but reverted to their Trades and settled the areas today known as: Grahamstown, East London and Gqebera (Port Elizabeth). A group of them also continued on to kwaNgcobo (what became known as Natal) in KwaZulu, in the time of King Shaka, and are some of the Merchants who established Durban.

The 1820 Settlers are commemorated in Grahamstown by the 1820 Settlers' National Monument which opened in 1974 and is supported by the 1820 Settlers' Association which was founded in 1920. There are genealogic sites on the Internet dedicated to Keeping their Ancestral Lineage alive.

- The 1822 Proclamation which provided for the gradual establishment of English in place of Dutch, as the official language of the Cape Colony, irked the Afrikaner Community which had already firmly established Afrikaans as the official language there.

Below is the **Manifesto of the Emigrant Farmers (1834)**, Copied from Wikimedia, public user license. The Wikimedia Author copied it from the original document as published in the Grahamstown Journal (February 2, 1837). It read thus:

A document has been handed to us, with a request to give it publicity, purporting to be the causes of the emigration of the colonial farmers – of which the following is a literal translation:

Numerous reports having been circulated throughout the colony, evidently with the intention of exciting in the minds of our countrymen a feeling of prejudice against those who have resolved to emigrate from a colony where they have experienced for so many years past a series of the most vexatious and severe losses; and as we desire to stand high in the estimation of our brethren, and are anxious that they and the world at large should believe us incapable of severing that sacred tie which binds a Christian to his native soil, without the most sufficient reasons, we are induced to record the following summary of our motives for taking so important a step; and also our intentions respecting our proceedings towards the Native Tribes which we may meet with beyond the boundary.

1. We despair of saving the colony from those evils which threaten it by the turbulent and dishonest conduct of vagrants, who are allowed to infest the country in every

part; nor do we see any prospect of peace or happiness for our children in a country thus distracted by internal commotions.

2. We complain of the severe losses which we have been forced to sustain by the emancipation of our slaves, and the vexatious laws which have been enacted respecting them.
3. We complain of the continual system of plunder which we have ever endured from the Kaffirs and other coloured classes, and particularly by the last invasion of the colony, which has desolated the frontier districts, and ruined most of the inhabitants.
4. We complain of the unjustifiable odium which has been cast upon us by interested and dishonest persons, under the cloak of religion, whose testimony is believed in England to the exclusion of all evidence in our favour; and we can foresee as the result of this prejudice, nothing but total ruin of the country.
5. We are resolved, wherever we go, that we will uphold the just principles of liberty; but whilst we will take care that no one shall be held in a state of slavery, it is our determination to maintain such regulations as may suppress crime and preserve proper relations between master and servant.
6. We solemnly declare that we quit this colony with a desire to lead a quieter life than we have heretofore done. We will not molest any people, nor deprive them of the smallest property; but, if attacked, we shall consider ourselves fully justified in defending our persons and effects, to the utmost of our ability, against every enemy.
7. We make known, that when we shall have framed a code of laws for our future guidance, copies shall be forwarded to the colony for general information; but we take this opportunity of stating, that it is our firm resolve to make provision for the summary punishment of any traitors who may be found amongst us.
8. We purpose, in the course of our journey, and on arriving at the country in which we shall permanently reside, to make known to the native tribes our intentions, and our desire to live in peace and friendly intercourse with them.
9. We quit this colony under the full assurance that the English government has nothing more to require of us, and will allow us to govern ourselves without its interference in future.
10. We are now quitting the fruitful land of our birth, in which we have suffered enormous losses and continual vexation, and are entering a wild and dangerous territory; but we go with a firm reliance on an all-seeing, just, and merciful Being, whom it will be our endeavour to fear and humbly to obey.

By authority of the farmers who have quitted the Colony, (Signed) P. RETIEF.

Column 2: A practical illustration of Retief's Point 1

Evidence taken at Fort Beaufort (summary): Farmer Johannes (Jan) H. Engelbrecht, who resided at Christian Bester's farm, Kat river, was found murdered. A young farmer, Hercules Marx, found that Engelbrecht's horse had returned at sunset to the farm with saddle and bridle, but without a rider.

Engelbrecht's body was discovered thanks to the barking of his dogs, being hidden in thick brush atop a hill near the Klukoo, about half an hour's ride from Fort Beaufort. From the spoor present, and traces of gunpowder, it was deduced that three Hottentots ambushed Engelbrecht from the cover of a Spekboom.

Engelbrecht was shot five times. A Fingo cattle herder, Boko, confirmed meeting a party of seven Hottentots in the area, six of them armed with muskets, who claimed to be searching for spoor of Kafir insurgents. https://commons.wikimedia.org/wiki/File:Retief_manifesto,_2_Feb_1837,_Grah am%27s_Town_Journal.jpg

The groups Settled the Land and created Republics (which are most of today's South African Towns) as follows:

- Andries H. Potgeiter's group established Orange Free State and passed beyond the Vaal River and settled in what became known as the Transvaal.
- Adam Kok's amaGriqua went North to Orange Free State.
- Piet Retief's group crossed the Drakensberg and began to occupy parts of Zululand and Natal in regions. Other Boer Voortrekkers in this party, allied with baTswana and amaGriqua armies, defeating amaNdebele, who relocated to Bulawayo in southwestern Zimbabwe.
- Louis Tregardt's group Trekked North to what is today Limpopo and Louis Trichardt renamed Makhado;
- Maritz's group went to Kwa Zulu but did not penetrate deeply.
- Insidiously, the Afrikaners and British, took complete control of new areas by force. They created Republics and Colonies and imposed European laws over the inhabitants of the conquered Territories. The people became indentured labour and sometimes outright slaves. These settlers excluded the indigenous inhabitants from political participation, choosing to see them as foreigners to "their" newly established Colonies and Republics. This began the process of alienating "Bantu" amaNguni from their land and the creation of the Migratory Theory of "Bantu farmers" into South Afrika, from some Northern region.

Below are all the Republics created by the Trekkers. All these Republics Represent a Conflict with baTwa first in the Cape Colony followed by amaXhosa in the historic 100-year war against both VoorTrekkers and later British. Followed by amaZulu and almost at the same time in various areas: baShoeshoe, amaNdebele, baPedi, vhaVenda in succession as well as all other Nguni Nations from 1795 to 1885.

Boer Republics

- Republic of Swellendam (1795): Khoe Nations and baSan
- Republic of Graaff-Reinet (1795-1796): amaXhosa
- Zoutpansberg (1835-1864): vhaVenda
- Winburg (1836-1844): amaNdebele
- Potchefstroom (1837-1844): amaNdebele
- Natalia Republic (1839-1843): amaZulu
- Winburg-Potchefstroom (1844-1848): amaNdebele
- South African Republic/Transvaal (1852): baTswana; baPedi, vhaVenda
- Utrecht Republic (1854-1858): amaZulu
- Orange Free State (1854-1902): baShoeshoe (baSotho)
- Lydenburg Republic (1856-1860): amaSwati, amaZulu, amaNdebele
- Klein Vrystaat (1876-1891): baShoeshoe
- State of Goshen (1882-1883): baTswana
- Republic of Stellaland (1882-1883): baTswana
- United States of Stellaland (1883-1885): baTswana
- New Republic (1884-1888)
- Republic of Upingtonia/Lijdensrust (1885-1887): baTswana

Republics of amaGoringaicona (amagriqua)

amaGoringaicona's Notable Leaders were Adam Kok and Nicolaas Waterboer.

- Griqualand East (1862–1879). as New Griqualand: baSotho and amaZulu
- Griqualand West (1870-1871), Capital: Kimberly: Khoe Nations, baSan and baSotho
- Philippolis/Adam Kok's Land (1826-1861): Khoe Nations, baSan and baTswana
- Waterboer's Land (1813-1871): Khoe Nations, baSan and baTswana
- amaGriqua Trekked even further North to Namibia
- Consideration must be taken, into the fact that, in the late 1700s and 1800s, the various amaNguni people were federated Nation States and not an

Amalgamated Nation as suggested above with the broad Names used instead of various family Nations that existed at the time (Example: baRolong, baKwena, baLobedu...)

- amaGriqua/Korana (Goringaicona) lost all their Land under Apartheid when they were designated Coloured and removed from their lands to Coloured designated areas. Their Lands were allocated to Afrikaner Farmers.
- On 24 April 2014, Political party: Front Nasionaal (FN) submitted the below land claim to the Land Claims Commissioner in Pretoria on behalf of the Afrikaner nation.
- The claim pertains to the land described in the National Archives of South Africa, File: R117/1846, "From Ohrigstad to the north till the Olifantsrivier, then downwards to the Delagoa Bay line; to the south till the Crocodile River; to the west to Elandspruit till the 26 degrees' line; east till where the Crocodile River joins the Komati River." *(Author Note: This Land is Today's Mpumalanga Province to Mozambique. To give Credence to this Claim, South African History is written in such a way that amaNdebele of Mpumalanga are "a mysterious Nation whose origin is not known" and who are therefore not legitimately of the Mpumalanga area)*
- FN states that the sale of said land was between King Masous (representative of the Zulu) as seller; and Commandant SJZR Burg (representative of the Dutch South African nation) as buyer. *(Author Note: This sale could only have happened in late 1700s when Boers began to Trek. The List of amaZulu Kings from that time, do not List a King Masous who would have presided over such a large area and as noted earlier, abaNtu do not sell Land)*
- FN further states that the land was legally bought and paid for on 25 July 1846 as an ethnic group *(Afrikaner)* and not as individual landowners and was only in custodianship of the pre-1994 government as they were regarded as descendants of the ethnic group. *(Italicised bracket is Author's emphasis. Author Note: It would be interesting to see if 6 Million pounds was paid for the land? To atleast make this sale as legitimate as the purchase of the Cape Colony)*
- There was, therefore, no legal right, to hand this land over, to a foreign government *(Black Afrikan)*, in April 1994, and away from the original *(Afrikaner)* ethnic group. *(Italicised bracket is Author's emphasis. Interestingly, Afrikans have become Foreigners and the Boer has become an Ethnic group)*
- However, as at 2020, The new land claims process had not yet been finalised https://alchetron.com/Boer-Republics

The British, were not interested in expanding the Cape Colony, due to Financial Implications. However, in order to Control the Trekking Afrikaner Boers, they Annexed all their Republics, until the Formation of the Union of South Africa. Sometimes, these annexations followed gruesome wars, in which concentration Camps were established. In these Camps, Afrikaners were given very little Resources and thousands died of Starvation, Exposure and Diseases. Although the most known Concentration Camps are those of Afrikaners, baTwa and amaNguni who did not co-operate with the British, or who co-operated with the Afrikaners were also held in Concentration Camps by the British. The British also employed the Scorched Earth tactics, wherein Farms would be burnt, immediately destroying the Assets of their opponents and making them vulnerable to Sickness, Exposure and Starvation. The Annexations of the Afrikaner Republics were prompted by the Economic benefits created by the Afrikaner such as the Discovery of Diamonds in the Orange Free State and the Transvaal and later the discovery of Gold.

The Annexation of Boer Republics, worsened Dutch (Afrikaner)-English Hostilities. It is also the Reason why some Afrikaner Boers are still looking to be independent from South Africa, as exemplified by the Afrikaans only Community of Orania in the Northern Cape, The Land Claim by Boer descendants above and the Story I shared earlier regarding the dream of an Afrikaner Mono Motapa. (Orange is the Colour of the Dutch Royal Family. The Lineage of the Current Dynasty, the House of Orange-Nassau, dates back to Willem van Oranje (1533). This is why the naming of Orange Vry Staat and Orania. The desire to establish a Dutch Settlement in Muwene we Mutapa remains...)

The Prolific Creation of Republics, which are Today's Towns and Cities in South Africa, prompts the Claim by Afrikaners, that: "South Africa, was built on the backs of Afrikaners". This Claim, albeit True, does not take into consideration, the fact that the Land on which the Towns/cities were built, belongs to the Native amaNguni, baSan and baKhoe Nations, who also laboured in the Construction of the Infrastructure and who also allied themselves with the Afrikaners in their wars against the English. It is as if Afrikans are a Nonentity in the Story of the Boers and the English in South Africa. This is why they imagine an Empty Land. Afrikans were in the Land. They were not passive by-standers, they Resisted and fought for their Land and when conquered, they were either enslaved or indentured into servitude and conscripted to fight wars they had little interest in. Afrikan lives and their interests were and are disregarded.

In 1835, a meeting attended by the full complement of the 15 settlers of Durban at the time, proclaimed a town and named it in honour of the then Governor of the Cape, Sir Benjamin D'Urban. 100 years later, in 1935, Durban would be granted city status after a number of satellite suburbs are incorporated into the town.

1836 – Boers defeat Mzilikazi's amaNdebele at Vegkop and Mosega. baRolong and amaGriqua ally with Voortrekkers under Andries Potgieter, Piet Uys and Gerrit Maritz against amaNdebele. amaNdebele are displaced to the North of the Limpopo River (Vhembe in luVenda) in November 1837 into what is today Zimbabwe, Mozambique and Malawi, displacing the Nations there.

In 1837, a Contingent of Boer Voortrekkers under Retief visited King Dingane at Umgungundlovu to have him sign a Transfer of large tracts of Land to them. (This is part of the Land the Boers want to reclaim that I spoke about earlier) Amongst amaNguni, Land is inalienable and the King is only a Steward and has no Authority to "Sell or Transfer" the Land. He can only give a concession for settlement for a generation, after which land should be returned. King Dingane felt Trapped by this request from the Voortrekkers, which was reminiscent of the earlier Appropriation of 6000 square km by the British, following an agreement with King Shaka. He understood this approach as an act of war, and decided to go on the offensive, by having Retief and his companions killed. He followed this with attacks on the nearby Voortrekker encampments. In 1838, Voortrekkers then try to take Umgungundlovu forcefully, but amaZulu Successfully defend their Territory in what became recorded as the Battle of Italeni. This is followed by the Battle of Blood River, in which the Voortrekkers led by Andries Pretorius sought to avenge amaZulu for what they saw as the Retief "Massacre". The battle took place on Sunday, 16 December 1838 on the Bank of the Ncome River. The River is said to have turned red with Blood as 3000 amabutho fell and the Boers won the battle. This is recorded as the greatest battle ever fought in South Africa. The Boers then settled in the lands they had wanted King Dingane to sign over to them and declared Natal the Republic of Natalia, founding Pietermaritzburg as their Capital in 1939. Thus the Ulundi vs Pietermaritzburg battle for the Capital of KwaZulu Natal in the Democratic epoch. A Railroad was established to Connect all the Boer Settlements from Pietermaritzburg and for the Transportation of goods from the Port to the various Colonies and Republics and delagoa Bay in Mozambique.

The date 16 December is now Celebrated as Day of Reconciliation. It was previously known as Dingaansdag, then it became, the Day of the Vow, because prior to the war with Dingane, the Voortekkers had made a vow to honour God with a Monument, should He give their enemies into their hands and protect them. The Voortrekker Monument in which this battle and the Great Trek are immortalised, was built in Pretoria to honour this vow. In 2016, The Voortrekker Monument and the Freedom Park Which Commemorates the Struggle history of South Africa, as well as the Heritage Foundation, signed a Memorandum of understanding, to Consolidate and Strengthen ties between the organisations as well as to promote mutual knowledge, experience and understanding amongst the citizens of South Africa...

The Retief matter and subsequent loss of the Blood River battle created rifts in the Monarchy. King Dingane's brother, Mpande, then allied himself with Andries Pretorius and challenged the throne. King Dingane is murdered at the Battle of Maqongqo in January 1840 and Mpande becomes iNkosi ya maZulu as a Vassal state of the Boer Republic of Natalia. This Alignment and the earlier Henry Fynn Relationshios as well as ubuNtu, has made the amaZulu Nation positively disposed toward the Settlers and long lasting relations endure in certain quarters. Few however have yielded any real Economic Empowerment for amaZulu, or enduring Family Relations, apart for non-institutionalised Educational Scholarships. Mpande leads amaZulu from 1840 to 1872 without much disturbance from the Boers. He is succeeded by iNkosi uCetshwayo after the succession battle of Ndodakusuka between Mbuyazi and Cetswhayo that elevated Cetshwayo, the younger brother, to succeed his father when he died in 1872.

In the meantime, in 1841, David Livingstone arrived in llHui! gaeb (Cape Town) through the London Missionary Society. "David Livingstone, I Presume?" became a quote because of the man's Prowess in Afrika.

When the Natalia Republic was established, Boers also wished to establish a Trade port, separate from the British settlers at Durban. A war ensued between the two nations at Congella (a Traditional amaZulu outpost established to Spy for invading foreigners: "Khangela amankengana"). Dick King rode 950km across some of the toughest terrain in that day to Grahamstown in 10days, to get help for the embattled Durban Town. The British arrived, defeated the Boers and Annexed Natal in 1843. Dick King Street opposite 163 Anton Lembede Street is named after him. Subsequent to this, Boers under the leadership of Andries Pretorius and W.F Joubert moved from Natalia to the Transvaal. The first wave of Voortrekkers, led by Hendrik Potgieter, had arrived in the area in the early 1800s and settled as farming communities amongst the Native vhaVenda and baSotho by concessions, given to them by the Kings of these Nations.

After wars with King Sekhukhune, King of baRota and later King Makhado King of vhaVenda, they settled the area Trans of the Ligwa River (Vaal river) and named the territory Transvaal. Rivalries between the earlier Voortrekkers of Potgieter and the later Trek Boers of Pretorius and Joubert prevented the Boers from forming a strong government in the Transvaal.

Early Afrikaner and amaGriqua Trekkers had also arrived in the Southern part of what would later be named Orange Free State early in the 1800s, living with the local baSan, baKhoe Nations and the various Nations that had amalgamated as baSotho under Kgosi Moshoeshoe during Dimfecane. In 1845, with increased settlement of Boers in the area, a battle ensued, known as the Battle of Zwartkoppies, between Voortrekkers and amaGriqua wherein Voortrekkers wanted to take Griqua lands. This was followed by a battle between the British and Voortrekkers near the Orange River, as the British defended amaGriqua. The British Proclaim Griqua West a British Protectorate. A Landdrost based at Winburg then Administered the Northern part of the area, after displacing the Various Native baSotho; baKhoe and baSan Nations through bitter war, so that the Northern part of what would later become the Orange Free State Republic, became predominantly, Afrikaner. This Northern part, would later come into federation with Potchefstroom and eventually join the South African Republic, after assisting the Transvaal to repel the British in several campaigns.

1846: 7th amaXhosa War, An Axe Event, wherein an umKhoe escort who was transporting an umXhosa man to Grahamstown to be tried, was accused of stealing an Axe and was attacked and killed by a group of amaXhosa raiders. amaXhosa refused to surrender the raiders and war broke out between the Colony and amaXhosa (amaNgqika), led by Kumkane Sandile Mgolombane, amaNdlambe and abaThembu. Pre and post war, Robert Godlonton used his Newspaper to Agitate Settlers in the land of amaXhosa to take Land from amaXhosa. Stockenstrom is dismissed as Governor of the area, leading to Further amaXhosa Land Appropriations, Wherein Scorched Earth Tactics are used and Cattle are taken. This leads to the establishment of British Kafferaria (Today's Eastern Cape). amaXhosa are left Landless and are forced to indentured labour and Capitalism begins, wherein amXhosa have to purchase their Resources from the British who now own the means of Production: Land, Labour and Law. amaXhosa, as described by my daughter, G.O, uNomathemba Mchunu, begin to "Work to live...", This is a position, wherein one is Never able to amass any wealth as one's earnings are enough only for them to go to work (Transport) Rent a Space to live in and buy some food with no margin to enable one to invest in anything...

In 1848, during the 7th Xhosa-British war, Sir Harry Smith, a British high commissioner, annexed the area between the Fish and Kei Rivers, as British Kafferaria.

1849–52 Sponsored immigration brought more British settlers to Natal.

1850 - 1853: 8th amaXhosa War, in the height of a Drought and a bitter winter, Governor Harry Smith orders the displacement of amaXhosa from Kat River region.

Prophet Mlanjeni exhorts the people to Resist as Bullets would not harm them. It is, unfortunately, a Bloodbath and amaXhosa are defeated. Governor Harry Smith then deposes Kumkani Mgolombane Sandile when the latter refuses to submit to the Governor's demands and declares him a fugitive. He also attacks and annexes the Boer lands in what would become the Orange Free State and hangs the Boer Resistance Leaders. This alienates him from all the Allies of the British: amaMfengu; Khoe Nations and the Trekkers, allowing initial victories by amaXhosa against him. These, however, are deflated when Re-enforcements are sent to Harry Smith from the Colony on land and by Sea. The Town of Harrismith, is named in his Honor.

1851– Territorial War ensues over the Boer- baSotho boundary at Caledon which was created by the British when they annexed the area. Kgosi Moshoeshoe's Army that was also Armed (Having procured arms from the Portuguese at Delagoa Bay) and also on Horseback, defeats the British. Kgosi Moshoeshoe offers Andries Pretorius an Alliance against the British. The British sign over the baSotho Land beyond the Caledon, to the Boers, who name it, the Republic of Orange Free State. This destroys the fragile friendship that had just been created between baSotho ba ga Moshoeshoe and Boers. baSotho decide to disregard this Cession and continue to graze their Cattle across the Caledon River, as they continue to do, to date.

In 1852, Hendrik Potgieter led a commando out against Kgoshi Sekwati wa baRota (baPedi) in order to take over his land and extend Transvalia. The Boers besieged the baPedi stronghold but baPedi were able to get resources at night in spite of being besieged, leading to a retreat by the Boers, who then raided baPedi cattle. This experience made Kgoshi Sekwati to move his capital to Thaba Mosega (Mosega Kop). At Thaba Mosega, he signed a treaty with the Boers declaring the Steelpoort River the boundary between the lands of baPedi and the boers in Lydenburg.

In 1852, on the 17th of January, the British who did not see this new Afrikaans Transvaal Republic as a threat, and who had no interest in expanding the Cape Colony because of the cost implications, Recognised the Transvaal Republic under the terms of the Sand River Convention. A Constitution was drafted in 1855 by the Boers. The earlier Voortrekker Communities, which were centred around what became known as Pretoria, Potchefstroom and Rustenburg, joined the Transvaal Republic and it became known as the South African Republic ZAR. The first president of the ZAR was Marthinus Wessel Pretorius, elected in 1857. He was the son of Boer leader, Andries Pretorius, who had commanded the Boers to victory at the Anglo – Zulu War of Ncome (Blood River) in KwaZulu. The capital of the South African Republic was established at Potchefstroom and later moved to Pretoria. The parliament was called the *Volksraad* and had 24 members. The discovery of diamonds and gold deposits 1868–74 along the Vaal River and other sites, heightened British interest in gaining control of the region.

The 1854 Bloemfontein Convention recognized the independence of the Orange River Sovereignty and it became the Orange Free State Country, which was located between the Orange and the Vaal Rivers and modelled upon the U.S. constitution, but restricted franchise to white males.

As a British Colony, in 1856, Natal separates from the Cape Colony and becomes independent. As Merchants, the British had Settled Natal, seeking a better life with better Business opportunities. They had established a Port for the purpose of exportation of Afrikan Resources to Europe as well as to sell to the Captive Afrikan Market and for their own use. Farms were also established to supply themselves, Europe and the Captive Afrikan Market that had lost its Settled Farming Lifestyle. Labour was needed for these Industries. amaZulu did not willingly join the Labour Market, only War and Famine finally forced them into the Labour Market in small numbers. Alternative Labour was sought from India, and in 1860, the first Indentured Labourers from India arrived. These were followed by Indian Merchants, who paid their own way to come and Establish Businesses. Laws were created to control and protect Indians and also to ensure that they are not competition for the English Merchants. Laws were also, created to Control movement and activities of the Kaffirs ("Coloureds, amaZulu, Slaves").

Native Locations were created for the Settlement of the Native amaZulu, outside of the cities, but near enough, for the natives to be able to work there.

In 1857: In a desperate but "self-defeating" attempt to resist European incursions, amaXhosa killed their cattle. This was in response to a millennial prophecy given by 16-year-old Nongqawuse. It is estimated that as many as two-thirds of the population died as a result of the killing of cattle and the livelihood they represented. Nongqawuse, a 16-year-old niece of an iqgirha had a vision. She encountered spirits of her Ancestors who told her that the Nation needed to Cleanse itself of ubuthi (uncountable witchcraft) by Sacrificing their Livestock and burning their crops. If this is done, the Ancestors would return and enable amaXhosa to return to their Glory days when they were Prosperous and owned Land, Cattle and Food. The Europeans would be driven back into the Sea. At first people are sceptical but the Prophecy takes root and over a year, People Protest European Occupation by burning their crops and killing their Livestock. This Resistance takes off When Kumkani Sarhili begins to Kill his Livestock as People become convinced and they follow suit. Initially a Day for the fulfilment of the Prophecy was not given, but under pressure, Nonqawuse and her uncle give a date. The Day arrives for the Prophecy to be fulfilled and nothing happens, leaving people disillusioned. Nonqawuse was imprisoned at Robben Island by the British who accused her of destabilising the amaXhosa Nation (There is a school of thought that believes she had been used by the British to destabilise amaXhosa and that this arrest was meant to ensure that she does not confess to this consipiracy).

1858 – JN Boshof, President of Orange Free State (OFS), declares war against Moshoeshoe, because of the Cattle Rustlings, wherein baSotho continued to graze their cattle in what had now become the Orange Free State, and he is defeated, as baSotho prove to be formidable and the Thaba Bosiu Stronghold is impenetrable.

In 1861, Kgoshi Sekhukhune succeeds his father, King Sekwati I, as the King of baRota who became known as Northern Sothos and baPedi during his reign. Not only was his throne challenged by his brother Mampuru, but also by the Political changes taking place in Mutapa (What would become South Africa) at the time, the Boer settlers, the British empire, as well as the Christian Missionaries who sought to undermine his Chieftancy to further their Mission of Christianity as Sekhukhune seemed to be against conversion to Christianity.

1865: Natal Exemption Law created Afrikan Classism amongst amaZulu as those who were European Educated were granted exemption status. Exemption Status meant they could: Take Alcoholic Spirit, Read Newspapers, have better freedom of Movement and live in Townships that were closer to the City. They became known as amaZamtiti and those remaining in Indigenous Knowledge Systems became amaQaba. The Law Provided that Afrikans desiring to be released from Native Law had to Produce Proof of Literacy and take an oath of allegiance to Britain, whereupon they could be given *some* of the privileges of Natal citizenship. This together with the later settlement of learned Afrikan Americans in the Cape Colony, who also obtained exemption status, is what has created the "Better Black" Notions.

1865 – The Orange Free State Launch a second Offensive on baSotho, using Canons which destroyed most of the baSotho Strongholds, but they were unable to take Thaba Bosiu. This war ended with a Peace Treaty, which did not last long. It is followed by a new Boer offensive over the murder of 2 boers in Ladybrand and Kgosi Moshoeshoe's refusal to hand over the killers. The Boers overran the entire Land of baSotho, but again, could not penetrate Thaba Bosiu. Moshoeshoe approached the British for Protection, and on the 12th of March 1868, the land of baSotho was annexed and baSotho became British subjects with Basotho land becoming a British Protectorate. The Borders of Present day Lesotho were defined in 1869, according to the Convention of Aliwal North. Kgosi Moshoeshoe died two years after this and was buried at the Summit of Thaba Bosiu.

In 1867, diamonds were discovered in the Orange Free State and by 1870, there were sufficient reserves of diamonds to stimulate a "rush" of several thousand fortune hunters. Mining of Diamonds in the Orange Free State is Responsible for the Famous "Big Hole" (Die Groot Gat) in Orange Free State. Other important Orange Free State exports that gained a wider world market during the 1860s, were: ostrich feathers and ivory, which was obtained by hunting the region's elephants.

The expanding commercial trade prompted the United States to complete its first international agreement with the Orange Free State: The Convention of Friendship, Commerce and Extradition of 1871, which served to recognize the young Republic.

Full diplomatic relations between the United States and the Orange Free State were never established, however, an unofficial relationship has persisted between the United States and some Afrikaners, over time, which makes it easy for Afrikaners to Access American Media, Tuition and Business.

On 16 May 1876, President Thomas Francois Burgers of the South African Republic (Transvaal Republic) declared war against baPedi ba ga Sekhukhune for their land. Kgoshi Sekhukhune defeated the Transvaal Army twice until they signed the Merensky Treaty at Botshabelo. The British took advantage of this defeat, to Annex the Transvaal (South Africa) Republic, on 12 April 1877, because it was bankrupt from its wars with Sekhukhune. This was done by Sir Theophillus Shepstone (honored with Shepstone building at UKZN) who was at the time, the Secretary of Native Affairs in Natal and who favored Confederation of British Colonies. The Boers were promised internal Self-Governance. Although the British had first condemned the Transvaal war against Sekhukhune, after the annexation, they picked up arms against him. In 1878 and 1879, three British attacks were successfully repelled by Kgoshi Sekhukhune. Finally, a large army of British, Boer and Swati soldiers was deployed against King Sekhukhune and he was subdued on 02 December 1879.

Kgoshi Sekhukhune was captured and imprisoned in Pretoria, but later released on the strength of the Pretoria Convention, whereupon, he left for Manoge, where he was Murdered by his brother, Mampuru. Mampuru was captured by the Boers who tried him for murder, found him guilty and hanged him, in Pretoria on 21 November 1883.

Sekhukhune's death was reported by the London Times of 30 August 1882 wherein his resistance against the British and Boers was Acknowledged and recorded as follows:

"... We hear this morning ... of the death of one of the bravest of our former enemies, the Chief, Sekhukhune... the news carries us some years back to the time when the name of Sekhukhune was a name of dread, first to the Dutch and then to the English Colonists of the Transvaal and Natal https://en.wikipedia.org/wiki/Sekhukhune).

1877 - 1879: 9th amaXhosa War, British Empire's Confederation dream... (The same policy had been successfully applied in Canada, entailed a Process of uniting the English Colonies of Natal, Eastern Cape and Western Cape into one federation). This Confederation scheme required that the remaining independent Indigenous Native States be annexed, to create one seamless Confederation with no intervening Native States. A frontier war was seen as an ideal opportunity for such a conquest. During this period, the Drought began to highlight the fractures that had developed amongst amaNguni, baSan and baKhoe, especially amaMfengu, abaTembu and amaGcaleka, where amaGcaleka attacked amaMfengu at a wedding and at a Police Post. Sir Bartle Frere used the incident as a pretext for British conquest of the land of amaGcaleka... He summoned Kumkani Sarhili wa maGcaleka to answer for the attacks. When Kumkani Sarhili declined the invitation for fear of arrest and coercion, Sir Frere wrote to him to declare him deposed as King and at war. He stoked and did not quell fires amongst radical British and Afrikaner settler groups who desired British intervention and cheap labour from amaXhosa to work their farms. On his side, Kumkani Sarhili faced intense pressure from belligerent factions within his own government and had to mobilise his armies to move to the frontier for the war. Local Paramilitaries of Boer Commandos, abaTembu and amaMfengu were deployed by Prime Minister Molteno, led by Commander Veldman Bikitsha and Magistrate Charles Griffith. The commandos swiftly engaged and defeated an army of amaGcaleka gunmen. The war was over in three weeks and amaGcaleka were conquered. Sir Frere brought in Imperial troops to enforce the disarmament, and then to invade the land of amaGcaleka once again. This time to annex it and occupy it for the purpose of white settlement. amaGcaleka and amaNqika combined their armies and laid waste to the frontier region. amaMfengu towns and other frontier settlements were sacked, supply lines were cut and outposts were evacuated as the British fell back. Frere's next move was to appeal to the authority of the British Colonial Office to formally dissolve the elected Cape government, which was now stubbornly standing in the way of the British Empire, and assume direct imperial control over the entire country. Frere still had access to the frontier militia and amaMfengu regiments of the Cape Government he had just overthrown. These forces, again under their legendary commander Veldman Bikitsha, managed to engage and finally defeat amaGcaleka, the last independent amaXhosa Nation on 13 January 1879.

1879 signals the end of the 100-year Resistance by amaXhosa against their displacement from their Land by the British Colony and the advancing Trek boers. amaXhosa offer themselves as indentured labour to the Cape Colony. This phenomenon of going to the Cape Colony for work, has continued to date, prompting the, then Premier of the Western Cape (Helen Zille), to call Students who travel from the Eastern Cape to study in the Western Cape, "Education Refugees."

Post War, AmaXhosa are under British Colonial Rule and Magistrates are appointed over their Chiefs. The Chiefs continue to lead their people in their Traditional manner but The Colonial Law is Supreme. There are forced Removals Whenever British Rule seeks to Appropriate Land for their use. This is the Era of, Her Royal Highness, Queen Nonesi, whose Speech I quoted for Part 3.

Eight (8) Anglo-Zulu Wars ensue in 1879, between the British Empire and amaZulu, led by iNkosi uCetshwayo at Isandlwana. Rorke's drift, Intombi River, Hlobane, Kambula, Umgungundlovu, Eshowe and Ulundi, wherein the British seek to wrest land off amaZulu. amaZulu resist them, and also retaliate. The British finally defeat amaZulu, razing the Capital, Ulundi, to the ground, as part of the same confederation dream that ended the Xhosa wars.

Hence the British established Natal from the Indian Ocean to Pietermaritzburg and the uThukela River under British Law. They successfully reduced the Zulu Kingdom to an enclave in the North. Some amaZulu were under British Administration whilst others were under Tribal Authority. British Rule determined what happened in the Tribal Authority of amaZulu Kingdom, this is the reason why the Democratic Government now, has power over the affairs of Royal Households and carry the Budgets for these.

The Boers and amaZulu have a tenuous relationship, allying with each other against the British or other amaZulu Dynasties, fighting with each other, when Boers Appropriate land, whilst, at other times, amaZulu permit Boers to set up their Republics. Boer Republics, expanded further in the Kingdoms of amaZulu, amaNdebele, baRota ba ga Sekhukhune, vaTsonga, amaSwati and vhaVenda on the North Eastern part of the Land. amaSwati sought protection from the boer invasion by becoming a British Protectorate in 1906.

In 1880, the Afrikaners revolt against the British as promises of internal Self-Governance of the Boers do not materialize. In 1881, they defy the Annexation of the Transvaal in four (4) battles. The British were finally defeated by the Boers at the Battle of Majuba Hill and the Independence of the South African Republic was restored, with certain conditions. Paul Kruger became the Republic's first president.

1886 – The Three Ships Distillery (reminiscent of Janze van Riebeeck's three ships), was established in Wellington, South Africa. Since 1652, Alcohol has been an Economic and Political thorn to the flesh, Creating Wealth for some, being a means of survival for Afrikan Women who run Shebeens and destroying the lives of untold multitudes in car crashes and through Alcohol addiction. Alcohol producers do not have a recognisable footprint in the support of Alcoholics, understandably so, because to do so, is to admit that one's product is Addictive. Legally, they are bound to say: Not for sale for persons under 18, but their Adverts, which are allowed on TV and Radio, compared to the banned Cigarette advertisements, target the Tweeny audience, associating Alcohol with Glamour and unity. According to www.thedtic.gov.za, "65% of the population in South Africa has never consumed Alcohol." This is among the highest rates of Teetotallers in the world. However, the 35% that consumes Alcohol "are some of the heaviest drinkers globally", according to www.businesstech.co.za (2019), Consuming 28.9L of pure Alcohol per capita/year (2.4L/month or 3Tots every day). This number excludes Beer and Wine which is consumed in heavier amounts. This Consumption level is the 5th highest Consumption rate in the world, with Tunisia being number 1, followed by Cook Islands, Eswatini and Namibia (All Afrikan Nations). Ninety (90) Billion Rands was spent on Alcohol by South Africans in 2014 which equates to paying University fees for 1 125 000 Students @ R80 000 per Student.

The discovery of large gold deposits in the Witwatersrand area in 1886 resulted in a greater influx of miners and fortune seekers, primarily English and Germans amongst whom was Cecil John Rhodes. The mines at Kimberley were already producing 95% of the world's diamonds. This wealth tripled the customs revenue of the Cape Colony from 1871 to 1875, enabling the Cape Colony, to become Self-Governing in 1872 (Not needing British Support). Cecil John Rhodes became its 7th Prime Minister in 1890. Its population doubled and allowed it to expand its boundaries and railways to the north.

In 1888, Rhodes co-founded De Beers Consolidated Mines with Alfred Beit, after buying up and amalgamating the individual claims, with finance provided by the Rothschild family, French and British Banks. He also established the British South Africa Company which received a Royal Charter, similar to that of the British East India Company, to promote Colonisation and Economic Exploitation of Africa. Thus, followed the colonisation of Dzimbabwe (Mashonaland), which became known as Rhodesia (named after Rhodes), followed by Botswana and Zambia.

The Afrikaner disdained the British and German Settlers as foreigners, calling them Uitlanders. The Uitlanders eventually came to outnumber the Afrikaners 2:1 in the Transvaal, but Kruger refused to grant them voting and other rights. This led to Cecil John Rhodes, in his capacity as Prime Minister of the Cape Colony, to Conspire with Leander Starr Jameson, (who was the Magistrate of the British South Africa Company and Administrator of Rhodesia) to Raid the Transvaal, using the Company "Police" to do the raids. The Plan was botched, and when the Conspiracy was exposed, it led to Cecil John Rhodes having to resign from his position as Prime Minister of the Cape Colony.

In 1894, Indian people led by Mohandas Gandhi, a legal agent for Indian merchants in Natal and the Transvaal, formed the Natal Indian Congress aimed to fight discrimination against Indian people in South Africa and to resist the increasing discriminatory legislation through satyagraha, which in luVenda is: Tshikhuna (Non-violent Non-compliance).

1897: 18 years after the last amaXhosa Resistance Wars, Enoch Sontonga Composes: Nkosi Sikelel'iAfrika as isiXhosa is reduced into the written language.

amaXhosa Authors, such as Tiyo Soga, Bud Mbele and John Tengo Jabavu in his Weekly Newspaper, Imvo Zabantsundu, Narrate some isiXhosa History. These sowed Seeds of the later Resistance Movements of the early 1900s. Influences by the African American and West Indian Blacks who had settled in the Cape Colony in the 1800s and who, because of their Western Education, were Exempted from being classified as Black, encouraged many "black" people to desire Western Education. This influential "black" Community was granted Political Franchise and was American and British Educated. Ngcukaitobi, T: The Land is Ours (2018), gives a concise history on their Contributions in the formation of the South African Resistance Movement. Some of them were Lawyers and others were Doctors. They Exposed in various platforms, mainly in England, the Human Rights Atrocities taking place against black people in South Africa, with the Pass laws and the conditions of labor, which were akin to Slavery in the Mine Compounds; the Railways and in the building of City Infrastructures. Notable amongst these Activists are Dyani Tshatshu, Mrs. Kinloch and Sol Plaatje who spent many years in England criss- crossing the Country to expose these atrocities. The Pan African Conference whose Committee members included: Booker T. Washington, W.E.B du Bois and J.T Jabavu took place in July 1900 and would influence Pan Africanism of Kwame Nkrumah and later, Robert Sobukwe and many others.

In 1899, the Orange Free State declared war upon the British and fought alongside its sister Boer republic, the South African Republic (Transvaal), during the Anglo-Boer War of 1899-1902. The British occupied the capital of Bloemfontein in 1900. The 1902 Peace (Treaty) of Vereeniging, which ended the Boer War, annexed the Orange Free State to the British Empire.

In 1899, 20 000 Uitlanders sent a petition to Queen Victoria, recounting their grievances and requesting Military Support to take over the South African Republic. When the Troops arrive, The Boers give the British Colonial Government an ultimatum to remove the Troops. When this is not complied with, War ensues in a Series of about 30 battles known as Anglo-Boer Wars, in the Transvaal and Orange Free State between the British and the Boers. Fighting between the Boers and British continued, until the resources of both Boer republics had been broken by unceasing strain against superior forces. Lord Kitchener, The British commander, used the scorched earth tactics against the Boer commandos and the rural "black" populations supporting them, Placing them in Concentration Camps. Some 25 000 Afrikaner women and children died of disease and malnutrition in these camps, while 14 000 "blacks" died in separate camps. 25 000 Prisoners of war were shipped off to India (Britain had deployed its Indian British Army to assist in the War) where they were placed in prison camps. Whitehead, A. How India helped Britain win its dirty war (May, 31, 2020) as published on The Wire, www.thewire.co.uk . The Wars ended with a Boer defeat in May 1902. The Treaty of Vereeniging Negotiated by Lord Kitchener and Sir Alfred Milner *reflected* that the British had won the war, paving the way toward the creation of the Union of South Africa under the administration of Sir Alfred Milner. During this time, Europe was Carving up Afrika in what became known as the Scramble for Africa.

The Union of South Africa was the Union of: The Cape Colony, Natal Colony, Orange Free State Republic and the Transvaal Republic. It Transferred 87% of Mutapa into British hands and later Afrikaner hands whilst pushing the Native Black (baKhoe, baSan, amaNguni) Land owners to the 13% Reservations, just like it had been done in the New worlds of: America, Canada and Australia. They were considered Aliens in "South Africa", and had to carry a Pass Book that identified them as those who could legally live in "South Africa" for work purposes. Indian People and Mixed Heritage people could live in "South Africa" as they were considered to be Landless.

In 1841, David Livingstone had arrived in llHui! gaeb (Cape Town) through the London Missionary Society. "David Livingstone, I Presume?" became a quote because of the man's Prowess in Afrika. It was presumed that if one met a European person in some deep Afrikan Country, living amongst the Native people, that person would be David Livingstone. He became Legendary for the work he did in Afrika. He was a Scottish Physician and Pioneer Christian Missionary with the London Missionary Society. Medical Doctor, Missionary, Explorer. Dr Livingstone is famous for being the first European person to Cross the Afrikan Continent from the Zambezi in Mozambique to the Atlantic. He was Obsessed to discover the Source of the Nile River, in order to end the Arab-Swahili Slave Trade on the East Coast. He is Considered a Martyr even though he died of Natural causes, because he was considered to have disappeared until he was later found dead, having been disembowelled. His servants reported that they found him dead in May 1873 at Chitambo (Named Livingstone after him) in a kneeling position at his bedside. The Servants, who apparently wanted to keep his legacy alive in Afria, and to ensure that his body could be Transported without decomposing, proceeded to embalm him. They removed his viscera and heart, which, were then buried on Afrikan Soil.

Dr Livingstone's Exploration of the Continent unfortunately was Instrumental in the Colonial Penetration of Afrika in the 1880s as Europe became more familiar with Afrikan through his expeditions. The Close proximity to the Afrikan people enjoyed by Missionaries was manipulated, by their sending Governments who insisted on using Missionaries to achieve their imperialistic goals. The Zeal of the Missionary to share the unadulterated Gospel was from a dismissive Dominions perspective, which served to undermine much of the Afrikan Societal fabric such that ubuNtu was erased from Afrikans and they became dehumanised, without Identity. This is seen in Today's Society where many are beginning to question their Christian or Islamic beliefs as these do not answer their deep longing for Carnal identity and Human Relations.

The Bible is so white-washed that they battle to recognise the History of their fathers in it. When they raise a character, an Achievement or a Contribution in the Bible as being Afrikan, they are met with: the "But not Bantu" rhetoric. When they try to find themselves in their Culture, they are labelled Syncretic and demonic. Worst of all, they are finding that very little Authentic Institutional Cultural Memory remains to Train them in the ways of their fathers. Being a Bible believer myself, and having been raised within a preserved Culture that was able to navigate the do's and dont's of culture within Christianity, and having experienced the grief of not finding myself in Historical narratives, I was called to this journey, to look for my ancestors in the shadows of the past. "Write about ubuNtu" was the Instruction. As I began, "Write about Bantus", You can't write about the Spirituality of a People whose History you do not Know..." Thus began my journey to pour out that which had been collected consciously and subconsciously over the past 12 years. I hope that every person who picks up this book may find the words that will Re- Humanise them and help them locate themselves in the writings of their Sacred scriptures, be they: Oral, Quranic, Baha'I, Vedas, Upanishads, Rigveda, Bhagavad Gita, Bible or many other rich Texts handed down to them from Generation to Generation...May you find your History, the History of your Ancestors with their God. May you Re-Humanise and become umuNtu. So that, umuNtu abe ngumuNtu ngabaNtu. (so that you may re-discover your personhood in the Collective of the People as one) To Re-Humanise, we have to be brutal with the Truth. It will Not Kill us... It Sets Free. Camagu!

The Union of South Africa

By the time the 1880 Scramble for Africa took place, Muwene we Mutapa: Namibia; Botswana; Zimbabwe; Zambia; Lesotho; Swaziland and South Africa was firmly in British hands mainly through the work of the Trek Boer and Cecil John Rhodes and his British South Africa Company. Namibia became: South West Africa; Botswana became Bechuanaland; Lesotho was Basutoland; eSwatini was Swaziland and Zimbabwe was practically owned by Cecil John Rhodes and was named Rhodesia whilst the balance of Muwene we Mutapa became the Union of South Africa.

1899 to 1902, A Series of about 30 battles in the Transvaal and Orange Free State between the British and the Trek Boers during the Scramble for Africa, end with the formation of the Union of South Africa on 31 May 1910 under British Control. The South African War which had ended with a Boer defeat in May 1902 and the signing of the Treaty of Vereeniging paved the way toward the creation of this Union of South Africa under the administration of Sir Alfred Milner.

The Union of South Africa Act of 1909 which was passed by the British Parliament in Westminster, London, United Kingdom, was created for South Africa to set out the enactment of the Union of the various British and Boer Republics into one Country. The Union rendered the two British Colonies of the Cape and Natalia as well as the two Boer Republics of the Transvaal and Orange Free State into Provinces of the Union of South Africa. Settling British and Trek Boers gained control over the whole of South Africa. South Africa therefore did not form part of the Scramble for Africa as it was already in "European Hands." It became a Member of the British Commonwealth and was recognized as an Independent Union under the Statute of Westminster in 1931.

Lesotho and Swaziland remained as British Protectorates and did not form part of South Africa, retaining their "sovereignty". All these decisions were made and Acts passed to Regularise them in the Absence of amaNguni, baKhoe and baSan.

This is the reason why abaNtu will have difficulty hearing the voices of their Ancestors or seeing their faces in South African History and why South Africa Remains More European than it is Afrikan.

Supported by the majority party in each province and by the British government, Louis Botha of the South African Party formed the first union government on 31 May 1910, by a Constitutional Convention in Durban. This Convention made provision for future inclusion of: Basotho land; Bechuanaland; Southern Rhodesia and Swaziland into the union of South Africa. It was a Bicameral Parliament with Proportional representation members and 8 Nominated members, four of whom should be reasonably acquainted with the wishes of the coloured population.

The Sovereignty of the Country lay with Parliament but Safeguarded by British Royal Prerogative as the Union becomes part of the British Common Wealth. The Rt. Hon. The Viscount Gladstone represented the Monarchy with Louis Botha as its Prime Minister.

The Union of South Africa was part of the British Common Wealth, one of the world's oldest political associations of states whose roots are the British Empire. Countries around the world who were ruled by Britain became members of the British Common Wealth. This effectively meant, a Country still had to "Submit" to the directives of Britain and its government and be patterned after the wishes of the Monarchy. Thus, the Leaders of such Countries Were Prime Ministers instead of Presidents.

In the New Union of South Africa, Voting was only for European Men except in the Cape where non-white men could vote, with IIHui! gaeb (Cape Town) becoming the Seat of Parliament, Pretoria the seat of Administration; and Bloemfontein in Orange Free State, the judicial capital, the seat of the Appellate Division of the Supreme Court"

During the second South African War, The English had rallied support from amaNguni Kings by promising them: "Equal laws, and Equal liberty" for all races. At the Treaty of Vereeniging however, this Promise was violated, stimulating political protest. Various organizations were formed to counter the impending union of white-ruled provinces whilst uniting Afrikans "ethnically" and regionally.

The South African Native Convention was then held in Bloemfontein and became a precursor to the birth of the African National Congress in 1912 on 08 January, led by John Langalibalele Dube and Pixley ka Isaka Seme. Reverend John Langalibalele Dube became the first President. In KwaZulu, amaZulu led by iNkosi uBambatha had earlier (1906) taken up an armed struggle: Impi ka Bambatha, to resist the poll tax. Many people perished and even more were imprisoned.

In IIHui! gaeb (Cape Town) the African People's Organisation had been formed in

1902 and was led by Abdullah Abdurrahman to lobby for coloured rights.

As mentioned earlier, In the Transvaal, Indians led by Mohandas Gandhi, a legal agent for Indian merchants in Natal and the Transvaal who had formed the Natal Indian Congress in 1894 to fight discrimination against Indian people in South Africa also resisted the increasing discriminatory legislation through satyagraha (Non-violent Non-compliance) Methods

These Non-European Organisations had links with each other at times. They were influenced by earlier Organisations formed from 1836 onward through the influence of the exempt Blacks and people like Dyani Tshatshu, Mrs. Kinloch and Sol Plaatje and J.T Jabavu.

Governor Milner, who had relocated from Cape Town to the Transvaal's Responsibility was to bring about the Post War Reconstruction of South Africa, which entailed creating an Efficient Administrative Structure that according to www.britannica.com was made up of Milner and a group of young Cambridge Graduates as administrators known as "Milner's Kindergarten" This Administration Ensured that under the Union of South Africa, White South Africans finally found Rest. They had successfully Invaded and Occupied this part of Muwene we Mutapa and Afrikaners had finally possessed the Promised Land. For the next 84 years they would enjoy Peace, Safety, Security and Wealth as it is today, albeit many feel insecure and ill at ease because of the burgeoning poverty of the black masses on their door step and their lack of familiarity with the people. Others are angry at having lost control of the Government and live in fear of the imagined Day when Black people will oppress them in the form of Reverse Apartheid which they prophesy every time a new law that appeals to Restitution is promulgated.

Milner and his Kindergarten quickly got to work to answer the "Native Question". He set the South African Native Affairs Commission (SANAC) and the Following were its Recommendations as detailed in Britannica encyclopaedia at: https://www.britannica.com/place/SouthAfrica/Reconstruction-union-and-segregation-1902-29, Retrieved March 2020

- Territorial separation of black and white land ownership
- Systematic urban segregation by the creation of black "locations,"
- Removal of black "squatters" from white farms and their replacement by wage labourers, and the segregation of blacks from whites in the political sphere
- Education in English,
- Post war Settlement of British Settlers in the Transvaal (This did not succeed due to: few English being willing to settle in the Transvaal because of Their past experiences wherein the English experienced Afrikaner hostility as the latter saw them as "Uitlanders" who want to take over). Some British people also left South Africa Post-war following the Post War Economic Depression
- The Transvaal becomes the Financial, Agricultural and Industrial Capital, spending £16 million to return Afrikaners to their farms and equip them through the creation of the Land Bank.

- Ensuring that Settler minorities would prevail over the black majority as Black societies were policed and taxed more effectively, increasing pressure on blacks to work for white farmers.
- The new constitution excluded blacks from political power,
- Development of Racial Segregation begins as Town Planning, Public transport, Housing, and Sanitation Spheres proceeded from the principle of separating white and black workers.
- Good Relations between Afrikaner Politicians and English Mining Capitalists that consolidated Economic dominance of Gold was developed (what is today termed State Capture). This State of Affairs helped Calm British worries over the Afrikaner win of the elections later on in 1910 as it was realised that both Botha and Smuts understood the economic Pre-eminence of Mining Capital and "a policy of reconciliation between Afrikaans and English-speaking whites was promoted." According to Terreblanche, S. (2018), Without this symbiotic relationship, both systems (Political and Business) could not have lasted for almost a century. It is for this reason that Terreblanche suggested a Wealth Tax in his TRC Testimony. TRC (2003 [1998])
- In order to increase Profitability of Mines by reducing Overheads, Milner ensured the 1904 Transvaal Labour Importation Ordinance was Created to facilitate the importation of indentured Chinese labourers who were willing to work for less pay than what Afrikans were willing to accept. Many Afrikans lost their jobs as 60 000 Chinese labourers were imported. The Ordinance stipulated that the Chinese could be employed only in the exploitation of minerals within the Witwatersrand district, excluding them from any other occupation. This is the reason Chinese who came to South Africa before 1910 are Classified as Black (Historically Disadvantaged Individuals) within the Democratic Dispensation's Broad Based Black Economic Empowerment Laws.

These Structures set in Motion an Economic Sector Which Today is the 2nd Richest in Afrika and one of the Most Unequal in the World with a 2014 Gini Coefficient of: 63, Where 80% of the Wealth is in 20% of the Population who are also White.

The Separate Development Strategy of Milner meant White People never had to interact with Black people except as Servants in their homes. They were never exposed to the hardships of black people and they never had to understand what Apartheid was. This is the reason why, most "white" South Africans now Claim to never have been involved in Apartheid or else just dismiss it as something their Grandparents did and that they have no Responsibility for.

The Media was a Government Propaganda Machinery and Reported News through the Lens of the Government, ensuring that News was only about White People and Afrikan (Black) People were only Reported on if they were involved in some ghastly Act, entrenching the view of Afrikan people as Barbaric

The British Separate Development Policy put in place by Milner was a precursor of the Afrikaner Apartheid Regime which Formalised it into a Policy of Government.

- How did these Measures Enrich White People whilst Impoverishing Black People?
- They Created a Police State in which White People lived in Safety in their own private Communities whilst Black people lived in Fear of being Stopped and Arrested for anything the Police may deem befitting on the Strength of the Pass Laws. This promoted "Political Stability" in the Country, with its attendant Economic growth. It is this Legacy that makes some people feel they have a right to question the presence of Afrikan (Black, Indian and Coloured) people in some Establishments or Suburbs with rude questions of: "What do you want here?"
- White People received Reparations for Loss of Slaves when the Slave Trade was abolished. They were also given Reparations for the 2nd South African War. The Land Bank was set up and it gave Farmers Loans and Grants to Support Farming. (slavery.iziko.org.za/end of enslavement)
- Indentured Afrikan, Indian and Chinese Labor maximized their profits
- International Industrialisation boom and Open International Trade for white people meant that they could sell their products to the International Market supported by Britain and the Government and they could also import International goods which helped to create White Monopoly Capital in Manufacturing and Retailing. Britain opens up the British Market to South African Commodities.
- Free Extraction of Mineral Resources. (Since 2008, the Royalty Act is in place to ensure that the community within which the Mine operates does get some Royalties). To date, Gold Mines Are Taxed in a special way and they also get Rebates for input Tax.
- Job Reservation for White people wherein all Senior Positions were always occupied by White people regardless of their qualifications. An Afrikan could not be a Manager to a White person. White people also attracted a disproportionately higher Pay compared to other races. (90% more pay than Afrikans, for the same work. Albeit Constitutionally this has changed, White people are still paid 30% more than their Afrikan Peers for the same position.
- Further, white people were assured of a Job in Government, Whilst White Owned Business were assured of Government Contracts. To date, in spite

of BBBEE, The Government and its Parastatals still award more Tenders/ Contracts to white Companies than Afrikan (Black) Companies. Moreover, the structure of BBBEE codes make it easier for White companies to score higher than Black companies because they have more Employees, who happen to be predominantly Black, albeit in the lower rungs of the Company. This coupled with Fronting defeat the purpose of BBBEE which has only managed to change the fortunes of less than 10% of the Afrikan Black populace. Mind you, this 10% includes Indian and Chinese Companies who tend to get the bigger Contracts. Black and Coloured Tenderers get the least of this Slice. Thus Broad Based White Economic Empowerment lasted 80 years and unfortunately still persists. (www.sahistory.org.za/Job Reservation Cruel), yet, 18 years into BBBEE there are already demands for it to be scrapped.

- Access to Funding: Lenient and Preferential Government Grants and Bank Loans at Low interest rates and Lenient Lending Covenants were offered to white people and at Banks, this Practice still happens and white people on average pay less interest on any loan than Afrikan Black people as interest rate is determined based on Risk perception.
- The Education they were allowed to pursue ensured that they are Leaders in every sector with greater earning capacity whilst "Blacks" were only allowed to do certain jobs and were not allowed to be more educated than White people by law, regardless of ability.
- Law protected white people, creating an enabling environment for them, whilst Criminalising Afrikans through Tax Laws, Pass Laws and other criminal laws including detention without Trial.
- White People gained a Superiority Can Do Attitude and Outlook on life created by the Subjugation of blacks, whilst "Blacks" gained the opposite.
- Westernisation and a demand for Afrikans to live a Western Lifestyle as well as their working conditions (Early to work and late to home, meant that Afrikans were unable to sustain their agrarian Lifestyles) and guaranteed a captive "Black" Labor and Consumer Market, whilst increasingly becoming Absent parents at a time when their Family Structures and support were severely attacked by Religion and the Migrant Labor system
- Preferential White Treatment wherever black and white compete for a commodity.
- Transfer of Wealth from Black people to White People through the Transfer of Means of Production: Land, Law and Labour. This Transfer impoverished Native Afrikans (Black and Coloured) greatly and remarkably reduced the ability of

Indian and Chinese people from being competitive with white People in the Economic Sector.

Land and Labour:

- Land has created an immense Capital Accumulation for white people from (1652 to 2020: 368 years) Creating incredible generational wealth for most, where some currently live only on these dividends., or are educated with them.
- The ability to sell off and/or Lease out these Assets to the now affording black middle Class at a premium, continues to create wealth for white people. Some have converted these into Game Farms for International Tourism, with Rooms that cost as much as R15000 per night.
- 87% of the Land was reserved for White people who were apparently 17%? of the Population at the time (Current statics show: 8.9%).
- The Dispossession that Started in 1652 culminated with Laws Being Passed to Legally effect the Appropriation, starting with the Glen Grey Act of 1894; the Natives Land Act of 1913; The various Apartheid Laws from 1948.
- The prohibition of Afrikans (Black and Coloured) from being able to redeem their land outside the reserves even through purchase, cemented the Dispossession of Land and permanent Transfer of this Land to white people. It is alleged that in 1994 when Government changed hands, most of these lands were still in Government hands and were Clandestinely transferred to white government officials as No Proper Asset Register was kept for the Land. This is why some can still claim purchased land from King Masous. According to the Land Audit Report of November 2017, 94% of South African Land is in Private hands.

The Impact of Land Dispossession on Afrikans had the following Consequences:

- ***Loss of Assets:*** Fertile Land and Water Sources; Homes; Material possessions; as well as Livestock, with every forced Removal. Most people were moved 2 to 3 times. The Loss of Assets not only forced them to look for employment as Cheap Labour but robbed them of 368 years' worth of Return on Investment. White Farmers love producing Title deeds for the Land the Government sold to them for a pittance/gave them for free, Land that the Government Appropriated without Compensation from Afrikans (Black and Coloured). Some have re-mortgaged these over and over and always bring up the dilemma of the mortgaged farm into the Re-Appropriation Conversation.
- The other Assets lost were: Intellectual; Social; Political and Spiritual Equity. This Loss disoriented Afrikans (Black and more so, Coloureds) as will be elaborated in Scrambled eggs section.

- Confinement to the most Arid parts of the Land, made it impossible for Afrikans to Maintain their Lifestyles, reducing them to labourers and captive Consumers. Not only did they work for less pay, which enriched their white Masters, but now they could no longer Produce what is required to Maintain their lives, they had to buy these, again from their white Masters further enriching them and because the pay was so low, they were bonded to the work, with no opportunity to Innovate as their Time and Talents were fully absorbed by the employer. The balance of what they made was absorbed by the disproportionately higher Taxes levied toward them.
- Typically, people would and still do, leave their homes at 04h30am to be able to arrive at work by 07h00 or 08h00, having changed Taxis 2 and sometimes 3 times. They get written Warnings for being late. After work they arrive home around 19h00 and then only can they see to their family needs. This they do daily sometimes six days a week only to get 21days' leave per year (if at all). When does one get time to Dream and envision innovations?
- These Labourers "Work to live and live to work" because Their Entire Pay can only achieve the following: Transport; Rent; Food. There is no surplus to Invest in any way, form or format, which keeps them as Captive Labour for their entire lives, only to retire Poor and without any of the Benefits enjoyed by Retirees. The Government now offers a Pension at below the Minimum Wage level and for which Tax payers who did not ensure the labourers have a Pension, complain about when SARS makes us Pay. This inability to maintain oneself post retirement is what necessitates so-called Black Tax, where the Children now have to work and support their Parents and their Siblings who did not manage to go to school, Keeping the "Black" Middle Class trapped in poverty and unable to venture into business.
- The Land Dispossession further meant they could not stake a Claim on the Mines so developed on their Land nor benefit from them except as indentured labourers. Mines also created a Migrant Labour System which destroyed families of Afrikan (Black, Indian and Coloured). The Destruction of families meant Children were raised without their Culture, Spirituality and Nurturing.
- Men lost their Traditional Schools which became corrupted as we see with some of today's Circumcision schools. For more than 10 generations now, Afrikan Men have lost Training on what it means to be a Man, The Responsibilities of a Man, Relations of Men toward Women in general and women as their wives; toward their Children; toward each other and as Leaders and Members of Society in general. Thus we see a sharp rise in Gender based Violence.

- This Loss of Cultural Wealth has left us with the rampant scourge of: Divorce; Gender based Violence; Incest; Child Abuse; Rape; and all forms of Crime. The Imprisonment of Afrikan Men because of these crimes as well as the Crime of being "Black" (Tax and Pass Laws) worsened the cycle of poverty and inequality.

Law and Labour:

- Segregation Laws and the Pass Laws, Solidified the segregation of South Afrikans from each other, and making it impossible for Afrikans to Learn, Innovate and Participate in the Economic Activities in the cities. The Process and Supply Chain of the Production of goods and services was and is Shrouded in Secrecy.
- Bantu Education which has yet to be decolonised ensures that Afrikan (Mainly Black and Coloured) graduates are unable to Start Manufacturing, Wholesale and Retail businesses, not for lack of funding, but for lack of Access to information on where to start and where to procure Raw Materials. The only ones they can get into are Franchises that are effectively a Transfer of wealth to White people as Franchise owners. These have become prohibitively expensive for Afrikan (Black and Coloured and Indian), who have to get loans in order to purchase, which loans Banks do not give easily to "Black" people.
- The Negative Regulation of Marriages of Afrikans through section 22(6) of the Black Administration Act 38 of 1927, made it impossible for them to Create Generational Wealth because for a Civil Union, if the couple did not specifically state 1 month before marriage that they wished to be married in Community of property, they would not be so married and the wife stood to lose everything to the husband's family upon the death of her husband. Customary Marriages were unrecognised at Law but administered by the same Act and seen as a contract between two family groups rather than two individuals.
- Native Labour Regulation Act unified laws making breach of contract a criminal offense and outlawed Afrikan strikes; it also regulated conditions of employment but had the effect of depressing wages for Afrikans. It also gave White Employers Carte Blanche power over their Afrikan (Black, Indian and Coloured) Employees including Criminal procedure for Desertion, insolence, drunkenness, negligence and strikes. People could be jailed for Deserting work and gain a criminal record. This had the effect of hardening people into criminals who were otherwise not and thus today's high criminal statistics. The Crime of South Africa is a Crime of anger and vengeance at these generational injustices. There are people who do not see what they do as criminal any longer

and feel justified in their actions of "Re-appropriation". This is why one will find that Townships are very safe as far as Theft crime is concerned compared to so-called "white suburbs".

- Tax Laws ensured that Afrikans paid significantly higher Taxes than White people and that they could be imprisoned for failure to pay these Taxes. Besides Income Tax, which was disproportionately higher for Afrikans than that of their white counterparts in spite of Afrikans earning a tenth of the salary of white people, Afrikans were also Taxed for being Male and older than 18 (Poll Tax); For living in a Local area (Local Tax); For owning Dogs (Dog Tax); For owning a Hut (Hut Tax, taxed per number of huts one possessed). They were also Levied for everything that white people were not levied for: Educational levies, dipping fees, grazing fees, Pass Fees and Compound fees. These Taxes and Levies not only provided a disproportionately large slice of the income necessary to create a system of first tier local administration in the rural areas (Blue Books on Native Affairs 1880) but it also created the need for people to sell their Livestock to pay taxes to avoid imprisonment. Families lost generational wealth because of these Taxes and had to go into towns in order to earn the money for its payment. Native Taxes transferred Afrikan Wealth into European hands through direct payment of Taxes and through the Cheap Labour they Created. My own conservative estimates at 40 million population estimates of 1900, 80% of whom were black and 25% of whom were male and over 18, at an average annual tax of 10pounds per person puts: 80 million pounds in government Coffers annually from Black people. Money which financed the Infrastructure that served only white people bar the development of locations for blacks.
- The Cheap Labour of Afrikans Mined the Minerals, Built the Industries, Built the Railroads and Roads, Built the Towering Sky Scrapers, Farmed the Land and also Served in the Private homes and Gardens, Freeing White Minds to be Innovative and Creative and Industrious. This too is Wealth Transfer.
- The Migrant Labourers were housed in Hostels which are still functional today and that house up to 5000 people. Some have been upgraded into family units but have not been handed over to the occupants, creating a situation where they have no owner and therefore are not Maintained and are largely left to dilapidate, entrenching a Mind-set that Afrikans do not know how to take care of Property.
- These Hostels have been breeding grounds for Political Violence. They were followed by the creation of Townships, the oldest of which is Alexandra Township, created 109 years ago in 1911. Town planning was such that each Township was

self-contained, with only one Entrance/Exit for ease of control. If that Entrance/Exit was blocked (by Police), no one could leave the township undetected. This was the same pattern with Sections within the township. The Townships do not communicate with each another. To Access the next Township, one has to go to town first in order to get transport specific for the next Township. The Houses (2 bedrooms that open into a Lounge and Kitchen area) remained the property of the government. Inhabitants paid Rental on these houses in a Rent to buy Scheme. Most people to date do not have title deeds to these homes they have lived in and paid for, for generations. The Townships are underdeveloped with houses lacking a sewer system and the so-called "Bucket system" which was a health hazard in every manner, being used. There was no Electricity and Coal or Paraffin was used for energy needs. Roads are underdeveloped, Narrower and of poorer quality than the suburbs. Sadly, this legacy still remains. The yards are small with houses abutting on each other; In some areas, especially coloured areas Flats were preferred, hence the famous Cape Flats, although all areas did have Flats. There are fewer schools and Clinics per population compared to the white suburbs. These are also poorly serviced in terms of Garbage collection, Consistency of water availability and Maintenance of Infrastructure. There are no Parks. Children play in the dangerous streets. Land for religious institutions was only allocated for the government recognized European-led churches (Dutch; Anglican; Catholic...), as such, independent Afrikan-led Churches are unable to find Land to build churches in the Townships and are forced to Rent Exorbitantly in Cities, where they pay business Tariffs as their premises can't be rezoned for Church because they have no Parking space. These are by-laws that if People knew how to lobby Government for change, they should be changing. But, Alas... They are ill-equipped. Laws get passed under their Noses and they are None-the-wiser for it.

- World war II caused a relaxation of the Pass laws, so that Government could get more Afrikan men to war. This caused an influx of Afrikans into the Towns, Land invasion and a Mushrooming of Informal settlements in the form of shacks that can mushroom overnight, Mushroomed. These were illegal, overcrowded and un-serviced. They are erected by people who come to look for work in the towns and do not have a place to stay in the Townships. Although the living conditions of the shack settlements are poor, they have the advantage of being Rent free and unregulated by the Police.
- Later, the government stopped building houses in the Townships and only availed plots for people to build their own houses or allowed a developer to develop houses that people could buy directly from the developer. Thus many

Sections of each Townships were developed with Umlazi having as many as 52 Sections and more. By 1950, a substantial proportion of the urban black population lived in Townships with a large Shack Settlement. The emergence of the Black (Coloured, Black and Indian) Middle Class saw a Mushrooming of Big Beautiful Mansions Develop in the Townships.

- Townships are still largely unregulated with Houses Constructed without Town Planning and No Service Delivery and on Disputed land, making Property Investment in the Township uninviting and therefore with the dawn of Constitutional democracy, Most Middle and Affluent Black, Indian and coloured people moved into the previously white owned Suburbs, to buy previously white owned houses that the Government had largely helped them build, at 100x the prices for which they paid 30 to 50 years earlier and which they have completed 2 mortgages on, putting children through university and investing in business from these mortgages. A House they paid R25 000 for then, now sells for 1.5m and sometimes even 2.5m, depending on Location. The white people then move into exclusive gated communities, using the Cash obtained from the sale of these houses, so that they upgrade their Asset Portfolio without a debt.
- Unfortunately, not all White South Africans are Wealthy. There are many who are of the Middle Class and even in Poverty with many Trapped in the Inner Cities and others Living in Squatter Camps and Townships Today, with few living on the Streets. However, even amongst these white people who did not fully benefit from the Colonial and Apartheid Epoch, the Privilege of Superiority still makes them more industrious than their Afrikan counterparts in the same circumstances. The Unequal Pay and Preferential treatment from Banks still give the White Middle Class an upper hand.

Current South Afrikan Economy by Sector:

Natural Resources: Mining which Contributes the following numbers of the world's Resources: Platinum: 77%; Kyanite: 55%; Gold: 11%; Diamonds: 5% According to www.mineralscouncil.org.za, Mining is a significant contributor to employment in SA, with 457 698 of the Country's Employed individuals in this sector.

Agriculture and Food Processing: According to bizcommunity.com (2018), Agriculture and Food Processing are a significant contributor to employment in SA, with 13698 of the Country's Employed individuals in this sector.

Manufacturing: Mainly Automotive as Textile buckled. 36 000 of the Country's Employed individuals in this sector.

Service Industry: This industry Employs 73% of all employees.

Tourism: Tourism is a significant contributor to employment in SA, with over 400 000 of the Country's Employed individuals in this sector.

Financial Services: South Africa has a Sophisticated Financial Sector with the JSE ranking 18th in the world in terms of Total Market Capitalisation of $1.2 Trillion as of March 2018 according to World Federation of Exchanges.

Informal Sector: Excluded amaNguni, Coloured, baKhoe and baSan Economic activities are considered as the Informal Sector and remain largely unsupported and unregulated.

According to the South African Local Economic Development Network, South Africa's informal sector contributes 8% of the country's GDP and supports 27% of all working people. and does not enjoy much Local Government Support. This number does not include Network Marketing, Township Spaza shops and Shebeens and it explains why the unemployment rate is higher than expected because people in this sector do not consider themselves employed even though they do have an income.

Part 5: Political Change

"Whites fragmented the Africans into separate tribes and drove them as far away as possible from areas inhabited by whites, to prevent them functioning as one cohesive group." Du Preez, B (2003:81)

The Genesis of Apartheid

1914 to 1918, South Africa was involved in the First World War by virtue of its dominion status. When England declared war on Germany, it meant that South Africa, Namibia, and other countries were automatically at war, and its troops mobilized to invade Germany.

Of the 229 000 South Africans who participated in this allied effort against Germany and its allies, 21 000 were black. They were however not allowed to hold a gun against a European, so, they served as unarmed support to the army in the dockyards and the rail roads. Prime Minister DF Malan would later say: "To every Afrikaner, the use of black troops against Europeans is abhorrent" (Mail & Guardian, Staff Reporter, 14 May 2017: Memories of black South African Soldiers who bore arms and fought in War II). 1120 died during this war and 250 of them perished in the Delville battle which is described as one of the most brutal battles of world war I. They were buried in Arque-la-Bataille in 1916 in France, separate from their white compatriots who also perished in the same battle and country. These were buried in Delville Woods. Their Contribution remained unrecognised by the Apartheid government until the Constitutional democracy recognised them in 2016. Their Heroics in the SS Mendi that sunk off the Coast of South Africa are only now being recorded.

In the later World War II, 334 000 Men volunteered for full time service in the South African Army of whom 211 000 were white, 77 000 black and 46 000 coloured and Indian (Indian and Coloured people tended to be lumped together in Apartheid Statistics). 11 023 are known to have died during this war. Although the Black soldiers went to war armed only with their imkhonto (Assegais/Spears), In the thick of battle, the South African army forgot their country politics and fought as one, Blacks were armed with guns and used grenades to repel their opponents in the battles in El Alamein Egypt and in Abyssinia (Ethiopia) against the Italians. Their heroics were not celebrated because if these became known, "Smuts could lose what support he had in Parliament".

For more on these wars, read, Honikman, M (2016): There should have been five. Honikman uses Transcripts of Research done by Vincent Moloi on the role of blacks in these wars. Moloi is a Film Maker whose most known works are: Tjovitjo, Hotel Rwanda, African Metropolis and Skulls of my people.

After world war I, Louis Botha's Administration was dogged by Wage Strikes from all population groups especially in the Mining Sector. These were met with fire from the Military. The Rand Revolt of 1921 is the most commonly known of these Strikes. This period of unrest facilitated the enactment of several Employment Acts and paved the way for more Strenuous Apartheid Laws which were more onerous than the predecessor laws passed since 1660.

Most Prominent Apartheid Laws were:

<u>Land:</u>

Glen Grey Act of 1897; Native Land Act of 1913; Native Administration Act of 1927; Native Trust and Land Act of 1936; Asiatic Land Tenure and Indian Representation Act of 1946; Group Areas Act of 1950; The Establishment of Bantu Self-Government Act of 1950; The Promotion of Bantu Self-Government Act of 1959; Bantu Investment Corporation Act of 1959; Bantu Homelands Citizenship Act of 1970; Bantu Homelands Constitution of 1971; Independence Status Acts for the TBVC States; Bantu Authorities Act of 1951; Group Areas Development Act of 1955; Coloured Persons Communal Reserves Act of 1961; Rural Coloured Areas Act of 1963; Preservation of coloured Areas Act 31 of 1961; Aliens Control Act of 1973.

<u>Pass laws and influx control:</u>

Slaves Pass Act of 1760; Kaffir Pass Act no. 23 of 1857; Natives Act of 1923; Natives (Urban Areas) Consolidation Act of 1945; Prevention of illegal Squatting Act of 1951; Native Laws Amendment Act of 1952; Natives (Abolition of Passes and co-ordination of Documents) Act of 1952;

Natives Resettlement Act of 1956; Natives (Prohibition of Interdicts) Act of 1956; Urban Bantu Councils Act of 1961; Black local Authorities Act of 1982

<u>Political:</u>

South Africa Act of 1909; Representation of Natives Act of 1936; Population Registration Act of 1950; Reservation of Separate Amenities Act of 1953; Separate Representation of Voters Act of 1951; Prohibition of Political Interference Act of 1968; Suppression of Communism Act of 1950; Public Act of 1953; Riotous Assemblies Act of 1956; Unlawful Organizations Act of 1960; Indemnity Act of 1961; Internal Security Act of 1982 which enabled: Bannings and Detentions without Trial.

Job reservation; Education and Economy: Mines and Works Act of 1911; Native Building Workers Act of 1951; Native Labour (Settlement of Disputes) Act of 1953; Industrial Conciliation Act of 1956; Various Business Licensing Acts; Alcohol prohibition Acts; Bantu Education Act of 1953; Extension of University Education Act of 1959; Coloured persons Education Act of 1963; Indians Education Act of 1965.

Civil Life:

Immorality Act of 1927; Prohibition of Mixed Marriages Act of 1949; Bantu Administration Act; Bantu Marriages Act.

Coloured people were largely exposed to the same laws as Black Afrikans but were exempted on some of the laws. Indian people and Coloured people later gained Franchise and became part of the Tricameral system. This was designed to create Tension between Afrikans, Indians and Coloureds further increasing the Insecurity of Afrikans and entrenching them as the underdog. These Tensions and suspicions linger, wherein Indian and Coloured people are seen as deputy whites by their Afrikan counter-part.

There is not much Written to describe the impact of Apartheid on everyday Life, which is why Black people are always asked: "Why are you still barking up that Tree?" "How Long will you blame everything on Apartheid?" "How did Apartheid affect you personally?" Chinese, Indian and Coloured people are not even allowed to Claim injury from Apartheid, especially because the laws applied on the various Nationalities were deliberately divisive, so that there is no sense of togetherness amongst: Indians, Blacks, Coloureds and Chinese. A hierarchy was created wherein Chinese were treated better than the Indians, who were treated better than the Coloureds, who were treated better than the Blacks. Each group fought for their rights separately and never became fully aware of the pain of the other and worst of all, fought each other more in a Xenophobic manner. These negative feelings toward each other escalated to an all-out "war" on Indians in KZN. Black people hated Coloureds for their lighter and Softer hair and their "Proximity" to Whites, denying them their "Black" heritage and divorcing themselves from them in an "injured leopard syndrome." (See Prologue)

Apartheid, was not just an Institutional and Legalised Segregational Policy. It was a devastatingly Destructive Spiritual, Psychological, Social, Political and Economic onslaught on Afrikans in their Land.

Unfortunately, These Traumas of Superiority and Inferiority have been passed on Generationally and are still very acutely etched in the Psyche of South Africans who treat each other according to these legacies. The Daily Micro Aggressions Levelled against Afrikans (Black and Coloured) and the Backlash they always provoke are worsening 27 years post-Apartheid.

The Truth and Reconciliation (TRC), that was meant to allow people an opportunity to understand the impact of the Settlement of Muwene we Mutapa by Europeans and their System of Governance was aborted. Its Scope was very narrow and limited to the Period of the Institutionalised Apartheid Era and focused on Victims of Political Suppression and the perpetrators thereof for the purpose of those people receiving Reparations on the one hand and Amnesty on the other.

It did not interrogate: The balance of the Atrocities meted against Afrikans in general and since the Invasion of Muwene Mutapa in 1652, neither did it interrogate the Social Engineering and legal Institutionalisation that was necessary to entrench Apartheid, leaving many things unsaid and festering. The reason why People find the EFF and its President, Malema attractive, is that he says for Afrikans, that which should have been said and Addressed and that they find difficult to articulate. Mr Malema's articulation of them, is not the issue, the issue is that there is no Platform to Ventilate these matters and for people to find each other in a Safe Space, without anger, therefore when he articulates them, it comes across as someone who is Anarchist. Like everyone in South Afrika, Mr Malema is looking for the Settled Lifestyle of his Ancestors, that the Europeans, Chinese and Indian People also came to Muwene we Mutapa looking for. We are all looking for the same thing, but it evades us because we will not be Truthful and acknowledge what went down and how it hurt us and still hurts us, so that we can forgive one another and find one another and build a Prosperous Amalgamated Nation. It is possible. It can be Uhuru... only if we will listen without being defensive and without attacking.

The TRC was set up in terms of the *Promotion of National Unity and Reconciliation Act*, No. 34 of 1995.

The hearings started in 1996 and ended in 1998. The mandate of the commission was:

- To bear witness to,
- Record,
- Grant amnesty to the perpetrators of crimes relating to human rights violations,
- Offer reparation and rehabilitation to the victims in some cases,

- Establish a Register so that ordinary South Africans who wished to express regret for past failures could also express their remorse,

The commission was empowered to grant amnesty from Criminal Prosecution to those who committed abuses during the apartheid era as Apartheid was Classified as a Prosecutable Crime against Humanity by the UN General Assembly in 1973. Amnesty was offered to Witnesses for whom it was deemed that their crimes were politically motivated, proportionate, and had given full disclosure.

Both Government and the Liberation forces were exposed to the TRC Enquiry and Amnesty Applications were considered from both sides.

Of those who Applied to be heard (Many were unaware of the Process and multitudes more chose not to Apply because they disagreed with the Mandate of the Commission, whilst others felt it would be a futile exercise) The Commission found more than 22000 people had been victims of gross human rights violations. The Commission voiced its regret that there was very little overlap between those seeking restitution and those seeking amnesty, which showed that the full extent of the Atrocities was not being heard.

The TRC was a Reconciliatory rather than Restorative Justice Mechanism. It was the first in the world and has been used by many governments since. It gave Mandela and the Chair of the TRC, Arch Bishop Desmond Tutu the Iconic Status they enjoy to date all over the World. It also served to brand the New South African Democracy very positively and engendered high Investor Confidence in the Country.

Some of the Recommendations the Commission made are:

1. Financial, Social Economic and Health Care Reparations
2. A List of 300 perpetrators of Apartheid who had not sought Amnesty and who it was deemed should be prosecuted (List created from the Testimony of those who sought Amnesty. To date, these have not been prosecuted)
3. Steps for Restoring dignity of People
4. Equalising the Playing field

The Democratic Government led by the ANC has tried to Address some of these Recommendations thus:

- According to a statement made by Minister Masutha in 2018 on SABC News (18 December 2018), symbolic reparation tokens of R30 000 per person have been paid to 17 000 of the eligible 22 000 applicants.
- Repealing of Apartheid Laws (Some are still hidden in the Social Engineering and do not at face value seem Segregationist, but remain impediments to Afrikans),
- Bill of Human Rights Drafted,
- New Constitution Created,
- Employment Equity Act and BBBEE to redress Economic Injustice Promulgated into Law and Applied from 2003.
- Various Social Grants Engineered
- Free Housing; Free Healthcare; Free Education (Which is being extended to tertiary) offered
- Recognition of those who were persecuted under Apartheid (Not everyone has been recognised however and mechanisms for ensuring that people are recognised are not clear and/or universally known),
- Building of Memorials: Apartheid Museum (Which is privately owned), Constitutional hill, Freedom Park,
- Change of Place Names back to their original amaNguni names. Khoe and San Names are still largely unrecognised. Most of these name changes have however been successfully legally overturned by White people. The latest name change is: Port Elizabeth, which is now Gqebera
- Change of National Symbols, which although designed by the previous government officials and service providers are more representative of the South Afrikan History and its people: Coat of Arms (designed by Iaan Bekker), Flag (designed by Frederick Bronwell). The Mace was redesigned in a more inclusive and Consultative manner by a Team of people who represented the Rainbow Nation including Honourable Members: Frene Ginwala, Baleka Mbete and Mr Schreiber.

Visit www. Parliament to read the interesting facts about these National Symbols which should be used to build understanding, Respect and Reconciliation amongst South Africans.

Post War Progress

In 1918 Spanish Flue Reportedly Claimed 200 000 people in South Africa. The 2019 Covid 19 has claimed 53 000 lives (February 2020 to March 2021) thus far. The disease exposed the Inequity that prevails in South Africa 27 years post Democracy.

In1919 South Africa was given a League of Nations mandate to rule German South West Africa (Namibia). This propelled South Africa into border wars and paved the way for later Conscription of White Men into the Army.

The African National Union organized burning of passes as protest against the invasion of Namibia

1919–21 Severe drought coincided with post-war boom and collapse of agricultural prices in South Africa, driving many White Afrikaners off the farms to become urban workers.

1920 Nationalists won the largest number of seats in the general election, but Smuts stayed in power by an alliance with the Unionists; election showed the growing appeal of White Afrikaner Nationalism. The Witwatersrand University was chartered and Students at Fort Hare burned buildings in protest against unequal Education policies.

The Communist Council of Action briefly gained control of the Rand (a Place, Witwatersrand)

Afrikaans was recognized as an official language of South Africa, on par with English and Dutch. In 1923 Afrikans hold conferences at Bloemfontein and Pretoria to protest the constant changes to their rights.

During this time, with the growing number of Afrikan Legal Minds, The British Government is Petitioned for the return of Land to Afrikans. Ngcukaitobi T (2017: 112) publishes an excerpt for one of the Petitions made by Lawyers at this time:

"Referring to the Native Laws and Treatment, your Petitioners have experienced with great regret that High Commissioners and Governors General who are the True Representatives of your Majesty, have merely acted as disinterested spectators whilst responsible government parties of various names and Associations are interpreting the Laws in Class Legislation to Suit their purpose.... Your Petitioners pray that your Majesty be pleased to hand back the so-called unalienated land to the family of the late King Lobengula (King of amaNdebele Nation) in Trust for the Tribe according to Bantu (sic) Custom and the right of Chieftainship therein to be restored and acknowledged." (This may be the same land alluded to earier, that the Boers are planning to Claim in the Land Claims Courts)

I encourage the reader to read Ngcukaitobi's book (The Land is ours), that details the war waged by abaNtu Lawyers to #Bring Back the Land.

The June 1924 election propelled Hertzog to the position of prime minister through a coalition between the National and Labour parties known as the Pact government.

1936, April 7, Natives Representation Act Passed, which removed the Cape Afrikan franchise and set up the advisory Natives Representative Council (NRC); Natives Trust and Land Act was also passed, which added land to native reserves and required six months' service of Afrikan tenants on white-owned land (Forced Labor of Afrikan People who live on land determined to be "White owned Land"). These types of Structural anomalies have engendered deep wounds that are currently seething as the Atrocious and brutal Farm Murders.

As part of the British Common Wealth, South Africa participated in the 2nd World war in Europe and North Afrika as narrated earlier. This loss of life and impoverishment in the service of Britain, further disgruntled White South Africans who support White Afrikaner Nationalism.

1948

The National Party comes into power and formalizes Segregation in its Policy of Apartheid.

Interestingly, this is the same year that the State of Israel is Proclaimed by David Ben-Gurion, the head of the Jewish Agency and the American President Harry S. Truman recognized the New Nation on the same day. (office of the Historian, US department of State). The Afrikaner Nationalist Sentiment is that Israel and Afrikaners experience the same hardship in trying to acquire God's Promised Land (Kanaan for the Israelites and Muwene we Mutapa for the White Afrikaners, both of whom in their thinking believe they have God's blessing to displace the "cursed Black people").

On 13 January 1949 an Indian store-keeper in central Durban assaulted an African youth. This incident resulted in a wave of violence from Durban to Pietermaritzburg, wherein a Total of

142 people of all races died.

This Violence was re-lived in the 2021 Phoenix Massacre that followed widespread looting and Arson in KZN and Gauteng.

On Monday 12 July 2021, South Africa erupted in Anarchy following the 15month incarceration of former president Jacob Zuma on 11 July 2021 for a Contempt of Court Ruling passed by the Constitutional Court that demanded that he appear before the Zondo Commission. The Zondo Commission, had been established by the past President, to look into the matters of alleged State Capture. Past President requested that Judge Zondo recuse himself when it was his time to give evidence as he felt that Judge Zondo was conflicted. When Judge Zondo refused to recuse himself, Past President Zuma also refused to Testify in the Commission, attracting a 15 month prison sentence from the Constitutional Court.

What started as a Stay away in protest of the former president's incarceration quickly escalated into full-blown Anarchy with widespread looting and Arson of businesses. The Government's paralysis in responding to the massive scale Anarchy led Communities to defend themselves against looters as they attacked businesses indiscriminately and the threat of attack of personal property became a real fear for most.

In some Indian Communities and predominantly Phoenix, the Protection of Community became a Massacre as 40 Afrikan people were confirmed as having been violently murdered in broad day light for driving or walking on the Phoenix highway. At the time of this writing, 100 were still reported as missing.

Bishop Dube captured the Massacre in an Opinion piece on the Sunday Tribune Newspaper's insider section of 25/07/21 in this manner:

We must learn to live together as brothers or perish together as fools."

Martin Luther King, Jnr's words came to mind when I saw the damage done to people's lives in Phoenix in particular.

In Phoenix, we are not counting the damage of property and burnt buildings during looting but the damage of racism and hatred that erupted in the name of protecting property. Black African brothers and sisters were shot and clubbed to death, just because they were walking around the area at the time the looting was taking place.

Indeed, what happened was not only in Phoenix and Chatsworth but even Lotus Park. It was evidence of the deep-seated tension that has not been spoken about openly, for fear that it would raise tension.

Historically, we know that Indians having lived together with Africans as brothers and sisters, were removed from the Inanda area, not out of their will but because of apartheid laws of segregation. I don't think that matter was dealt with in a proper manner. There has always been that hidden hatred for a few.

We must remember that apartheid has taught us that we, Black Africans, are not the same, we were made third-class citizens while Indians were regarded as second-class citizens. We cannot bury our heads in the ground and behave as if we did not see the damage of the mind done by racist regime of pre-1994.

Was there a time after 1994 where we paused and reviewed the damage that was done in our minds when we were separated? Why do we shun the truth, that we have been using derogatory words toward Indians and called them "C**lies" and "c**rros" while they will call Blacks "K**fer"?

What we see in Phoenix is as a result of a damaged mind. How did people who were living together a day ago become such enemies, so that any Black person walking around Phoenix is shot at as an enemy?

Looking at some of the videos, one can see black people were hunted and shot at like targets at a shooting range. Their cars were stopped, they were pulled out and clubbed to a cheering crowd, that cheered whilst other people were being killed.

That was a damaged mind full of racism and hatred revealing itself.

We were too quick to call ourselves a "rainbow nation"

Yesterday, we were enemies and, the next day, we were supposed to clap and sing together.

Looking at what was done in Rwanda to undo the damage must teach us how we can rebuild relationships. We quickly wanted to show the world that we are a forgiving nation, yet there were no institutions fully established to teach the people what it means to live together as a united nation. Some black people were advantaged by money and be able to buy houses in the Indian communities, yet we did not allow ourselves the time for healing the wounds inflicted by racism.

It may be true that, in some case, that Indians took a stand of self-defence due to the internal damage of thinking that they are a soft target for the poor because of the state of socio-economic conditions. There was element of fear when the looting started. The Indians and whites thought they would be easy targets. It is understandable but forming the barricades of one race when in other communities we live together was as the result of what racism can do.

Why is it that when we are under attack, we quickly forget that we live in a country of united people? Why group yourselves according to race and begin to shoot Blacks? Is it because they have never trusted Blacks all the time but were not able to speak about it? Or is there another reason for this deep-seated racism that was entrenched in people's minds?

There has been an outcry of failure of our leadership as the ruling party. People are accusing us of a loud absence. Where were the community leaders, traditional leaders, religious leaders and political leaders in this crisis? People believe that when it's time to vote, we are too visible and during the time of crises, our presence cannot be accounted for. Maybe one of the truths is that, as leaders, we were not taught or trained on how to handle crises in leadership. This is something we must learn.

When all is said and done, we have a major task of rebuilding again. We have to destroy the seed of racism, not just to chop the roots. We have to engage on social cohesion, not in theory but on the ground. We have to re-establish the moral regeneration course. We need to relook at the Reconstruction and Development of the soul.

In the same paper, Ela Ghandhi Reflected on the Lessons learnt during the 1949 Riots as follows:

"I was 9 years old when I witnessed the horrific 1949 riots. At the time, I was gripped with fear, disbelief and anger. We lived at the Phoenix settlement in the then eNanda, established by Mahatma Gandhi and over the nine years of my life, I had only seen friendship, love and mutual respect among the local African and Indian Communities. Suddenly what happened? My little mind could not fathom."

At that time, 1949, Ela Recounts that the violence led the leaders to come together and work together to try and find a solution. Chief Albert Luthuli and Dr Monty Naicker were amongst those who brokered peace. This coming together would strengthen the bond amongst all the oppressed, culminating in the later Defiance campaign of 1952 and the organization of the Congress of the people in 1955 and later the UDF. In 1985, another horrific attack occurred eNanda as Indian homes and property were looted and burnt. Phoenix settlement was also burnt down and occupied.

Ela believes "the hidden hand of Apartheid" orchestrated the violence and she believes again there was a hidden hand in the 2021 systematic attacks in KZN and Gauteng to destabilize (South Africa). In each of these three circumstances she witnessed, "It is clear that in the front line were poor and vulnerable people whose hunger and poverty rendered them easy prey to be used by those with wealth and power."

According to Ela Gandhi, "History has shown that peaceful societies exist where a sustainable partnership between all sectors of society and the state exists." In the past decade Inequality, unemployment and poverty have grown while rampant corruption and Looting of state resources became endemic and service delivery reached an all-time low. These circumstances, she believes created an ideal situation for the use of divisive tactics by those who still harboured racist attitudes.

"Fear, Anger and aggression gripped the people as they saw their Livelihoods snatched from them" She says.

"From my earlier experience and from the words of our leaders, I see clearly that our resilience against any future unrest can only be built if we are able to heal the wounds of the past few days and unite as South Africans. If we work together constructively on issues of poverty and unemployment; discard Materialism, corruption and greed; build a humane culture of non-violence with compassion and love; and cherish the values of our constitution, then we will be able to avert any future occurrences such as the one we have witnessed" she concluded.

1950: Populations Registration Act enabled the formal Classification of People on the basis of their "race" into: White, Coloured, Bantu and Other (which was later changed to Indian. Chinese people are quietly "assimilated" to the White Class or unclassified)

The Act Enabled the Grand Apartheid Strategy which involved rigid political, territorial, and economic segregation by race in order to entrench white domination and White Afrikaner Nationalist power. The Groups Areas Act furthered this concept by rigidifying urban segregation and excluding black and Indian traders from central business districts. Later, Indian people were allowed to Trade in certain parts of the CBDs whilst Blacks were outlawed. This is why one finds various Business quarters in a CBD. The Center is White-led and the Outskirts are Indian-led, whilst there is neither Coloured nor Black areas in the Towns and Cities. Thus Black people who are now (Post-Apartheid) taking up business in the City and Towns, have to Rent Exhorbitantly from either white or Indian Landlords.

The Classification went as follows:

Bantu (Black; African; and/or Native): All Native People: amaNguni, baKhoe and baSan Nations "a Bantu is a person who is or is generally accepted as a member of any Aboriginal race or tribe of Africa..."

This effectively alienated Afrikans from their Afrikan Land. Afrikaners deemed it improper to name Afrikans as Afrikans because Translated to Afrikaans it would be Afrikaners and they had already Appropriated this Afrikaner identity for themselves. The former derogatory Kaffir remained an unofficial derogation and later "Bantus" was reserved for Academic purposes as a Philological Classification

Coloured: All Mixed Heritage People who are Not White Passing

"A Coloured is a person who is Not a White person or a Bantu."

The very Painful Test of White Passing was done with various methodologies of which the Pencil Test is the most remembered.

Methods of Testing:

- Skin Colour (Looking for Melanin Tones)
- Facial Features (Looking for Breadth of nose and Thickness of Lips)
- Home Language, and especially the knowledge and Accent of Afrikaans
- Area where the person Lived, their family, friends and acquaintances (Are they Black or White)
- Employment and Socio Economic Status (Poor vs Middle Income and or Wealthy)
- Their Eating and Drinking Habits. (Type of Cuisine: African or Western. That is our Children to date will say: "I don't eat that African meat" when served with Offal or the various unfarmiliar African cuisines)
- "Pencil Test" wherein a Pencil is used to confirm whether one was of European or Mixed race descent. This tested the characteristics of a person's head hair and other body hair. If a Pencil placed in one's hair fell off without being entangled by Curly hair when one shook their hair after a pencil was placed in their hair, one would be Confirmed as "White"

If the Pencil was entangled in the curly hair, one was proven to be of mixed descent and thus designated "coloured". This Test divided families as some members of European descent now had Khoi, San and African abaNtu blood and the gene for curly hair would not necessarily appear in all members of the family. Under the Act as Amended, Coloureds and Indians were formally Classified into various subgroups: Cape Coloured; Malay Coloured; Griqua coloured; Chinese coloured; Indian coloured other Asian and other Coloured. *Interestingly, the sub classification never included Native/Bantu coloured.*

White: All White People

"A White Person is a person who in appearance is obviously White and who is generally not accepted as coloured or who is generally accepted as white and is not obviously Non-White". Provided that a person shall not be classified as a white person if one of his natural parents has been classified as a coloured person or Bantu..." thus including most Afrikaners who have earlier mixed heritage of abaNtu, Khoe and San, whose immediate parents did not look like their grandparents or great grandparents. This is why some people who identify as white look Coloured and why there have been a few cases of throwback genes, where white people have given birth to "coloured" or "Black" children. You might want to watch the film Skin, a British-South African 2008 Biographical film about Sandra Laing, a South African woman born to white parents who was Classified as Black in spite of being the child of at least three generations of ancestors who had been regarded as white, because she failed the Skin tone and pencil Test. She was expelled from her all white School and separated from her family, to live a harrowing life of rejection during the Apartheid era. www.journeyman.tv the spiritual journey of Sandra Laing is a shorter and easily accessible version.

Indian and Chinese People: were Initially Classified as "other", Negating their Personhood and Legitimacy in South Africa as People. Later they became Asians, then Indians and Chinese.

Indians: Indians were Classified as South Asians from the former British India and their Descendants regardless of their mixed heritage.

The Population Registration Act was used for Political, Social, and Economic Purposes. Allocating White People Towns and Suburbs to live in; Giving them Political Franchise; Creating Separate Amenities for people; Protection of White People and Granting Privilege and Access to Means of Production to White people as well as to control social relations between the "Races" criminalizing Interracial relationships and marriages so that those involved would be charged. The White people would get a fine and the black people would be jailed.

In the Western Cape (eMbekweni), Black people were either forcefully removed or designated Coloured. This was done to further reduce the population of Black people in the Western Cape and increase the Coloured population. This population had previously been deliberately increased through the strictly and exclusively controlled intermarriages between Dutch and Khoe Nations at Genadendaal and Humansdorp Mission Stations (1738).

It was possible for one person to be assigned different Racial categories and for different people in a family to belong to all Racial groups: White, Indian, Coloured and Black. These families have suffered untold Trauma to their Emotions and Spirits as they are invalidated and rejected on several levels.

Derogated and denied by All: "Bantu", "White" Indian and Chinese people. As it is today, most "Coloured" people can only trace their genealogy to their Grandparents and sometimes they can't associate with them as they are either White or Black. This fostered deep wounds of Superiority and Inferiority which still feed the Racial Tensions today.

The Act and its disastrous consequences was met with Protest Campaigns and the Creation and Launch of the Freedom Charter which was a Collaboration of various Organisations (The ANC- African National Congress, The Indian People's Congress, Coloured People's Congress and Congress of Democrats).

In December 1951, the African National Congress at a Conference held in Bloemfontein presented the Defiance Campaign. In 1952 Non-Violent Mass Demonstrations, Boycotts, Strikes and Acts of Civil Disobedience were organized.

The Defiance Campaign was organized as a joint effort across the Racial bar and the participation of other Organisations: The Indian People's Congress, Coloured People's Congress and Congress of Democrats).

The South African Government viewed the protests as acts of anarchy, communism, and disorder. 8000 black people were reportedly arrested for defying Apartheid laws and regulations. The "Swart Gevaar" and "Kommunisme Gevaar" became words that white Children were raised with, learning to fear Black people and see them as evil and thoughtless Barbaric Vagrants who are out to get them. The Communist Party of South Africa is driven underground and It Reforms as: The South African Communist Party (SACP), having recruited people from all "races".

In 1955 The Congress of the People (Not to be confused with the Post-Apartheid COPE) also known as the South African Congress Alliance is formed. It is made up of the African National Congress, the Indian Congress, Coloured People's Congress and the white liberal South African Congress of Democrats.

The ANC sent out 50,000 volunteers into townships and the villages to collect "freedom demands" from the people of South Africa. These were synthesized into the final document by ANC leaders including Z.K Mathews; Lionel Bernstein; Ethel Drus; Ruth First; and Alan Lipman, whose wife Beata Lipman wrote the original Charter by Hand.

It is apparently the Only and unique Freedom Charter of its kind in the World. A Charter Memorial has been erected in Kliptown to Commemorate the Charter. The Charter was officially adopted on Sunday 26 June 1955 at a gathering of about 3,000 in Kliptown Soweto, 17km South-West of Johannesburg. For each Section read out, the People Would Shout: **¡Afrika! Mayibuye!**

The Freedom Charter Started with these words:

"We, the People of South Africa, declare for all our country and the world to know: **that South Africa belongs to all who live in it, black and white,** and that no government can justly claim authority unless it is based on the will of all the people; that our people have been robbed of their birth right to land, liberty and peace by a form of government founded on injustice and inequality; **that our country will never be prosperous or free until all our people live in brotherhood, enjoying equal rights and opportunities;** that only a democratic state, based on the will of all the people, can secure to all, their birth right without distinction of colour, race, sex or belief; And ***therefore, we, the people of South Africa, black and white together - equals, countrymen and brothers*** - adopt this Freedom Charter. And we pledge ourselves to strive together, sparing neither strength nor courage, until the democratic changes here set out have been won."

The "Freedom Demands" were synthesised into the following Demands, each with a brief Summary of what the Demand Meant. Refer to the website www.historicalpapers.wits.ac.za/FreedomCharter-Wits-Historical-papers to see one of the original Complete Copies of the Charter.

- The people shall govern
- All national groups shall have equal rights!
- The people shall share in the country's wealth!
- The land shall be shared among those who work it!
- All shall be equal before the law!
- All shall enjoy equal human rights!
- There shall be work and security!
- The doors of learning and of culture shall be opened!
- There shall be houses, security and comfort!
- There shall be peace and friendship!

The Reading was Concluded with these words:

"Let all who love their people and their country now say, as we say here: These freedoms we will fight for, side by side, throughout our lives, until we have won our liberty."

Sobukwe, a lawyer who was a Lecturer of African Studies at WITS University, Founded the Pan Africanist Congress. He had joined the ANC Youth League as part of the Student Leadership of Fort-hare but was increasingly critical of what he saw as the organisation's "liberal-left-multiracialist" policies, Himself being Non-Racial Pan Africanist. This led him to Form the Pan Africanist Congress(PAC) in 1960. As President of the newly formed PAC, Sobukwe was key in organising protests against the Pass laws, which had intensified from their earlier Appearances in the 1700s now they demanded that all Afrikan Males carry a Pass Book that people called: "Dom Pas" which attested to bearer's eligibility to be in a certain area. Failure to produce a Dom Pas was a criminal offense and meant immediate Arrest without Trial, rendering the entire Afrikan populace potentially Criminal.

In the late 1950s, the pass laws had been extended to include Afrikan women. Both the PAC and the ANC responded with nationwide civil disobedience campaigns. On the morning of 21 March 1960, Sobukwe left his home in Mofolo, Soweto, to lead a small crowd on an eight-kilometer march to Orlando police station. The crowd had one goal: To be arrested.

Sobukwe and his comrades were trying to expose the absurdity of the Pass laws by forcing the authorities to arrest them, thereby gridlocking the system and hopefully breaking it down if the process was repeated often enough in various locations. The Marchers were arrested as expected.

The Marchers from Sharpeville however met with a different fate. As a crowd of 5 000 peaceful protesters approached the local police station, police opened fire. 69 people were killed and more than 200 were wounded, many of them shot in the back as they fled. This Sharpeville Massacre, became a turning point in the Apartheid History of South Africa. It made International headlines and intensified international pressure on the apartheid state.

In its aftermath the government imposed a state of emergency, banning both the ANC and PAC as illegal organisations and detaining 18,000 people.

The liberation movements responded by abandoning passive resistance for military struggle, with the ANC forming its armed wing Umkhonto we Sizwe, and the PAC its armed wing Poqo.

On 1 April 1960, the United Nations Security Council passed Resolution 134 after a complaint by 29 member states regarding "the situation arising out of the large-scale killings of unarmed and peaceful demonstrators against racial discrimination and segregation in the Union of South Africa". The resolution voiced the council's anger at the policies and actions of the South African government, and called on the government to abandon apartheid. The UN Resolution 134 became a powerful weapon for the international anti-apartheid movement.

The Apartheid Regime regarded Sobukwe to be more dangerous than Nelson Mandela because his ideology of Non-Racialism meant equality of people, as opposed to the Multiracial potentially unequal people, which did not threaten them. This threatened the Apartheidness of Apartheid as an ideology (a United People Stand... whilst a divided people fall...) After his arrest on 21 March 1960, Sobukwe was sentenced to three years in prison. He refused the help of an attorney, and would not appeal the sentence, on the grounds that the court had No Jurisdiction Over him, as it was neither a court of law nor justice. Just as his three-year term was coming to an end, the South African government passed the General Law Amendment Act on 3 May 1963, which contained a special clause that later became known as the Sobukwe Clause and that was ever applied only to him, allowing the minister of justice to prolong the imprisonment of any political prisoner indefinitely. Sobukwe was moved to Robben Island, where he served a further six years in solitary confinement.

He had separate living quarters and was denied contact with other prisoners. But he was allowed books and study materials, and during this time earned a degree in Economics from the University of London. In 1964, a year after his sentence was supposed to have ended, Sobukwe was offered a job by the National Association for the Advancement of Coloured People in the US. But John Vorster, then the minister of justice and later prime minister of South Africa, refused to allow him to leave the country.

Sobukwe was finally released from jail in May 1969 and banished to Galeshewe outside Kimberley, 500 km away from his familes in Mofolo and Graaff Reinet, where he was held under house arrest for 12 hours a day, and forbidden from taking part in any political activity.

He was again offered a job in the US by the University of Wisconsin in 1970 and again denied permission to leave the Country. While under house arrest Sobukwe studied law, completing his articles in Kimberley and opening his own legal practice in 1975, But soon fell ill with advanced Lung Cancer which he could not get effectively treated for because of the terms of his house arrest. He Succumbed to Cancer On 27 February 1978 and was buried in Graaff Reinet, the town of his birth.

The Mounting Resistance begins to grab the attention of White People and some members of the United Party, which is the official Opposition Party, break away, to form the Progressive party, to fight Apartheid legislation as it is brought in to Parliament. They win one seat which is occupied by Helen Suzman, the Leader of the party.

Ms Suzman uses her seat in Parliament to oppose Apartheid from within, campaigning against pieces of apartheid legislation put before Parliament. She fights against detention without trial, pass laws, Group Areas Act, and forced removals. In 1967, Helen Suzman visits Mandela at Robben Island and uses her power in Parliament to ensure that the horrific Prison Conditions begin to improve. Upon his Release, Mandela acknowledged this initiative by Helen Suzman. Ms Suzman was also by Mandela's side when the new South African Constitution was signed in 1996. The Democratic Alliance which evolved from the Progressive Party has used this Relationship to *Appropriate* Mandela into their Movement and they use his pictures in their campaigns and website. It is appropriation because, Mandela is acknowledged apart from and without the consent of the Organisation that made him the Phenomenal "Mandela", the ANC.

Under International Scrutiny, on 5 October 1960, White Voters are called upon to hold a referendum to decide whether South Africa should Remain in the British Common Wealth or become an Independent Republic. The intention was to become a Republic whilst retaining Common Wealth Membership. 52% were in favour of a Republic. Then Prime Minister, H.F Verwoerd attended the Conference of British Commonwealth Prime Ministers to give a formal notice that South Africa wished to change from a Monarchy to a Republic, whilst requesting permission to remain a Member of the Commonwealth. The effect of this request if granted would mean that Britain could not veto decisions made by the South African Government. This request was strongly opposed by other Afrikan States, India and Canada because of South Africa's policy of apartheid. South Africa was granted its desire to become a Republic but was ejected from the British Commonwealth. It became a Republic in 1961. South Africa was welcomed back into the Modern Common Wealth which is now open to all Countries in 1994. With South Africa being an Independent Republic from the Common Wealth, Apartheid laws intensified and this reciprocally increased the Momentum of the Resistance Movement.

Republic of South Africa and Anti-Apartheid Movement

The Resistance Movement builds up Momentum with Boycotts; Strikes and Stay at Home Campaigns. These were sometimes enforced brutally on those who did not want to participate.

The Youth League of the African National Congress led by Nelson Rolihlahla Mandela campaigns its mother body for the uptake of an Armed Struggle.

A Plethora of Documents documenting the Armed Struggle is available from the Nelson Mandela Centre of Memory.

http://atom.nelsonmandela.org/index.php/nelson-mandela-centre-of-memory-south-africa

Umkhonto we Sizwe was finally formed with these sentiments:

"The White State has thrown overboard every pretence of rule by democratic process. Armed to the teeth it has presented the people with only one choice and that is, its overthrow by force and violence. It can now truly be said that very little, if any scope, exists for the smashing of white supremacy other than by means of mass revolutionary action, the main content of which is armed resistance, leading to victory by military means."

Nelson Mandela was captured at Howick on 05 August 1962 in relation to his activities in umKhonto we Sizwe and his Trial began: 09.10.1963 – 12.06.1964. Known as the Rivonia Treason Trial, it takes place at the Palace of Justice in Pretoria, leading to the imprisonment and sentencing to Life at Robben Island of: Nelson Mandela and others as enumerated below who were convicted of State Sabotage, with the following Charges:

- Recruiting persons for training in the preparation and use of explosives and in guerrilla warfare for the purpose of violent revolution and committing acts of sabotage;
- Conspiring to commit the aforementioned acts and to aid foreign military units when they invaded the Republic;
- Acting in these ways to further the objectives of communism;
- Soliciting and receiving money for these purposes from sympathizers in Uganda; Algeria; Ethiopia; Liberia; Nigeria; Tunisia and elsewhere.

<table>
<tr><th>Trialist</th><th>Results</th><th>Lawyers</th></tr>
<tr><td>Nelson Rolihlahla Mandela, umXhosa
ANC Youth Leader</td><td>Life Imprisonment at RobbenIsland. Released 27.8 years later and became 1st DemocraticPresident of South Africa</td><td rowspan="13">The presiding judge wasDr Quartus de Wet, judge-president of the Transvaal

The chief prosecutor was Dr Percy Yutar and DeputyAttorney-General of the Transvaal

Nat Levy was attorney of record in Pretoria for Mandelaand the other accused, with theexception of Kantor

Their Team
Joel Joffe: instructing attorney

Bram Fischer Advocate, leadcounsel

Vernon Berrangé Advocate George Bizos Advocate Arthur Chaskalson Advocate

Harold Hanson Advocate

The defence line-up for Kantorwas:

John Coaker Advocate Harold Hanson AdvocateGeorge Lowen Advocate

H. C. Nicholas Advocate Harry Schwarz Advocate</td></tr>
<tr><td>Walter Sisulu, umXhosa of mixed Xhosa and European descent</td><td rowspan="2">Both received Life Imprisonment at RobbenIsland.
Came out after 26 years</td></tr>
<tr><td>Elias Motsoaledi, MoPedi, ANC Trade Unionist</td></tr>
<tr><td>Lionel Bernstein, Jewish, SACP Member. Deemed as the Architect of the Plan</td><td>Placed under house arrest.Later, fled the country.</td></tr>
<tr><td>Denis Goldberg, JewishEngineer. Leader of theCongress of Democrats</td><td>Imprisoned at PretoriaCentral Prison for 22 years</td></tr>
<tr><td>Arthur Goldreich, Jewish</td><td>Escaped from jail</td></tr>
<tr><td>Bob Hepple, English</td><td>Hepple fled the country, without testifying, and stated"that he never had any intention of testifying" and hewas Removed from Accused Roll</td></tr>
<tr><td>Harold Wolpe, Jewish Prominent Lawyer & Activist</td><td>Escaped from Jail</td></tr>
<tr><td>James Kantor, Wolpe's Brother in law. Jewish</td><td>Discharged: Judge Quartus de Wet ruled that he had nocase to answer. He died in 1975 of a Heart Attack</td></tr>
<tr><td>Ahmed Kathrada, Indian,Muslim</td><td>Life Imprisonment at RobbenIsland. Came out after 26 years</td></tr>
<tr><td>Govan Mbeki, umXhosa</td><td>Life Imprisonment at RobbenIsland. Released after 24y</td></tr>
<tr><td>Raymond Mahlaba,umXhosa</td><td>Life Imprisonment at RobbenIsland. Came out after 26 years</td></tr>
<tr><td>Andrew Mlangeni, moPedi</td><td>Life Imprisonment at RobbenIsland. Came out after 26 years</td></tr>
</table>

The government took advantage of legal provisions allowing for accused persons to be held for 90 days without trial, and the defendants were held incommunicado during which they endured beatings and torture. This is what fuelled the Escapes. The trial was condemned by the United Nations and Nations worldwide, with some Applying Sanctions on South Africa.

At the Trial, Mandela gave the Speech in which these Iconic Paragraph is found:

"During my lifetime I have dedicated my life to this struggle of the Afrikan people. I have fought against white domination, and I have fought against black domination. ***I have cherished the ideal of a democratic and free society in which all persons will live together in harmony and with equal opportunities***. It is an ideal for which I hope to live for and to see realised. But, my Lord, if it needs be, it is an ideal for which I am prepared to die." Nelson Rolihlahla Mandela at the Treason Trial, speaking in the dock of the court on 20 April 1964

The Treason Trials galvanised the International Community against South Africa until finally in 1986 Sanctions were Applied to the Country.

When Nelson Mandela was eventually sentenced in 1964, to life imprisonment, Winnie was left to raise their two small daughters, Zenani and Zindzi, on her own. In spite of Winnie Supporting her husband during his imprisonment in Robben Island and her extensive campaigns for his Release, the years of separation and tremendous social and political turmoil irrevocably damaged the Mandela marriage and the two separated in 1992 after Mandela's Release.

Monitored by the government, Winnie was arrested under the Suppression of Terrorism Act and spent more than a year in solitary confinement, where she was tortured. Upon her release, she continued her activism and was jailed several more times.

Following the Soweto 1976 uprisings, in which hundreds of students were killed, she was forced by the government to relocate to the border town of Brandfort and placed under house arrest. She described the experience as alienating and heart-wrenching, yet she continued to speak out, as in a 1981 statement to the BBC **on Black South African economic might and its ability to overturn the system.**

In 1985, after her exilic home in Orange Free State where she was exiled between 1977 and 1985 was firebombed, Winnie returned to Soweto and there continued to criticize the regime, cementing her title of "Mother of the Nation." Her youth group, the Mandela United Football Club, garnered a reputation for brutality. In 1989, 14-year-old Stompie Moeketsi was abducted by the club and later killed. Winnie was found to have been: "Negligent in that she failed to act responsibly in taking the necessary action required to avert his death."

Winnie appeared before the Truth and Reconciliation Commission in 1997 and was found responsible for "gross violations of human rights" in connection to The killings and tortures implemented by her bodyguards.

Winnie was elected president of the ANC's Women's League and in 1994 became the deputy minister of arts, culture, science and technology. However, due to affiliations and rhetoric seen as highly radical, she was ousted from her cabinet post by her husband in 1995. The couple finally divorced after a 4-year separation in 1996.

While ANC leaders kept their political distance, Winnie still retained a grassroots following. She was re-elected to Parliament in 1999, only to be convicted of economic fraud in 2003. She quickly resigned from her post, though her conviction was later overturned. Winnie Madikizela served Parliament again from 2009 until her death on April 2, 2018, in Johannesburg. She is the Mother of the Nation.

To enforce the government's stance against: Liberation Movements; anti-apartheid activists (Swart gevaar) and the 'communist threat' The Defence Amendment Bill was passed on June 1967 to make military service compulsory for White young men. Conscription was instituted in South Africa in the form of 9 months of service for all white males between the ages of 17 and 65 years old. Conscripts became members of the South African Defence Force (SADF). The Conscription demands kept changing to suit the needs of the State especially in the Townships and Namibia until the service time was increased to 2 years followed by 30 days of Service annually for 8 years.

Whilst Studying Medicine at Natal Medical School (Now, N.R Mandela School of Medicine), Bantu Stephen Biko developed the Black Consciousness Movement. Having joined the National Union of South African Students, he became disillusioned with its Paternalistic ethos toward the Black Struggle. He developed the view that to avoid white domination, black people had to organise independently. He Founded the South African Students 'organisation (SASO) in 1968, whose Membership was open only to Black People: Bantu, Coloured and Indian. Although He was careful to keep his movement independent of white liberals, he opposed anti-white sentiments.

Biko and his compatriots developed Black Consciousness as SASO's official ideology. The movement campaigned for an end to apartheid and the transition of South Africa toward universal suffrage and a **Socialist economy**. It organised Black Community Programmes (BCPs) and focused on the psychological empowerment of black people. Biko believed that black people needed to rid themselves of any sense of racial inferiority, an idea he expressed by popularizing the slogan "Black is Beautiful" When Biko extended his ideology to the wider Population, the Government began to see him as a subversive threat and placed him under a Banning order in 1973, severely restricting his activities. He remained politically active, helping organise BCPs such as a healthcare centre and a crèche in the Ginsberg area. Following his arrest in August 1977, Biko was beaten and pulled behind a moving car and he died, whilst in

Custody, from Multi organ failure following the Blunt Trauma and Contusions he had suffered. Police claimed that he hung himself in Custody. His Funeral was Massive, Attracting Over 20,000 people who attended his funeral.

A 1978 biography by his friend Donald Woods formed the basis for the 1987 film: Cry Freedom

The Apartheid Government Created Bantustans for Afrikans to further alienate them from the Land and force them to the 13% of Land that had become reserved for them from 1913, with territories being finalised in the 60s and these Bantustans being formalised so that Muwene Mutapa can become a White South African Country and Afrikans can live in Independent Reserves as it had been done in the Americas wherein the Natives live in Reserves and America is a Land of white people, with all others in the Minority and treated like Aliens. These separate Developments were also calculated to divide and rule. baKhoe and baSan were not included in these developments as they had been erased by being designated Coloured and generally disregarded as though they had become extinct, especially because their Land in what is Now the Western Cape had been fully Appropriated as the land of White people, the Cape Colony. Thus they were left Landless.

The Bantustans Solidified Tribalism and false National federal amaNguni States of VhaVenda; baPedi, baLobedu and some amaNdebele as Northern Sotho; baTswana; vaTsonga; amaNdebele; ba Sotho as Southern Sotho; amaZulu and amaXhosa with proposed Homelands and who were offered Independence from South Africa. The so-called TBVC States: Transkei, Venda, Bophuthatswana, and Ciskei Accepted their Independence from South Africa serially. Other territories, such as Kwa Ndebele; KwaZulu; Leboa; Kagwane and QwaQwa, were treated as such even though they did not Accept the independence:

In 1973, to Pacify the growing Anti-Apartheid Sentiments, The Information Minister hatched a Plan to sway Public opinion through positive Pro-Apartheid Media. He is given a green light to vire R64 000 000 from the Defence Budget to Slush funds to Bribe International News Agencies as well as to Buy an International paper: The Washington Star and to establish a Local government controlled newspaper, that was "owned" by Louis Luyt: The Citizen. These were meant to push a positive Propaganda about South Africa, Silencing what was perceived as the "Hate South Africa Crusade". When investigations into this matter were complete, it was found that the extent of the Corruption and financial irregularities amounted to 72 Million USD in 1978 (about one Billion Rands today) Murphy, C. (September 30, 1980): Rhoodie's Fraud Conviction

Reversed in South African Scandal, The Washington Post online. Some sources blame the introduction of the General Sales Tax in 1978 on this looting of State coffers, necessitating the Government to look for other avenues to create income. The General Sales Tax became Vat in 1991.

The Media of South Africa still suffers the wounds of the Propagandist Apartheid Regime and Reports to sway the opinions of South afrikans, rather than to inform them of the News. News have become Opinion Statements as each Agency seeks to peddle its opinion position or that of its sponsors. Public Media tries to be independent, but ultimately its budget comes from Government. Private Media blows its independence horn but as seen with the Citizen above, it is possible for it to be bought. Desperate for a Mouth that would Champion his Voice, Past President Zuma also created a Media Network hosted on Multichoice. Once this became clear, Multichoice did not renew its contract with Afro Worldview. Although Multichoice shows great BBBEE score cards, the considerable BBBEE Shareholding, does not carry the necessary mandate for Policy Change. Most importantly, Most Afrikans who hold these shares hold them as an investment, they are not aware of the potential Decision-making power they possess, so they do not attend Annual General Meetings.

In KwaZulu, Mangosuthu Gatsha Buthelezi who was also the Executive councilor of KwaZulu and the Prime Minister of amaZulu Nation founded the Inkatha Freedom Party as a Cultural Movement and Political Party when he resigned from the African National Congress in 1975. It was formed as an Anti-Apartheid and Black Nationalist Party.

On 4 January 1974, Gatsha had met Harry Schwarz, leader of the liberal- reformist wing of the United Party and the two had Created what became known as the Mahlabathini Declaration of Faith.

The Declaration entailed 5 points:

- Negotiations involving all people to draw up constitutional proposals stressing opportunity for all with a Bill of Rights to safeguard these rights
- Constitutional Democracy ensuring equal opportunity for all
- Bill of Rights
- Non-Violent Political Change
- Federal System of Government

It was the first agreement by acknowledged black and white political leaders in South Africa that affirmed to these principles and was heralded by the English Media as a breakthrough in race relations in South Africa. Shortly after it was issued, the declaration was endorsed by several chief ministers of the black homelands (Bantustans). The National Party, the Afrikaans Media and the conservative wing of the United Party however vehemently opposed it, preferring the Status quo. The Declaration would sow seeds for the later Negotiated Settlement of South Africa.

By the early 21st century Inkatha claimed to have more than 1.5 million members. Inkatha did not expand much beyond its amaZulu base however (Although it has always and continues to attract some committed members from the Indian, coloured and Afrikaans communities). The organization was criticized as being collaborationist and ethnically divisive by members of the ANC. In the late 1980s and '90s followers of the two movements were regularly involved in bloody clashes (Black on Black Violence). In 1991 the South African government admitted that it had secretly subsidized Inkatha in the latter's deepening rivalry with the ANC. (Online Britannica)

In South Africa's first post-apartheid elections (1994), the Inkatha Freedom Party won a decisive victory in KwaZulu-Natal. Nationally, the party won 10.5 percent of the vote and 43 seats in the National Assembly. Buthelezi was subsequently appointed home affairs minister by President Nelson Mandela.

The Bantu Education Act of 1953 had established a Black Education Department in the Department of Native Affairs, which had to compile a Curriculum that suited the "Nature and Requirements of the Black people" Hendrik Verwoerd felt that "Natives (Blacks) must be taught from an early age that equality with Europeans (Whites) is not for them" (Northern Cape Government,16/06/2016)

Black people were not to receive an education that would lead them to aspire to positions they wouldn't be allowed to hold in society. Instead, they were to receive education designed to provide them with skills to serve their own people in the homelands or to work in laboring jobs under whites.

Because of the government's homelands policy, no new high schools were built in Soweto between 1962 and 1971. Students were meant to move to their relevant homeland to attend the newly built schools there. According to: Boddy-Evans, Alistair (28 January 2020) in their article: "16 June 1976 Student Uprising in Soweto." Published online. www. thoughtco.com/student-uprising-soweto-riots- part-1-43425,

In 1972, the government gave in to pressure from business to improve the Bantu Education system to meet business's need for a better trained black workforce. 40 new schools were built in Soweto. Between 1972 and 1976 the number of pupils at secondary schools increased from 12,656 to 34,656. One in five Soweto children were attending secondary school.

This increase in secondary school attendance had a significant effect on youth culture. Previously, many young people spent the time between leaving primary school and obtaining a job (if they were lucky) or in gangs, which generally lacked any political consciousness. But now secondary school students were forming their own, much more politicized identity. Clashes between gangs and students only furthered the sense of student solidarity.

In 1975 South Africa entered a period of economic depression. Schools were starved of funds. The government spent R644 a year on a white child's education but only R42 on a black child. The Department of Bantu Education then announced it was removing the Standard 6 year from primary schools. Previously, in order to progress to Form 1 of secondary school, a pupil had to obtain a first or second- degree pass in Standard 6. This served to reduce the numbers that would proceed to High School. Now the majority of pupils could proceed to secondary school without any hindrance. In 1976, 257,505 pupils enrolled in Form 1, but there was space for only 38,000. Many of the students therefore remained at primary school, disgruntling many learners who were highly politicized.

The African Students Movement had been founded in 1968 to voice student grievances, changed its name in January 1972 to the South African Students Movement (SASM) and pledged itself to building a national movement of high school students who would work with the Black Consciousness Movement (BCM) and SASO helping students to understand themselves as black people and thus helping to politicize the students.

When the Department of Education issued its decree that Afrikaans was to become the medium of instruction for black Schools, the Students objected to being taught in the language of the oppressor.

These events built momentum until in 1976, Through the Student formations, Several High Schools were Mobilised to Protest this New decree. About 20,000 students from Soweto's high schools decided, in secret, to participate in the protest.

Though the protest had been planned secretly, one of the organizers leaked details to the media in order to guarantee coverage. Sam Nzima, a 42 -year- old photojournalist with *The World* newspaper, was sent out to cover it. Unfortunately, the Government also got a Tip off and were ready for the Students.

A few Minutes into the Protest, Police fired Live Ammunition into the Crowd of Students. Amongst the Casualties was Hector Petersen whose limp body in 18-year-old Mbuyisa Makhubo's arms with Antoinette Sithole (Hector's sister) running beside Makhubo was caught on Camera by Mr Nzima and it made Front Page on the World Newspaper.

"No one was prepared for the impact!"

The World Newspaper, had a relationship with international wire agencies, and by the next day, Nzima's photo was splashed across the front pages of newspapers from New York to Moscow. Suddenly the world could no longer ignore the horror of apartheid. Almost overnight, international opinion hardened against South Africa's apartheid regime. The U.S. government condemned the shooting, and activists worldwide began lobbying for economic sanctions, which eventually brought the apartheid government to its knees. In South Africa the picture helped launch a civil uprising and emboldened the black liberation movement. According to: Online Time Magazine's Aryn Baker (June, 15, 2016), "The protest was about Afrikaans in school, but it raised eyebrows for other countries that, *this is not right...* "How can kids be killed for claiming their rights?"

The Hector Pieterson Memorial and museum opened in Orlando West, Soweto in 2002, not far from the spot where 12-year-old Hector was shot on June 16, 1976 during the Soweto uprising.

uPoqo and Umkhonto we Sizwe which had been conducting Campaigns against the Apartheid Regime over the years now increased their Recruitment efforts amongst the Politicised youth and later the Trade Unions, UDF and Religious Organisations. A lot of young People would leave for School and never return home, having "fled the country to go underground in exile" through: Swaziland, Lesotho and Mozambique to: Russia, Uganda, Tanzania, Mozambique, Tunisia, Morocco, Algeria and many other Countries for Military Training. They could also Study and some became Doctors, Lawyers and Economists on these Placements. Once in a while a Terror attack would be carried out on strategic targets meant to send a Message: Military Bases; Malls; Post Office... The Penalty for the Bomber if caught, was death. One such young person who was killed by hanging at the age of 15, was Andrew Zondo, who detonated an explosive in a rubbish bin at the Sanlam Centre Shopping Mall in Amanzimtoti, Durban's South Coast on 23 December 1985. These people who are regarded as Struggle icons, have been largely forgotten and some languish in poverty. We do not get to hear about them and their Secret Missions. Being secret and acts of War and Terror, they have remained shrouded until the Ashley Kriel MK Detachment decided to write a Book on their experiences: Voices from the Underground by Ashley Gunn.

In 1982, a Johannesburg man who contracted HIV whilst in California Tests HIV Positive and randomized Tests show a 12.6% prevalence rate amongst White Johannesburg Gay men. Although at first it was described as a disease of white Gay men, this disease would prove to be burdensome amongst Afrikan people of all sexual orientations in the 1990s.

In 1983, with the Bantustans established, it was time to solve the Coloured and Indian question. The Apartheid Government thus devised a new Divide and Rule Strategy by introducing the Tricameral system which gave Indian and Coloured people Suffrage whilst excluding Blacks, following a Referendum in which 66% White Voters supported a change of the Constitution and to adopt the Republic of South Africa Constitution Act. A Tricameral Political System was instituted from 1984 to 1994 wherein a limited political voice was given to "coloureds" and "Indians". The majority Black population group outside the Bantustans was ignored.

The Commonwealth Eminent Persons group led by Olusegun Obasanjo and Malcolm Fraser persuade the South African Government to Dismantle Apartheid but is unsuccessful. This mobilizes new Resistance in the form of the United Democratic Front (Churches; Political Parties and Trade Unions)

With the ANC Banned and its Leaders in Prison, Rev. Allan Boesak introduced plans for a New Political Organisation at a conference of the Transvaal Anti-South African Indian Council Committee (TASC) on 23 January 1983. The part of his speech calling for a "United Front" of " Churches, Civic Associations, Trade Unions, Student Organizations, and Sports Bodies" was unplanned, but well received. In his Speech, he also called for Inclusion of black people in Government. The United Democratic Front was thus inadvertently formed.

The Party was formally Launched in Rocklands Community Hall in Mitchell's Plain, on the day of the Launch of the new Tricameral Constitution, 20 August 1984 to Shouts of: **UDF Unites! Apartheid Divides!**

After a conference of delegates from 575 organisations, a public rally was held and was attended by about 10,000 people. Reverend Frank Chikane, the first major speaker, called the day "a turning point in the struggle for freedom."

The UDF and its affiliates promoted Rent boycotts, School protests, Worker stay-aways and a Boycott of the Tricameral System. In 1989, UDF sent delegates to the USA and UK to discuss what foreign countries could do to help end apartheid.

Throughout its existence, the UDF demanded the release of imprisoned ANC leaders, as well as other Political Prisoners. In 1985, the UDF announced at a rally of 2,500 people, their campaign, to see: "The release of Nelson Mandela". This became an International rallying call that saw International Musicians organize Concerts for the Release of Nelson Mandela. The World Reverberated with: "Release, Nelson Mandela!"

However, the UDF was never formally attached to the ANC, and did not participate in the armed struggle.

The Congress of South African Trade Unions (COSATU) was formed in 1985, uniting various worker's Movements. This intensified the Struggle further.

On February 19, 1985, several UDF members, including Albertina Sisulu; Frank Chikane; and Cassim Saloojee, were arrested on high treason charges in what became known as the Delmas Treason Trial. They were part of 22 people arrested of whom: Moses Chikane, Mosiuoa Lekota and Popo Molefe were known as the big 3. The UDF was accused of being a "shadow organization" for the African National Congress. In November 1988, eight of those accused of treason were acquitted of all charges, while five activists were found guilty of terrorism. The Judge also ruled that the UDF was a "Revolutionary Organization" that incited violence in black townships in a bid to render South Africa ungovernable. The convictions were overturned by the Appeal Court in Bloemfontein in 1989, releasing the five activists.

The Townships were burning. Umkhonto we Sizwe agitated for change through violent means; Black on Black Violence increased with counter allegations of impimpi and the atrocity of Tyre Necklacing reached its peak, wherein those suspected of being impipi (sell outs) were summarily burnt in broad day light in the street, by having a Tyre wedged around their neck and shoulders, Petrol poured on them and that, set on fire...

The Country became increasingly ungovernable and its Economy was greatly weakened, Necessitating the Declaration of a State of Emergency with Military

Patrols and curfews. During this period "official murder and torture" become common. Many were detained without Trial, Tortured and Murdered in Prisons. Police Raids Were Common and the "Yellow Mellow" sent Children Scattering off the Streets. "Nansi Mellow Yellow!" Echoed in the Streets, and ultimately a song, in True kiNtu, immortalising Historical events in Song whilst creating emotional connections to them to ensure they are never forgotten, as people warned each other of impending Police raids.

Black People lived in Terror as Disappearances became commonplace. As a Black person in South Africa, one had absolutely no Rights. The Police and Army were not protectors, but agents of Terror and Death. They had absolute power to detain, Torture and murder for any Suspicion of Terrorism and almost any one with Political opinion was labelled a Terrorist. You probably know someone who was Detained, Tortured or even murdered... This wound is responsible for the negative opinion many South Africans have of Law Enforcement.

More people from the White Community get drawn into the UDF through the Church, notably the South African Council of Churches as well as the End Conscription Campaign, which sought to end the Conscription of white males into the Army. There had always been a Movement of Anti-Apartheid Activists amongst white people from the entire population spectrum with the Black Sash being the most prominent organisation whilst most people used their positions of power, to do their Activism.

Desperate to Contain the Raging fires in the Townships, The Government begins to meet Mandela in Secret. These talks were driven by the National Intelligence Service, until Mandela was moved to Polls Moor Prison in 1982.

They were Talks about Talks... "Would it be possible to have a Negotiated Settlement?" was the Question on everyone's mind. These talks created a wedge of suspicion between Mandela and the other Prisoners and eventually, they had to also be brought in. Talks began to happen on International Soil: Dakar, Senegal and also in Germany.

It was during this time that Arch Bishop Desmond Tutu became the Voice of Hope in the Wilderness. Comforting the bereaved, burying people under Police Guard and with bullets flying. He Spoke Truth to Power. As the Bishop of Johannesburg and Secretary general of the South African Council of Churches, He was a Unifying figure in the Non-Violent Campaign to resolve the problem of Apartheid in South Africa. He was awarded a Nobel Peace Prize in 1986 for this Role as a Human Rights Activist.

Foreign Donations started coming in, to support Anti-Apartheid Activism and to support victims thereof. The Most well-known funding is that given to Dr Allan Boesak's Peace and Justice Charity, which was affiliated to the UDF. The Organisation received the sum of 1 000 000 USD in 1985 from the Dan Church Aid Fund. The Government, fearing that support of NGOs would be sufficient to destabilize Government, prohibited the UDF from receiving further foreign funds and the organization became banned, restricting its actions. By late 1987, majority of its activists were imprisoned.

In 1999, Dr Allan Boesak was Charged and found guilty of Misappropriating the funds that his organization had received. Dr Boesak maintained that the Banning of the UDF had something to do with why the funds he was accused of Misappropriating could not be Accounted for. He received a Presidential Pardon on 15/01/2005, having served 1 out of his 3-year Jail term.

The same year in August 1986 the Commonwealth leaders agreed on a programme of economic sanctions against apartheid-era South Africa, helping to galvanise international action against the apartheid regime. Sanctions included a ban on both air travel and investments in South Africa, as well as a ban on agricultural imports and South African tourism. Bank loans to South African companies were banned as well as imports of coal, iron, steel and uranium from the country. Consular facilities were also withdrawn under the agreement. In their communiqué, the heads of government called for "the dismantling of apartheid and the establishment of a non-racial and representative government in South Africa as a matter of compelling urgency." "The Commonwealth cannot stand by and allow the cycle of violence to spiral, but must take effective concerted action," the leaders said. "We trust that the authorities in Pretoria will recognise the seriousness of our resolve."

The following 7 Leaders of the Common Wealth were present at the Sanction Decision Making Summit in 1986:

- President Kenneth Kaunda of Zambia,
- Prime Minister Robert Hawke of Australia
- Prime Minister Lynden Pindling of the Bahamas,
- Prime Minister Brian Mulroney of Canada,
- Prime Minister Rajiv Gandhi of India and
- Prime Minister Robert Mugabe of Zimbabwe, as well as
- British Prime Minister Margaret Thatcher.

These Leaders concluded that: "There has not been the adequate concrete progress that we looked for." The United Kingdom, however led by Mrs Thatcher, declined to sign up in full to the agreement and instead offered a "voluntary ban" on investment and Tourism in South Africa. Secretary-General Ramphal, speaking at a conference a few weeks later, insisted that the sanctions were intended "not as punitive but as corrective". "It is a programme to impress on Pretoria, and those in South Africa who support the regime that apartheid must be dismantled and a future for all South Africans that is truly non-racial and democratic within a united and non-fragmented country (must be pursued)."

In 1989, the UDF and the Congress of South African Trade Unions (COSATU) began cooperating more closely in a loose alliance called the Mass Democratic Movement, following restrictions on the UDF and COSATU by the apartheid government. The loose nature of the MDM made it difficult for the apartheid government to ban it.

In 1989, upon winning the elections from PW Botha, FW de Klerk inherited a Government in Distress which according to the Daily Maverick was in the red with a debt to the tune of US$23 billion — in other words, bankrupt."

Whether motivated by the Talks about Talks, The Plight of the people; The Ungovernability of the Country, the Ardent Prayers of many believers everywhere who prayed for the end of Apartheid or the dire Financial state of the Country or all of the above, President F.W de Klerk began Negotiating for the Dismantling of Apartheid. He unbanned Political parties and released Political Prisoners.

In February 1990, the ANC, the SACP; the PAC and other organizations were unbanned, and according to the UDF: "it became clear that the need for the UDF no longer existed". In March 1991, the decision to disband was made and the UDF held its last meeting on August 14, 1991 in Johannesburg.

On February 2 1990, former president FW De Klerk announced in his speech at the opening of parliament, the unbanning of the ANC and all other proscribed political parties; and the release of Nelson Mandela and all other political prisoners. On February 11 that year, after 27 years in jail, Mandela was released from Victor Verster prison.

This is what he had to say on his Release. (Retrieved from: www.timeslive.co.za/IN-FULL/Nelson -Mandela's-February-11-1990-Speech)

Amandla! Amandla! iAfrika! Mayibuye!

Friends, comrades and fellow South Africans, I greet you all in the name of peace, democracy and freedom for all. I stand here before you not as a prophet, but as a humble servant of you, the people.

Your tireless and heroic sacrifices have made it possible for me to be here today. I, therefore, place the remaining years of my life in your hands.

On this day of my release I extend my sincere and warmest gratitude to the millions of my compatriots and those in every corner of the globe who have campaigned tirelessly for my release.

I extend special greetings to the people of Cape Town. This city, which has been my home for three decades.

Your mass marches and other forms of struggle have served as a constant source of strength to all political prisoners.

I salute the African National Congress. It has fulfilled our every expectation in its role as leader of the great march to freedom.

I salute our president, comrade Oliver Tambo, for leading the ANC, even under the most difficult circumstances. I salute the rank and file members of the ANC. You have sacrificed life and limb in the pursuit of the noble cause of our struggle.

I salute combatants of Umkhonto we Sizwe, like Solomon Mahlangu and Ashley Kriel, who have paid the ultimate price for the freedom of all South Africans.

I salute the South African Communist Party for its steady contribution to the struggle for democracy. You have survived 40 years of unrelenting persecution. The memory of great communists like Moses Kotane, Yusuf Dadoo, Bram Fischer and Moses Mabhida will be cherished for generations to come. I salute general secretary Joe Slovo, one of our finest patriots. We are heartened by the fact that the alliance between ourselves and the party remains as strong as it always was.

I salute the United Democratic Front, the National Education Crisis Committee, the South African Youth Congress, the Transvaal and Natal Indian congresses, and Cosatu, and the many other formations of the Mass Democratic Movement.

I also salute the Black Sash and the National Union of South African Students. We note, with pride, that you have acted as the conscience of white South Africans. Even during the darkest days of the history of our struggle you held the flag of liberty high. The large-scale mass mobilisation of the past few years is one of the key factors which led to the opening of the final chapter of our struggle.

I extend my greetings to the working class of our country. Your organised strength is the pride of our movement. You remain the most dependable force in the struggle to end exploitation and oppression.

I pay tribute, I pay tribute to the many religious communities who carried the campaign for justice forward when the organisations of our people were silenced.

I greet the traditional leaders of our country. Many among you continue to walk in the footsteps of great heroes, like Hintsa and Sekhukune.

I pay tribute to the endless heroism of the youth. You, the young lions, have energised our entire struggle.

I pay tribute to the mothers and wives and sisters of our nation. You are the rock- hard foundation of our struggle. Apartheid has inflicted more pain on you than on anyone else.

On this occasion, we thank the world, we thank the world community for their great contribution to the anti-apartheid struggle. Without your support our struggle would not have reached this advanced stage. The sacrifice of the front-line states will be remembered by South Africans forever.

My salutations will be incomplete without expressing my deep appreciation for the strength given to me during my long and lonely years in prison by my beloved wife and family. I am convinced that your pain and suffering was far greater than my own.

Before I go any further, I wish to make the point that I intend making only a few preliminary comments at this stage. I will make a more complete statement only after I have had the opportunity to consult with my comrades.

Today, the majority of South Africans, black and white, recognise that apartheid has no future. It has to be ended by our own decisive mass action in order to build peace and security. The mass campaigns of defiance, and other actions of our organisations and people, can only culminate in the establishment of democracy.

The apartheid destruction on our subcontinent is incalculable. The fabric of family life of millions of my people has been shattered. Millions are homeless and unemployed. Our economy, our economy lies in ruins and our people are embroiled in political strife.

Our resort to the armed struggle in 1960, with the formation of the military wing of the ANC, Umkhonto we Sizwe, was a purely defensive action against the violence of apartheid.

The factors which necessitated the armed struggle still exist today. We have no option but to continue. We express the hope that a climate conducive to a negotiated settlement would be created soon so that there may no longer be the need for the armed struggle.

I am a loyal and disciplined member of the African National Congress. I am, therefore, in full agreement with all of its objectives, strategies and tactics. ***The need to unite the people of our country is as important a task now as it always has been.*** No individual leader is able to take on these enormous tasks on his own.

It is our task as leaders to place our views before our organisation and to allow the democratic structures to decide on the way forward. On the question of democratic practice, I feel duty-bound to make the point that a leader of the movement is the person who has been democratically elected at a national conference. This is the principle which must be upheld without any exception.

Today, I wish to report to you that my talks with the government have been aimed at normalising the political situation in the country. We have not as yet begun discussing the basic demands of the struggle. I wish to stress that I myself have at no time entered into negotiations about the future of our country, except to insist on a meeting between the ANC and the government.

Mr De Klerk has gone further than any other Nationalist president in taking real steps to normalise the situation.

However, there are further steps as outlined in the Harare Declaration that have to be met before negotiations on the basic demands of our people can begin.

I reiterate our call for, inter alia, the immediate ending of the state of emergency and the freeing of all, and not only some, political prisoners.

Only such a normalised situation which allows for free political activities can allow us to consult our people in order to obtain a mandate.

The people need to be consulted on who will negotiate and on the content of such negotiations. Negotiations cannot take place above the heads or behind the backs of our people.

It is our belief that the future of our country can only be determined by a body which is democratically elected on a non-racial basis.

Negotiations on the dismantling of apartheid will have to address the overwhelming demands of our people for a democratic, non-racial and unitary South Africa.

There must be an end to white monopoly on political power and a fundamental restructuring of our political and economic systems to ensure that the inequalities of apartheid are addressed and our society thoroughly democratised.

It must be added that Mr De Klerk himself is a man of integrity, who is acutely aware of the dangers of a public figure not honouring his undertakings.

But as an organisation we based our policy and strategy on the harsh reality we are faced with. And this reality is that we are still suffering under the policies of the Nationalist government. Our struggle has reached a decisive moment. We call on our people to seize this moment so that the process towards democracy is rapid and uninterrupted.

We have waited too long for our freedom. We can no longer wait. Now is the time to intensify the struggle on all fronts. To relax our efforts now would be a mistake which generations to come will not be able to forgive.

The sight of freedom looming on the horizon should encourage us to redouble our efforts. It is only through disciplined mass action that our victory can be assured.

We call on our white compatriots to join us in the shaping of a new South Africa. The freedom movement is a political home for you too. We call on the international community to continue the campaign to isolate the apartheid regime.

To lift sanctions now would be to run the risk of aborting the process towards the complete eradication of apartheid. Our march to freedom is irreversible. We must not allow fear to stand in our way.

Universal suffrage on a common voters' role in united democratic and non-racial South Africa is the only way to peace and racial harmony.

In conclusion, I wish to quote my own words during my trial in 1964. They are as true today as they were then. I quote:

"I have fought against white domination and I have fought against black domination. I have cherished the ideal of a democratic and free society in which all persons live together in harmony and with equal opportunities. It is an ideal which I hope to live for and to achieve. But, if needs be, it is an ideal for which I am prepared to die."

In May 1990, and other meetings Mandela and FW de Klerk Met and Agreed on:

- The resolution of the existing climate of violence and intimidation
- Removal of practical obstacles to negotiation including immunity from prosecution for returning exiles
- Release of political prisoners.
- Suspension of the armed struggle by the ANC
- An end to the state of emergency

August 1990, ANC suspended the armed Struggle and began negotiations with the Government

1991

After 5 years and with some conditions having been met toward ending Apartheid, Sanctions are immediately lifted in 1991

In February 1991, The lone voice of Prophet Benjamin Ithuteng-Tshiamo addressed a few hundred people from the Steps of the Durban City Hall and Proclaimed: "South Africah, is a Wounded Nation. Our Leaders Are Wounded. If these wounds are not healed, it may appear as if all is well, but later, a Stale mate will be reached wherein, no Political Solution Will Triumph unless the people be healed first, for the Higher than the Highest, Regardeth."

The South African Democratic Teacher's Union (SADTU) is formed and then a young Teacher at the time, my Husband helps to found the Midlands Region of SADTU and is elected as Chairperson. SADTU is ANC Aligned and was very instrumental in Activating Students and Teachers Politically, entrenching the Organisation in the Grassroots.

14 September 1991 Representatives of twenty-seven political organisations, National and Homeland governments sign the National Accord to prepare the way for the CODESA negotiations.

All Party Negotiations in the form of CODESA (The Convention for a Democratic South Africa) start in December 1991. My Dad, Dr M.C Neluvhalani is one of the representatives for Venda in these talks. These were not easy talks and broke down several times, following the Boipatong Massacre, Rolling Mass Action and

Bisho Massacre. They were boycotted by the Conservative Party and the Pan Africanist Congress.

When CODESA broke down, bilateral Negotiations continued between ANC's Cyril Ramaphosa and NP's Roelf Meyer. These two could also not find common ground until Joe Slovo finally brought common ground with the proposal of Sunset Clauses that allowed compromises on both sides.

Some of the Sunset Clauses were:

- Formation of a Government of National Unity to include all parties with a 10% vote or more. This was meant to ease Loss and avoid a winner take all situation.
- Afrikaner Civil Servants loyal to the National Party to be retained for the first 5 years of Democracy. This is the period it is thought Mass looting of unknown Government Assets took place.
- Ensure Representation of the National Party in Cabinet and a Deputy President from the National Party until 1999

A White Referendum on the Dismantling of Apartheid showed an overwhelming majority in favor thereof. This Strengthened the Government's Resolve to a Negotiated Settlement.

On 26 September 1992 the government and the ANC agreed on a Record of Understanding which dealt with the formation of: a constitutional assembly; an interim government; Release of political prisoners; Revitalisation of hostels; Release of dangerous weapons and Mass action and it restarted the negotiation process after the failure of CODESA

On 1 April 1993 the Multiparty Negotiating Forum (MPNF) gathered for the first time. The fact that the NP and ANC already had talks and had reached some Agreements that the other parties had to agree to at the risk of being left behind, disintegrated these talks as well and International mediators helped persuade the IFP by guaranteeing special status of the Zulu monarchy, and to Prince Mangosuthu Buthelezi, the promise that foreign mediators would examine Inkatha's claims to more autonomy in the KwaZulu area.

On 10 April 1993, the assassination of Chris Hani, leader of the SACP and a senior ANC leader, by white right-wingers again brought the country to the brink of disaster, but ultimately proved a turning point, after which the main parties pushed for a settlement with increased determination.

In the June 1993 Negotiations Meeting, the right-wing Weerstandsbeweging (AWB), led by Mr Eugene Terreblanche stormed the World Trade Centre in Kempton Park, breaking through the glass front of the building with an armoured vehicle and briefly taking over the negotiations chamber... to Paint slogans on the wall, Urinate on Furniture and harass delegates.

The Police finally got the situation under control and the AWB left. This actions however did not deter the Negotiators who were determined to see them come to a fruitful end. The MPNF finally ratified the interim Constitution in the early hours of the morning of 18 November 1993 after which a Multiparty Transitional Executive Council was formed to partner the Government until the elections of a New Parliament. The elections finally took place on 27/04/1994, Freedom Day. All South Africans, Indian, Coloured, Black and White had Political Franchise/Suffrage.

Constitutional Democracy

1994

In April of 1994, the first Democratic Elections wherein all South Africans older than 18 years regardless of Gender and Race could vote for the political party they wished to represent them in Government. The Bantustans were dismantled and their political parties also participated in the General Elections which were held under the watchful eye of the International Community who declared the Results Free and Fair, Representing the will of the People. The Republic of South Africa became a Constitutional democracy.

It was an Historic Moment as people from all walks of life and areas of the Country woke up early in the morning to patiently wait their turn in kilometers-long winding queues, under the scorching sun, with all the patience in the world, to cast their vote... Universal Suffrage had been Attained!

The Results were as follows:

ANC: 63%; NP: 20%; IFP: 11%; Others: 6%

Nelson Mandela was Nominated and subsequently elected President of South Africa. The first Democratically Elected President of South Africa.

He Established the Government of National Unity - GNU (ANC was Majority Party and could Govern unopposed, but for the Sunset Clause). He also Appointed Two Deputy Presidents: Thabo Mbeki and FW de Klerk, with Cyril Ramaphosa as the Chairperson of the Constitutional Assembly, in an effort to build National Cohesion and satisfy another Sunset Clause.

South Africa was then re-admitted to the United Nations and the Common Wealth.

1996 to 1998

NP withdrew from the GNU to become an opposition Party in 1996. Subsequently, the Party changed to become the New National Party (NNP) in 1997 and subsequently in 2005, it merged with the ANC by the "crossing of the floor" provision, so that the ANC gained Ministers from the NNP who had not gone through the Ranks of the ANC and did not have the necessary Cadre Training. The NNP subsequently imploded.

The Truth and Reconciliation Commission as narrated upon earlier, was established to provide a public forum for the personal Accounts of human rights abuses during the Apartheid years. Attendees could Apply for Amnesty from Prosecution

A New Constitution was approved in 1996 and was signed into Law in 1998.

On 08 May 1996, then Vice President Thabo Mbeki gave this Speech on behalf of the African National Congress in llHui! gaeb (Cape Town) on the occasion of the passing of the new Constitution of South Africa.

I am an African

I owe my being to the hills and the valleys, the mountains and the glades, the rivers, the deserts, the trees, the flowers, the seas and the ever-changing seasons that define the face of our native land.

My body has frozen in our frosts and in our latter-day snows. It has thawed in the warmth of our sunshine and melted in the heat of the midday sun. The crack and the rumble of the summer thunders, lashed by startling lightning, have been a cause both of trembling and of hope.

The fragrances of nature have been as pleasant to us as the sight of the wild blooms of the citizens of the veld.

The dramatic shapes of the Drakensberg, the soil-coloured waters of the Lekoa, iGqili noThukela, and the sands of the Kgalagadi, have all been panels of the set on the natural stage on which we act out the foolish deeds of the theatre of the day.

At times, and in fear, I have wondered whether I should concede equal citizenship of our country to the leopard and the lion, the elephant and the springbok, the hyena, the black mamba and the pestilential mosquito.

A human presence among all of these, a feature on the face of our native land thus defined, I know that none dare challenge me when I say - I am an African!

I owe my being to the Khoi and the San whose desolate souls haunt the great expanses of the beautiful Cape - they who fell victim to the most merciless genocide our native land has ever seen, they who were the first to lose their lives in the struggle to defend our freedom and independence and they who, as a people, perished in the result.

Today, as a country, we keep an inaudible and audible silence about these ancestors of the generations that live, fearful to admit the horror of a former deed, seeking to obliterate from our memories a cruel occurrence which, in its remembering, should teach us not and never to be inhuman again.

I am formed of the migrants who left Europe to find a new home on our native land. Whatever their own actions, they remain still part of me.

In my veins courses the blood of the Malay slaves who came from the East. Their proud dignity informs my bearing, their culture a part of my essence. The stripes they bore on their bodies from the lash of the slave master are a reminder embossed on my consciousness of what should not be done.

I am the grandchild of the warrior men and women that Hintsa and Sekhukhune led, the patriots that Cetshwayo and Mphephu took to battle, the soldiers Moshoeshoe and Ngungunyane taught never to dishonour the cause of freedom.

My mind and my knowledge of myself is formed by the victories that are the jewels in our African crown, the victories we earned from Isandhlwana to Khartoum, as Ethiopians and as Ashanti of Ghana, as Berbers of the desert.

I am the grandchild who lays fresh flowers on the Boer graves at St Helena, The Bahamas, and the Vrouemonument, who sees in the mind's eye and suffers the suffering of a simple peasant folk, death, concentration camps, destroyed homesteads, a dream in ruins.

I am the child of Nongqawuse. I am he who made it possible to trade in the world markets in diamonds, in gold, in the same food for which our stomachs yearn.

I come of those who were transported from India and China, whose being resided in the fact, solely, that they were able to provide physical labour, who taught me that we could both be at home and be foreign, who taught me that human existence itself demanded that freedom was a necessary condition for that human existence.

Being part of all of these people, and in the knowledge that none dares contest that assertion, I shall claim that - I am an African.

I have seen our country torn asunder as these, all of whom are my people, engaged one another in a titanic battle, the one to redress a wrong that had been caused by one to another and the other, to defend the indefensible.

I have seen what happens when one person has superiority of force over another, when the stronger appropriate to themselves the prerogative even to annul the injunction that God created all men and women in His image.

I know what it signifies when race and colour are used to determine who is human and who, sub-human.

I have seen the destruction of all sense of self-esteem, the consequent striving to be what one is not, simply to acquire some of the benefits which those who had imposed themselves as masters had ensured that they enjoy.

I have experience of the situation in which race and colour is used to enrich some and impoverish the rest.

I have seen the corruption of minds and souls as a result of the pursuit of an ignoble effort to perpetrate a veritable crime against humanity.

I have seen concrete expression of the denial of the dignity of a human being emanating from the conscious, systemic and systematic oppressive and repressive activities of other human beings.

There the victims parade with no mask to hide the brutish reality - the beggars, the prostitutes, the street children, those who seek solace in substance abuse, those who have to steal to assuage hunger, those who have to lose their sanity because to be sane is to invite pain.

Perhaps the worst among these, who are my people, are those who have learnt to kill for a wage. To these the extent of death is directly proportional to their personal welfare.

And so, like pawns in the service of demented souls, they kill in furtherance of the political violence in KwaZulu-Natal. They murder the innocent in the taxi wars. They kill slowly or quickly in order to make profits from the illegal trade in narcotics. They are available for hire when husband wants to murder wife and wife, husband.

Among us prowl the products of our immoral and amoral past - killers who have no sense of the worth of human life, rapists who have absolute disdain for the women of our country, animals who would seek to benefit from the vulnerability of the children, the disabled, and the old, the rapacious who brook no obstacle in their quest for self-enrichment.

All this I know and know to be true because I am an African!

Because of that, I am also able to state this fundamental truth that I am born of a people who are heroes and heroines.

I am born of a people who would not tolerate oppression.

I am of a nation that would not allow that fear of death, of torture, of imprisonment, of exile or persecution should result in the perpetuation of injustice.

The great masses who are our mother and father will not permit that the behaviour of the few results in the description of our country and people as barbaric.

Patient because history is on their side, these masses do not despair because today the weather is bad. Nor do they turn triumphalist when, tomorrow, the sun shines.

Whatever the circumstances they have lived through and because of that experience, they are determined to define for themselves who they are and who they should be.

We are assembled here today to mark their victory in acquiring and exercising their right to formulate their own definition of what it means to be African.

The Constitution whose adoption we celebrate constitutes an unequivocal statement that we refuse to accept that our African-ness shall be defined by our race, our colour, our gender or our historical origins.

It is a firm assertion made by ourselves that South Africa belongs to all who live in it, Black and White. It gives concrete expression to the sentiment we share as Africans, and will defend to the death, that the people shall govern.

It recognises the fact that the dignity of the individual is both an objective which society must pursue, and is a goal which cannot be separated from the material well-being of that individual. It seeks to create the situation in which all our people shall be free from fear, including the fear of the oppression of one national group by another, the fear of the disempowerment of one social echelon by another, the fear of the use of state power to deny anybody their fundamental human rights and the fear of tyranny.

It aims to open the doors so that those who were disadvantaged can assume their place in society as equals with their fellow human beings without regards to colour, to race, to gender, to age or to geographic dispersal. It provides the opportunity to enable each one and all to state their views, to promote them, to strive for their implementation in the process of governance without fear that a contrary view will be met with repression. It creates a law-governed society which shall be inimical to arbitrary rule. It enables the resolution of conflicts by peaceful means rather than resort to force. It rejoices in the diversity of our people and creates the space for all of us voluntarily to define ourselves as one people. As an African, this is an achievement of which I am proud, proud without reservation and proud without any feeling of conceit. Our sense of elevation at this moment also derives from the fact that this magnificent product is the unique creation of African hands and African minds.

But it also constitutes a tribute to our loss of vanity that we could, despite the temptation to treat ourselves as an exceptional fragment of humanity, draw on the accumulated experience and wisdom of all humankind, to define for ourselves what we want to be.

Together with the best in the world, we too are prone to pettiness, to petulance, selfishness and short-sightedness. But it seems to have happened that we looked at ourselves and said ***the time had come that we make a super-human effort to be other than human, to respond to the call to create for ourselves a glorious future, to remind ourselves of the Latin saying: Gloria est consequenda - Glory must be sought after.***

Today it feels good to be an African. It feels good that I can stand here as a South African and as a foot soldier of a titanic African army, the African National Congress, to say to all the parties represented here, to the millions who made an input into the processes we are concluding, to our outstanding compatriots who have presided over the birth of our founding document, to the negotiators who pitted their wits one against the other, to the unseen stars who shone unseen as the management and administration of the Constitutional Assembly, the advisers, the experts and the publicists, to the mass communication media, to our friends across the globe - congratulations and well done!

I am an African.

I am born of the peoples of the continent of Africa. The pain of the violent conflict that the peoples of Liberia, and of Somalia, of the Sudan, of Burundi and Algeria is a pain I also bear. The dismal shame of poverty, suffering and human degradation of my continent is a blight that we share.

The blight on our happiness that derives from this and from our drift to the periphery of the ordering of human affairs leaves us in a persistent shadow of despair.

This is a savage road to which nobody should be condemned. The evolution of humanity says that Africa reaffirms that she is continuing her rise from the ashes.

Whatever the setbacks of the moment, nothing can stop us now! Whatever the difficulties, Africa shall be at peace!

Thank you very much.

www.gov.za/Constitution of the Republic of South Africa, 1996 The Preamble states that the Constitution aims to:

- **Heal the divisions of the past and establish a society based on democratic values, social justice and fundamental human rights;**
- Improve the quality of life of all citizens and free the potential of each person;
- Lay the foundations for a democratic and open society in which government is based on the will of the people, and in which every citizen is equally protected by law;

- Build a united and democratic South Africa that is able to take its rightful place as a sovereign state in the family of nations.

Founding Provisions:

South Africa is a Sovereign and Democratic State Founded On the Following Values:

Human dignity; The achievement of equality; The advancement of human rights and freedom; Non-racialism and Non-sexism; Supremacy of the Constitution Universal adult suffrage: a national common voters' roll, regular elections and a multiparty system of democratic government to ensure accountability, openness and responsiveness.

Fundamental Rights:

The fundamental rights contained in Chapter 2 of the Constitution seek to protect the rights and freedom of individuals. The Constitutional Court guards these rights and determines whether actions by the state are in accordance with constitutional provisions:

South Africa's Constitution is one of the most progressive in the world and enjoys high acclaim internationally. Human rights are given clear prominence in the Constitution.

The Constitution of the Republic of South Africa, 1996 was approved by the Constitutional Court on 4 December 1996 and took effect on 4 February 1997. **The Constitution is the supreme law of the land. No other law or government action can supersede the provisions of the Constitution.** Thus, many a law have been overturned in the courts when the opposition deem them to be in violation of the Constitution, leading others to bemoan that we are ruled by the courts, instead of just getting researchers to ensure that our Policies are structured in such a way that they do not violate the Constitution. In 2020, a Supreme Court of Appeal declared the Preferential Procurement Policy Framework regulations invalid... This may quickly escalate to this Policy of Transformation and Restitution being declared unconstitutional on the basis of the ability of lawyers to argue their cases.

In 1997, Mandela Stood down as President of the ANC and was succeeded by Thabo Mbeki, he subsequently retired from the Presidency in 1999. He Rested with his Fathers (Ancestors) on 05 December 2013 and was interred at his birth town of Qunu. 1 Kings 2:10

The ANC has been the Ruling Party since 1994 to date (2020), and currently holds 230 of the 400 National Assembly Seats. The opposition has grown, led by the Democratic Alliance with 84 Seats followed by Economic Freedom Fighters which is an ANC Splinter with 44 Seats, Inkatha Freedom Party retains 14 Seats whilst the Freedom Front Plus holds 10 Seats and the balance of the chairs are shared amongst 9 parties.

As for the other events of the Democratic era from 1994 to date, are they not written in the Public Domain of the Media?

27 years into Democracy, The Challenges from the Legacy of Apartheid which South Africa must Overcome and which have mired our Democracy remain and can be dismantled by:

1. Restoration of ubuNtu to help Heal the Fractured Society and form the bond of Brotherhood and build Patriotism;
2. Political Literacy for the General Population to be informed and Active Participants in Democracy;
3. Economic Transformation through Shareholding;
4. Legal, Police and Judicial Transformation so that all languages of South Africa can be languages of the court and so that the Police and courts are re-oriented to their role of Protectors and Supporters of Citizens.
5. Find Solutions to end Private – Public Corruption and State Capture (Learn from those who Claim to have done so in the world). If Nobody has, then...
6. Transformation of the Media and its Re-orientation to report News from the Position of ubuNtu rather than the position of the Criminal Procedures Act no. 40 of 1828.

Part 6: Scrambled Eggs

"England and France will rule Africa.
Africans will dig the ditches and water the deserts.
It will be hard work and the Africans will probably become extinct.
We must learn to look at the Result with composure, it illustrates the beneficent law of Nature, that the weak must be devoured by the Strong"
Reade, WW (1864)

commons.wikimedia.org/wiki/File:Punch_Rhodes_Colossus.png#/ Public Domain.

This "Rhodes Colossus" Cartoon of Cecil John Rhodes, was made by Edward Linley Sambourne in 1892, eight years after the Berlin Conference. It shows Rhodes measuring the distance from the Cape in South Africa, to Cairo in Egypt "as the crow flies". He used the telegraphic line, to illustrate the ease with which it would be, to Traverse and connect Afrikan Resources to Britain. This was part of his broader "Cape to Cairo" concept for British domination of Afrika. Rhodes set to achieve this dream through his

British South Africa Company. At that time, Britain was the Imperialist in both South Africa, since (1795) 1806 and Egypt, which it occupied in 1882.

It has been suggested in some academic circles that the wealth produced at Kimberley was a significant factor influencing increased British Hegemony in Africa through the Scramble for Africa. The Relentless Appropriations of Land by the British South African Company, South to North, made the other Iberian Peninsula Countries of: Portugal, France, Belgium and Germany to Scramble for African Holdings of their own. First on the Scene was Portugal, who planned to get an East to West Corridor from Mozambique to Angola as their Ports were already established on the coasts of both these Countries. The Corridor would be, through, Present day Countries of: Zimbabwe, Zambia and Congo.

These Plans were foiled by King Leopold II of Belgium, who explored Kongo in 1885 to colonise it for its Rubber and Ivory. Upon learning of this mission, the French followed suit and raised a flag over what they named, Congo Brazaville, so that Kongo was Colonised by both Belgium and France

Portugal, which had a longstanding relationship with Kongo, and which had already established a mission station there, in 1490, also Claimed the area. Portugal then moved swiftly to safeguard its Monopoly on the Atlantic Seaboard from Belgium. Britain, Portugal, France and Belgium then jostled for the greatest control of the Afrikan Continent, spiking fears of another European War.

To avoid European War over Afrikan Resources, Portugal Requested a Conference of European Nations, that would help Establish guidelines for the Acquisition of Afrikan Territory by Europe. The so-called: "Peaceful" Colonisation. The Conference was thus convened in Berlin in 1884, by German Chancellor, Otto von Bismarck. This is usually referred to as the ultimate point of the Scramble for Africa and Colonial Imperialism.

<u>What was this Scramble?</u>

The **Scramble for Africa** was the formal Division, Invasion, Occupation and Colonisation of Afrikan territory by European powers: Britain, France, Portugal, Germany, Netherlands, Spain, Italy, Brandenburg, Sweden and Belgium between 1881 and 1914. The Occupation would remain until 1952, which is the year of the first Independence and early 1990s the year of the last Independence (Namibia). South Africa is still not Independent. It only experienced a change of Regime. Unless if one considers its Independence from the British Common Wealth in 1960 or the earlier formation of the South African Union in 1910 or its recognition as an Independent Union under the Statute of Westminster in 1931. If not, then what is the date of our

Independence day? Is it any wonder that every President in South Africa has to go to England and Courtesy upon Assumption of the Presidency? When we speak of State Capture in South Africa, we are saying, the Economic orientation of the Government is no longer Western but Eastern or Internal. We are not talking about Corruption, because as I mentioned earlier, that was set in motion in 1652 or earlier when the DEIC Charter was formulated. I have alluded to the fact that a simple matter of being able to get a Tax Clearance Certificate tempts one to corruption. How about the Medical Aid system? Life cover? Municipal utility bills? Subscription fees? Insurance? Public Finance Management Act (PFMA)? Companies Registration Act? xxx? At every turn, the system is so Capitalistic, so Beaurocratic and so Burdensome and unfarmiliar, that fraud and corruption become easier.

Almost 95 percent of the continent was colonised, with only Ethiopia, a portion of present-day Somalia and Liberia remaining independent. This Partitioning of Afrika is responsible for the division of Afrikan abaNtu/baTwa into Different peoples that seem Disconnected due to Loss of Linguistic Integrity, Social Cohesion, Cultural, National and Continental Identity. Africa has been Independent for a Total of 31 years or 1 generation and at most 2.5 (Egypt's 69 years). Kehona rebula Mehlo...! (We are becoming Woke)

The Scramble is Responsible for the formation of:

- The Creation, on a Paper Map, of artificial Countries in Afrika by people, whom some of had never set foot on Afrikan Soil, and the Declaration of those Countries as belonging to some European Imperial power without Consultation and or formal war with the Citizens of those areas. The same way one cuts up a piece of cake... "We have been engaged in drawing lines upon maps, where no white man's feet have ever trod; We have been giving away mountains and rivers and lakes, to each other, only hindered by the small impediment that we never knew exactly where the mountains and rivers and lakes were" Lord Salisbury, 1885
- Tribes, Ethnic Groups, Surnames, Race and Countries in Afrika;
  All foreign Concepts applied to Afrikan abaNtu/baTwa in an Attempt to understand, package, divide and Rule over them. These have enabled: Wars, Genocides, Xenophobia and general Intolerance;
- Generational Statelesness, Wherein Afrikans do not belong to any State within the Afrikan Continent, because they are unregistered in the territory they find hemselves living in for various reasons, including being displaced by War and illegal Migrant Labour of their parents. In 2015, there were more than 1 million

people who were Stateless just between 3 Afrikan Countries. These people are unable to access any services of the country they live in legitimately and it exposes them to crime, fraud and corruption as they try to fit in to a society that denies their existence. How can an Afrikan be Stateless in Afrika? This is the full impact of the Migratory Theory and its attendant Scramble for Afrika.

- Appropriation of: Land, Culture, Resources, Language, Knowledge, Institutional Memory and Civilisation. These were Extracted, Processed, Repackaged, Monetised and Sold back to Afrika at highly inflated prices.

My brother Ramulayo makes this Joke whenever we watch Science Fiction Movies: "Vha do ni tswela na vhuloi hanu…!" ("They will Appropriate even your witchcraft…"). He says this whenever we watch in amazement, as all Afrikan Spiritual Wisdom and Understandings as well as their rituals, that we were demonized for, are now woven into American Blockbuster Movies as Virtues and powers to be desired, without any acknowledgement of the origins of those concepts, let alone casting of an Afrikan Actor.

Reasons for the Scramble

In Literature, these are always said to be Complex. In Truth though, the Scramble was and is about: God, Gold and Glory.

God:

The Almurabitun's Dream of Islamic World Domination and the "Re-Conquista of Iberia" and the Crusades, set the Stage for one Religion to set itself above all others. European/American-driven Arabic enslavement of Afrikans was at its Peak, and only recently abolished (1833 and 1865 respectively). The Anti-Slavery movement became the Rallying Call to "Save" Afrika from Slavery and Damnation through Civilisation and Christianity. This Call, was Motivated by Rudyard Kipling's "The White Man's burden" as well as the Pseudoscience of the day, which portrayed Afrikans as lesser beings, who are "Child-like" albeit, Savage and Barbaric, needing the Paternalistic protection and guidance of "Civilised superior Europeans". The Paternalistic attitude, is responsible for the superiority complex that is still pervasive in some sectors, wherein Afrikans are Studied, Classified and Written about without their input. It is also responsible for: giving Children the audacity to call our mothers and fathers: "Girl and Boy", when referring to them as their servants.

The Missionaries for their part were quick to go to work, building Churches, Schools and Hospitals. They helped to bring Control to Tropical diseases, especially Malaria and the Tsetse disease, which were killers for the foreigners. These Medical Advances however, served to make European penetration into Afrika Easier and faster. Coming from a Eurocentric Dominions Worldview and Perspective, which made them believe that theirs was the only and right path, made Missionaries complicit in Creating a Captive Afrikan Consumer Market, that is still enriching Europe to date wherein, European products were Christian and Civilised, making them objects of desire for the Afrikan Christian who had to become European in order to be Christian: Warneck (1879) as quoted in sahistoryonline said: *"According to a calculation made by the missionary Whitmee, every missionary sent to the Polynesian islands produces an annual trade-revenue of at least 200,000 marks. Of course (sic), the trade is organised by merchants, but the missionary originates it." (1888).*

Gold:

Afrika Represented a Cheap Investment Opportunity for European Surplus, whereby cheaply extracted raw materials could be shipped and Processed in Europe, Keeping the Source Country Ignorant of what their Resources are able to Produce and How. This created a wider Consumer Market for Afrikan Sourced and European Processed Products: Europe, Afrika and the world;

In order to make this Investment opportunity a reality, Afrika's Trade Routes and Networks had to be abolished and or taken over, so that Afrika's previous Trading Partners: China, India and the now Arab World would be supplanted. Thus the formation of New Trading Routes by Rail and Road Systems as well as the Control of the Continental Waterways, `Rivers: Nile, Niger and Congo; Lakes: Nyasa, Tanganyika and Nalubaale (Victoria) and Lake Chad; The Suez Canal and All Coastal Ports that went from Source (Afrikan Area) to Mouth (Europan Country), Reducing Travel time and avoiding Taxes for the Transport of Raw Materials, to increase the Profit Margins.

Britain's Cape to Cairo Rail to the Suez Canal; British Control of Southern African and East Afrikan Ports as Stop overs to Asia and India; Portugal's Coast to Coast land acquisition; The French Niger River to Nile River Dream and control of Fort Fashoda in the Sudan as well as Britain and France's need to Control Egypt and the countries of the Source of the Nile River, being the prime examples.

Glory:

Europe, Consciously or Subconsciously used Afrika to feed her Sense of Self by Deprecating others especially Afrikans. Whiteness became the Standard of Normalcy,

Intelligence, Righteousness, Wisdom, Innovation, Beauty, Goodness and Superiority. Other Nations were then layered beneath this Standard with Black, Afrikans of the Dark Continent being the lowest Rung of this Hierarchy. Caucasoid, Mongoloid, Negro... White, Black.... Christian, other Religions..., and then within Afrika: Shemitic, Hamitic... Light Skin, Dark Skin... Pointy Nose, Broad Nose... Thick Lips, Thin Lips... Round eyes, Epicanthic eyes..., Coarse curly hair, Smooth long Hair, Short stature, Tall Stature... This Social Hierarchy was entrenched through Caricature of Afrikan people, wherein Afrikans were portrayed as ugly, undesirable, of "abnormal proportions", inferior and unintelligent. More of Animal than of Man. This was done systematically in the Entertainment Industry with entertainment companies raking in Millions. This created in the Hearts and Minds of Europeans a sense of Greatness as compared to the Lowliness of Afrikans. It cemented the notion that Afrikans were Sub-human and Less than. Until recently, this (and still persisting really), this theme remained in Most Movies, where Afrikans are always cast in roles wherein they are belittled, Killed off first, the villain, the sloppy, the stupid, the broken home, the infidel, the slave, the servant, the poor, xxx and the Criminal. In a Bullying tactic, Afrikans were bullied in order to Boost European ego... Giving Europeans the Audacity to Dominate and Lead and Subjugate Afrikans because as Reade, W. puts it, "it illustrates the beneficent law of Nature, that the weak must be devoured by the Strong".

Some of the Most famous victims to be Caricatured are: Saartjie Baartman, a Khoekhoen woman from what is now South Africa. She was displayed for her curves and what was regarded as abnormally big buttocks; Ota Benga, a Mbuti man from Kongo, was displayed for his short stature and dark complexion, He would be placed next to an orangutang, as an example of the Darwinian Missing Link and to demonstrate that Afrikans are more of ape than of man. This Tradition of exhibiting Afrikans continued into the 19th century when, in 1899 Frank Fillis took 200 Natives of South Africans, a number of Boer families, representatives of the mounted police and a number of animals to perform daily shows at the Empress Theatre, to prove the savagery of the "Blacks", as this "Cast" was made to re- enact the Anglo-Zulu war of 1879.

Colonies were used for "Balance of Powers" wherein a Colony's Resources: Human and otherwise, could be used to Satisfy whatever power bargain the Colonial country required (Collateral) in order to maintain its Position of Glory amongst its Peers.

Import Slavery was replaced with Colonial Occupation Slavery disguised as Employment, wherein the Colonialist could now Appropriate not only people, but their Lands and Resources as well by means of Imperial Law. This Indentured people and created Migrant Labour practices. When Afrikans refused to work under these circumstances, they were (and still are) referred to as "Lazy and unwilling to work". How does one Work to Survive/Live? Would you do it?

Consequences of The Scramble

The Consequences of the Scramble for Africa are:

Division and Trauma

The Formation of Boundaries, Mutilated Nations, Communities and Familes, leaving them Bleeding with Deep Spiritual and Emotional Traumas, whose PTSD, is unraveling daily in the form of: Civil war, Coups, Genocide/Ethnic Cleansing, Low Value/Regard for life and properties of others, Self-loathing, Xenophobia, Inferiority.

The Arbitrary Naming of Countries, without Regard for local History and the subsequent renaming, of original indigenous Place Names, with European Names, has Appropriated Afrikan: Land, History, Heritage and Identity contributing to further "Ethnic" Tensions, Wars and Genocides.

Creation of Ethnic groups, Tribes and Clans as well as the Comparisons between these, that regard some "Tribes" or "Ethnic" groups, as more European than others, more Semitic than others or "worthy" of House jobs whilst others are suitable only for outside jobs, has left Afrika with deep Tribal/Ethnic Wounds. Because of this, countries keep dividing into new nations as each ethnic group seeks sovereignty. This has led to the post-colonial birthing of new Countries along Tribal lines (Sudan, Biafra...). The Congolese Civil war as well as the ongoing North Eastern and North Western Conflicts of Tigray and Western Sahara are also compliments to these divisions. The Rwandan Genocide and the South African Xenophobia demonstrate them well. Most Countries also experienced Civil Wars and Guerilla wars fought with foreign Artillery, after Independence, as Monarchies sought to depose each other from the Presidency and assert themselves as legitimate governments.

Use of Different orthographies based on the Colonial country of origin made language dialects seem like separate and different Languages, dividing and severing related people further, who today do not recognize each other as family and have phantom limb syndrome. Medically and at an individual person level, Phantom Limb Syndrome continues to be a difficult condition to understand and treat. Imagine what it is like on a Continental Scale. Fortunately, if Patients understand the source of their pain, even if it is untreatable, they can learn to live with it and find new ways of coping.

Interference with Development Potential

Colonialism Interfered with the Trajectory of Afrika's Development and Civilisation. Nations in Afrika had Political Order; Technology; Economy; Social Structures and Law, which enabled them to understand themselves and the world they lived in, so that they thrived without outside intervention. These systems which would have evolved as greater contact with other people occurred through trade and Media, would have evolved and developed in a different trajectory than the current one had they not been disrupted. Let us say for example that your name is Benedito and you live in Angola and your wife and Children live in South Africa. It is 2020 and Countries are in Covid 19 Lockdown. You have not seen your family in 10 months and you are desperate to see them. There are various options that lie ahead of you about the course of Development you could take to satisfy your needs. If someone comes and kidnaps you at night, puts you in a chartered Aeroplane, bribes some Airport officials in both South Africa and Angola, flies you to South Africa and delivers you on the door step of your family, would you have arrived home? The person then proceeds to Bill you R250 000.00 (Angola to South Africa Flight is usually under R10 000.00) How would you feel? Would you have arrived home? Is Home where you wanted to be? Would you be grateful? Would you be willing to pay? Is that the Trajectory you would have taken had you been given an opportunity to decide? What if the borders opened the very next week after this? What if you were tracked down and imprisoned for Bribery and Illegal entry into a foreign land?

Colonialists had *Carte Blanche* power to decide what was relevant to be noted as Historical fact and what was not. Who was relevant and who was not. These decisions were based on whom/what was the flavor of the month for them as they had the power, what laws should govern the Land; What Political System should be in Place; What Economy should be used... This has left the Afrikan feeling, Effaced, Dehumanized, Dazed, Rootless, Floating and Unable to make sense of their world, Strangers in their own land where foreigners feel more comfortable and at home than the Afrikan does.

Foreign rule, which did not Validate Afrikan Civilisation, led to Loss of Institutional Memory and Intellectual Property of: Technology; Spirituality; Politics and Government; Industry and Economy; Social and Emotional Intelligence as these were rejected for new European values and standards. Tradition and Culture – Afrika's Way of Life (kiNtu) and its Spiritual Philosophy of ubuNtu were rejected and replaced with that of the Colonial Master, so that, there can be congruency between Master and Servant at the expense of the Internal Congruency of that Servant. This has Created a Dependency by the Afrikan, on the European, as the Afrikan is forced, to define themselves in the Colonial Worldview of the Master, that is hailed as the Right, Good and Godly Worldview.

State Capture and Corruption

Control of Royal Succession Practices by Missionaries and the Courts, ensured Colonial Rule by extension. This Interference sometimes put despots and foreigners on the Throne, to further colonial aspirations.

Upon Independence, The State was Captured, to do the bidding of Europe, whether overtly or Covertly. The Colonial powers set up Administrative Apparatus which guaranteed, continued European Extraction of Raw Material, as well as the Support and Protection of these activities, by Government. The Afrikan Leaders so appointed were not Trained first in the Democratic Structures they were now being made to run. Some turned dictator as they Straddled Democracy and Royalty.

To date there are No Training Institutions dedicated to the Democratic systems that Afrikan Leaders are finding themselves having to Navigate whilst actually leading, neither are these Democracies reflective of Afrikan Values and Culture. These Leaders relied on ethnic divisions, a centralized authority and patronage system that feed into the ethnic divisions to maintain their stranglehold on power, fracturing the fledgling "Nation" and creating a perfect Storm that decries any Nation building efforts. Thus, many coups followed immediately after independence of Afrikan States.

Having watched the enormous Looting of their Resources to Colonial Nations as a desirable Norm, Come Independence, the Political Elite saw an opportunity to also "Eat" and thus the culture of state Looting, which is tied to Nepotism developed in Afrikan Nations. The deposing of one Party for another has been about deposing of one "Tribe" for another so that it can be the time for the next "Tribe" to eat. They are sucked into endemic Systemic cycles of Corruption and the support of external imperial patrons, as Captured States, because a Popular vote can seat anyone on the Presidential seat...and money can sway the popular vote. This Instability feeds detrimentally into the Country's Poor development as resources are channeled to the Military (to Protect the Incumbent Leader) rather than development, so that:

Colonial Powers protected their "Investments" in Afrika with Sunset Clauses when they "Relinquished power" at Independence. These dictated how countries should be run post-independence and basically maintained Colonial rule under an Afrikan leader, Tying that Country's Economy to the Economy of the former Imperialist through: Language, Culture, Currency, Law and Media

The Former Coloniser, still held Assets and Investments in the former Colony that continued with the Extraction of wealth from Afrika to date. This ensured that development was Europe-driven, to serve European Needs, creating an Economic dependency with the Constant threat of Sanctions, Economic downgrades to Junk Status and Disinvestment to errant governments and in worst case scenarios, a change of Government through assassinations, coups, imprisonments of leaders, vilification of leaders through the media or coups.

The Afrikan Countries inherited enormous Debts with the International Monetary Fund at high Interest Rates and Credit lines with punitive covenants. Ratings Agencies further punish these Countries to force them to comply with Western Monetary Regulations. South Africa for example was Bankrupt when the Democratic Dispensation of 1994 took over Government. According to Oscar van Heerden in his article on https://www.dailymaverick.co.za/opinionista/2018-09-19-once-we-were-bankrupt-the-uncomfortable-truths-of-history/When the ANC took over government in 1994, it found the fiscus in a dire state. The country was in the red, in debt for: US$23 billion. Over the past 24years, the Post-Apartheid Government reversed the deficit and now has healthy foreign exchange reserves which in July 2020 were US$57.8 billion, in spite of Covid 19. Yet, from the beginning of 2014, the Country has continually been down-graded by rating Agencies until Junk Status (2019) because the West is not comfortable with the Political Climate of the Country.

Western Economic Meltdowns become Afrikan Melt downs. During these Melt downs, Western Economies have their Credit Lines extended whilst Afrikan Economies are relegated because they are a credit Risk. Economic Poverty has left us with the Triple Malady of: ***Unemployment, Poverty and Inequality*** which together with the other types of poverty create a perfect Storm of Greed, Theft, Fraud, Murder, Violence and Substance Abuse. The book, Confessions of an Economic Hit Man by John Perkins available on Amazon, details the Tactics used to keep Afrikan Nations poor.

The Infrastructure in Afrika is 120 years old and was developed for 20% of the population for purposes of Exporting goods. It is not suited for the Spatial Planning that was created for divide and rule. Now that infrastructure serves 100% of the population. This has Strained all Infrastructure leading to: Poor Water and Sanitation; Poor Health Infrastructure, Failing power utilities and high burden of disease. Infrastructure, which were built with the Imperialist in mind, rather than the population of the country, now buckle under the increased traffic volumes.

Effacement/Dehumanisation of abaNtu

The Process:

- The Coloniser Asserts Dominion over the Colonised;
- The Colonised Accepts what the Coloniser tells them as truth and a superior way of doing things, as they are subdued into following instructions;
- The Colonised Loses their Self Esteem and Suffers the Consequences of Worthlessness: Hopelessness, Insignificance, Fear, Anxiety, Anger, Depression, Schizophrenia, Inferiority, Loss of Voice, Loss of Innovation, Loss of Faith, Physical ill-health, Resignation, Murder, Violence, Substance Abuse
- The Colonised begin to Comply with the purpose for which they are brainwashed and therefore fulfill the objectives of the colonizer;
- The Colonised lose All sense of Purpose and Vision as they Accept their Status of being Oppressed;
- The Colonised Emulates the Coloniser and wishes to be them in a Stockholm Syndrome Shift;
- The Colonised abandons their Identity, Language, Culture, Standards and Spirituality in favor of the Coloniser's, as everything Colonial is deemed Better, Holy and Trustworthy (Holesome, Good and Godly)
- The Colonised "dies" as they become fully Colonised and Encultured and gains Colonised Worldview and begin to pursue the purpose of the Coloniser rather than their own and Speak the Language of the Coloniser with the Values of the Coloniser as their own, completely Shifting their Cognition from Communal to Individualistic;
- The Colonised Despises everything Afrikan, mistrusts it and prefers to consume, associate with and support everything from the colonizer as everything Afrikan becomes Backward and uncivilized.
- The Colonised loses empathy and patience for what is understood as Ineptness, backwardness, barbarism, lack of education, utter Stupidity, Greed and xxx;
- The Colonised becomes Effaced from ukuba umuntu (ubuNtu) and becomes deHumanised (Other than Human), without Identity, Culture and Spirituality... forever emulating the Coloniser and never becoming like the colonizer... ever Consuming, ever Chasing, Never Arriving. Every time the Afrikan reaches a European Milestone, the European shifts from it to another. We see this often The Capitalist Nigger by Dr Chika Onyeani (2000), book captures this sentiment very well.

<u>The Impact of Effacement and deHumanisation</u>

Economic Poverty:

Dispossession of the Means of Production: Land, Law and Labor leads to Economic Poverty.

Land: Dispossession of Land with all its Resources – Earth and its Resources; Air (Wind); Sun (Fire); Water: Oceans, lakes and Rivers and their Resources leaves the Afrikan incapable of Production and Manufacturing, especially since the Intellectual property to do so has also been lost.

Law: Introduction of foreign Economic Policies concomitant with destruction of Afrikan Economic policies and Relations entrenched poverty and demonized ubuNtu practices of Reciprocity and honor of Authority.

Tax Laws are unsupportive of Afrikan and new Business entities. Many an Afrikan venture has been sacrifice on the Altar of Tax, leaving entrepreneurs disillusioned, indebted and impoverished.

Labor Laws entrenched Poor Wages and Working Conditions of workers. In Afrika we are Laborers and Menial workers, whilst people who do the same work in Europe are Artisans. The European Laborers have an opportunity to turn their Skill and experience into a thriving business because they understand the language, spirit and workings of the Law, but in Afrika, they remain trapped in the role of being employees or temporary workers because they are not supported to navigate the various legislations of business. Google any service company in South Africa. Look for one owned by a white person, call them for a Service, see who turns up at your door... It will be an Afrikan, capable of providing whatever service you require, with or without the requisite Formal Training. Unable to get Licensed on their own. The person may even be an illegal immigrant. Find out how much they earn versus what you are charged. Put the same person (the one who turned up at your door) in a Company of his own, if that company survives, it is a Miracle. Why? Law, Funding, Management. There is an ubuNtu way of running this business. You are White, you are Empowered, you know the basic principles that make a business succeed, you know your work, but there is only one of you and you need to expand, it is simple. Offer some Ownership shares to your employees. Skill them in Management or Centralise Management and let them find a territory where they can reproduce the business. They call it Franchising I believe... with a spin of course. It is Skills Transfer, Empowerment and Sharing in the wealth of the Country. It is ubuNtu and very easy to implement. What about the instance where the employee is an illegal immigrant? Work with them to help them become Legal. How can an Afrikan be illegal in Afrika? You know why...

Social Poverty:

Patriarchy: We lost Afrikan Patriarchy and inherited Western Patriarchy which destroyed Afrikan Matriarchy and All forms of Female Societal Roles. Colonisation reduced Matriarchy only to the context of Migrant Labor, which robbed Families of a father figure and introduced the violent suppression and oppression of women, outside the Protection of the extended family as families became Nucleated. Men took out their anger at the injustices they suffered on their Women and Children through abuse, without fear of the Cultural consequences of such behavior since all Cultural Structural Support is destroyed. Thus the Scourge of Gender Based Violence. In Afrika of yore, abusive men were dealt with in the manner I described in the Prologue with the story of the dragon and Madondido.

Use of Surnames and Colonial Names: The Consequence of this, was loss of History and Genealogy. It makes our families seem young because our surnames only go back to the 1850s. Through surnames alone, one is unable to recognize next of kin. It is better for those who have not lost Totemic knowledge as they can somewhat follow the lineage to the 100 AD and maybe beyond. Some families still retain Genealogical records of fathers that can go back to 1000 BC (100 generations. The Author is blessed to be able to recount hers that far back) but few can go further. If you sit your Great Uncle down or even Grandmother, you will be surprised by how many generations of your family lineage you can reconstruct. This is Wealth. Ensure it is kept for your generations. Digitalise it. Create a Website... Otherwise you will be denied or Erased, like your Egyptian Ancestors. Do this Not only for your family, but also for the "Tribe" that you now belong to. Do not re-invent the wheel, Collaborate. Re-birth the Community.

The lack of recognition of one's brethren, effaces ubuNtu from one, so that they have no feeling for another as they fail to identify themselves in the other. This is the cause of Xenophobia.

The Renaming of Place Names Exacerbated this poverty because Place names were Historical Records, that helped people dwell in the Land, connected to it. Alienation to the Land makes it bear thorns and thistles for us, since neither recognizes nor acknowledges the other. Have you ever wondered why War is always followed by Drought and Famine...? Creation Groans for the Manifestation of the sons of God.

Innovative Poverty

Colonialism undermined the Afrikan Education system, discrediting all Afrikan learning and indigenous knowledge systems and rendering them irrelevant and then using the opportunity to bottleneck us in Education Institutions Created solely to turn us into Servants. The Education of Afrikans is structured to make us followers and fearful compliers. Very few Graduates exit the system after 17-22 years with any Innovation or viable Business Plan. 99% exit to go and look for a job, only to find that they are overqualified, inexperienced and costly and therefore unemployable.

The Best Learned Afrikan is Learned in *"How to serve"* the Agenda of the West, How to Comply with its Legal Systems and Accounting Systems, How to Produce the Products the West wants and Values, How to Report News that Europe wants to hear, How to Speak with the European (American) Accent, How to Prescribe European Remedies, How to Emulate and fit into the European Worldview, How to have space at the European Table… **NOT** how to Innovate for Afrika or Create a Table for Afrika as my daughter Tehillah is fond of reminding me. "Mommy, Remember, you are creating your own table, you are not looking for space at other people's tables. They worked hard for their tables and they are not about to change what is working for them and pull up a chair for you to sit and have a voice. Build your own Table… Afrika, must build her own Table, so that we your children, can find space".

Spiritual Poverty:

- Spiritual Poverty is entrenched in the Lack of a place/foundation/locus on which Afrikans can Place or build things. This Poverty has created Substitute Foundations which are the basis of much social dysfunction.
- Displacement of Afrikans from their kiNtu, displaced them from their Spiritual Locus of ubuNtu.
- Ninety (90%) of Sub-Sahara Africans have become Christian and they Practice Spirituality within this Context, of God being that Locus upon which their Life foundations are built.
- God in the Christian context however was packaged in European Constructs, complete with the picture of his White son, Making the Afrikan Conflicted in their Spirituality as they could not see themselves in the Narrative of Christianity.
- Christian Missions were also Country aligned, making us: English; French; Spanish; Portuguese; German; Dutch or Belgian in our Afrikan Countries and Churches. This went as far as the entrenchment of European Church divisions and rivalries in Afrika, creating a Body of Christ that is divided and Competitive,

devoid of Christlikeness (Preaching Love, Unity and Brotherhood but paddling Division, Suspicion and Anger).

- The spirit of division within the church furthered divisions into Racial, Classist and Gender spheres within and without the church.
- Further Spiritual Poverty entrenched our Low Self Esteem as our Foundation/ Locus/ became Europe and its Constructs, Instead of God. Even for those of us who became Muslim, our Locus became the Arabic Culture instead of God.
- Europe as a Locus upon which to build came with the Acceptance of New Foreign Identifiers that divorced us from the Land and Married us off to an inferior Slave Mentality as "Black" with the resultant Colorism and Self- Loathing. Having a European name and speaking a European language further entrenched that Europe was the God Locus and Foundation, Making everything European Goodly and Godly. Thus the Consumerism as we try to become European by Material extension, instead of becoming God-like in the Spirit of ubuNtu.

African Consumerism:

Having Lost kiNtu and ubuNtu, Western Lifestyles and Materialism have become the Locus/Foundation upon which Most of us as Afrikans build Value for our Lives. Mass Media has successfully entrenched White superiority and trapped Afrikans in their pursuit to attain everything "white" in order to have Value and be worthy.

- Western products, produced with the West in Mind in terms of Design, Fit, coloring etc. are Mass produced and sold in Afrikan Markets with no regard for our Tastes, Sizes and Shapes.
- Afrikans contort themselves to fit into Clothes stylized, Stenciled and designed for Western figures and then are criticized for wearing Clothes that do not fit them or that are to revealing and contouring. To fit into their Clothes, we have to take them to the Tailor after purchasing them, to Snatch the Waist, Expand the Hips and Breast, Lengthen them and...
- Western Brands such as: Brooks Brothers; Nike & Converse both owned by Nike inc; Tommy Hilfiger which Sells American-themed apparel, fragrances, eyewear; Calvin Klein; J.Crew; Polo; Ralph Lauren; Levi's; Abercrombie & Fitch and its new Teen Focused Hollister Brand; Nike; Banana Republic; Coach; Gap & Old Navy; Victoria's Secret; Gucci; Benetton; French Connection; FCUK; Austin Reed; Louis Voutton; Jimmy Choo; Lacoste; Prada; Armani are all Brands that 90% Afrikans Know, Love and aspire to own as status symbols which confirm that one "has arrived" (Possibly at being White). These Brands which have

no bearing on Afrika nor are they produced in Afrika or with Afrika in Mind are idolised and bought by people who have to spend their entire salaries to afford them. Most of these brands were created between 1890 and 1960, Coincidentally The same years during which Afrika was colonized and the extraction of its Raw Materials began? Their worldwide operations rake in between 25bn Rands and 800bn Rands (2020 USD-Rand exchange) and their public company shares are not on offer in Afrika.

- This Consumerism *is in every respect:* The homes we live in, the Vehicles we drive, the food we eat, the Hair we wear... Although Afrikans have always worn protective hairstyles, we were discouraged from these and taught to prefer European looking silky styles that are still manufactured overseas and whose raw materials we have no clue of. We become Addicted to our Wigs, which cost anywhere between R3000 and R10 000 (You can get cheaper in Mozambique) in our quest to fit the model of beauty that has been cast.
- This Consumption extends to Food. Afrikans consume more Fast food and foreign food than other Countries. Most Afrikans are allergic to most of the food Additives in western Fast Foods leading to Fast Food Addictions and Morbid obesity. The Sugar, Salt and Oil Contents of these foods are dangerous to Afrikan people. Add to this the Genetically Modified Organisms used to Mass produce the food and the Recreational drinks and drugs: Alcohol; Cigarettes and Street drugs, whose raw materials are extracted from Afrika and manufactured in the West or Western Owned Plants in Afrika and sold in Afrika at exorbitant prices. Based on the Prices published by www.financesonline.com, in an article by Russo-Baltique named: Top Most Expensive Vodkas in the world, There are bottles of Alcohol that cost the amount it takes to: Build a luxury home, Buy 2 luxury vehicles, Take 4 children to a private school from Grade zero to Tertiary and still save some money in a Trust for some philanthropic work. As an example, Billionaire vodka costs R66 600 000.00...! It is like paying your oppressor to kill you and impoverish you, whilst flaunting it on social media so that you may feel like you are seating at his Table.

Colonisation therefore matters in that it Entrenched the settling and occupation that began 2500 years ago in North Afrika and 370 years ago in Sub Sahara Afrika as well as the Slavery that increased from 2000 years ago and climaxed 300 years ago and the Apartheid that was formalized in 1948 and which though repealed as law, resides in the hearts and minds of many in 2021. It Completely Destroyed Afrika and it is not a small matter that we can "Just get over it!" "Why do you blame everything on that? It has ended, Move on...!" The Question is: Has it? Ended? The only Person who can end it, is you. #NO LONGER SILENT!

Salungano

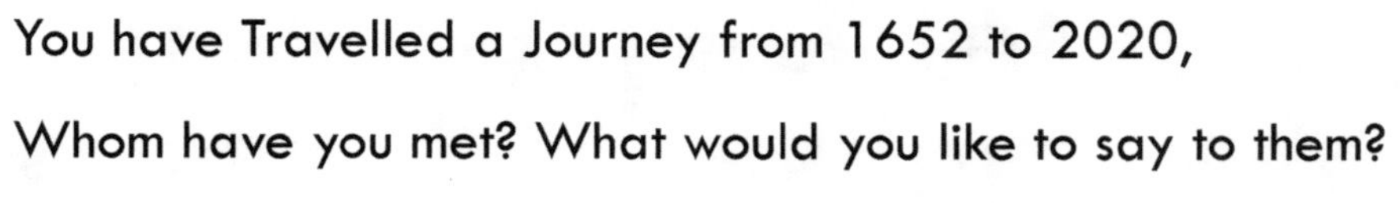

You have Travelled a Journey from 1652 to 2020,

Whom have you met? What would you like to say to them?

Now that you understand, what will you do?

Create Policies, to help Make an Omelet from the Scrambled eggs.

Part 7: New Beginnings

Muthu ndi muthu nga vhathu, tombo a li na Ndevhe.
Umuntu ngumuntu ngabantu, itshe kalinadlebe. Motho ke motho ka batho,
Leswika ga lena tsebe. umNtru ungumuNtru ngabaNtru ilitshe alinandlebe
Munhu hi munhu hi vanhu, ribye rihava ndleve.
I become human when I relate to you, Rocks have no ears.
Ek is, Want Jy is, Rotse het nie ore nie.

New Beginnings

This has been a Narration of the origins and untold HiStory of the First Nations of (South)Africa since Creation. The Indigenous Aboriginal Autochthone and Native ababaNtu (People) of Afrika. Those who have been Classified as: Black, Coloured, KhoiSan (Bushman and Hottentot), Pygmies, Bantus, Caffer, Kaffir and Negroid/ Negroes, Berber, Arab and who originated/were created in Afrika and who persisted in Afrika since Creation/Emergence and who Populated the Afrikan Continent, the Islands and the Diaspora and who are the Progenitors of all Human Beings in all Continents of the Earth.

Since the Out of Africa Exodus is a Theory, regardless of the Genetic markers that seem to support it, one day, it may be proven to be off the mark. As it is, Nations are combing their Soil Heaps to see if Life does not perchance Start in their Continent?

For Afrikans, that is not a Problem. Whether we started here or there, we were here first and or we were with those who came here first, and we have persisted here. When the world evolved technologically enough to be aware of people on other continents, we were here... In Afrika. We have been here for 300 000 years, or Biblically 13025 or 6025 years... Thus we Assert ourselves as Afrikans and as Aboriginal, Indigenous and Autochthone the entire Continent, not just one area or the Colonially dermacated areas. Ri vha Muno. We are of Here. Singa ba la! (We are of Afrika)

We also Acknowledge our European Afrikans; Indian Afrikans; Chinese Afrikans; xxx, as Afrikans. Karibu!

According to Bs. Dube, The Story of origins, will never end. As it ends, a new one begins. New evidence surfaces. New understanding comes, Hypotheses are ditched in favor of New ones... It is for this reason that this Narrative Synthesises all revealed Truth, Oral Evidence based on Indigenous Knowledge Systems as well as Evidence based Science and Scientific Hypotheses.

Although one does not walk forward whilst looking backward, it is hoped that Afrikans can look backward through this Afrocentric Lens, to re-Appropriate their, History, Culture, Heritage, Identity and Land in order to learn from their Mistakes so that from these they can build a better future. Afrika must benefit from the wisdom of Hindsight by understanding her History, so that by wisdom she may be built and by understanding she may be established.

The Buddhists say: "Whatever your Attention lands on, Grows, whatever you feed, Grows." Thus, as we look back this time, may our Attention be on our: Blessings, Abilities, Wisdom and Contributions to Humanity rather than the atrocities meted against us except to acknowledge these and release them once and for all.

It is imperative that we understand that the unrecognized past evils committed on Afrikan soil are Responsible for this Scrambled Egg Condition that Afrika is in. Genocide; War; Xenophobia; Racism; Poverty; Anger; unhappiness; Anxiety; Depression; Gender based Violence; general Violence; Murder; Theft; Fraud, Corruption, Substance Abuse; Materialism; Corruption; Dictatorship; Poor Progress; Poor Service delivery; High Burden of disease; Dehiscence of Family Structure to name but a few of the symptoms of our deeply wounded Soul.

Whilst it would be nice to Receive a Global and International Apology for the Systematic and Brutal Colonisation and Appropriation of Afrikan: Soil, Air, Water, Sun, Minerals, Fauna, Flora, People, Culture, Spirituality, Philosophy, Civilisation, Identity and History from all Parties Concerned, this may not be Forthcoming for several reasons, such as: Fear of Retribution, Unwillingness to Restitute and Pay Reparations or just Sheer Ignorance, Lack of Understanding and Arrogance...

Afrikans know based on their Spiritual Philosophy of ubuNtu that an Apology is Not Necessary for them to Forgive. Afrikans as the First amongst men and with the benefit of aeons of Wisdom, choose to be the bigger person and Forgive. Afrikans Choose to Forgive because we Can... We have the capacity.

Afrikans also forgive because we realise that it is the only way to release ourselves from being enslaved to anger and bitterness. It is the only way for us to Free ourselves from burdens that prohibit us from being able to Re-imagine a new Afrika. #The Afrika we want (AU Slogan)

As Afrikans, we can Choose to Feed our Wounds or our Future; We can Choose to Attend to our Past and allow it to stifle our future; We can Hold a Grudge and Poison ourselves with its bitterness; We can Stress ourselves, Loathe ourselves and others, Detain and paralyse ourselves, in the Past hoping for an Apology to come and help us go forward that is not Forthcoming or we can Look at the Past, Learn from it, Repent for our role in it, Forgive its Injustices, Release its Grasp and hold on us, and begin, to Look forward, to Build and to Establish ourselves, our Families, our Nations, our Countries and our Continent.

One may bring a Donkey to a River, but one can't force the donkey to Drink. One may Scream and Shout at the Donkey and even beat it, to try and get it to Drink, but if it does not want to, it will not. Fortunately, God has built in it, a Thirst Mechanism. One day, it will be Thirsty... At that time, it will Drink without being asked...

abaNtu say: "Nama Khombetshedzwa iphula khali" (If you force Meat into a Pot, it will ultimately break the Pot – Clay Pot – but then again... a pressure cooker could conceivably burst as well...). Do Not Be Deceived: God cannot be mocked; a man reaps what he sows. Be sure of this: The wicked will not go unpunished, but those who are righteous will go Free. Galatians 6:7

Whether Afrikan Colonisation was deliberate or Accidental, Whether the descendants of the Imperialists knew or did not know, partook or did not partake Benefitted or did not benefit... The Question today is, As Part of Humanity, located within a "Black" Person, what do you hear, See and Feel? Anguish, worthlessness, defeat, Anger, vengeance and retribution... It is not about whether YOU did anything wrong... It is not about Condemnation, it is about Learning and Growing Forgiving, Repenting and Going Forward. It is about being Human...Is it too much to Ask? That we all just pause for a Second and be the other person... be Human? Can you feel it? That, is ubuNtu.

Whether Afrikan Colonisation was deliberate or Accidental, whether you lived through it or not, whether you have been brutally violated or not, The Question today is: As Part of Humanity, located within a "White" Person, what do you hear, See and Feel? Fear, Anger, Self-preservation, guilt, Shame, Defensiveness...It is not about whether YOU were wronged or not... It is not about getting even, it is about Learning and Growing Forgiving, Repenting and Going Forward. It is about being Human...Is it too much to Ask? That we all just pause for a Second and be the other person... be Human? Can you feel it? That, is ubuNtu.

When I was 10, my Dad, who was always in his Study, called me into the study one day and sat me down on the Couch across from his Table. The Reclining Couch had a Spectacular (10-year-old eyes) View of the Garden past the Study Desk through the Glass Door and Wide Window. There was a Jacaranda Tree with beautiful Pink/Purple? Flowers and bright green leaves (and the occasional Green Mamba... or was it a Green Water Snake that I had a scary encounter with once? Most likely the latter).

The Yard in front of the Study Seemed like a Football court to those eyes... and through the fence, one could see neighbors Pass on the road on their merry ways.

When he called, I had Come into the Study and Knelt in front of him, head bowed. Aa! I had answered. "Take a Sit", He'd offered. Then, I Immediately took my favorite position of the Couch.

"What would you do" he began, "If when you wake up tomorrow morning, you do not find me in the house?"

I would go and Look for Mom, was my quick Response. What if you Could not locate her?

Oh, I would look for my Siblings.

And what if they were not there, he Pressed. I Hesitated... Confused...

I.... I will – go – and – check – our – neighbors, I Stuttered... My Breathing was becoming labored and my heart was racing as this scenario played out vividly in my head... I felt my Chest Tighten and my Mouth go Dry, Nga Phiswa same Time!

What if they are also not there?

I feel a knot in my Tummy and my Voice Catches... "I will go to the Police Station?" (At that, I realized I did not know where the Police Station was!)

What if the Police are not there?" Came the Response I Burst into Tears...

My Dad sat up Straight in his chair and looked me squarely in the eye and proceeded. "Nwananga, Muthu ndi muthu nga vhathu, tombo a li na ndevhe. Hone, Vhathu ndi mapfura vha a doliwa." (Daughter, Your existence is meaningless in the absence of other Humans. Immerse yourself in them, they are your Wealth).

As I write this Book, Afrika is at the Brink of a new Era. An Era of beginning, Again!

In this Conclusion, I wish to propose a few Strategies that we can Adopt to help us Recognize ourselves in each other... Locate ourselves in the other...Appreciate one another, Accept one another and Immerse ourselves in each other, in order for us, to Begin again... To learn to live together and rebuild/reconstruct Afrika for Global Impact, as we did in the beginning of Human History. We Collaborated then... We can Collaborate Now.

Afrika is one Continent and we are One People. We are Afrikan; Continental Afrikans, Diaspora Afrikans; Arabic Afrikans and Afro-Arabic people; European Afrikans and Euro-Afrikan people; Indian Afrikan and Afro-Indian people; Chinese Afrikans and Afro-Chinese people; Berbers; xxx... We are one. Cairo to Cape, Senegal to

Mozambique, Windhoek to Djibouti, Durban to Djelfa! We are Related sons and daughters of the same original 4 African fathers who became 26, 120 and then 10 000 and populated Africa, when their brethren Populated other continents. We are also the sons and daughters of those who have Chosen Afrika as Home. We are One! Islandic, Continental, Diaspora and the Grafted... We are one.

Let us safeguard our History for Posterity and build a sense of Continental and National Identity that will foster the Cohesion Prophesied in South Africa by Arch Bishop Tutu's: Rainbow Nation.

This Cry of baKhoe and baSan, is the Cry of Afrikans:

- Recognise us as the First Nations of Afrika
- Recognise all our Languages as official Languages
- Return our Land
- Abolish the divisive terms: White, Black, Indian and Coloured

It has been 2600 years since the first continual foreigners sat on the Egyptian Throne (100 generation); 368 years since Janze van Riebeeck set foot on South Afrikan Soil (15 generations); 135 years since the Scramble for Africa (6 generations); 69 years since the first country received its Independence (2.5 generations) and 26 years since South Africa became a Democracy (1 Generation) .... Collectively therefore we have been Oppressed for 100 generations Free for only 1 Generation.... It will take time to Restore Afrika to her former Glory. Thank God that a Nation can be Born in one Day... Thus we will work with God to birth this Nation in one Day. He does not bring to the Time of Labor only to Close up the Womb... We are Woke and We Are #NoLongerSilent!

It is imperative that we have a distinct grasp of what our Future Glory looks like, so that we are not chasing Europe (Including all their "New Found Lands"), Arabia or Asia in their Vision of their Future Glory. These Nations are where they are, because they Began and they are focused on their Visions. Let us therefore take a Resolute Decision to Cast our own Vision. The Afrikan Vision. #TheAfrikaWeWant

I do not Presume to Speak for all of Afrika. But since I am writing the Book, I will Suggest some things... Just so that we can begin having conversations and Agitating and breaking the shackles...

The Afrikan Vision

My Daughter, Ruth Suggests this:

Afrikans are Rising up, Re-Humanised by ubuNtu, achieving their Wildest Dreams, Living the Life, Happy and Content in their beloved Continent.

Mission

The Holistic Empowerment of Afrikan People Toward a Reconstructed Afrika for Global Impact

Objectives

Background

The Scramble for Africa was the taking of one whole Afrikan Egg with a Distinct Yolk and Albumin composed of various cells, substrates, substances and fluids encased in a Shell and Cracking the Shell open, Discarding it, Scrambling its Contents and further separating these into little pockets of colonial countries and consuming them in a Socio-Politico-Econo-cultural hegemony.

This Historical Narrative, was an effort to identify the various cells, substrates, substances and fluids of Afrika as well as its Shell in order to unscramble her.

The Shell, is Our Protective Cover which is Our Continent. The Soil, The Air, The Water, The Minerals, The Fauna and The Flora.

The Yolk and the Albumin: Our People in their Diversity.... One Seamless whole, with different parts, looks and callings.

The Albumin is the Substrate that makes us Human: our God, Lingo-Cultural Heritage, Spiritual Philosophy of ubuNtu

Unscrambling Afrika is Possible if we will borrow the Wisdom of Genesis 11: 6 "If as one People, Speaking the same language, they have begun to do this, then NOTHING they Plan to do WILL be IMPOSSIBLE for them."

Pan Afrikanism is a Necessity as we Reclaim our Continent. It was Pan Afrikan 2600 years ago. Pan Afrikanism need not abolish the Countries that it has taken us 2.5 Generations to get used to. The African Union is Sufficient as an Organ of Pan Afrikanism for now, which may become the Government of Afrika with Countries becoming Federal States.

The Reason for Pan Afrikanism is the Need for Nation Building which to borrow the language of the above Genesis 11:8 verse gives us examples of the Objectives we could adopt:

1. <u>One People:</u>

This speaks to A Continental Identity which is, Afrikan (No Arab Afrika, No Sub-Sahara Afrika, No Maghreb, No Sahel, No East Afrika, No West Afrika, No Central Afrika and No Southern Afrika... Just Afrika) Are Afrikans big enough to ditch our divisive labels created to keep each other outside? Can we learn to accept that the whole realm of Afrikan History and Legacy belongs to all Afrikans?

Further we should Appropriate the given Country Names and borders that we have become accustomed to as our Location Identity. Within these Country Identifications we should Identify by Nationality: Berber, Afrikaans, English, Tamil, Gujerati, Hindi, Xhosa, Tsonga, Chinese, Arabic, Luwo, Igbo, Akan, Tuareng, Fulani, Mbuti, Tigrinya, Kikuyu, Chechewa, Shona, Ovimbundu, Khoekhoengowab, !Xoo, Kongo, Bemba... xxx just to give you an Example. I am sorry that I can't write out all 10 000 and more Nations here. After writing 10 000, It may be that I still haven't acknowledged another 10... We are Countless in our Multitudes and we are all Legitimate. What is important is that you become farmiliar with your Nation and their Language. This will help us to Identify Each other Across Borders. Further than the Language we could identify by Totemic and Genealogical Lineages as a measure of Keeping Family History and Honoring those who came before (our Fore fathers/Ancestors).

If I were to use myself as an example: This is How I would Identify:

I am Takalani Dube, Mukololo wa (Princess of) Luvhalani, I am an Afrikan, South African of the vhaVenda Nation.

Further I can locate myself within my family Genealogy and History as follows:

Ndi muNgona, Mudau wa Mapungubwe. (I am a part of the Farming Community who prize the Nguni Cattle: amaNguni/Bakone) whose Dynastical and Totemic Identity is a Lion and whose last Precolonial Ancestral Royal Citadel was Great Mapungubwe.

Where necessary to Remind myself that God has walked with me from the first of my Ancestors in time immemorial until today, I may then List my Ancestral Lineage:

Ndi nwana wa (My Fathers are): Mvumi Matshikhiri a Nndwa, Vele, wa (son of) Tshavhungwa, wa Ramulayo, wa Ratshiuvhu, wa Tshidziwelele, wa Phuthaluse, wa Ramadenga, wa Muregu, wa Ranwedzi, wa Thovhele, wa Tabumvenda, wa Malupazwifho, wa Lavhengwa, wa Nevhulozwi, wa Luti, wa Matevhutevhu, wa Vembalanwali, wa Tshavhumbwa, wa Bwerinofa, wa Ranwedzi, wa Musholommbi, wa Mungona, wa Khangale, wa Mpofu, wa Mushungwa, wa Thavhadziawa, wa Musingadi, wa Dzolokwelamidzi, wa Mamidzavele, wa Mupetanngwe, wa Ramisho, wa Murathangwena, wa Nemapungubwe, wa Neluongwe, wa Saselanwali, wa Sase, wa Malimandila, wa Tshifhavhadzimu, wa Thavhadzalundwa, wa Naledzivhungu, wa Mungona, wa Denga na kupa, wa Malinda thakha ya nwali, wa Shiri ya Denga, wa Vhanwe vhanzhi na (Many others including) Misraimi wa (K)Ham wa Nukhu (Noah) na vhanwe uswikela kha (and many others until) AddamuNtu, wa Nwali (Adam spirit son of God). Matthew 1 (Bible)

To Embolden myself if need be, and root myself in God, others and my Environment, I will sing or Speak my Family Praises. This is a way to Acknowledge the Journey God has caused my people to travel since creation in the Land he allocated me to live in, to reassure myself that the God who was with my Ancestors and with me in the Past, will continue to be faithful to me and my descendants forever. Exodus 15 (Bible).

My Family Praises:

Kha Dzule zwawe Dau, Mudau Mudamane, Ratshiembe! Nkhwatshivhula wa gumba lamipfa livaya vhatshilaho; Mungona, Senzi, Shiri ya Denga, Denga na Kupa;
Nganiwapo, Tshidza tshapo, Ntangiwakugala;
Mudabe wa mitshilinzhi ya Venda;
Venda la ha tshika muroho li sa ladzi nwana na ndala;
Razwipo, wa Mudzimba abva, u vhuya na muhwalo mabweni a Matongoni; Muthu wa shango la Nama na Vele;
Mulondwa nga Radabe lamavhanga; Muregu wa Tshiala tshitswu; Nwana wa ngozwi ntswu;
Tshiala tsha khanga vhanna; Nangana ya tshipembe, Muregu ha di reguli...

Do your own Research and Identify yourself in a way that is authentic to you and honours you, your God, your God-given Ancestral heritage, God's walk with you in your Ancestors in your Continent(s).

2. Speaking One Language:

Speaking one Language is Proxy for Identity.

Psychologists Claim that being able to do Identify ourselves by Connecting ourselves to God, Ourselves, the Land, our Ancestors who came before us, to our contemporaries as well as Past and Current Events, gives us a sense of continuity and permanence, which lends itself to Confidence in the present and the future, motivating us to be Creative and lessening our Anxiety and tendency toward Isolation and Depression.

Understanding the Continuity and Permanence of our existence further frees us to see others as part of the pack and as collaborators rather than competitors. It capacitates us to understand how everything is connected and our role in the whole. Understanding that one is a portion of the whole and not the whole, frees one to focus only on fulfilling their role in the whole, confident that others will fulfill the balance incrementally and generationally rather than in one generation through one person.

Thus Afrika should have a Language that all its Citizens Speak. One of the oldest written Afrikan Languages is Kemitic ((K)Ham's language), Coptic is a derivative of this language and a Plethora of writings exist written in Coptic. The Rosetta Stone has enabled us to decipher Kemitic and its Alphabet is now Available.

Several Medutus on Rocks and Papyrii exist for us to have literature to read. The Egyptian Government has created a Digital Library of the Library of Alexandria and this should prove invaluable. In Kemitic, People (abaNtu) are: Wanu. This tells the reader that they should be able to identify many more words similar to their vernacular language in Kemitic, making it an easy language to learn. Afrikans Should therefore adopt Kemitic as our Continental Shell Covering Language and we should all be fluent in it. This will be our Pan Afrikanist Language.

According to the UN Geopolitical Map, we can then have 5 secondary Languages of:

- North Afrika: Arabic, Berber and Tamazight
- East Afrika: Amharic, Maasai, Gikuyu & Kiswahili
- West Afrika: Yoruba and Hausa
- Central Afrika: kiKongo, Fulani, Tshiluba
- Southern Afrika: isiZulu, Shona, Chechewa, N|uu
- Islands: Malagasy

Although Kiswahili is not a 100% Afrikan Language, it is the best language that demonstrates the ability of Afrika to Love, Forgive and Accept the Stranger in her Midst and Heal herself. Kiswahili Contains Most abaNtu (Bantu) words as well as

Arabic and French. This being a commonly spoken and written language that is readily accessible can be used as our early (1st) Pan Afrikanist language, It is already spoken by 150 000 000 people and contains words from most of our Languages.

Each Country should ensure that its indigenous Languages and Colonial languages are preserved and spoken in the Country. Where possible, all the Languages should be recognised as official languages. South Africa recognises 11 official Languages including sign language, but has yet to Recognise baKhoe and baSan Languages such as: Khwendam, N|uu, Khoekhoengoab, !orakoab, Xirikobab, !Xunthali and many more. At the bare minimum, N|uu, which is now being taught by Mama Katrina Esau as assisted by Sheenah Shah and Matthias Brezinger should be Recognised as a representative official language of baKhoe and baSan, the same way that the 8 Nguni Languages are a representative of the Multitudes of Nguni Languages such as kiLobedu, siPhuthi, xiTonga, isiHlubi, siBhaca, siNhlangwini, isiNrebele, isiMpondo, sePulana, siTlokwa, seHananwa, SeKgalaka/Tshikalanga, siLala... and many more that still cry out for recognition...

Speaking One Language enables people to Recognise (locate) themselves in the other which helps them to readily Acknowledge, Love and Accept each other. Language being the Transmitter of Culture, Wisdom and Spirit, will enable the breaking of boundaries and the Understanding of Brotherhood to emerge organically and easily. (Just look at how abelungu who speak Vernacular are celebrated by Afrikans as a "Curtain" lifts from our eyes and we stop seeing a white person and begin to see ourselves in that vernacular speaker to love them and Embrace them. The same happens when any recognisable "outsider" speaks the language of the people in whose land that person is. This is why the French suddenly become helpful to you when you speak in their language in their Country. It is a well-known thing... If you want help in France, Speak French... Language will enable Afrika to Relinquish Xenophobia and Racism and Help build united Communities that "See" each other. Language will make Pan Afrikan Trade possible again and it will help us Standardise our Accounting and Legal Standards.

People who speak one Language Can Collaborate, Problem Solve and Innovate better.

Language is the main Transmitter of Culture, which encompasses Social and Spiritual Identity.

It is imperative that we deliberately ensure that our Vernacular Tongue is Transmitted to our Children perpetually. There is No European who speaks luVenda as their first

Language and who has forgotten their Mother tongue and does not bother to ensure that his progeny knows the language. The French won't even speak English and yet they are neighbors and descend from the same Ancestor. Let alone Indian people, Japanese people and Chinese people who are advancing technologically whilst coding all their technology in their mother tongue. We Must insist that All our Schools Teach Communication Proficiency Vernacular and we must encourage rather than laugh at those who missed out on learning vernacular in their childhood.

3. <u>With a Common Speech:</u>

A Common Speech speaks to reading from the same Book... A Common Picture as encapsulated by:

Vision, Mission and Culture

A Pan Afrikanist Vision and Mission is required that will help all Afrikans understand what we Stand for and unite us in Focus. I have proffered my suggestion above.

Individual Countries can use the Vision and Mission to inform their Objectives and Policies which would help inform:

- Politics of Afrocentric Democracy
- Law: Pan Afrikan, Afrocentric Law
- Economic Principles: Standardisation of Accounting Practices that can factor in ubuNtu. Standardised Regulatory Bodies; Agreement on Trade and Economic Zones: Farming; Technology; Manufacturing; Mining and Energy. (Afrika became a Free Trade Zone in January 2021: The African Continental Free Trade Area (ACFTA))
- Travel: Standardisation of Movement... Connecting: Road, Rail and Air with no Visas and less cumbersome borders designed to control rather than Restrict.
- Afrikan Technology and Cyber Identity (Afrikan Silicon Valley)
- Continental Social Relations based on principles of ubuNtu (We can have a set of 60 Social Laws, with each country Contributing 1 Most Cherished Ideal and 6 from all Diaspora and Dependencies) These Laws should be taught in School to help establish Patriotism. Each Country can then have their own set of 12 (1 for each Month)

Culture and Tradition root us in our Land. It also encompasses the roles we play in our society and family, our past memories, and our hopes for the future, informing our Work, hobbies and interests. It allows us to have common ground, which fosters

Goodwill and Peace. It reduces Stress, Anxiety and Depression by creating a sense of Belonging (Acceptance, Understanding and Confidence), Being Part of a Pack: Loved, Appreciated, Needed, Protected and Assured of Nourishment. People outside a culture and tradition are left feeling like outsiders who do not fit in and who do not belong and who never feel accepted nor confident in anything, leading to a sense of worthlessness, anxiety and Depression. This has been the plight of our Private School Children, where one may find just 10 Afrikan Children in a Class of 50 or more pupils and where the school rules do not take into consideration their specific needs. It is for this reason that more instances of Racism are reported in these schools, where no special effort is made to include the Afrikan Children and where their Lingo-cultural heritage is minimised and uncelebrated, so that they are always feeling Left out, Unseen and unheard, which injures their spirit and fosters Rejection. So that these children feel effaced every day, leading to high Suicide and Substance Abuse amongst them as they are misunderstood at home, school and the community, and who do not have sufficient numbers to form a supportive community of their own. Some become reclusive, never achieving their potential, they drop out of school, they become rebellious, they leave the country and go overseas, where they feel more at home (My daughter, who was Private school schooled, visited America for 6 weeks. When she came back she said: I felt at home. I am American. Everything felt so familiar... for once I felt like I belong. What she did not know, is that she identified with Americans because of the level of affluence and Media exposure, which have created a Lingo-Cultural atmosphere that validates her, and that this is not the experience of the general African American in America).

Let us Ensure that our Children Are Afro-Enculturated, regardless of which schools we afford to take them to... We must ensure that they Understand the basics of kiNtu and ubuNtu as shared in this Book, which are sufficient to enculture anyone at the current level of Afrocentricity. We must stop delegating Enculturation to the teachers, who will Enculture our children in what is familiar to themselves... their own Culture. The Lack of Lingo-Cultural Heritage amongst Continental and Diaspora Afrikans is what causes us to find ourselves caught up in the extremes of all Societal ills: Generational Poverty, Homelessness, Violence, Crime, Substance Abuse, Sexual Permissiveness, Gangsterism (which is a deviant Lingo-Culture born of Negligence and Rejection), Low Literacy rates, Unemployment, Vulnerability to Pandemics, Intolerance, Abuse of Women, Children and the Elderly, Spiritual abuse of Church members and amaThwasa, Mental Health illnesses, Lifestyle Non- Communicable diseases, xxx.

- All Religions and Spirituality can be followed within kiNtu. kiNtu and ubuNtu are not Religions.

- Decide for yourself which Cultural, Traditional and Spiritual Values Are Meaningful for you and enshrine them in your family Tradition for posterity. You might Consider Traditions of:

UpWard Posture:

- Faith or Religion or Spirituality to follow and how to practice that.
- Genealogic Preservation
- Parental Care and Support
- Support of family Members
- Support of Progeny
- Support of Community InWard Posture:
- Self-care Traditions: Emotional, Spiritual, Social and Physical Care OutWard Posture:
- Traditions to Commemorate Life stages: Birth; Childhood; Menarche and Semnarche; 21st Birthday or other Birthday Celebrations; Marriage Negotiations and Wedding Celebrations, "Adulting" Transitions, Menopause and Andropause Celebrations, as well as Celebrations of End of Life as examples. Follow these to be aligned to your Spiritual Faith (Religion)
- Child Naming and Welcoming Traditions and/or Rituals (To Assist... Ritual is defined as a religious or solemn ceremony consisting of a series of actions performed according to a prescribed manner or order). Create these to be aligned to your Spiritual Faith (Religion)
- Social Etiquette and Communication Norms such as Kneeling to show Respect to parents and the elderly; Types of Eye Contact when communicating with various people; Strategic Repulsive Responses to Sexual grooming and Harassment; Answering when one is called; Addressing the elders and Attending to them...
- Communalism for Family, Neighbors and Community
- Political and Economic Activism DownWard Posture:
- Environmental Ethics and Activism
- Commemorative Museums and Memorials
- Reconstruction of the Education System

4. <u>Begin to do...Let us Build a City (Reconstruction):</u>

It must be the Responsibility of every Child, Young person, Adult, Parent, Entrepreneur, Environmentalist, Social Leader, Technological Leader, Political leader, Religious Leader, Media Leader, Judicial Leader, Educator, Artist and every other type of Leader and Creative in every field, to ensure that we Love Afrika, believe in Afrika,

Promote Afrika and share knowledge about Afrika from a deColonial perspective that locates all the first peoples in the center stage of Afrikan History and Development.

deColonial Perspectives: A few General Suggestions:

Reconstruct Lingo-Cultural Hegemony:

As part of Acknowledging her Colonial Past and Reconstructing herself from its negative impact, Afrika should make her Environment attest to the autochthoneness of her people through the construction of Commemorative Museums and Monuments unto Healing and Restoration:

- Museums of Natural History from Creation should depict Afrikans as Progenitors of all Humanity, the first to "evolve" from Hominids or the first to be Created by God. It should demonstrate the Out of Africa Migration and showcase the settlement of Afrikans in Afrika Precolonially and the changes of those settlements with Colonisation from 1600 BC to the 1900s AD and conclude with the current Post Colonial Map, whilst Reminding people of the connectedness of the various people (by preserving their Nationalities) who are now bounded in various countries in order to foster a sense of brotherhood and eliminate xenophobia and racism.
- Museum of our Colonial Past including Slavery and Apartheid (There is a Holocaust Museum in Israel and a Monument in Germany) This should be done in order to explain the patterns of Economic disparities that exist and to illustrate how these can be reversed and to avoid reverse injustices from occurring.
- Settled Lifestyle Villages should be funded or encouraged as the new "Gated" Residential Community Models, complete with Modern Day Amenities in Afrocentric Architecture and setup and "Tribal" Councils as Body corporates...
- History Textbooks should be re-written to include precolonial Afrikan History and remove languaging of Bantus, Negros, Blacks, Caffer, Kaffirs, Pygmy, Hottentots, Bushman, Berber and other derogative remarks in naming Afrikan people except where these are a reflection of the History itself. Racial Classification of Afrikans as: White, Indian, Coloured and Black should be removed from History books and be scrapped from all Communication altogether. I elaborated on how people can be identified by Continent of Origin if it is necessary to know that. The Text Books should also remove the Pseudo Theory of the Migration of Bantu Farmers into South Africa or any other Afrikan Country and Acknowledge

all Afrikans as part of the first peoples of South Africa.

- Afrikan History Should Be Compulsory for all learners from GRRR up to Grade Nine
- Education should also be styled according to the calling of a Person with early Practical exposure and Apprenticeship.
- Afrikans are naturally gifted with Creativity. Subjects like Coding and Software and Application development should be offered as part of Life Orientation at School from Primary level and those gifted in Technology be supported to pursue their calling and begin these studies in High primary and High School, the same way that Mathematics is taught to all Children.
- Universities should not be coerced into discriminatory processes where Mathematics is used to exclude people from entering the field of their calling. In real life, if one is not gifted in Mathematics or whatever, they hire that skill to come and offer the requisite skills. As an Example, Medicine hardly uses Mathematics that is more advanced than Mathematical Literacy, yet people are disadvantaged from following their calling of Healing through Western Medicine because pure Maths is a requisite to entry. This is the reason why one finds brilliant doctors with no sense of people skills in Hospitals, leading to untold misery for both the doctor and the patient. It is the same for coding and Property development to mention but a few. Precedence exists where in order to enable more students who are not good with Mathematics to enter into the

B. Commerce Stream, Universities have found innovative ways of creating Streams such as: B. Com Innovation, B. Com Economics etc. so that those who do not qualify for Accounting because of the pure Maths requisite can still do parts of B. Com that do not require this skill and that they are naturally gifted in.

Reconstruct Political Hegemony

As Afrikans we have Accepted Constitutional Democracy as a Representative, Just and Fair Governing System.

We have Accepted the Colonial Boundaries that have been created.

We have Accepted the Legal System that comes with these Colonial Legacies.

Going back to our Traditional Political Systems and Judiciary will be as much a harrowing journey as the Colonial journey thus far has been. We should however

Transform certain things in our Political and Judicial systems that are not enabling for Afrikan people and that are devoid of Righteousness, Justice and ubuNtu.

We should Transform our Political systems in such a way that anyone can stand for office. (South Africa now allows for Independents to Stand for office). Those who are so gifted, should run for office and stop pointing fingers at those who are running. Active Citizenship speaks to every citizen taking their role in society seriously and participating in the various political structures and ensuring that their views to build the community can be heard. Democracy is a Government of the People by the people for the People. Our leaders need to hear from us, not us from them... It is our Government and we put the incumbents into office, so that they can govern us as we wish, not as they imagine we wish and handcuffed by disabling archaic colonial laws. When we choose to relegate our responsibility, they have no choice but to Lord it over us without any accountability.

We need to Educate our masses in the workings of this Democratic Political system both at School through the History and Life Orientation Curricula, Online and in Various Social groupings such as Religious and other organizations as well as in our various Political Parties. Each Citizen should be confident that they can get their voice heard and be able to Mobilise the Community for changes of Laws that disadvantage them. We should be confident that we are able to engage with government and have our voices heard in matters of Service Delivery.

We should Aim for a 90% Voter turnout whenever we go to the polls. We should also ensure that our Royal Houses remain intact and are able to contribute politically, reminding the Country of its National of its Identities.

We Should Teach the Freedom Charter; The Constitution and Principles of ubuNtu at Schools to build a Patriotic and United Generation

As Citizens, we should starve the Corruption Child that we have nurtured all this time since it first arrived in Boats on our shores. If all of us whistle blow and refuse to give bribes or receive them, the baby will soon die. Corruption Steals Service delivery money and starves the Poor whilst enriching a few. We must demand the Summary removal of corrupt CEOs and Directors of Private companies who corrupt Public officials and Politicians.

<u>Reconstruct Economic Hegemony:</u>

Means of Production are: Land, Law and Labor

Land:

6% of the population produces what is consumed by 94% of the population.

In South Africa, 60 000 people own 80% of the Land. Land must be restored to the people (of all "races") without crippling the economy nor the capacity to produce food. There are many Clever ways we can do this and the government must deliver on this Mandate. South Africa has a Land area of 1,22 million Square kilometers.... At a population of 60 million people, thus, every current living individual can own 20square kilometer of Land (The same size as a small farm). Those so gifted can figure out the semantics. The Alternative is to make the Government Custodian of the Land as our Kings used to be, and then whosoever wishes to Lease the Land can do so for the Public good. The Revenue to Government from leasing out Land can be exclusively used for Social grants in order to relieve the Tax purse.

Spiritually, We Must Claim and Call back our Land to ourselves. If we disown our Land or Neglect it, we will continue to lose power over it until it no longer Responds to our Creative Authority, bearing Thorns and Thistles for us. This is why there is drought and Famine across Afrika, especially the areas inhabited by Afrikans... The land no longer recognizes us. Just Walk around proclaiming out loud, "You are the Land of my Ancestors, a Gift of God to me. Know me and support me and my Offspring!"

Law:

Our Law is enabling and will build a robust, Transparent and globally competitive Economy once all people are educated and supported through its extensive Compliance requirements. BBBEE is still needed for the transfer of wealth, but it can only do so, as far as Government Tenders are concerned. It does not really work for Private Wealth Transfer. For Private Wealth Transfer, Afrikans have to begin to build their own tables and stop waiting for the Crumbs that fall from the Tables of others. Wen'o wa bona inja ilinde ithambo...

Labor and Consumption:

Labor is the greatest Economic Transformation tool that is at our disposal for Economic Transformation. It will be effected by our own Actions and Habits.

The Labor Industry is predominantly Supplied by Afrikans. We Supply Labor for both the Private and the Public Sectors. In the Public Sector (Government):

We Enjoy Permanent Jobs with Packages. Government is a Company just like any other... It provides goods and Services.

The Difference is that its Revenue does not come from the sale of goods and services except a few... but comes mainly from Taxes paid by the citizens that the Employees of Government should serve. As Shareholders in our Government Company, Citizens are the most important people who also happen to be our Customers, they should therefore be treated with the utmost respect. Our services as Government are sorely needed by the masses who have suffered the most and who can't afford to purchase goods and services in the private sector. Much of what Government Company provides can be replaced by Private institutions: Education, Health, Housing, Energy, Water (to a limited level because it is protected by law), Sewer and Refuse collection can all be provided by Private Companies, leaving us without customers and at risk of losing our jobs. If we are Permanent Employees, it means we "own" this Government Company and we must ensure it thrives. We Must:

- Love Government and be Proud to be its Employees;
- Love our Jobs;
- Ensure that we are Skilled in our work and take advantage of various trainings that are offered for our upskilling;
- Keep Working Hours diligently and go beyond the call of duty;
- Love the Community we serve and give them our best Service even according to our Batho Pele Code (SA);
- We must actively Engage both the Public and The Legislatures to make them aware of the problems we are experiencing in our endeavor to serve them;
- We must whistle blow on all manner of corruption;
- We must avoid being involved in corruption.

In the Private Sector, the same Principles advanced above for Government apply. However, we can do more. We can Learn how the Business works, we can organize ourselves as Employees and raise money to buy Shares in the Company we work for. Shares of companies can be worked out through readily available Accounting Methodologies. If our offer is refused, As Employees, we can use the funds so raised to set up our own company in that same Industry and Market it among our people for support.

The Labor Force is also the Biggest Consumer of goods and services produced by the Private Sector.

Mazidl'ekhaya is an isiZulu saying based on an Idiom meaning: "People, must Consume what they Produce"

As Consumers, we need to come together, Raise Capital and offer to buy Shares of Companies whose products we most Consume. If our reasonable offer is Refused, we must set up those companies and be loyal to buy only from ourselves. If we demand that companies open up affordable shareholding to us so that as we buy products, we are confident that we are investing in ourselves. Where owners do not want to open up their companies, we must stop supporting such businesses and learn how to produce what they produce and buy from ourselves.

The Following Industries should be our Targets for Transformation and Development in the next 10 years.

<u>Banks:</u>

- Currently, Banks give Afrikans the highest Interest rates for Credit. They are also quick to Sanction Afrikans for failure to pay, Repossessing our possessions in spite of years of regular payments. They then Claim from Insurance for our failure to pay and still proceed to sell those Assets at current values, Making Profit 3x, whilst impoverishing us at a faster pace than for other sectors of society. We must demand the lowest possible rates. We are the biggest Clientelle in any Bank and we must be treated with the respect afforded everybody else.
- There are a few emerging entrants in the Banking sector owned by Afrikans but these lack infrastructure and footprint, whilst we wait for them to grow, we can support them by depositing money in them. We must also raise capital so that we can buy Shareholding in them to help grow them to become the major Banks or buy out the current major Banks. Building our own Banks, especially Credit Banks is also important, so that we can have easy access to the capital that we are currently denied by traditional banks.

<u>Farming:</u>

- Farming, Food Processing and Manufacturing

At 55 Million People, Afrikans are the Majority demographic in South Africa, whose Total Population is estimated at 60 million People.

All of us eat food we neither produced nor processed. Neither do we retail this food. The entire value chain is in the hands of other Nationalities, with a negligent sprinkling of Afrikans contributing. The Re-appropriation of land will apparently happen without compromising food security. This means productive farms will not be re-appropriated.

Whilst this is desirable and recommended, those farms should offer shareholding to their employees who are predominantly Afrikan and government should give these workers loans to be able to buy this shareholding.

The same can be employed with Manufacturing, Processing and Retailing. In order to give other Afrikans an opportunity, Community Shareholding should also be made available for people in whose community the Farms, Factories and Shops are found. All people in the Community regardless of their Nationality would then benefit from this shareholding opportunity.

Where Afrikans are able to procure land as in the example where government is leasing out its land to "Blacks", those who are successful in procuring these farms should receive government support to ensure that they are able to make the Lands productive.

Property:

55 Million people represent upward of 10 Million families, all these people live in homes and as their children grow, they will need decent housing.

Afrikans must develop the areas where they live so that they are attractive to live in. Rather than building houses for people, government should focus on giving people Land and a Minimum amount for the people to empower each other in their own communities as owners take responsibility of appointing architects and builders for their homes. Each Community Can Register the available companies in the community that government can approve and monies can be paid directly to service providers. Those who choose to use their own service providers can do so and bear the burden of proof of compliance.

In the CBD, Afrikans Tenants should form Property schemes and buy up property in the CBDs where they are currently the largest suppliers of Tenants. Where they already own Units, they must educate each other on the running of Body Corporates, get involved in these and actively participate in them.

Fashion and Hair

Let us build a Clothing Manufacturing Plant that produces Clothes for our Body Shape. Each Community can come together to support people in the Clothes Manufacturing Industry.

I love my Weave and my Wig... But it is time we wore Hair whose origins we knew and understood and hopefully can even benefit from. We should get to know what synthetic materials are used and how to manufacture this. Most Afrikan Countries already have Trade agreements with china. Let us understand these and ensure that we can get shareholding in Chinese Companies that we bring to our Countries to produce the products that we consume.

<u>Alcohol:</u>

We do not own any of the favorite Alcohol Brands that we love to consume so much and we are quickly losing the intellectual Property on our own Brewing skills for Amarula, Umqombothi, amaHewu, utshwala... whilst preferring wines, spirits and Beers. Look up any Brand you love and see who owns it. Need I say more? Yes, there are a few Afrikan Wine labels... Most are just that, labels, not producers. Be that as it may, At least let us start by supporting these labels whilst we work our way to producing. Schools, Hospitals, Professionals... Mazidl'ekhaya, bakithi

Granted, Afrikans may not meet your Service or goods Standard... but how will they improve unless there are customers holding them accountable and demanding growth from them? A 3-year-old Brand can't compete with a 150-year-old product.

Conclusion

All these Reconstructive Strategies I have presented here, are not Revolutionary. The Indian, English, Greek and Jewish Communities in any Nation employ these strategies... especially where they are the Minority. The Indian Community in South Africa has employed them since they arrived in South Africa in the 1860s. They were as marginalized as we are, but today they are more prosperous than most European South Africans. They came 160 years ago as a community of 152 184 people between 1860 and 1911. Today there are 1 300 000 people of Indian Descent in South Africa. Most of them live a decent lifestyle with several being Multi-Millionaires and having managed to preserve their Religion and Culture. The Strategies I have presented above are a modification of what enabled them to get where they are today. The Afrikaner and English Communities have also done the same.

The Beautiful thing about what I have suggested is that it does not require Regime Change; It does not Require war; It does not require new Laws; It does not Require any Demonstrations; It does not require looting and Stealing and Killing. It requires None of that. It only Requires us coming together as Families and Communities, Churches, Temples and Mosques. That's all... Come to therefore, let us build ourselves a City, whose tower reaches to the heavens, so that we may make a name for God!

How long will we keep trying to get space at other people's Tables? Is it not time for us to Build our own Table? Many may be unhappy with us trying to build our own tables... but many more will rejoice that we have finally been set free and stand shoulder to shoulder with them as brethren in the Human Family.

I know that in South Africa, the Afrikaner Community is quiet keen to become part of the Afrikan Continent and finally find a place of Rest in the "Promised land" without guilt, fear and anxiety and that they are willing to share the lessons they have learnt in Self-preservation and wealth creation with their fellow Afrikan brethren, so that they may live peaceful lives in "South Africa, our Land!". The Indian Community having experienced Marginalisation and always at the mercy of both the Afrikan and European Communities, are also ready and willing to share their Learnings... So do the English and other Communities.

The Unfortunate events of 12 to 16 July 2021 have taught South Africans that "United we Stand and divided we Fall". They have taught us that we can't continue on our current Gini Coefficient trajectory if we are to be a peaceful and progressive Rainbow Nation. We may not get a Chair at the Tables of others, but Many are willing to show us where to Source the Material for building our tables as well as How to build the

Table and even to collaborate with our tables once these are built.

It is the Will of God that we may have Life in Abundance and the resources of South Africa are Abundant enough for the few of us... only 60 million people. The Resources of Afrika are abundant for the few 1.35 billion of us. It is no longer necessary for Afrika to enrich the world at its own cost... Charity must begin at home and then spread out... Jerusalem, Judea, Samaria and the uttermost World. Blessed be Africa (Egypt) my People, Assyria my handiwork and Israel my Inheritance. Ashiya 19:25

May Afrikans Rise up, Re-Humanised by ubuNtu, to achieve their Wildest Dreams, Live their Lives, Happy and Content in their beloved Continent, Afuruwaika, Afrika.

umuNtu ngu muNtu ngabaNtu.

Camagu!
(The Divine Ntu in me greets the Divine Ntu in You and wishes you well!)

This, is the untold HiStory of Afrika and her People: abaNtu

Amandla!

Gratitude

"Though I seem empty, in my Emptiness I am in Purposeful and Meaningful Existence I seem invisible, yet in my invisibleness, I am Profoundly Present, nothing that happens, can happen without my empty invisibleness." Mma S.P Neluvhalani

To all of you who have given be the Privilege of Encountering you... Everything about you has been Profoundly Meaningful and has served to be the auto correction I needed to keep on the Path. Thank you

The List of People who made this work Possible is an entire Chapter. Forgive me if I have not mentioned you specifically, I hope that as you read the book, you were able to see yourself and acknowledge yourself in the bigger pictures that I have painted.

I ask that in the spirit of ubuNtu, you help me Honor these heroes by reading their

names out loud as a prayer...

Mulalo! Shalom! Salaam! Salamu! ukuThula! uXolo! Khotso! kuRhula, Rugare!

Gratitude to:

God my Father and Creator, YHWH, without whom I have no, essence, Being or Purpose, who from Antiquity put the purpose of Restoration of Vhathu (abaNtu) in the Genetic Material of my Ancestors, each of whom served Him in this manner in their generation and passed on the Baton to the next generation until our Dad, **Mukololo, Mvumi, the Commissioner, Dr Matshikhiri a Nndwa, Christopher, Vele Neluvhalani, Mudau, Mudamane, Nemapungubwe, Nelukungurubwe, shiri ya Denga**, who in turn passed the baton onto us his son daughters and by extension son-sons.

We too shall pass this work to our Children and our Children's Children until the day of our LORD **Yeshua ha Mashiach,** The word of God. Without whose word, every other is meaningless. The Way, The Truth and the Life, without whose Truth, every other way is Darkness, and who redeemed me from Darkness into His Marvelous Light. The Light that shines in the Darkness, which Darkness cannot overcome. This Light, is the Life of Men. **The Holy Spirit,** my Teacher, Friend and Companion who revealed Purpose to me, opened my eyes to see and coaxed me into this Speech.

My Dad, the 81-year-old Computer guru, whose baton, my siblings and I have received. This is the work of our father. Without the tedious lifelong work of his

Doctoral Thesis that he completed in 2017, this work would have been impossible. We stand on the Shoulders of those who came before us.

My Mom, Maligana Litshavha, Shonisani, Patricia Neluvhalani. Mukololo wa Luonde, who taught me Wisdom, Dedication, Persistence and Resilience. Thank you for creating space for me in your 5-star Hotel home and for the refreshments you kept bringing like Clockwork at your Grand age of 74. Thank you for the Oral History. Khazwiande!

My Mom in Love, MaDuma. The Personification of ubuNtu. uMamezala onjengawe akajwayelekile. Ingane zakho zi zo Phumelela... Kanjalo ne sizukulwane Sakho sizo sukuma njalo sisho sithi: ngubani o njengaye!?

My Siblings: Tshiwela na Mawonga; Mhlantla; Mbuso no Busi Dube; Celuzuze MaDube Mazibuko; Vhonani e Benedito Caquece; Ramulayo Neluvhalani; Mutanuni Matenzhe na Vhafuwi Mulatedzi Netshimbupfe; Mashaka a havha vhathu vhothe na vhana vhavho u swikela lini na lini ngahusafheliho, Amen

Vhoni, Thank you for Editing this work and making it Scholarly and Professional.

Your Input has been invaluable

eThekwini Community Church,

Our sons and daughters in Yeshua ha Mashiach! your love and support to fulfill the vision of God through us, humbles us. It is your support that enabled me to obey God to write this work. This Book, is for you and your descendants after you throughout all your Generations. May I single out **Sharon** for Proof Reading the English and ensuring that my clumsy sentences become readable.

My Friends... All of you! Thank you for your Encouragement and Prayers and Faith

The family of Believers everywhere in the World, who hold the Word of God in High esteem and who want to see it authentically taught to empower mankind to relate to one another and to worship the Father in Spirit and in Truth...

Papa le Mama Khutsoane, thank you for Teaching me the concepts of Oppression, Suffering, Carnal and Spiritual Mindedness and Dying to Self. Your Offering has come up before the Father as a Memorial Tower.

VhoMme Khorombi, Ndi a vha Funa... Thank you for healing me nga vhuthu

Vhafunzi vho Nevhutalu,

I would have never understood African Traditional Religion if you had not Schooled me.

Our Oversight Bishops:

M. Habile; P. Mkhize (RIP); A. Kitonga; F. Edwards.

The Faith Organisations and Churches who raised us: UKZN Student Christian Fellowship; Lutheran Church; Presbyterian Church; Charis Missionary Church; Kingdom Power Dimension Outreach Centre and Durban Christian Centre. You opened my eyes to the Word of God. Thank you!

Mashaka anga othe **Luvhalani na vhathambi** vhothe and all connected to you. Aaaa!

Luvhalani, Tshakhuma tsha Madzivhandila...vho Nemashango and the descendants of my Grand uncle: **Ernest, Fhedzisani Neluvhalani Mudau**, who in 1971 told my father, "Knowing Your Genealogy and your Roots in this Continent from Creation, is your Inheritance. Therefore, Write, so that we can find each other."

Mr Tshigabe of Nzhelele who after hearing my father teach about the Autochthoneness of vhaVenda as part of the, Vhangona and abaNtu Nation, showed my father the human foot print on Lwala (Igneous volcanic rock) at Kokwane in 1980, as well as the throngs of then U.E.D Students at UL (Then, the University of the North) who gladly accompanied my Dad in the excursions to Kokwane. Amongst them, **Pioneering Ladies: Matamela; Masiagwala, Now Mrs Rambani and Ms Hulisani Mangoma.** The Throngs of Young men who enthusiastically encouraged my Dad by allowing him to take them on these excursions: **Netshisahulu; Rambani, Ravele and Milubi** as well as scores that my Dad's 80-year-old mind can't remember by name but whose register is available as **U.E.D Alumni of University of the North (Limpopo).**

The Scores of **vharwa/baTwa and Vhangona, Bakone, amaNguni Nationals** who shared wisdom, oral History and Knowledge that allowed my Dad to research further for us today to be able to Reconstruct the History of abaNtu, their Way: kiNtu and their Spiritual Philosophy: ubuNtu. This is the Remnant God Preserved for Himself for a time such as this, For He works in all things for the Good of them that love Him and are called according to His Purposes.

The Scores of **descendants of L'afet (Japhet) and Shem** who have been writing about Afrika from various perspectives throughout the years from every possible trajectory and Motive.

All Archaeologists who have unearthed our Ancestral homes throughout the Continent and who will continue discovering many more as they choose to hear and do the Will of God with open hearts.

My Dad's Thesis Promoters, The Midwives who tried him and Tested him and allowed him to come out as a True Mubikwanaive, ive la vhibva, muvenda a sala, as they helped him navigate his Pregnancy and ultimate birth of his work: "Examining the Migration Theory of Black Africans into South Africa: a deColonial Perspective. Doctor of Philosophy. April 2017. Centre for African Studies, School of Human and Social Sciences, University of Venda

Professor Masoga and Professor Makgopa for your rigorous work.

Your Names are surely written in the Lamb's Book of Life

Herewith my deepest Appreciation to you the Reader:

May you Prosper and be in Health, even as your Souls Prosper.
May your enemies who come against you in one Direction, be defeated before you and Flee from you in seven directions.
May you be above only and never beneath.
May you be ahead and not at the Tail end.
May everything you begin, never die again in your hands.
May it live on in your Posterity...
May you receive the Desires of your heart.
May you be at Rest on every side...
May your Children be taught of the LORD and Great may their Peace be.
May they be Great in the Land of their Ancestors, to Re-Possess it and to Advance the Purpose of UmveliNqaNqi, uYHWH for this Great and beautiful Continent until the Day of our LORD. Amen

Bibliography

Leopards are territorial	www.sanbi.org/animal-of-the-week/leopard
Muwene we Mutapa:	Chanaiwa, D. The international Journal of African Historical Studies, Vol. 5, No.3 (1972: 425-435): Politics and Long Distance Trade in the Muwene Mutapa Empire during the sixteenth Century www.wikipedia.org/wiki/kingdom of Mutapa
Rock Art	www.wits.ac.za/about-rock-art-south Africa
Portuguese Trading Ports on African Coasts	www. Colonialvoyage.com/east-africa-list of Portuguese colonial forts www.wikiwand.com/list_of_portuguese colonial forts
Kushite Queens	www.girlmuseum.org/the-kushite-Queens www. National geographic.com/The Nubian Kingdom
Arabic General Trade and Slave Trade	link.springer.com/content/pdf/Nineteenth century Arab Trade: The growth of a Commercial Empire Bone, S.D. Journal of Religion in Africa (1982:126-138): Islam in Malawi, Brill Malawi Yao Culture: www.ghi.llu.eedu/files/docs/Malawi Brown, B. (1971) Muslim Influence on Trade and Politics in the Lake Tanganyika Region
San Name for Cape Town	www.apc.uct.ac.za/ancestral-stories/place names of Precolonial origin and their use Today/archives & Public Culture
iNkosi uShaka	www.history.com/Shaka-Zulu
Nonqawuse	Peires, J. The dead will arise (2013), Published by Jonathan Ball Publishers
King Sekhukhune	www.news24.com/voices/our story, no.6: Sekhukhune, the great Pedi King
Makhado Wars	Nemudzivhadi, MH. 1975. Makhado Wars and the South African Republic in 1895. Pretoria: University of South Africa. Unpublished MA Dissertation

vhaLemba and other Black Jews or Black Israelites	le Roux, M. The Lemba, a Lost Tribe of Israel in Southern Africa? UNISA (2003) Wade, N. (1999) The New York Times (www.nytimes.com)/DNA Backs a Tribe's Tradition of early descent from the Jews. Lane, B. A. et al. (October 2002), Genetic Substructure in South African Bantu-Speakers: Evidence from autosomal DNA and Y-Chromosome Studies Konner M.J, (2005) Jewish Diaspora in the Ancient World, Africa, and Asia. In: Ember, M., Ember, C.R., Skoggard I. (eds) Encyclopedia of Diasporas. Springer, Boston, MA The Books of Genesis and Judges in the Bible Mudau, E. and Motenda, M.M 1958. Ngomalungundu na Ramabulana. Pretoria: Government Press.
Precolonial Horses	www.farmersweekly.co.za/horses in Africa
Metallurgy	Childs, T. S. (2003) Indigenous African Metallurgy, Nature and Culture
Precolonial Africa	www.cega.berkely.edu/assets/Ecology, Trade and States in Pre-colonial Africa
Writing on Clay Pots	www.academia.edu/in_Pots_we_Trust Smith, A. (2016: 1-21) Cambridge Archaeological Journal: Pottery ad Politics: Making sense of pottery traditions in Central Africa
vhaVenda Cuisine	Neluvhalani, S. P (2015), Zwiliwa zwa VhaVenda, unpublished handwritten notes
89 Generations since Adam	www.answersingenesis.org/genealogy
Kruger National Park	www.krugerpark.co.za/first-warden-of-kruger-national-park
Poverty	Fanin, F. The Wretched of the Earth (1963:27) New York Grove Blamoied, C. African Governments must take Responsibility on Poverty, Financial Times, October 6, 2014
The Scramble	Wikipedia: The Partition of Africa. 1880s Scramble for Africa. https://en.wikipedia.org/wiki/Scramble_for_Africa
4 Ancestors of Africans	Phut, Canaan, Misraim and Cush add your / Name at https://www.biblicalcyclopedia.com/
Consumerism	William Leach, *Land of Desire: Merchants, Power, and the Rise of a New American Culture* (1993). www.whowhatwear.com: 12 European Clothing Brands women in their 30s love, 10 Jan 2020 www.usatoday.com: Most successful American fashion brands, 26 August 2019 www.wealthygorilla.com: Most expensive Alcoholic drinks in the World, by Matt Mcintyre

Bantu Migration debunked	Rwawiire, S. &Tmkova, B. (2014) Thermo-Physiological and Comfort Properties of Ugandan Bark Cloth from Ficus Natalensis, The Journal of the Textile Institute, 106(6), 648-653 Neluvhalani, M.C (2017) The Examination of the Migration of Black Africans into South Africa: A deColonial Perspective https://keyamsha.com/2017/04/10/the-melanin-dosage-test-by- cheikh-anta-diop/ Pennisi, E. (2017), First Big efforts to sequence ancient African DNA reveal how early humans swept across the continent. Published in www.sciencemag.org Semo, A. et al: Mozambican genetic variation provides new insights into the Bantu expansion. www.doi.org/10.1101/697474 Schuster, S.C et al: Complete Khoisan and Bantu genomes from Southern Africa. www. ncbi. nlm.nih.gov De Fillipo, C. (23 May 2012): Bringing together linguistic and genetic evidence to Test the Bantu expansion. https//doi.org/10.1098/rspb.2012.0318 www.khanacademy.org/the spread of farming in Sub-Sahara Africa: The Bantu Migration Ehret, C. (1972) Outlining Southern African History: A re-evaluation A.D. 100-1500, published in Ufahamu: A journal of African Studies. UCLA Ehret, C. (January 1972), Critique and Interpretation, Published in the Trans African Journal of History, Vol. 2, No. 1 pp.1-9 Ricquier, B. (2014) The History of Porridge in Bantuphone Africa, with words as Main ingredients. https://doi.org.10/4000/afriques.1575 Miller, H. (1980) Testimony of the Rocks, Arno Press Samwiri Langa-Lunyiingo: The Bantu Problem Reconsidered, Published in Current Athropology (Volume 17, Number 2) https://www.journals.uchicago.edu/doi/abs/10.1086/201717, Accessed 18 February 2020 www.theodora.com/George-McCall-Theal de Luna Kathy M (2014), Bantu Expansion https://www.researchgate.net/publication/287217490
Identity	Shroff & Fordham (2010): Do you know who I am? Exploring Identity and Privacy. https://www.researchgate.net/publication/262345097 Solomos, J. Black, L. 1996. Racism and Society. London: Mac Millan Press Ltd. Saunders, C. (1988) The Making of the South African Past. Major Historians on race and class. Johannesburg, David Phillip publishers

Religion	Ukpong, J.S (1984): The Emergence of African Theologies https://doi.org/10.1177/004056398404500305 Chidester, D. (2014) Religions of South Africa (Routledge Revivals) Khathide, A.G,
Colonial Slavery and Child labour	Lance van Sittert (2016) Children for Ewes: Child Indenture in the Post- Emancipation Great Karoo: c. 1856–1909, Journal of Southern African Studies,
Civilisation	de Heinzelin J (1962): Ishango. Scientific American 206.6 Ben-Jochanan, Yosef. AA 1988. Africa: Mother of Western Civilization. Baltimore. Black Classic Press Cory, Geo E. 1930. The Rise of South Africa: A History of the South African Colonisation and of its Development Towards the East from the earliest times to 1857. Vol V. London: Longmans, Green and Co. Tellinger, M & Heine J. 2009. Temples of the African Gods: Decoding the Ancient Ruins of Southern Africa, Zulu Planet Publishers. Waterval Boven. Mpumalanga https://www.biography.com/inventor/granville-t-woods Olanrewaju Lasisi (August 2916): New Lights on the Archaeology of Sungbo Eredo, South-Western Nigeria Published on researchgate: https://www.researchgate.net/publication/335013603 Diop, Cheik Anta. 1974. The African origin of Civilisation. New York. Westport (Can be purchased from Goodreads) Hermel, H. Black Sumer: The African Origins of Civilisation (2012) https://blackhistorystudies.com/shops/the-great-mighty-wall/eredo- the-largest-city-in-the-ancient-world/

Origins	Collins, FS. 2006. The Language of God, a Scientist Presents Evidence for belief: Free Press, New York Norling, B. 1960. Towards a better understanding of History. London: University of Notre Dame Press. Tobias, PHV. 1995. The Communication of the Dead: Earliest Vestiges of the origin of Articulate Language. Johannesburg: University of Witwatersrand Rito T, Viera D, Silva M, Conde-Sousa E, Pereira L, Mellars P, et al. (March 2019). "A dispersal of Homo Sapiens from Southern to Eastern Africa immediately precede the out-of-Africa Migration" Gibbons, A. (2017) World's Oldest homo sapiens fossils found in Morocco. https://www.sciencemag.org/news/2017/06/world-s- oldest-homo-sapiens-fossils-found-morocco What did the Bushman actually eat, retrieved 20/10/20. www.peregrinenutrition.com https://www.smithsonianmag.com/smart-news/heres-how-europeans- quickly-evolved-lighter-skin-180954874/ Recent evidence supports the late appearance of the light complexion in Europeans.
African History	Shillington, K. 2005. History of Africa. Revised second Edition. New York: Macmillan Publishers, Davidson, B. (1994): Modern Africa: A Social and Political History, Longman, London, New York Oluyitan, F.E (2019): Snapshot of Past and Present Historical Events in African Countries, Author house, Bloomington https://www.bbc.com/timbuktu manuscripts https://en.wikipedia.org/wiki/Herodotus Harris, JE. 1972, Africans and their History. New York. New American Library Times Mirror Fage, DJ. 1970. Africa discovers her past. London. Oxford University Press Shillington, K. 2005. History of Africa. Revised second Edition. New York: Macmillan Publishers Limited

Ancient African Civilisation	Hermel, H. Black Sumer: The African Origins of Civilisation (2012) Johnson, J.E. Did Ancient India feel African Influence? (1990), New York Times Ansari, M et al. Comparative Visual Analysisof Symbolic and illegible Indus Valley Script with other Languages. Punjab University, Lahore, Pakistan Stearns, P.N, Langer, W.L (2001). The Encyclopedia of World History. Houghton Mifflin Burstein, M.S. State Formation in Ancient NorthEast Africa and the Indian Ocean Trade Sadiq Ali, S (1996). The Afrrican Dispersal in the Deccan: From Medieval to Modern times. Orient Blackswan Diop, Cheik Anta. 1974. The African origin of Civilisation. New York. Westport https://faculty.georgetown.edu/jod/texts/pliny.html Winters, C.A (1986). "Dravidian Settlements in Ancient Polynesia", India Past and Present 3, no2:225-241 Winters, C.A (2007). Did the Dravidian Speakers Originate in africa? BioEssays, 27(5):497-498
Jesus Christ	https://www.theguardian.com/ is this the face of Christ?
Missionaries	https://www.sahistory.org.za/article/european-missionaries-southern- africa-role-missionaries
South Africa	Joyce, P. (2007) The Making of a Nation. Zebra Press Gilomee, H & Schlemmer, L. 1985. Up Against the fences of Poverty. Passes and Privilege in South Africa. Johannesburg, David Phillip. Van Jaarsveld, FA. 1975. From Jan van Riebeeck to Vorster 1652- 1974: An Introduction to the History of South Africa. Johannesburg: Presor Publishers https://www.newsweek.com/sub-saharan Holden, William Clifford. (1866). *The past and future of the Kaffir races*. The author. Retrieved April 2020 from https://library.si.edu/digital- library/book/pastfutureofkaff00hold https://www.britannica.com/place/South-Africa/Reconstruction-union- and-segregation-1902-29 https://www.ekon.sun.ac.za/sampieterreblanche/wp- content/uploads/2018/04/SCIS-Wealth-Tax-for-SA-2018-SJT.pdf www.mineralscouncil.org.za/Mining -employment Van Heerden, O. (19 September 2018): Once we were bankrupt, The Uncomfortable truths of History https://www.dailymaverick.co.za/opinionista/2018-09-19

	Sampson, C.G (1974) Stone Age Archaeology of Southern Africa. New York. Academic Press Nemudzivhadi, M.H. 1977. The Conflict between Mphephu and the South African Republic (1895-1899). Potchefstroom: University of Potchefstroom. Unpublished Doctoral Thesis Muller, C.F.J. 1981. Five Hundred years: A History of South Africa. Third revised Edition, First Impression, Pretoria: Academic Mattingly, D. (2007). An Impeial Posession: Britain in the Roman Empire, 54 BC – AD 409. Penguine UK.
kiNtu, ubuNtu, Settled Lifestyle	vhaNgona Cultural Movement Oral Evidence Dube Family Oral Evidence Muthambi Family Oral Evidence Mr Gwamanda Oral Evidence Mrs Ndemera Oral Evidence Mr S. Phiri, Oral Evidence Ms. N. Mchunu, Oral Evidence Mutwa, Vusamazulu Credo. 1964. Indaba my Children. Finland. WS Bookwell.
	Neluvhalani, MC 2018. The Banguni-Bakone-Bangona and San as the autochthones of South(ern) Africa on: Land (Re)Claim. Sasavona Publishers Neluvhalani, M.C. 1987, Ifa lahashu la Maambele with English Rendering. Moria: Sasavona Publishers and Booksellers Neluvhalani, M.C. 1992, The Teaching of Luvenda Drama in the Senior Secondary School with Special Reference to Venda Schools in the Northern Transvaal, Sovenga: University of the North. Unpublished M.Ed. Dissertation Neluvhalani, M.C. Ifa lahshu la Mirero with English Rendering, Moria: Sasavona Publishers and Booksellers Van Warmelo, NJ and Phophi, WMD. 1948, Venda law Part ii. Pretoria: Government Printers Holden, William Clifford. (1866). *The past and future of the Kaffir races.* e Book. Retrieved April 2020 from https://library.si.edu/digital- library/book/pastfutureofkaff00hold Masoga, Mogomme and Musyoki, A. 2004. Building on the indigenous. An African Perspective. Pretoria. National Research Foundations
Maps	See Credits in Text where the Map Appears Movie: Gore Verbinski (2013) The Lone Ranger: "Something very wrong with that horse"

Salungano

What are your Thoughts?

What Political Decisions do you need to make?

What Economic Decisions do you need to make?

What Socio-Cultural-Spiritual Decisions do you have to make?

Ndi u fa ha Lungano!
(What Seemed like Myth is actually Truth)

Matshikhiri Cocludes!

Now it remains for us to be #NolongerSilent...

CPSIA information can be obtained
at www.ICGtesting.com
Printed in the USA
LVHW061040280921
698914LV00002B/3

9 781638 714521